Praise for *A New Dawn Rising*

"Very fast paced and will be enjoyed by readers of early American fiction and romance."

—Naomi Theye, Historical Novel Society, Historical Novels Review Online

"The plot is exciting and moves along rapidly, keeping the reader fully engaged.... A thoroughly-researched novel ... a first effort of which the author can be genuinely proud."

—Barbara Watson, The Medicine Hat News Book Club

"The author adds just enough circumstance to entice the reader into wanting more. The book will take the reader through a range of emotions, serving as a cumulative and breathtaking mirror to the world of the South. The characters are intriguing and develop in pace with the plot. The final twists follow one another in dramatic crescendo."

—Corene Kozey, The Saskatchewan Library Forum

"*A New Dawn Rising* is a compelling read with characters that linger in your mind weeks and months after you read the final page. It paints a picture of a time and place so far removed from contemporary Fort McMurray that you have to wonder how this talented writer was so effectively able to bring it to life."

—Russell Thomas, *The Fort McMurray Today*

A New Dawn Rising

A NEW DAWN RISING

A NOVEL

Patricia Marie Budd

iUniverse Star

New York Bloomington Shanghai

A New Dawn Rising

Copyright © 2006, 2008 by Patricia Marie Budd

iUniverse Star
an iUniverse, Inc. imprint

iUniverse books may be ordered through booksellers or by contacting:

iUniverse
1663 Liberty Drive
Bloomington, IN 47403
www.iuniverse.com
1-800-Authors (1-800-288-4677)

Because of the dynamic nature of the Internet, any Web addresses or links contained in this book may have changed since publication and may no longer be valid.

This is a work of fiction. All of the characters, names, incidents, organizations, and dialogue in this novel are either the products of the author's imagination or are used fictitiously.

ISBN: 978-1-60528-004-2 (pbk)
ISBN: 978-0-595-60010-6 (ebk)

Printed in the United States of America

Acknowledgments

No one does anything alone—nor would I want to. The guidance and counsel I have received from family and friends over the years have helped make me a better person, and a better writer. Many of you out there have guided me along the road of life and your ability to love and support me is astounding. I salute you!

Simon John Budd. You are the love of my life and the fire in my soul. Without you I would be nothing. Thank you for loving me. On a more practical level, thank you for building my Web site!

Christine (Bluto) Scott. You have been my mentor over the years and I love you! You have read everything I have ever written, offering advice and criticism without fail. You are my greatest influence.

Robert Wilson. Thank you for the year of toil you volunteered. Your editing services helped shape my novel.

Irene (Mom) Budd, Corene Kozey, Lorna Dicks, Marichal Binns, Shonna Barnes, Patsy Sharron. Dearest family and friends, you read my first draft. You read my second draft. You encouraged me to continue when hope was darkest. I will never forget your unwavering support. I love all of you!

Patricia Marie Budd

CHAPTER 1

▼

A NEW DAWN RISING

On a bitter winter day, mid-January, John Connolley stood overlooking the swamp that washed over the northeast edge of his land. His land! The thought warmed his belly like the orange glow that caressed the line of clouds over the muddy waters of Laurel Creek. The sun's rays peeked beneath the crooked arm of the old live oak that stretched for yards over the murky bog, Spanish moss dripping down every limb. From its gnarly branch, new trees sprang, roots digging deep into the mud. John stood awed by its majestic beauty. *That's what I'll call my land,* he thought—*Majestic Beauty, as it will be my beauty after today.*

He scratched the head of the old coon dog that stood at his heel. "So, what ya figure, Amos? Could ya be happy livin' out here with me?"

As if in agreement, the dog howled. He had followed John out to the swamp, having leaped to his feet as soon as he heard the man rustle inside the tent. Where John went, the coon dog followed. John trusted the old redbone with his life and viewed the dog as a friend. Amos's head and shoulders were as rusty as the hair on John's head. The only difference between the two manes was that the fur on the dog sat straight, while John's hair was a mass of unruly curls, something his mama said he had inherited from his daddy. John wished he could have known his father, but it was laid down years ago that there was to be no crossing of paths. As it was, John's daddy, the deceased Lieutenant Connolley of the British army, would never influence the young man's life. That responsibility landed on the shoulders of Mister Jacob Barlow, John's owner. Lieutenant Connolley's untimely death and the enslavement of John's mother could not be undone. Although white, John was a slave as a result of their actions, but he did not blame them. Today was a new day. Today was the day John could finally work for his freedom.

Amos's dark back twitched, and he let out another howl as John stepped forward into the swamp. The dog had no desire to romp around in frigid water. Amos pawed lightly at the water before joining his master. John stepped forward, his boots slowly sinking into slightly hardened mud. He had tucked his pants inside his boots so as not to get them wet. John still had a trip into town to make before noon. He was not wearing the shirt he planned to wear later, but those pants were his only pair. *A little mud ain't going to hurt them*, John figured. *They're dirty brown anyway.* Nor was he worried about the boots, as he had another pair. John stood beneath the upper reach of the old oak's gnarly arm. The branch stretched forward from the original trunk, dropped down to near the big man's knee, then reached up again, high enough for even John to stand underneath.

Standing six feet five, John's head lightly scratched the rough bark. More than likely, he would have hit his head if his feet had not been sucked deep into the mud. Habitually, John's eyes scanned the waters for alligators—foolish this time of year, really, as it was too cold for pike heads, but John liked to stay in the habit. Gators had been known to show up in colder temperatures from time to time, though John had never seen one this deep into winter.

Bracing against the cold, John moved past the branch, deeper into the swamp. Digging rice canals on his own would be quite the job, but if he were to make a decent profit this year, he would need to grow something other than tobacco. Cotton was always a sure bet, but that was too much work for just one man. The same advantage and disadvantage applied to rice. Not that it mattered, anyway; Mr. Barlow was dead set against him planting anything but tobacco. Likely Mr. Barlow wanted him to stick to tobacco because of its low market value.

True enough, the land to the south was better suited to tobacco. Still, John wanted to grow another crop, and even rice brought a higher price these days. John figured he had enough land in his swamp for a decent rice field. He knew growing rice would be arduous, but John believed that with determination a man could overcome any obstacle. That belief did not seem to matter to Mr. Barlow; he kept insisting tobacco was the easiest crop for a man to plant and harvest without the help of Negroes. *I ain't taking on no slaves nohow*, John reminded himself. *I don't care what Barlow says.* It would not be easy making a profit without the help of slaves, but John had to do it. He just had to. John couldn't picture himself owning anyone. It was not his way.

Amos let out a warning howl, and John turned to see Mr. Barlow standing at the edge of the swamp, on solid ground. Mr. Barlow was a mighty handsome man. Even at sixty-six years of age, he attracted the eye of many a lady. He had been a real dandy in his day—still fancied himself one, at that. He wore a neatly trimmed goatee which helped to lengthen an otherwise round face, and even though his hair was gray, it was still as thick and bushy as it had been when he was twenty.

Mr. Barlow looked down at the muddy swamp. As he did not fancy getting his gator boots dirty, Mr. Barlow stayed right where he was, looking at everything beneath him with a commanding eye, as a powerful overseer would peer down on a field of slaves. Besides, Mr. Barlow was dressed in fine attire; he no longer owned work clothes. His bone-white suit was made of coarse silk that had been brought all the way across the world, from China. His shirt, made of fine oxford cotton, had been dyed an earthy brown. Black onyx links adorned French cuffs; gold buttons, carved with the Barlow family monogram, lined the front of his jacket.

Mr. Barlow had connections with Raymond Poitras, a trading baron. Mr. Poitras owned trading companies as far south as New Orleans and all the way north to Boston. The son of French immigrants who had settled in New Orleans, Poitras had helped secure French assistance during the American Revolution. This action, in turn, helped Mr. Poitras secure loyal customers and alliances, allowing him to expand his empire all across the Atlantic coastline of the new United States. Because Mr. Barlow was one of Mr. Poitras's better customers—Mr. Barlow had helped him set up his business in Savannah and had introduced him to his wife, then Miss Delilah Ogelthorpe—Mr. Poitras always secured Mr. Barlow the finest of just about anything from all over the world, including Mr. Barlow's impressive suit.

Amos's tail waved foolishly for Old Man Barlow, and the dog leaped out of the swamp to greet him. The dog splashed some swamp muck onto John, but John took no notice. Mr. Barlow did, though, and stepped back quickly to avoid being soiled by the impending mudslinging. When the dog finished shaking himself off, Mr. Barlow stepped forward to pat the fellow on the head. After receiving his greeting, Amos raced back to join John, splashing even more of the muddy water on his master.

Mr. Barlow's voice echoed across the water to John. "Checking out the swamp, I see."

"Yes, suh," John replied, the edge in his voice belying the calm he wished to portray. Mr. Barlow's presence had shattered the morning's tranquility, but John was not about to let him know—or at least he thought his distress was well hidden. John was on the verge of becoming his own man. Feeling like a piano string that anticipated the hit of the hammer, already almost vibrating as it waited for its music to resound, John was tuned and ready for the sweet sound of freedom … but Mr. Barlow was a sharp reminder of the sour note that could ruin John's private concert.

Jacob Barlow was not fooled by outer appearances; he had known the young man too long for that. Hell, he had practically raised him! "Relax, son. This here is a fine piece of land."

John lowered his head and dug at the mud with his boot heel, rice canals forming in his mind.

"I got my start here," Mr. Barlow resumed. "Built my empire, I did. Yes, suh."

John nodded, having heard this story long ago, throughout his youth, and very recently, during the ride in from Savannah. They had arrived after dark, so John had not seen much of the place. He had tried to rise early, well before Mr. Barlow, so he could scout things out on his own.

Mr. Barlow, a light sleeper, had heard John rise. "Are you still thinking about planting rice, John?"

Looking down to avoid Mr. Barlow's eyes, John nodded.

"Well, rice is fetching a good price these days, that's for sure. Makes for fine eating, too, especially mixed with red beans … and this here stretch of land is perfect for it. Rice needs lots of fresh water. I had seriously considered clearing out the swamp and planting rice when I first bought this section of land, but I knew the task to be too daunting … and I had me a Negro to boot! Whereas you, son … you are insisting on doing it all on your own. That is too much work for just one man, even one as strapping as you. Now," Mr. Barlow persisted, "if you take my offer of a—"

John snapped, "No, suh! I ain't takin' on no slaves." Catching the sudden rise in Mr. Barlow's brow, John slipped back into proper vernacular. "I will not be an overseer!"

Mr. Barlow smiled wryly, flashing shiny white teeth, and made his offer one more time.

"No gifts, especially Negroes," John insisted. "I swear I ain't …" John's voice quieted until it was nearly inaudible as he muttered an oath. He hated having to watch his tongue for that man. "I will not be an owner!"

Mr. Barlow's laugh rumbled deep inside. He was not a portly man; he retained a muscular shadow of his youth. Having been a bare-knuckle boxer in

England before arriving at the colonies, Mr. Barlow had kept up his training, and he had pushed John in the ring. As strong as Mr. Barlow was, his age and short stature made him appear slight next to the towering John Connolley. John was a mighty pine stretching into the sky, caressing the clouds with his grandeur. Standing at six feet five, John Connolley towered over all men. John had always wondered if he had grown as tall as James Montgomery. Next to Mr. Barlow, James Montgomery had been the biggest influence in John's youth. He had met Mr. Montgomery when he was twelve. Few men stood taller than John, who had already surpassed six feet, even at his young age. When John met Mr. Montgomery for the first time, he had to crane his neck to look up at the man's eyes. Perhaps now, after seventeen years, John could safely say he had surpassed Mr. Montgomery's stature.

Even at twelve years of age, John had been big—not looming or overpowering, but skinny, like a willow that had grown up too fast, always bending at the slightest wind. John had been lanky back then, but not anymore—Mr. Barlow had seen to that. He had fed John well and worked him hard. A man needed weight and strength to survive in the ring—especially in the illegal ones, where, like cockfights, the outcome was often death.

There was no fat on John Connolley, but his bulk was a mighty sight. John's shoulders were broader than an oxen's yoke, his torso was as strong as a brick wall, and his legs were as thick as tree trunks. When John Connolley stood straight and strong, all men stepped aside for him. A scowl from John often brought shivers to the spines of onlookers.

John never did like folks shying away from him because of his size, but he never slouched to accommodate them. He never slouched—Mr. Barlow had seen to that, too. A man could not intimidate another in the ring if he slouched.

John only fought when he had to—which was still more times than even he could remember. Mr. Barlow was always tossing him in the ring over some bet or another. John's fighting had helped build Old Man Barlow a small fortune. Those forced matches were the only times John had ever laid a hand against another.

His cheekbones, having been crushed, gave him a dangerous look, much like a badger trapped in a corner. His nose, busted twice, angled to the left, suggesting the proud look of an eagle. Only his eyes were a reminder of his former good looks. They were a steel gray that sometimes shone a deep blue, depending on the light. His irises blended two colors together, an outer ring of blue lapping against an inner circle of gray. But when John Connolley smiled, his fighting injuries vanished and the warmth of his soul lit up his eyes. One could almost imagine the handsome face behind the disfigured one. Even the disfigurement seemed to give the man a rugged, handsome quality. Women admired John; he looked like a man who would protect a lady from any harm that might befall her. For women, John Connolley was a beacon of safety.

"Well, son"—John always winced when Mr. Barlow called him son—"I reckon your mind is made up, and I am not likely to change it. Still … my daddy always said every man needs a Negro." Mr. Barlow crossed his arms in front of his chest and looked the stubborn man up and down.

John inspected the mud beneath his feet; he roused a river frog from its hibernation. Mindful of others, he carefully packed the mud back on top of the frog, hoping the little thing survived. John was always saving the lives of critters. He had even picked up a spider once and carried it outdoors, rather than squishing it, as most folks would have done.

"No, suh," John replied. "I ain't gonna own no slave."

Mr. Barlow grimaced at John's slovenly vernacular. *How many times must I remind him that a man's speech helps to elevate his status? Instead he insists on talking like a slave.* John's stubborn use of low-class vernacular only served to heighten Mr. Barlow's guilty conscience. Self-recrimination always angered the man. He felt an urge to hit the young man hard. "You realize, I hope, that making a profit alone is going to be nigh on impossible."

John sighed. His biggest fear was that Mr. Barlow was right.

"If you are obstinately determined to do it all on your own, then you ought to think wisely about things. Growing rice is too hard a job for one man. I would advise you to consider tobacco. It's broad-leaved … you can harvest it on your own." Mr. Barlow noted John's discouragement, and a hint of anger hardened his voice. "Do not let me see you giving up before you have even begun. I will not have it. There are no quitters in my family!"

John desperately wanted to shout "We are not family!" but he let Mr. Barlow ramble on instead.

"Even just a dollar's profit will get you another year, boy."

John's back tightened at being called boy, but he kept his anger inside. He released it through his boots as he swirled the mud.

Mr. Barlow sensed his victory, and his voice echoed gaily. "Come on, son, get out of there. We have a long day ahead of us."

"Yes, suh." John made his way back under the knotted arch, with Amos trailing at his heels.

As the two men walked back toward John's house, Mr. Barlow continued with his monologue on the values of owning land. "Yes, suh. My sweet Louise and I started here with nothing but that little house and two Negroes … a man to help in the fields and a little girl to work in the kitchen. It was tough going that first year, but there were lots of small critters for us to eat. We fed mostly on coons and swamp rabbits that winter. When I was unable to trap any red meat, we still made do. You will find Laurel Creek stocked high with catfish. They make for mighty fine eating. Cook them in butter with pepper and lemon."

John shook his head unconsciously as he replied, "Yes, suh." He knew Mr. Barlow had never been without. Having been born into aristocracy, Mr. Barlow was a man who wanted for nothing. Still, Mr. Barlow's daddy had lived by a puritanical work ethic, and Mr. Barlow had inherited that mentality. In Jacob Barlow's mind, a man had to earn his empire, and even though he had wealth and power behind him, Mr. Barlow had worked with his own two hands to build up his plantation.

John looked over his shoulder to see the sun rising above the bayou. He smiled, remembering fondly what his mama used to say: "Son, life is made of new beginnings, an' every day is a new dawn risin'." *Yes, sir*, John figured. *This here is my new dawn rising.* He would grow rice—if not this year, then the next.

Mr. Barlow rambled on like a songbird; that man sure did love to hear himself talk. "Stay away from the snakes, though, as they are not as tasty as some folks say. We had us a big king snake one night. My poor, sweet Louise spent half the night with her head over the chamber pot, and her little Negro girl running back and forth from the outhouse, dumping the damn thing." Mr. Barlow laughed heartily at the memory. Wanting to fill John with as much advice as possible, he continued. "Try not to get any skunks in your traps either. It is not a pleasant experience, let me tell you. I caught me one once …"

John laughed along with Mr. Barlow. That was a story the old man had been telling since John was old enough to sit up on Mr. Barlow's knee. For a brief moment, they were like father and son. But Mr. Barlow pushed the moment too far by placing a hand on John's shoulder.

John shrugged it off with a quick turn, making it look as if he were scouting the land for wildlife. "I was plannin' on gettin' me some bigger game. Maybe a whitetail deer or a bear, come spring."

Mr. Barlow reacted some to the sting of John's rejection but managed to keep his voice steady; still, his hurt gave it a biting quality. "You may find a whitetail around here. More than likely, though, you'll have to travel inland, north to the mountains at the very least, for a bear. After getting there, it will likely take you a good week or two to bag anything." Looking at the old house, he added, "It seems to me you are going to be kept pretty busy just fixing up the ol' house and all." Not wanting to discourage John too much, Mr. Barlow softened his tone and acquiesced some: "Still, if you are lucky enough to bag a whitetail here and about, it should keep you the winter ... could hold you through 'til spring." Still reeling from the punch of John's shrug, Mr. Barlow added with a slightly derisive edge, "If you can still shoot, that is." Mr. Barlow had taken John hunting when he was a boy, but all that had stopped when John had turned fourteen.

John refused to listen to any of Mr. Barlow's subtle suggestions; he was too close now to owning his own. He knew what he wanted and what he needed to do. "I need to get me a rifle first, I figure." Before Mr. Barlow could utter an objection, John hurried on with his explanation: "That musket you gave me is real fine, suh ... but they are none too accurate for huntin'."

"Yes, suh," Mr. Barlow agreed. "It was not very accurate on the battlefield either." Slapping John on the shoulder to congratulate the man's wise decision, Mr. Barlow added, "Maybe the local merchant will take your musket for trade." He pulled his hand off instantly to avoid another rejection.

John hesitated slightly, then added, "I would like to keep it, suh, if that is all right with you."

"All right?" Mr. Barlow smiled, pride filling him and beaming out his eyes. It pleased him to no end that John Connolley, the man Mr. Barlow had raised, even if he was not blood, wanted something that had been an important part of Mr. Barlow's life. "Of course it would be all right!" Mr. Barlow was a proud man and loved to talk about himself. He added, "You know, I fought in the siege of Savannah with that very musket."

John smiled gingerly, remembering youthful hours spent listening to Mr. Barlow's incredible stories: tales of patriotism and battling the British to help secure freedom and independence. He could twist a tale into yarns of gold, Mr. Barlow could. Seeing John smile, even so slightly, warmed Mr. Barlow's heart, and without thinking, he wrapped an arm around John's shoulder. John left his arm there instead of shrugging it away as usual, and the two men hiked the incline toward the tent pitched next to the old house.

The old house stood high on a bluff overlooking Laurel Creek. Mr. Barlow sighed at the sight of it. "That little house sure has taken a lot of punishment over the years. I built it with my own two hands, I did." He paused a moment to smile at the memory. "Still"—he tightened his grip around John's shoulder like a father sending his son off into the world—"you can fix it up in no time. A few floor stones need replacing. I got them yonder in those hills." Mr. Barlow pointed to the southwest. "It was quite the job breaking them to the right size, but you are as strong as an ox. No need to worry about breaking them to an exact size either. I just filled in all the cracks with tabby." Pausing for a moment, Mr. Barlow shook his head. "Why I did not make the entire floor out of tabby is beyond me. It's easy enough to make, just a little sand, lime, and oyster shells. I guess it was for my sweet Louise; she was used to a finer lifestyle. I reckon you could just fill in all the loose spaces and holes with tabby."

John figured that was a fine idea. He might be as strong as an ox, but he had no intention of breaking his back unnecessarily. Tabby would work just fine; it would be much easier to fill the floor with the cement than break up stones. After thirteen years in the ring, John's body had enough aches and pains to last him a lifetime. *Besides,* he figured, *tabby's real fine. Them oyster shells give it a nice sparkle.*

Walking around to the front of the house, Mr. Barlow continued his inspection. "And those windows ..." He scratched his right ear and thought for a moment. "They must have been knocked out by the last hurricane. That is the problem with anything left unattended for a time: nothing gets replaced." Continuing his walk around the house, Mr. Barlow added, "Most of the roof is in need of repair, too." With that he laughed, remembering how badly the roof had leaked during the previous night's heavy rains. They had sheltered in the barn, of all places, until the storm ended. The barn had not been any drier, so John had pitched the oily canvas tent they had brought.

It had been years since Mr. Barlow had been to the old plantation. There had been no telling what shape things would be in. He had leased it out until two years ago, when it had been abandoned, but sharecroppers never cared for a place as well as an owner would.

Mr. Barlow smiled when he saw the tent John had pitched for them. Bringing it had turned out to be a good idea. When Mr. Barlow left, the tent could stay with John. As for tonight, Mr. Barlow planned to stay in town. *This here is John's land now. It is his job to rough it and make things work. Besides,* Mr. Barlow thought, *I am too old to sleep on the ground.* "Enough of this," Mr. Barlow grunted. "Get a fire going and cook us up some grits. I am as hungry as a bear in April. I could do with some good coffee, too."

"Yes, suh." John settled into making breakfast. He had had the foresight to soak some beans before going to sleep, so they would cook up fast and soft. After draining the water and crushing the beans, he tossed in some lard and leftover possum from last night's meal. He ripped up a few pieces of hard bread and set them on plates while he waited for their meal to warm. He set a pot of water on the fire to boil and tossed in some coffee grinds.

The two men ate in silence. When they finished, Mr. Barlow handed his plate to John and told him to hurry and wash up—they had to get to town. Before long, the two men were sitting in Mr. Barlow's wagon, riding eastward to Laurel Creek.

CHAPTER 2

▼

LAUREL CREEK

Normally Jacob Barlow would never ride in a wagon. He had a fancy carriage, one gilded in gold, to let folks know his station in life. (On a more practical level, the carriage protected him from the elements.) Still, Mr. Barlow had agreed to bring the cart, as John would need it to haul things in from town.

Mr. Barlow's wagon was hardly comfortable, even with the pillow he had brought along to pad his seat; still, it was practical, and John definitely needed it. Mr. Barlow was not expecting John to buy a wagon on his first day. In fact, John was talking about building one to save money. The only parts he could not make himself, John figured, were the wheels. John would buy them from the town mill, along with all the lumber and tools he would need.

As they headed onto the road, Amos howled—there was no way he was getting left behind. John smiled and said, "Come along, then." The old coon dog settled into a pace alongside the cart, and stayed with his master—for the most part. There was far too much new ground to scout for an old redbone to stick to the road.

The ride into Laurel Creek was beautiful; trees surrounded the road, and the Spanish moss added an elegant grace. John figured it would be a real pretty ride come spring. Along with laurel and black cherry, live oaks jutted up everywhere. There was also a good supply of magnolia, poplar, and dogwood. The poplar and dogwood trees looked like skeletons interspersed throughout. John noticed some bushes that looked like palmetto, blackberry, and huckleberry. *Come spring*, John figured, *all them flowers will make for a real pretty sight, and them berries mighty fine preserves … if the ladies in town are willing to sell their jams, that is.*

✳   ✳   ✳   ✳

Laurel Creek was a small but prosperous town. It sat on the crossroads between Laurel Creek and the Savannah River. The river lay to the east of town, and to the north were the southern banks of the creek. The small stream of Laurel Creek sprang up from an outcrop of rocks some thirty miles southwest. Legend had it the Lord flung a lightning bolt into the rocks to bring forth the waters of wealth. Indeed, Laurel Creek's swampy waters were surrounded by some of the most prosperous plantations in Georgia.

Mr. Barlow's plantation—Heartland, the most enterprising by far—nearly circled the little town, cupping it from the Savannah on the west, then swirling around and down past it on the southeast. Only a small portion of the town's edge was touched by another man's land—Kilmartin Glen, the property of Mr. Angus MacPhearson. Kilmartin Glen was the second-largest plantation in the area, and even it paled next to Mr. Barlow's two townships. Mr. Frank Crawford owned the third-largest property near Laurel Creek—Pine Grove, a mere twenty-two thousand acres.

Mr. Crawford had started out with five hundred acres when he first bought his Laurel Creek land. With big money behind him, though, he had been buying out—or rather, pushing out—his neighbors for the past five years. Pine Grove now brushed against the mighty Mr. Barlow's property. Mr. Barlow intended to sell John the five hundred acres that swooped to the southwest of Laurel Creek. Frank Crawford had been trying to get Mr. Barlow to sell him that land for the past two years, after Mr. Barlow's tenant, Mr. Edward Moores, passed away. But Mr. Barlow had refused to sell. His daddy had taught him to never sell land. "Son," the old man used to say, "land is more valuable than gold, and a man holds onto it once it is his own." Mr. Barlow, however, made an exception for John, as John was like family to him.

As a result of the great wealth surrounding the little village, much of its infrastructure was well tended. Two of the town buildings were even made of brick. The most impressive structure was Richardson's Inn. Even hurricanes found the building a formidable opponent. It had weathered more than a few mighty blows. Red brick with slate flooring (and Georgia marble in the lobby!), the inn stood a magnificent four stories high. Laurel Creek's small population had never generated enough guests to fill the inn to capacity. Mr. Richardson had agreed to house the town clock on the top floor, since his building stood higher than any other. His inn was also the center of town, so folks always walked by it. Many fine folk frequented the Richardson dining hall, as Mrs. Richardson was proclaimed as fine a cook as any in New Orleans. The Richardsons' stables were the best place in town to park a horse and cart.

Mr. Barlow had the whole day planned. They were to meet folk, and John was to buy supplies.

John paid the stable hand, Ol' Riley, a penny for his services.

The old Negro guffawed and waved a hand toward John as if to say, *ya sho is somthin' else Mista*. Ol' Riley continued to chuckle to himself as he shuffled back toward the barn.

When John rejoined Mr. Barlow on the street, the old man grunted to show his displeasure at the sight of Amos. "That dog will not be joining us, I hope."

John shrugged. He saw no reason to leave Amos behind. "I fail to see why not. Amos ain't gonna get in the way."

Mr. Barlow's gaze hardened into a scowl. "Clean your tongue. 'Ain't' ain't a word!" That was another one of his daddy's fine expressions. "I mean to introduce a gentleman to all the finer folk in this town. I most certainly will not be introducing your dog."

John turned and led Amos back to the cart. There was no point arguing. *Soon enough*, he figured, *I'll be on my own, and I'll take Amos any damn place I please.*

John's tour began with the jailhouse. The small building housed both the sheriff's office and nine cells for prisoners. Built of lumber, it was probably the most unpretentious building in town, even more humble in appearance than the hitching post out front. Alongside it was a gallows for three, made of pine. The office was cramped and barely accommodated a desk and chair. Next to the door was a collection of hooks for coats, hats, pistols, and holsters. Leading away from the office was a corridor to the cells. Three were empty, the others filled with vagrants. The sheriff, Artemus Sprague, was proud that he had not had a full jail in over two months. He ran a quiet town. Folks felt safe in Laurel Creek. Sheriff Sprague credited himself for that, and the town folk appreciated his services.

Mr. Barlow gave John a full tour of the village, introducing him to fine society and making everyone aware that he viewed John Connolley as a son. They now knew to treat John with the respect accorded to any Barlow. Mr. Barlow's introductions immediately placed John at a status equal to Angus MacPhearson. The Barlow name spoke louder than money or the size of one's land.

After showing John around, Mr. Barlow took him to the bank. "We are going to get the banker to witness the deed transfer," he explained. Then he added, "I reckon you brought along the cash to pay for this transaction?"

"Yes, suh," John replied. From the inner pocket of his jacket, John retrieved the thick wad of bills Mr. Barlow had given him the other day. This was all the money Mr. Barlow had held in trust over the years for John's laboring and fighting. John shuffled through the bills. "With enough left over to make it through the year," John added. That had been the deal struck between Mr. Barlow and John: John had to save up enough money to buy the land and make do for a year. In addition, the deal stipulated that John make a profit by the end of the year. John swore, come hell or high water, he would make that profit—even if it killed him.

"I know you brought it with you, son. I just wanted to see you smile, is all." Mr. Barlow laughed at the sight of the money. It was more money than John had ever held, and he held it with all the reverence reserved for the Holy Bible.

John had smiled, but not to please Mr. Barlow. He was so close now to owning his own land and being on his own for at least one whole year. Freedom was at his fingertips. This alone was reason to rejoice. His smiled exposed the teeth that had managed to survive beatings in the ring. His eyes glistened with anticipation, looking like crystal blue pools in the sunlight.

Standing in front of the bank, John looked up to admire the sign that spanned the width of the building, proudly proclaiming it to be The First Bank of Laurel Creek. Walking through the heavy oak doors, the two men made their way across the lobby to the banker's desk.

John was impressed. He had never been in a bank before. The banker's solid oak desk sat at an angle in the far corner, giving the portly man a clear view of everything, including customers, tellers, and the huge steel safe. Only one teller was working that day.

The banker, Joseph Atwell, peered up as the two men entered. He held a stubby cigar between his teeth. He twisted and rolled it between his fingers as he pondered who these two men might be. One was clearly a man of high standing, the other more destitute. Mr. Atwell grimaced at the sight of John Connolley. *This ruffian*, he surmised, *is certainly not here to deposit any money.* Standing, Mr. Atwell directed his attention to the gentleman of good breeding. "Good day, suh. How may I serve you on this fine day?"

Mr. Barlow reached a hand of greeting over the richly carved desk. "A good day to you, suh. It is truly a fine day ... a mite chilly with the winter wind, but the clear sky and the shining of the sun is enough to warm a man's heart."

"Indeed it is," Mr. Atwell agreed. "But it has been uncommonly cold. Why, there was even frost on the ground this morning. If you are chilled, good suh, come stand by the potbellied stove." Mr. Atwell gave his response in a most inviting manner; a closer look at Mr. Barlow's fine attire confirmed a huge sum of money was about to be deposited.

"No, thank you, suh." Mr. Barlow smiled. "We are warm enough."

Mr. Atwell invited them to take a chair before he sat back at his desk to do business.

The banker's oily face displayed a greedy smile that made John cringe. He could not trust a man who resembled a greased pig. Mr. Atwell's pasty white face produced beads of sweat that ran down his neck to be absorbed by his shirt collar. John figured Mr. Atwell was the kind of man who would sweat even if he were standing outside naked on the coldest day of the year.

Although Mr. Barlow scorned men like Mr. Atwell, he viewed him as a necessity and had dealt with his type before.

The banker drew deeply on his cigar, turning the ash to a red, hot glow. Exposing yellow teeth as he exhaled, Mr. Atwell commented, "No doubt, good suh, you are looking to deposit a sizable sum of money."

Mr. Barlow laughed. "No, suh. I am planning no such thing." Gesturing to John, he added, "It is this gentleman here who will be needing your services."

As suddenly as his smile vanished, Mr. Atwell managed to resurrect it, so as not to offend. Turning his attention to John, the banker inquired, "And what business is it you will be needing?" As he waited for John's answer, Mr. Atwell sighed, raised his brows, and eyed John suspiciously, once again reminding himself, *Clearly this oaf will not be making any sizable deposit.*

John noted the dismissal of his character, but he was used to such disrespect, and it concerned him little. "I need you to witness a business transaction, suh. We wish to transfer a land title. I am purchasing some property from this here gentleman."

Mr. Atwell's jaw dropped. *This lout has enough money to buy land?* Realizing he was betraying his shock at the events transpiring, the banker closed his gaping mouth. "All right then, gentlemen," Mr. Atwell said with impeccable composure, "y'all will be needing me to draw up new drafts of the land title then, am I correct?" Fixated on Mr. Barlow, Mr. Atwell did not even bother with a single sidelong glance at John.

"That would be good," John answered.

"I can accommodate your request," Mr. Atwell said. Leaning back in his chair, he reminded the men that his services required a small fee. Because he was disappointed the giant had not requested a mortgage, Mr. Atwell mentally inflated his fee. Addressing John curtly, he inquired, "Do you have ten dollars for the service fee?"

Without waiting for John to reply, Mr. Barlow exploded. He leaped to his feet, knocking back his chair. Only John's quick reflexes kept it from hitting the floor. "Are you out of your mind? Ten dollars ... why, that is extortion!"

Mr. Atwell was not ruffled by Mr. Barlow's explosion. He expected customer uproars over his extravagant fees. "Suh, my customers are among the wealthiest in Georgia, and my fees reflect the expertise I bring to this business. As you may know, my clientele represents the finest of southern gentility. In fact"—Mr. Atwell sat forward to emphasize his next point—"even Jacob Barlow"—he paused to let the weight of the name sink in—"even Mr. Jacob Barlow keeps some of his money inside my bank."

John stifled a laugh, turning his head to avoid dishonoring the man.

Mr. Barlow grinned wryly. "Is that so?" Pausing for effect, he ran a finger across the man's desk. "Well, Mr. Atwell, you are dealing with Mr. Jacob Barlow right now, and if you wish to retain my patronage, you will consider lowering your rates." As an afterthought, Mr. Barlow added, "I should have transferred that money to the Bank of Savannah decades ago."

Mr. Atwell blanched, his jaw dropping so wide his cigar fell to the floor. He did not move to pick up the burning ember, but sat there staring, dumbfounded, mouth hanging open like a fish held up by the gills.

Leaving the man to look foolish a moment, Mr. Barlow waited before adding, "Do you plan to pick up your cigar, suh, or are you going to let it catch fire to your fancy desk?" Mr. Barlow sat back down, knowing he was in control.

Quickly snapping his jaw shut, Mr. Atwell bent to pick up his cigar. With regained composure, he returned to the business at hand. "All right, then, gentlemen, who is selling what, and what is being purchased?"

As John leaned forward, Mr. Barlow interrupted him. "Not until we settle this matter of the ten dollars. We will be paying you a five-dollar fee, which is more than the banks in Savannah charge."

Mr. Atwell sat back and studied Mr. Barlow carefully before nodding in agreement. "Five dollars it is, suh."

Mr. Barlow smirked at having successfully bartered with the greedy banker; there was nothing like knocking a man off his high horse. Turning to John, Mr. Barlow nodded for him to speak.

"I will be purchasin' five hundred acres of Mr. Barlow's land just west of town."

For the third time, the banker's jaw dropped. Turning to Mr. Barlow with dismay, Mr. Atwell asked, "You are selling that land?"

Mr. Barlow nodded.

"I heard tell Frank Crawford has been trying to get you to sell him that land for nigh on two years."

"That is true, good suh. Mr. Crawford is as persistent as a blood-starved mosquito. But my daddy always advised me to hold on to land. Worth more than gold, he said. Gold's value fluctuates daily, whereas land will always increase in value."

Mr. Atwell scratched his head and pondered. "Your daddy gives sound advice, suh. So why are you not listening to it? Why are you selling land to this here"—he glanced over to John questioningly—"this here gentleman?"

Mr. Barlow slapped John's shoulder and smiled. "Because John is family. I practically raised the lad, I did."

John's head dropped slightly, hiding his anger. It was beyond comprehension that Mr. Barlow continued to view himself as a father figure, given the abrupt change in their relationship on John's fourteenth birthday. John had no intention of ever restoring those former feelings. This transaction could never pardon fifteen years of betrayal. Whether Mr. Barlow was aware of that, John neither knew nor cared.

The business deal only took a few minutes; the details had been determined long before their arrival at the bank. After Mr. Atwell was paid, John assumed they were done. *Nothing left to do*, he thought, *but wait for the new title to be writ. I'll return after lunch for the paperwork.* Before John could get out of his chair, though, Mr. Barlow slapped a wad of bills on top of Mr. Atwell's desk.

Mr. Atwell's eyes popped out farther than those of a big old horny toad. His eyes were bigger and rounder than a full-grown alligator's sticking up out of the water. A wet tongue flicked across razor-thin lips, licking off drops of sweat. "Why, suh … that is quite the sum of money you just planted there."

"Eleven hundred and fifty dollars, to be exact," Mr. Barlow bragged, adding, "to be deposited in an account under Mr. Connolley's name."

John was so mortified and sickened that bile fouled his tongue. Mr. Barlow knew John did not want that money, and here he was, trying to deposit it in John's name. Like a bear ready to attack, John growled at Mr. Atwell, "You *will not* be depositing that money in *my* name."

As only Mr. Barlow could, he said, "Mr. Connolley *will* be depositing that money in your bank, Mr. Atwell. It *will* be under his name, and it *will* be done today."

With fiery eyes and gritted teeth, John growled, "I ain't touchin' none a' that! I done tol' you so already!"

Curiosity consumed Mr. Atwell. *The buffoon is starting to show his true colors. Here he was trying to act like a proper gentleman, and now he is talking like the sloth he really is.* Mr. Atwell smiled, sat back, and watched.

Mr. Barlow stood, angered by John's defiance. "Now you listen here, boy!"

John received the word "boy" like a bayonet to the belly; Mr. Atwell's grimace revealed just how great an insult "boy" was, even for a hired hand.

Mr. Barlow barged on arrogantly. "This is your money! You earned it. And you will take it. Do you hear me, boy?"

John refused to answer, staring instead at Mr. Atwell's painting of a little boy in blue. Oddly, he wondered if it was a copy or the original. Some artists, he had heard, made money mimicking famous works.

"John!" Mr. Barlow shouted. "Do. You. Hear. Me?" Each word was a bullet shot from a gun.

John closed his eyes, lowered his head, and whispered, "Yes, suh."

It was evident which of the two men was in charge. Mr. Atwell had heard right: Jacob Barlow was a man who always got his way. Mr. Atwell made a mental note never to cross Mr. Jacob Barlow.

✳   ✳   ✳   ✳

After opening John's account, the two men were pampered at Richardson's Inn. Terrance Richardson and his good wife, Paullina, were titillated by the presence of the great man. When Mr. Barlow registered, they were overjoyed. No sycophant could have drooled harder. A coon dog gnawing on a roasted pork bone could not have salivated more. When John and Mr. Barlow were finally freed from the supplications and flattery bestowed upon them by the innkeeper and his wife, the two men headed for the general store. There they met Mr. Brian Hodson, the proprietor, his good wife, Dinah, and their daughter, Amanda.

"Why, Mr. Connolley," Amanda squealed. She was a slight child of thirteen, with black hair and dark brown eyes. "You've gotta be the tallest man I ever did see." Then, flashing doe eyes at him, she added, "An' so imposin'. Don't he look imposin', Mama?"

"Hush now, girl." Mrs. Hodson smacked Amanda on the behind and sent her running. "I am very sorry, Mr. Connolley," she quickly apologized. "Amanda is starting to think she is a lady already. Her sister married at fourteen, so she is thinking she can, too."

John blushed at the suggestion of marriage, especially to a little girl like Amanda.

Mrs. Hodson saw through his worry. "Now, do not fret, Mr. Connolley. We are not looking to find a husband for Amanda yet. She has to wait until she is at least sixteen." Wrapping her arm around John, she led him to the back of the store. "Now you come with me, good suh. Mr. Barlow gave me strict orders to measure you for work clothes."

Wandering the mercantile, Mr. Barlow collected flour, sugar, coffee, tea, and the like as Mrs. Hodson measured John in the back of the store. After Mr. Barlow finished, and while Mr. Hodson prepared the bill, John inquired about purchasing a rifle.

"Well, we have a couple here y'all might be interested in," the smiling proprietor replied. Considering Mr. Barlow's fine attire, Mr. Hodson presented them with the finely gilded Baker rifle he had on display. It was a real beauty, with finely cut ivory inlaid on the stock, and shiny engraved silver for the bolt and hammer. "Now, this is likely the finest rifle y'all are ever to see."

Whistling thoughtfully as he picked up the gun, Mr. Barlow braced it against his shoulder to line up the sights. "It sure is a beauty. Fits right nice in the hands, too." He smiled and tossed the rifle over to John.

Turning the rifle over, John eyed its sights and felt its weight. "How much are you askin' for it, suh?"

"Twenty-five dollars, Mr. Connolley," Mr. Hodson boomed, "and worth every penny, let me tell you! There is no finer crafted rifle than a Baker. It even has a percussion cap. It is the latest thing to come out of England."

Mr. Barlow whistled again, but he did not balk. There was no denying it: this Baker was a mighty fine rifle.

John, however, had no intention of spending that kind of money. "Y'all got anythin' a little more affordable for a workin' man?"

Mr. Hodson laughed, extending his apology. "Forgive me, suh. I am used to pulling out the finery for the wealthier folks in town."

John smiled. This man was not trying to slick him with oil; he was just good at his business.

"Let's see … I got me a Kentucky rifle up here somewhere. Or would you prefer a Hawkins, suh?"

"A Kentucky would be just fine."

"Here we go." Presenting the gun to John, Mr. Hodson added, "Just as good as the Baker, without all the fancy icing. It's a flintlock but will shoot straight, and you'll hit your mark, if you have a good eye."

"How much for this one, suh?"

"Five dollars."

John smiled.

After completing his transaction at the mercantile, John headed toward the lumberyard. Mr. Barlow chose not to join him: "I need to rest, son. I think I will head on over to Richardson's Inn. I am not as young as I used to be. Besides, you do not need me to help you pick out wood and such. You come fetch me when you are finished, and we will sup together."

"Yes, suh." John was elated. Alone, he could finally make his own decisions. The first thing he did was fetch Amos.

$$*\qquad *\qquad *\qquad *$$

After supper Mr. Barlow reminded John of their last appointment. They were to meet with Dr. Karl Odland come morning. John was to leave all the explaining to Mr. Barlow. John grimaced at the prospect of hearing his shameful story spoken aloud. Mr. Barlow was right, though: the story had to be told. What if something happened, and John needed the doctor's care? Better to be forthcoming with Dr. Odland now than end up swinging from a big old oak.

As expected Dr. Odland was disgusted by what he saw and heard. Not even Mr. Barlow's mighty storytelling could soften the horror. The look on Dr. Odland's face seared John's soul. Dr. Odland's reaction was evidence that he, John Connolley, could never be his own master, live a normal life, or marry a woman willing to bear his children. If word ever got out, John Connolley would never be his own man. He was branded for life. The only facet of Dr. Odland's reaction that mollified John some was that the doctor's look of disgust was directed at Mr. Barlow more so than at John. Finally someone had refused to be taken in by all of Mr. Barlow's finery. Even though he knew they could never be friends, John liked Dr. Odland. His respect for the man increased when Dr. Odland promised to keep his secret—something about a Hippocratic oath. John believed the doctor, as did Mr. Barlow.

"This is not something folks need to know about, now is it, John?" Mr. Barlow emphasized as they left Dr. Odland's office.

"No, suh," John answered.

Mr. Barlow had not expected a reply. He knew John was the last person willing to share family history. It would not be in John's favor to share this information with anyone. It was simply that John was used to responding "Yes, suh" and "No, suh" to everything Mr. Barlow said.

Saddened, Mr. Barlow looked at John, knowing he had ruined the man, destroyed his chances for prosperity. Still, he would give John back whatever he could. Changing the topic to appease his guilt, Mr. Barlow said, "It is time for me to head back to Savannah. You run along now, son. You need to start fixing up your house."

Looking at his feet, John shuffled them around a bit in the dust. "I was thinkin' … maybe I ought to ride back with you, suh." He paused slightly to look up at the sky, not wanting to appear concerned. "With highwaymen about, you ought to have an escort."

Mr. Barlow laughed deeply and freely, pleased that John was worried for him. "Do not fret over me, son. Richardson's eldest boy, Keith, will ride with me. He has some urgent business in town … a young lady, most likely."

John nodded and turned to unhitch his horse.

Mr. Barlow added, "I wish the best for you, John."

John stepped up and swung himself into the saddle, turning the horse to face his new home.

"I truly mean that, son."

There was a painfully long pause. The silence was agonizing, something Mr. Barlow wanted to struggle against, like a bear trap snapped against his leg, metal teeth stuck in the bone.

John kept his back to the old man, clicked his tongue, flicked the reins, and galloped off, his coon dog trailing after him. John was not looking back, no matter what kind words Mr. Barlow had to say.

CHAPTER 3

▼

ENTER THE ENEMY

Spring came late to Laurel Creek that year. Brown shades of winter still clung to the grass. Buds had yet to form on the trees, and the wind was a sharp reminder of cold weather. The lateness kept everyone on edge. Farmers had yet to till their spring fields or dig canals for rice. Their worries grew over whether crops would make it to harvest. Owners of smaller plantations were concerned about feeding their families next winter. This year had yielded the harshest of winters and the coldest of springs to hit Laurel Creek in years.

As a result of hard times, some of the more superstitious folk noticed John Connolley and suggested he had brought the bad weather with him. It was not long before the younger Frank Crawford, widely known simply as Junior, jokingly initiated a rumor that John Connolley was a bad omen, and soon feelings of resentment spread. Only the foolish believed it, but as the cold winter weather dragged on into March, they needed a scapegoat. John Connolley, a quiet man new to town, was a prime target for superstition and suspicion.

Still, most folk knew the suspicions to be tomfoolery and treated John decently to his face. Angus MacPhearson, for his part, guffawed at the notion, helping to keep the boiling pot to a simmer. John Connolley was respected as a man of wealth, which helped to legitimize his presence. Word was that Jacob Barlow himself had helped open the man's bank account, depositing over a thousand dollars. The banker held all transactions in confidence, but his wife was a notorious gossip, and Joseph Atwell told her everything. It was John's wealth, his connection to Jacob Barlow, and Angus MacPhearson's refusal to give way to nonsense that kept John Connolley in good community standing.

John did not carry himself as a man of wealth, which confused most folk. Had it not been for Gertrude Atwell's gossip, no one would have believed John owned anything but the shirt on his back. In fact, if it had not been Mr. Jacob Barlow himself who had introduced the man around town, no one would have believed a word that crazy old gossip said. Gertrude Atwell was known for gross exaggeration. She spread rumors as wide as her hips—and hers were pretty wide hips, especially compared to her height. Just shy of five feet, Mrs. Atwell had been a slight woman … until she married Joseph Atwell, that was. But a luxurious, sedentary lifestyle had padded her backside mightily over the years. Even though folks didn't always take Mrs. Atwell's gossip at face value, they knew John Connolley had bought Mr. Barlow's five hundred acres with cash.

John's plantation, although humble, was prime land. Stretching west along the south bank of Laurel Creek, it reached up into the hills. Old Edward Moores used to sharecrop the land. Since he had passed away, many a man had had his eye on it. None could afford it, though, except Frank Crawford and Angus MacPhearson.

Mr. MacPhearson was not interested in owning any more land, as he already owned a township. He was only as ambitious as his family needed him to be, and he had already acquired all that good society had to offer them. Frank Crawford, however, was always looking to expand. Power was important to him. Everyone knew Mr. Crawford had bid for Mr. Barlow's strip, and Mr. Barlow had refused to sell. Folks reasoned John Connolley must have paid a small fortune to convince Mr. Barlow to sell. That John paid for his land in full and still managed to deposit over a thousand dollars in the bank proved Gertrude Atwell's gossip to be true.

For a wealthy man, John Connolley lived in squalor. He lived in the original house. It had been a fine enough home when Mr. Barlow first built it, but after thirty years, it resembled a shanty. One would think a man with a thousand dollars to his name could rebuild, give himself a home to be talked about, but John Connolley saw no need for that. He did not require any more than the humble house provided. As far as John was concerned, it was a fine house now that he had fixed it up.

The front door opened into the parlor. To the left was a window seat that doubled as storage. In the corner was the most impressive structure, a stone fireplace jutting out three feet into the room. No cooking was done in this fireplace, as it was clearly for show. Atop the black slate mantel were two oil lamps with mirrored backing. Along the back wall stood a bookshelf that John had added.

He was a big reader, thanks to Mr. Barlow's influence, and kept a fair-sized library. Two wing chairs angled toward the fireplace, which John used for reading. Between the two chairs was a small table, where John kept an oil lamp and his current reading material, Thomas Jefferson's treatise on slavery.

John considered politics distasteful but remained current on political affairs. Jefferson, having held the office of president for two terms, had only just stepped down at James Madison's inauguration. John respected Thomas Jefferson, but Jefferson was inconsistent on the issue of slavery. Jefferson claimed to support emancipation, yet had stated that Negroes were inferior to white folk. According to Jefferson, Negroes lacked imagination and intellect. John knew this was not true. Besides, John reasoned, if Jefferson had truly wanted the South to abandon slavery, he should never have argued that Negroes are inferior. According to Southern logic and natural law, if Negroes were not human, then it was acceptable practice to enslave them. Slaves were so integral to the Southern economy that plantation owners were not likely to give them up readily.

John's kitchen housed a much larger, unadorned fireplace. It ran along the right interior wall, serving the dual purpose of heating the adjoining room as well as providing a place to cook. His kitchen had only one counter, with shelves above, and a table for two. John saw no need for more; he was a simple man.

A door in the kitchen led down into a small pantry, a recent addition to the house. The house was situated on a slight rise, so John had been able to dig deep enough for a semi-underground pantry that doubled as an icehouse. Currently very little food was stored there. John had no wife to prepare preserves. Mr. Barlow had purchased him a few jars of pickled vegetables and preserves, prepared by a Miss Katherine MacPhearson; she sold her wares at the Hodsons' mercantile. John hoped to get a garden going, but for now there was other work to be done. His main goal was to seed the land. He would plant tobacco this year, weather permitting. Anyway, gardening was women's work, and John had no wife. In the meantime, he would buy what he needed from this Miss Katherine MacPhearson, because she could pickle a mighty fine beet. Her peaches were so good, John had eaten his way through three jars already.

In back was a bathing room that housed the only brass tub in Laurel Creek. Mr. Barlow had given it to John for winning his last fight. When word of the bathtub got out, folks reasoned a man who owned a brass tub had to have more in the bank than merely a thousand dollars. Some even claimed he had as much as ten thousand dollars.

John's sleeping quarters were the same size as the kitchen. Two large windows revealed a view of Laurel Creek where two old oaks stood guard over the bank.

Their branches intertwined, forming an archway down to the creek. A rope hung from one branch; the Moores's son had used this spot as a swimming hole, swinging from the rope and dropping into the water. There were no window dressings, as John had an affinity for sunlight and nature. The sleeping quarters were sparse. Aside from a bed and dresser, all that furnished the room was a small wooden writing desk and chair. Atop the desk were an ink jar, quill, and stack of writing paper.

A small second bedroom had been occupied by the previous tenant's son, and later their help. The room felt too small even to John, and he considered building on to the house later on. For now he left it empty.

Besides the house, Mr. Barlow's plantation came complete with a small barn, work shed, and old plow. After thoroughly cleaning and sharpening the plow blade, John determined it still had a few good years left in it. The plow, however, lacked an ox, so he purchased one from Angus MacPhearson.

Originally John had planned to purchase an ox from the Crawfords. They were renowned for having the finest stock in the county. He changed his mind, for they were a most distasteful family. John had in fact gone to speak with Frank Crawford about the purchase. At Pine Grove, the Crawfords' plantation, John was directed to the barn. He was told he would find Frank Crawford there. Instead he found Frank Crawford Jr.

Junior was a wiry little man with blonde hair. He was twenty-five but barely looked a day over fifteen. Although Junior was handsome, there was a viciousness about him. All the Negroes had firsthand knowledge of his deep-seated propensity for violence. Junior did not just whip slaves, he enjoyed beating them. When John entered the barn, Junior had a bullwhip in his hand. He was thrashing a small Negro boy who could not have been more than ten years old. The metal-tipped whip had shredded the boy's back and splattered blood across the whole of the barn. The boy cowered into a corner, but Junior persisted with the beating, not only using the whip but his riding boots as well.

John was disgusted and outraged. He grabbed Junior's hand and held it back. Growling, John insisted, "The boy has been punished enough."

Startled by the sudden stop, Junior cursed. He turned to see the giant John holding him back. Sheer hate filled his eyes. Puffing up like a wild turkey during mating season, Junior shouted, "Get your filthy hands off of me!"

John looked down at the younger man. "Stop beatin' that child."

Junior struggled to free himself. "Do not tell me how to treat my niggas."

"I said the boy has had enough."

"I decide when my nigga has had enough!" Junior shrieked. Panic started to fill his voice, and his eyes bulged. There was nothing he could do to free himself from John's hold. Junior's voice took on a higher pitch. "Let me go!"

It was then that John decided he would never do business with these people. In disgust, he let go of Junior and turned his back on him. Before he could leave, though, the elder Frank Crawford entered the barn. He was a big man, nearly six feet tall. Prior to John's arrival in town, Mr. Crawford had been the tallest man in Laurel Creek. Unlike his son, who was short and soft, Mr. Crawford was rock hard. Junior, to his father's chagrin, took after his mother. Junior had gentle, boyish features and a sly smile that easily won over the womenfolk. The only feature the two men had in common was their brown eye color.

Mr. Crawford extended his hand in greeting. "You must be John Connolley. I am Frank Crawford. The help mentioned you were looking for me. Wanting to buy an ox, are you?"

John looked the man in the eye. "Not no more, suh. I was just leavin'."

Mr. Crawford raised a brow to his son. He could feel the tension between John and Junior. Mr. Crawford noted his son's bloody hands and the Negro boy crouched and bleeding in the corner. "Hell, boy, what fool thing have you gone and done now?" Snatching the whip out of Junior's hand, Mr. Crawford stormed over to the injured child. The whip's metal tip tore more skin off the boy's shoulder. The poor child howled in pain. "Well, Frank?" Mr. Crawford demanded in a rough tone. "What foolhardy thing has this miserable little nigga gone and done?"

Junior, facing his daddy, recited, "This here lazy whelp failed to brush down my horse after I ran him. Then the uppity little nigga, instead of cleaning the shit out of Tenet's stall, was found playing out back with Wilfred."

"Damnation, boy!" Mr. Crawford had no qualms about cursing. "You know the value of that horse." The boy backed against the stable wall, crouching in fear. Mr. Crawford rewarded him with another lash of the whip. After the boy finished howling, Mr. Crawford bellowed, "Junior plans to race that horse in the fall derby. I swear to you, boy, if he loses, I will lynch you. Now get in there and clean that stall proper! And when you are done with that, wash your dirty nigga blood off of my barn walls."

"Yessuh, Massa Crawford," the still weeping child barely managed to utter through gasps of pain.

Frank Crawford turned his attention back to John. "Well, suh, you came here to buy an ox, leastwise that is what I was told … and now suddenly you no longer wish to do business with me?" Mr. Crawford's tone became menacing. "Is my stock not good enough for you, suh? Did you not see them in the pasture as you rode up?"

John eyed the situation at hand: a boy cowering in the stall, Junior's bloody hands, and Mr. Crawford's scowl. John politely answered, "Your stock is in fine shape, suh. I just no longer wish to do business with y'all."

Mr. Crawford, glaring at the man suspiciously, snarled. "Well, suit yourself, mister. The only other farm you are going to find half-decent oxen for sale is Angus MacPhearson's. And his stock is nowhere near as hardy as mine. He works all his oxen to death. You best be buying from me while you still can."

"He is nigga-loving scum, Daddy," Junior piped up. "Do not sell him anything."

Mr. Crawford looked to his son. "Those are harsh words, Junior. What makes you say such a thing?"

"He interfered with my beating of Nathaniel here. He never even asked why I was punishing the little shit … he just grabbed my wrist and stopped me."

Turning on John, Mr. Crawford bellowed, "You, suh, have no business messing in my family's affairs. I do not tell you how to mind your dog. Do not presume you can instruct us on how to mind our niggas."

John tipped his hat. "Good day to you, suh." He left the barn, mounted his horse, and headed for Mr. MacPhearson's.

CHAPTER 4

▼

JUNIOR'S INTENTIONS

"Junior!" Mr. Crawford's voice shot out like a bullet. "Saddle your horse. I want you to head on over to Kilmartin Glen. Go the back way and cross the creek. Let Angus know what is coming his way."

"Yes, suh." Junior was eager to do his daddy's bidding. Making his way through the swamps and canals was muddy work, but worth it. The idea of fouling John's plans to purchase an ox satiated Junior's desire for revenge. It also provided Junior with the perfect opportunity to see Angus MacPhearson's daughter, Katherine—the woman he intended to marry.

The proposed union between Junior and Katherine MacPhearson was one agreed upon years ago by their mothers. Josephine Crawford and Mary MacPhearson had been fast friends since childhood. Their relationship deepened after Josephine married Frank Crawford. It had been a prestigious union, securing Josephine's entrance into Southern society. But it was not long before the dark side of Frank Crawford emerged. Mrs. Crawford spent a lifetime trying to placate her husband enough to avoid beatings. No matter how good a wife she endeavored to be, there was no pleasing Frank Crawford. He continued to beat her like a dog. The only predictable thing about Frank Crawford was that his anger was unpredictable. Only in public, and in the arms of her dearest friend and confidant, did Josephine Crawford ever truly feel safe. Her only refuge in the storm of her relationship was Mary MacPhearson. Being so close, the two women considered it only natural their children should marry. Such a union would secure their friendship throughout the generations.

Junior knew the mamas had agreed to this union, and his daddy certainly approved. If only Katherine and her daddy could be persuaded. Junior's was an unrequited love. Junior wanted Katherine badly and believed she would come to love him in time. It bothered Junior that he was nearing twenty-six years of age, and he still had not convinced Katherine to marry him. He wanted to marry her before she became an old maid. She was already twenty—far too old for a lady to remain single.

Katherine MacPhearson was a most alluring beauty. She was two inches taller than Junior, but that never bothered him. Her golden red hair cascaded, caressing her neck. Even Cleopatra and Helen of Troy would have been envious. Katherine was blessed with childbearing hips, and Junior desperately wanted to be the man to break her open. Junior envisioned her breasts, supple and ripe like Georgia peaches. He longed to hold her. Thoughts of Katherine MacPhearson always roused Junior's passion. After every visit with Katherine, Junior sought relief in the arms of one of Margarette's whores.

*   *   *   *

Unaware of Junior's approach to the plantation, Katherine was busy in the kitchen. Her family always teased her about debasing herself in this manner. "Little darling," her father jokingly commented, "you need to learn how to run a household, not work in one." Initially her mama was mortified, but softened some, as Katherine proved to be an exceptional chef. No one could tell Katherine she was merely cooking; she was practicing the culinary arts.

Her mama was in town, and her daddy was meeting with the overseer, so Katherine took advantage of her current run of the house. She had all the household slaves engaged in clearing and arranging the pantry, which she considered to be her domain. Even Abraham, who usually held the job of greeting and announcing guests, was occupied arranging jars. When there was a knock at the door, Katherine stopped Abraham from resuming his duties.

"Abraham," she ordered, "you stay right where you are. I will answer the door. You are to finish rearranging those jars for me."

"Yessum, Missy Katherine," the old Negro replied.

Ruth looked up, dismayed. "Missy Katherine, it ain't fittin' for a lady ta be answerin' de door."

"Never you mind, Ruth. It also 'ain't fittin'' for a lady to be working in the kitchen, but I always do. If I can pickle a beet, I can answer the door."

"Don't ya be lettin' her do your work, Abraham. De massa'd whip you's for sho."

"Ruth, do not threaten Abraham for obeying me, or I will whip *you*." Turning to calm the elderly Negro, Katherine cooed, "Do not fret, Abraham. If Daddy hears about this, I will explain what happened." Ruth received a warning scowl that suggested Daddy better not hear about it in the first place. "You have important work to do for me, Abraham. I do not want you wasting time answering doors."

"Yessum, Missy Katherine."

Ruth let out one last exasperated shout: "It ain't fittin'!"

"Oh, Ruth, you would think I was a China doll the way you act."

"You's supposed ta see yourself as one, Missy Katherine."

"Hush, and get back to work."

Katherine left Ruth to take out her frustrations on poor Abraham, slapping him on the head for putting a jar on the wrong shelf.

Katherine MacPhearson enjoyed visitors and looked forward to answering the door. But when she swung the door open, she was frightfully taken aback by the presence of Frank Crawford Jr.

"Junior." Katherine's voice was curt. "You know better than to come here unannounced. It is my daddy's expectation that I be chaperoned in your presence."

Junior smiled. "You mean to say you are alone?"

"I am, and I mean to stay that way. You are to leave immediately, suh."

With a bold arrogance, Junior pushed his way into the foyer. "I have important business with your daddy, and I mean to speak with him."

"My daddy is not here. I believe it proper for you to come back later."

"I cannot accommodate you," Junior replied smugly. "My daddy sent me on urgent business."

"If your urgent business is with my father, you can go down to the slave quarters, where he is meeting with the overseer."

Junior stepped uncomfortably close to Katherine. "I also have some urgent business to attend to with you." He pushed her against the stairwell. With Katherine pinned, Junior reached around her waist to undo her apron. Violating someone was always sexually arousing.

"You leave my apron be!" Katherine shrieked.

"You are a lady, Miss Katherine," Junior admonished her. Then, with a slur mimicking the slaves: "Y'all ain'ts ta be workin' like no nigga." Junior gripped the apron and ripped it off her body, as if he were tearing open a finely wrapped gift. Shoving Katherine harder against the stairwell, Junior attempted to kiss her.

Katherine slapped Junior's face so hard, silver flecks flashed before his eyes. A red welt with four thick fingers formed almost instantly. "You get your filthy hands off of me, Junior. I am not one of Margarette's prostitutes."

Junior flashed his winning smile. "I would never treat my wife like a whore."

"I would rather be auctioned off as a slave than be married to you, Mr. Crawford," Katherine scoffed.

Angered by the insult, Junior pressed hard against her. Driving his pelvis into her side, Junior forced kisses and fondled her bodice as he sneered, "You better get used to my touch, Miss Katherine, because you will be my wife one way or another." Feeling her squirming against him as she struggled to free herself caused young Junior to ejaculate in his trousers. A man weakened at a time like that, and his body went limp.

Katherine took advantage of Junior's loose grip to squirm away from him. She ran into the foyer and crashed into Ruth. A great clatter ensued as Ruth dropped the tray of jars she had been carrying. As soon as she saw her mammy, Katherine cried, "Oh, Ruth, hold me."

Startled by the sound, Junior turned to see Ruth, who was bigger than most men and had the size and strength to pull a plow. She was an intimidating force, and Junior's knees went weak at the sight of her. He swore he would see that woman whipped. After a good lashing, he would personally cut and strip a laurel branch to switch open her wounds. *Maybe splash a little salt water on them, too!* The very thought made Junior smile.

Abraham, a gnarled old slave with barely a tuft of white hair still on his head, came running upstairs, having heard the noise. "Hell's bells, Ruth, what be all de noise about?" Looking at the mess at Ruth's feet, he shot an accusing glare at the woman. "Ruth, what y'all gone an' done?"

Ruth turned her scowl on Abraham, and the man shrunk in his stance. "I ain't done nothin', ya ol' fool. Run along now, an' fetch Sarah ta clean up dis here mess. An' when you's done that, go find Massa MacPhearson." Looking Junior in the eye (he could not believe a Negro had the audacity to look him in the eye!), she added, "There be a situation here be needin' his attention." When it took Abraham more than a second to respond, Ruth barked, "Don't jes' stand there, ya ol' fool! Move!" Then her voice shifted instantly to soft cooing to help calm Katherine, who clung to her smock, crying as if she had been beaten.

Junior figured it was time to leave. *Knowing Katherine,* he reasoned, *she will likely exaggerate the whole thing, and that fool nigga holding her seems more than willing to believe her nonsense.*

Before Junior could depart, though, Katherine's mother, Mary MacPhearson, walked through the front doors. Mrs. MacPhearson, a stunning beauty, was an older, richer version of her daughter. She was dressed in a fine, cream-colored silk gown with yellow flowers dotted over the bodice. She wore a yellow lace shawl over her shoulders. Her golden red hair was tied up in a bun, with curls dangling.

She smiled when she saw Junior. "Why, Junior. What a pleasant surprise."

Junior bowed to Mrs. MacPhearson, thrilled at finally having someone in his camp for support.

Mary MacPhearson extended a gloved hand toward the young man.

Gathering her hand into his, Junior leaned forward and kissed it.

"My, my, you are a charmer." Then, turning her seraphic smile on her daughter, she added, "Junior is simply the paragon of gentlemanly behavior, is he not, Katherine?"

Katherine MacPhearson, still clinging to old Ruth's smock and using it to dab tears from her eyes and wipe her nose, replied, "No, Mama. I do not believe he is."

Ruth instinctively tightened her hold on the girl.

Mrs. MacPhearson took in her daughter's stance and Ruth's protective grip. "Oh, Ruth, let her go."

Ruth obeyed, but Katherine hung on.

"Katherine, you look like a fool, clinging to that old Negro like a baby to a wet nurse."

Junior laughed.

Katherine glared.

Mary MacPhearson noticed the mess at Ruth's feet. Her voice hardened. "Ruth, you let go of her this instant and clean that up!"

Katherine, not wanting Ruth beaten on her account, released her grip on the woman.

"Yessum," Ruth replied, as she bent down to pick up the tray and jars she had dropped.

Katherine stood straight, adjusted her skirt, and faced her mama square on with a defiant glint in her eye. She knew her mama was likely to side with Junior regardless, but she spoke out anyway, pointing her finger accusingly. "Mama, that man accosted me!"

Junior stepped forward. "Now, Mrs. MacPhearson, it was all pure innocence." With arms open wide, Junior flashed the smile he knew worked all too well on Katherine's mother. "I just tried to steal a little kiss, is all."

"Junior," Mrs. MacPhearson admonished with a smile, "you know that to be inappropriate behavior." Mary MacPhearson laughed along with the young man.

Indignantly Katherine stammered on. "It ... it was more than that, Mama ... he ... he had his hands all over me. Ruth saw it." Katherine turned, and her eyes pleaded with the old woman.

Ruth stood, her tray full and the floor cleared. She had not seen anything, and she hated lying, but she believed Katherine. "Y-Yessum, Missy Katherine," she stuttered. "I done saw it all."

Junior flushed with anger. "That nigga is lying!"

Mary MacPhearson turned on Ruth, her eyes glaring. "Surely you have some work to do?"

Ruth curtsied slightly. "Yessum, Mrs. MacPhearson. I sho do."

"Then run along, and do it!" When Mary MacPhearson issued a stern order, she expected her slaves to turn and run, which was exactly what Ruth did. As soon as Ruth was out of the room, Mrs. MacPhearson turned and admonished her daughter. "You are acting foolish, young lady. What is all this nonsense about Junior accosting you?"

"I am telling the truth, Mama," Katherine wailed. "You heard Ruth. She stood up for me."

Mrs. MacPhearson dismissed that bit of evidence. "Ruth is a silly old Negro who would say anything you told her to." Taking her daughter by the shoulders, Mary MacPhearson moved Katherine closer to Junior before continuing condescendingly, "Now Katherine, Junior is no lecher. He is just a passionate young man in love with a beautiful woman. He never should have tried to kiss you, but we can forgive him that little indiscretion."

Junior smiled, moved in closer to Katherine, and began patting her hand.

Katherine slapped his hand as soon as it touched hers.

Junior retracted as if he had been struck by lightning.

"Katherine!" Mrs. MacPhearson admonished her daughter. "This gentleman is to be your husband!"

"Not unless my sweet bonnie Kate agrees!" Angus MacPhearson's voice echoed through the room. He had come up the back way, taking the staircase up from the kitchen into the dining hall.

Angus MacPhearson was a burly man. His red, curly hair and massive chest were clear evidence of his Scottish ancestors. Still, he had married himself a fine

Irish girl, and all his children bore Irish names. He held a soft heart for his wife, but an even softer one for his youngest daughter, Katherine. She was the only one of his children to show any semblance of the Scot in her, not so much in looks as in temperament. Katherine had a temper, just like her daddy. Angus MacPhearson had overheard some of the conversation, as he had chosen to wait inside the dining hall before entering. He was curious to hear what Junior had to say about Katherine's accusations. He had already taken a moment to talk with Ruth. Mr. MacPhearson knew how to pull the truth out of her, and he knew she loved Katherine as her own. Mr. MacPhearson stepped slowly forward.

Junior carefully placed himself behind Mrs. MacPhearson.

"Do you think my wife is going to protect you, son?" Mr. MacPhearson asked, his anger evident in his voice.

Junior stepped to the side. "Ah ... no, suh."

"Why are you stepping behind her skirts, then? Have you done something you are afraid to get punished for?"

Junior turned white. "No, suh, I ... uh ... I just ... ah ... tried to ... ah ... steal a kiss from my sweet bonnie Kate, is all." He shuffled his feet and glanced a few times toward the door.

"Katherine is my sweet bonnie Kate," Mr. MacPhearson said gruffly. "She is Miss MacPhearson to her suitors. Assuming, of course, she wants you for a suitor."

"Of course she wants him—" Mary MacPhearson burst out, but before she could finish, Mr. MacPhearson silenced her with a wave of the hand.

Gently placing an arm around his wife's shoulder, Mr. MacPhearson moved her aside. "Just because you like him, Mary, does not mean Katherine wants him."

Katherine shot a smug look Junior's way. He could have screamed. Reaching for his hat, Junior edged toward the door. "I best be going."

Gripping Junior's shoulder, Mr. MacPhearson escorted the young man out to the veranda. He instructed the lad, "You are not to steal any more kisses from my little girl. Is that understood, Junior?"

Fidgeting, Junior replied, "No, suh ... I mean, yes, suh. I promise, suh."

"Stealing is a crime, Junior ... and you do not want to steal from me." Mr. MacPhearson glared down at the young man. "You are lucky your father is my friend. Otherwise I would skin you alive, then have you drawn and quartered." Gripping the young man tightly, he added, "And I would burn your entrails myself."

"Y-yes, suh." Junior was squirming worse than a catfish out of water.

Mr. MacPhearson turned the young man to face him. "You look at me when I am talking to you, Junior. Now, here is the way things are going to work."

Junior looked up. "W-work, suh?"

"If you want a kiss from my sweet bonnie Kate, you will have her hand in marriage first. Understood?" Mr. MacPhearson's eyes blazed with fury as he spoke.

Junior nearly wet his pants. Trembling like a leaf, he stuttered, "Y-yes, suh."

"Now, get on out of here, before I change my mind about stripping your hide." Mr. MacPhearson gave the lad a shove, and Junior stumbled down the stairs. Racing over to his horse, Junior was in his saddle faster than a frog could snap up a fly for its supper.

As he raced off on his gelding, Junior questioned recent events. *Why does that man hate me so? Angus and Daddy are friends. He should embrace me as the son of a beloved companion. But he refuses to. It is Daddy's scorn run over on him.* Junior knew, deep in his heart, that his daddy held him in disdain. It bristled down Junior's spine every time he was in the presence of his father. As a little boy, he used to cry himself to sleep at night, reliving all the horrible insults his daddy had slung at him that day.

The worst was when Frank Crawford called his son a baby girl. "You have the face of a baby girl." "You have the eyes of a baby girl." "You cry like a baby girl." "Lord, are you my son, or are you a baby girl?" When Junior was ten, he fell off his horse and bruised his shoulder. His tears had so angered Mr. Crawford that he had torn Junior's clothes off and made him walk around the rest of the day in a slave girl's dress. Shuddering, Junior recalled how the hands—even the Negroes—had laughed at him! *And Daddy refused to punish a single one!* It was the most humiliating experience of Junior's life. Every time Junior made a mistake, he cringed, thinking how his daddy would react.

Junior was halfway down the road when he ran into John Connolley. It was only then that he remembered he had failed to follow through on his father's command. He was scared his daddy would kill him. *Maybe*, he thought grimly, *I can lie my way out of this one.*

CHAPTER 5

▼

ENTER THE FRIEND

When John first arrived at Mr. MacPhearson's plantation, he was awed by its grandeur. One entered Kilmartin Glen, named for the small village in Scotland the MacPhearsons hailed from, through a live oak lane a full mile long. The lane opened into a well-manicured garden and pond. Encircling the pond was a path, with benches interspersed. Flowers, sculpted shrubbery, and oak, palm, and magnolia trees were carefully placed for effect. At the other end of the yard was the white MacPhearson plantation home, with its imposing Roman columns. The house stood a glorious three stories high, with a loving-arms stairwell inviting guests up to the second floor. John shuddered at the work required to maintain such a mansion.

The veranda was just as impressive as the rest of the house. It was furnished with large teak plantation chairs that overlooked the yard. Attached to the veranda was a magnificent gazebo, as large as a tearoom, where the family often took meals. John was intimidated. The MacPhearson home was even grander than Mr. Barlow's plantation house, and he wondered what it looked like on the inside. Quickly he wiped the dust from his clothes.

John knocked at the door and was promptly received by an elderly Negro. The slave was knotted up and bent over some. What little hair he had left was white and tufted up from behind his ears.

"Hello, suh. May I ask who's callin'?" the old Negro inquired, as he gestured for John to enter.

John walked past the old man, eyes widening. The foyer alone was bigger than his entire house. The floor was black slate inlaid with Georgia marble. The focal point of the foyer was the largest French chandelier John had ever laid eyes on. John did not even bother trying to count the candles. Continuing to scan the room, his eyes glanced through two massive doors that stood open to the ballroom. Inside, a large concert grand piano sat majestically. It was a beautiful sight. John had only ever seen one of its kind before, in a fancy New Orleans hotel. He remembered its sweet, rich tones, and his fingers itched to play the noble instrument.

"Excuse me, suh."

John, turning to face the scratchy voice, responded, "Sorry, my name is John Connolley. I have come to speak to Mr. MacPhearson."

The old man motioned for John to take a seat. "I'll go fetch Massa MacPhearson for ya."

"Thank you."

John sat, then resumed admiring his surroundings, particularly the ballroom.

"It's for parties and dances," chimed a lighthearted voice. "Mama loves to entertain."

John stood at the sight of Katherine MacPhearson. He had heard of her beauty, and every word proved true. She was tall for a woman, but short next to John. Her blue gown, which accentuated her white bosom, was made of fine muslin. Her golden red hair hung in curls past her shoulders. She wore it naturally, something John loved.

In a most alluring and calculated manner, Katherine swept toward John, fully aware of the effect she had on the gentleman. Extending a soft, white hand, she spoke softly, "My name is Katherine MacPhearson." Thick lashes extended to reveal sparkling green eyes. John had never seen emerald eyes before; he was mesmerized.

Katherine giggled, blushing crimson. "Do you not wish to kiss my hand, good suh?"

John's heart beat rapidly, as he bowed and gently kissed the back of her hand. "My name is John Connolley."

"I know." Katherine blushed again. "Everyone knows who you are," she explained. "You are quite famous in these parts, suh, for having bought Mr. Jacob Barlow's land."

It was John's turn to flush.

Sensing the gentleman's desire to change the subject, Katherine motioned toward the great doors. "Would you care to see the ballroom, Mr. Connolley?"

John nodded.

The room soared two stories high. "Daddy hired the best architect from New Orleans to design the house. He paid particular attention to the details of the ballroom. We have hosted many a fine party in this room. But surely you have come to my father's home for something other than a tour?"

"Yes, Miss MacPhearson." Uncomfortable in the presence of the beautiful woman, John cleared his throat. "I wish to speak with your father."

"Daddy is out back. Follow me … I will take you to him." Katherine turned, swaying her hips provocatively. Tilting her head slightly, she smiled, waving for John to follow.

Under his breath, John whistled at her beauty, the likes of which he had never seen. The freckles lightly spotting her face added color to a very healthy complexion. She was a good height, too, with her head just below John's shoulder. If John were allowed to hold her, Katherine's face would snuggle up against his chest. He blushed.

Katherine giggled, knowing what Mr. Connolley was thinking. She led him through the dining hall and down the back stairwell into the kitchen, where Negroes bustled about, preparing the midday meal. They finally emerged through the back door. There, Angus MacPhearson was working in the stable yard with two slaves, struggling to yoke an old ox.

Katherine stopped abruptly, causing John to bump into her. Katherine didn't react to this contact. She stood on her toes and whispered, "Daddy hates to be disturbed whilst he is working."

John smiled at the feel of Katherine's breath tickling his ear.

Katherine knew she had power over him, and her laughter bubbled up from inside. It was a hearty laugh, more than John had expected from such a slip of a girl.

Katherine's laughter attracted Mr. MacPhearson's attention. Looking up, he jokingly queried, "Katie, darling, what mischief are you up to now?"

"Nothing, Daddy. Why must a lady always be up to something when she laughs?"

"When you laugh like that, little girl," her father said, "you are always getting into trouble." Looking up from the yoke he was struggling with, Mr. MacPhearson noticed John. Eyeing John suspiciously, he asked, "And who might you be, good suh?"

"Ah … John Connolley, suh."

Mr. MacPhearson smiled. "The Connolley who bought Ol' Edward Moores's place from Jacob Barlow?"

"Yes, suh."

Stepping forward, Mr. MacPhearson extended his hand. "Pleased to meet you, Mr. Connolley. I am sorry I missed the opportunity for formal introductions in January, but I was busy entertaining my family in New Orleans. We always take a winter vacation in that lively city. The weather is much more pleasing down there at that time of year." Noticing the way his daughter was observing John Connolley, Mr. MacPhearson changed the cadence of his voice. "I see you have my daughter swooning over you."

Katherine blushed.

John inspected the ground between his feet.

"Get inside the house, little girl," Mr. MacPhearson ordered.

Katherine indignantly turned on her heels and marched defiantly back to the big house, keeping enough of a sway in her hips to hold John's attention.

"Never you mind that little girl," Mr. MacPhearson quipped to redirect John's attention. "She is my youngest and my darling. My good wife has lined her up to marry young Frank Crawford, so there is no use wasting your time."

Taken aback by this sudden censure, John stumbled in his speech. "I's … ah … I am sorry, suh."

"Surely you are here for more than courting my daughter?" Mr. MacPhearson queried.

"I am not plannin' to court your daughter, suh. I just come … I just came to buy an ox."

Mr. MacPhearson smiled. He had the man off balance. That always made for a most profitable business transaction. "Most folks prefer to rent."

"I would rather own, suh. I got me … I plan to do more than plow."

Angus MacPhearson politely ignored all of John's slips of the tongue but found it fascinating how the young man struggled to speak like a gentleman. He had to hold back his laughter—not because he found John Connolley to be a fool, but because John Connolley reminded Mr. MacPhearson of himself as a youth: young, penniless, and struggling to enter the aristocracy. "Sounds like you have grand plans for the old Moores place. I cannot say as I blame you. Still, oxen are expensive. Even this ornery fellow here is worth a hundred dollars."

John swallowed hard at the price.

Mr. MacPhearson pretended not to notice. "I keep the more docile beasts for renting, for they make a good dollar. Is it possible I could change your mind? I would prefer to rent."

"No, thank you, suh." John was adamant.

"Well, then, you can have this ornery ol' bastard for a hundred dollars, if you want him."

John winced at the price.

"I have to sell him high, son. Otherwise I will lose out on all the profit wrought from renting him."

John sighed.

"If my beast is too costly, you can always purchase an ox from the Crawfords."

John lowered his eyes, figuring Mr. MacPhearson already knew what had transpired, given John had passed Junior en route.

"You would get a much better deal from Frank," Mr. MacPhearson continued, "as he raises more oxen than I do, so he has more stock to choose from."

John's silence sat awkwardly.

Mr. MacPhearson laughed. "I see you met the wrong side of ol' Crawford."

Twisting his hat in his hand, John replied, "You might say that."

"Aye, he is a powder keg and easy to set off. You do not want to be on that man's bad side. Trust me when I say folks cower to him. His daughter married the sheriff, and the sheriff is more than willing to do Frank's bidding. You would be wise to make peace with Frank Crawford."

"I have done nothin' to apologize for, suh."

Studying John, Mr. MacPhearson warned him, "I see you are a proud one … and as stubborn as ol' Crawford too. Just remember this, son: Frank Crawford owns most of Laurel Creek. You do not."

John kicked at the dirt, wishing to complete both the transaction and the conversation. He was unable to hold his tongue, though. "I hold no respect for a man who owns a town. My only goal is to buy me an ox. I will never do business with Mr. Crawford."

"Well, those are noble ideals. How old are you, son?"

"Twenty-nine."

"That is a fine age. A little late to be starting your own plantation, but you clearly made something of yourself and possess a good bank account."

John interjected quickly. "I am just a simple man makin' his way in the world."

"Simple men do not have a thousand dollars in the bank, son … Don't look so shocked, Mr. Connolley. Mrs. Atwell cannot even say the word 'secret,' let alone keep one. And ol' Joseph is incapable of keeping anything hidden from his wife."

"I did not make that deposit."

"I understand it was deposited on your behalf by Mr. Jacob Barlow."

John winced at the mention of the old man's name.

"You have a mighty fine connection there, son. I must admit I envy that." Studying John, Mr. MacPhearson noted the reluctant bond. "What exactly is your connection to Jacob Barlow?"

"I grew up on his estate, suh. My mama was his cook." John scanned the horizon, looking for something other than Mr. MacPhearson to focus on.

Mr. MacPhearson thought it strange that Mr. Barlow would act as a benefactor to his cook's son. He took a moment to study the young man's evasive glances. "Who was your daddy, son?"

John looked at the man incredulously.

"I do apologize for such an abrupt inquiry but I like to know who I am doing business with."

John suspected Mr. MacPhearson wanted to know who his daughter was interested in. "I never met him, suh." John dropped his head in shame.

"Is your daddy dead?" Mr. MacPhearson inquired.

"I do not care to discuss it, suh."

Now that was odd. It left the mind open to suspicion. Mr. MacPhearson wondered whether John Connolley was really Mr. Barlow's bastard child. If so, he would have to keep John from his sweet bonnie Kate.

"I just came here today to buy an ox," John reiterated.

Not wishing to further John's discomfort, Mr. MacPhearson steered their discussion back to business. "Shall we settle up, then?" the man queried politely. "Do you have any money with you?"

John reached into his vest pocket and pulled out a fat money clip.

Mr. MacPhearson whistled. "Is this more of the ol' man's gift?" Mr. MacPhearson blanched at his own ignorance. "Forgive me, Mr. Connolley, my curiosity gets the better of me sometimes."

Indignant, John explained, "This here is my own money. I worked for Mr. Barlow since I was fourteen years old. I saved every penny I ever earned with the dream of ownin' my own land."

"A self-made man, are you? I can respect that. My money is hard earned, too." Not wanting to be too intrusive, Mr. MacPhearson redirected the conversation. "Enough of this. Come inside, and we will complete our transaction."

Once in the study, the two men sat down. Within moments Mr. MacPhearson had written up a bill of sale, along with the receipt for John Connolley's money. "There you go, Mr. Connolley. That ornery ol' bastard is yours now." With the transaction sealed, the two men shook hands. "Thank you for your business, Mr. Connolley."

Mr. MacPhearson smiled and gestured for John to follow him out. He liked puzzles, and John Connolley was an enigma. *Who is the lad's daddy? Is it Jacob Barlow? Why would a man give so much money and attention to the cook's son? And his face! This man is a fighter. My Katie sure likes her men to look rough. The complete opposite of Junior, I suppose. She is a foolish girl to attach such strong affections to a man she knows nothing about. A fighting man means a dangerous man. I must protect her at all costs.* Mr. MacPhearson swore he would piece John's past together one way or another.

For his part, John wondered whether he could apply the principles of taming a horse to the task of breaking an ox.

As they passed the ballroom, John glanced inside. Once again he admired the concert grand piano, vowing to own one someday.

Stepping out onto the veranda, the two men were greeted by the sweet melody of Katherine's voice. She hummed softly to herself; all her attention appeared to be focused on her painting. As John reached the steps, she sang out, "Daddy, are you going to invite Mr. Connolley to take lemonade with us? It is mighty hot out, and I am sure the man is parched."

Mr. MacPhearson smiled. It was not hot; the breeze was cool, and Katherine was wearing a shawl. The girl's father admired her tenacity. His daughter was a sly one. A pitcher of lemonade was placed on the table in front, with three glasses waiting to be filled.

"Let it not be said a man left the MacPhearsons' house thirsty. Mr. Connolley"—Mr. MacPhearson gestured to the chair next to his daughter—"will you join us for some lemonade?"

"Thank you, suh. That is mighty neighborly of you."

Setting her palette and brush aside, Katherine poured John a drink. "So, tell me, was your business deal successful, gentlemen?"

"Mr. Connolley purchased an ox from me."

"I do hope you sold him a gentle creature and not that wild thing you have been fighting with all day."

"I see you have been paintin', Miss MacPhearson," John interjected. "May I admire your work?" John was interested, but he also hoped to defer Katherine's fascination with his recent business deal.

Katherine, turning her picture to face John, explained, "It is a likeness of our pond, Mr. Connolley. I am almost finished. Do you like it?" She hoped to impress him.

"It is masterfully done. You have a very good eye." Turning to Mr. MacPhearson, he added, "You have a very talented daughter."

"The painting is yours, Mr. Connolley," Katherine announced. "When I am finished, it shall be framed and delivered to your home."

"I-I did not mean to suggest ..." John stuttered.

"It is my way of thanking you, good suh."

"Thanking me, Miss MacPhearson ... I-I don't ... ah ... do not understand."

Katherine's smile widened. "Why, for purchasing my pickles and preserves from Mr. Hodson's store. You are my first customer, Mr. Connolley." The young lady giggled with delight.

"You are her only customer, Mr. Connolley," Angus MacPhearson pointed out. "My daughter is an entrepreneur of the female persuasion. Clearly she believes one must give her customers gifts to keep them buying her products." Eyeing Katherine sternly, he inquired, "Do you plan to serve me some of that lemonade, little girl?"

Katherine ignored her daddy completely. "Mr. Hodson said you came back twice now. I actually had to send him more stock." Another giggle of delight led into her next sentence: "Daddy laughed at me when I decided to set up at the store, but you showed him, Mr. Connolley ... did he not, Daddy?"

"If I say yes, will you pour me a lemonade?"

"I am sorry, Daddy," Katherine sweetly cooed, as she poured her father a drink.

John's eyes were fixed on a point between his feet. His face was redder than a pickled beet. Katherine gently placed her hand on the armrest next to John's, her hand brushing his ever so slightly. John struggled to gain composure, but the feel of Katherine's hand was churning his mind into butter. "Ah ... you make mighty fine ... ah ... they makes for real good eatin', ma'am." John winced at his slip. This young woman had him so tongue-tied, he was starting to sound like a field hand. He tried again. "I especially like your canned peaches."

Katherine smiled, batting her eyes. "Why, thank you, Mr. Connolley."

John quickly pulled his hand away and rubbed the back of his neck, feeling the sweat trickle down his shoulders.

Katherine giggled, perceiving John's nervousness in her presence.

He was uncomfortable. Katherine's advances had not gone unnoticed by John—or her father. John observed Mr. MacPhearson's stance. His arms were crossed in front of his chest, and he had a surly expression on his face. He was sizing John up—no doubt, John reasoned, considering him an ill prospect for his daughter due to the uncertainty of his past. Katherine MacPhearson, too, was eyeing him, but for entirely different reasons ... reasons John knew he could never accommodate.

"I had best be goin'," John said suddenly. As he stood to leave, his legs knocked into the table, spilling the lemonade and breaking the glass pitcher. "I's … I am real sorry, Mr. MacPhearson … I will buy y'all another." Awkwardly John bent down to clean up the mess he created.

"Stand up, son." Mr. MacPhearson was annoyed. "We have Negroes for that sort of thing. As for the pitcher, forget it."

"Please do not worry yourself, Mr. Connolley," Katherine said soothingly. "It was just a silly ol' pitcher. We can replace that easily. Please sit down. I will have Sarah make us up some more lemonade."

"I think I have embarrassed myself enough for one day, Miss MacPhearson. I best be gettin' back to my work. But I thank you for your kind hospitality." John crossed over to his horse and quickly leaped into his saddle.

"Mr. Connolley." Mr. MacPhearson was laughing. "It has been a pleasure doing business with you, son. However, I do believe you should take the ox with you. Go around back. Lucas should have him ready."

As John disappeared around the side of the house, Katherine spun with delight to face her father. "Oh, my! What a fine gentleman. Would you not say so, Daddy?"

Mr. MacPhearson harrumphed, "Mr. Connolley is as fine as that ox is useful, and you are as foolish as it is ornery."

"Why, whatever do you mean, Daddy?"

"I am undecided whether or not that man may court you."

Katherine was distressed by her father's adverse reaction to Mr. Connolley. "But why?"

"There is a shroud of mystery surrounding that young man, Katie. Until I have a clearer picture of his lineage and connection to the Barlows, you will have to put a hold on your aspirations."

"Well, I certainly do not want to end up with Junior, but what am I to do? Junior has frightened off any potential suitors, and I do so want to have children. I simply cannot live as an old maid all my life."

"At least we know who Junior's daddy is. I have a sense that Mr. Connolley has something to hide. He is a man with a past … a past we know little, if anything, about."

"Well, Junior may have good lineage, but he is a scoundrel."

"Junior is not that bad, I suppose. Your mama likes him."

"Oh, Daddy, really! I have known Junior all my life and have felt nothing but disdain for him. I have watched him bully our Patrick, beat Negroes, and torture little animals, including his own dogs. Now, Mr. Connolley is the first man I have felt a sincere interest in. He is rugged and strong, not soft and pretty like Junior.

Mr. MacPhearson smiled. *The opposite of Junior.*

Katherine ignored her father's grin. "There is in him a goodness and respectability that only a woman can perceive."

"My sweet, bonnie Kate." Angus MacPhearson gently wrapped his arms around his daughter. "You must trust your father's judgment. I have only your best interest at heart."

"Oh, Daddy, I do so want to know the gentleman."

Unbeknownst to Katherine and her father, John Connolley was next to the veranda with his ox in tow. It was evident by his expression that he had overheard much of their conversation.

Katherine gasped as soon as she saw him.

Her father said nothing but managed to avoid eye contact with John.

John tipped his hat, bowed, thanked them again for the ox and lemonade, and immediately made his way down the drive.

Katherine ran inside, eyes wet with embarrassment.

Mr. MacPhearson grieved for his daughter. He knew full well that Junior was a rogue; he had no desire for his daughter to marry him. Still, there was too much uncertainty surrounding John Connolley. It was his duty as a father to protect his daughter's interest and security.

John rode on in stunned silence. He had never experienced anything of the like before. The day had started off peacefully enough. He had set out to buy himself an ox, got run off one ranch for being a *nigga lover*, and departed the other knowing Katherine MacPhearson could never be his wife.

CHAPTER 6

▼

SURPRISE VISIT

It was a fine Sunday afternoon. Spring had finally won over winter's harshness, and summer was in the air. The weather was not too hot, but hard labor made a man sweat. John wished he could take off his shirt, but he knew he could not risk it, lest someone pop in unexpectedly.

Shoving that thought aside, John raised his whip, cracking it just above the ox's back. The old beast, taking advantage of John's moment of reflection, had stopped working. John was tilling the quarter-acre garden out back, preparing to seed it with corn for hominy, onions, carrots, potatoes, beans, peas, squash, cabbage, and lettuce. A garden was essential, as he could not afford to continue purchasing Katherine MacPhearson's preserves. To continue with this extravagance, much as it would please Katherine, would require him to dip into the monies Mr. Barlow had given him. John swore he would never touch that money.

A few clouds drifted in front of the sun, providing a slight reprieve from the midday heat. John stopped and quieted the ox, taking a moment to stretch his back. He knuckled the muscles until he heard the crack and felt the tension drain away. Lord, but his body ached. Some days he felt like a crippled old man instead of a man of thirty. *I ain't giving in to the pain,* he swore, *'cause it's a helluva lot worse in the ring.*

"Well, Gator"—that was the name John had given the ox to match its temperament—"what say we take a ten-minute break? I could use me a little water, an' I'll bring you back a touch of sweet hay." Slapping the old beast on the back,

John made his way to the pump. Faithful Amos leaped up from his resting place to follow, afraid of missing out.

The pump was attached to a short trough that allowed Amos to rest his paws up on the edge and lap up excess water. Shooing the dog out of the way, John pumped water into his hands. Slurping steadily, he quenched his thirst. John removed his hat and stuck his head under the pump to rinse off the dust and sweat. The water dripped down John's shirt, and again he desired to take it off. Here, alone on his own property, he should be safe. Before foolishly giving in to his whim, John was shaken back to reality by the sound of Amos splashing around. Amos had jumped right inside the trough and was lapping up the water.

"Get outta there, boy!" John chastised the dog, behind a smile he was unable to hide. Man and dog shook off in sync.

The sound of approaching hooves lifted John's head. He saw Keith Richardson, the innkeeper's son, making his way up the road. John donned his hat, tipping it slightly. "Good day, Keith. What brings you out this way?"

"Good day, Mr. Connolley," Keith said, tipping his hat in return. "My daddy sent me to fetch you."

Perplexed, John queried, "Fetch me? What for?"

Keith shrugged. "He did not say ... just said it was important, is all."

John was annoyed by this disruption to his work. "How important? I am in the middle of tillin' my garden."

In self-righteous indignation, Keith asked, "You are working on a Sunday?"

John lowered his head, then, raising it defiantly, looked Keith in the eye. Refusing to give in to shame, he quoted the good book: "What man shall there be among you, that shall have one sheep, and if it fall into a pit on the Sabbath day, will he not lay hold on it, and lift it out? How much then is a man better than a sheep? Wherefore it is lawful to do well on the Sabbath days."

Keith sucked in his breath. "You are twisting the scriptures, Mr. Connolley."

"No, suh. I am quotin' the Holy Bible. That was Matthew twelve, verses eleven through twelve. The good Lord understands I cannot get everythin' done durin' the week."

Unable to conquer John's argument, Keith used a new tactic. "Pastor Kipper will not be pleased to learn you have been working on the Sabbath." Keith shook his head in both warning and condemnation. "He is always commenting when you are not in church. Last Sunday, I reckon, you were tilling something else."

John straightened his back, drawing himself up. He did not need some well-to-do judging him. "I was plantin' tobacco in the east field."

"Yes, well." Keith's voice became stern and judgmental. "I heard the good pastor asking the doctor to look in on you. The way Pastor Kipper sees it, if a man is not in church every Sunday, he must be sick."

John winced. Mr. Barlow was keeping an eye on him through the doctor. "I will try to make it next Sunday."

Keith tsked. "I would do more than try, Mr. Connolley. It is unwise, as well as improper, for a man to refuse to attend weekly services. Folks are starting to talk. Sunday is the Lord's day. The Sabbath is a day of rest ... and you, suh, have not been resting."

"A man has to eat, and this garden has to get planted. I can no longer afford to buy rations off Miss MacPhearson."

"Pardon me for being rude but according to Mrs. Atwell, you have nothing but money." Keith looked down on John. "The Lord is more important than being too cheap to spend it."

John gave no reply.

Keith persisted, "I know that ol' biddy ought not to gossip, but if what she says is true, then you have no excuse."

John looked to the south and fervently wished Mr. Barlow was farther away. Spitting on the ground, John tried to rid himself of this Barlow business and the foul taste it brought to his mouth.

"Well, I was not sent here to judge you," Keith intoned. Once he said that, the tension between the two men eased. "Daddy asked me to bring you back to the inn, and that is what I mean to do."

Turning back toward Keith, John asked, "Did your father say anythin' about why he needs me?"

Keith shook his head. "Not a word, Mr. Connolley, but he had a smile on his face that would stretch from here to Savannah. Whatever it is, it sounds like good news."

John took off his hat and slapped it against his leg, sending dust swirling around in small clouds. "Well, all right. Give me a minute to wash up and change. I cannot arrive lookin' like this, now can I? Not if it is important."

Keith winced; John was purposely taking his time, and Keith knew it. His daddy said to hurry, but making John Connolley move was like pouring molasses in winter. Still, John needed to dress proper for this occasion. "Shall I saddle your horse whilst I wait?" Keith asked.

John nodded. "I would be much obliged."

Keith turned toward the stable, and John made his way into the house. "Come along, boy," John said to his coon dog. Amos acquiesced with a bark and followed John inside. As he stepped over the threshold, John suddenly recollected that his ox was still yoked.

"Keith," John called, "how about givin' me a hand with my ox? It would be cruel to leave him sittin' in the sun and yoked all day."

Keith, wondering whether John would ever be ready, begrudgingly agreed: "I hate that ornery ol' bastard, but I will help if it will hurry you up." Everybody in town knew all about that old ox. They all laughed to beat hell after hearing John had purchased it.

"Gator is not so bad, I reckon," John replied. "I have him pretty much tame now."

Keith, rolling his eyes and raising an eyebrow, muttered, "Sure you do."

"Fine, leave me tend to him myself." Gazing back at Keith, John inquired, "How important is it we go see your daddy right away?"

Keith strangled a curse. "I said I would help you, and I will. But you ought to know, that damn ox scares me half to death."

Smiling at his victory, John added, "This will only take a moment of your time." Actually, had John done the task alone, it probably would have only taken a minute; Gator had grown accustomed to John and was willing to let him run the show. The sight of another man rankled the beast, and the smell of fear brought out the worst in him. He put up such a fuss, with his front hooves pawing the earth as if he were ready to attack, that the task took much longer than usual, but eventually John and the shaking Keith Richardson finished the job. Keith seemed concerned that they had not left yet, and he gestured to John to get moving. The two men turned and headed toward the house.

Keith removed his hat and shook his head in disbelief. "I swear, Mr. Connolley, I do not know how you do it. That ox is one ornery beast ... worse than Beelzebub himself."

John smiled, looking back at the old beast. "Gator is no kitty cat, but when he is latched to the plow, he can do the work of five oxen. Shoot, if you had not shown up like you did, I would have had my garden plowed and planted by now." Grimacing, John added, "How long do you figure your daddy plans to keep me?"

Impatiently Keith shot back, "I do not know, Mr. Connolley." Stifling back a curse, the innkeeper's son added, "But he has been waiting well over an hour already. Could you please hurry it up whilst I saddle your horse?"

John, enjoying the distress he was causing young Keith, turned back to his house, trying not to laugh out loud.

CHAPTER 7

▼

MR. BARLOW'S GIFT

The ride into town was uneventful. Keith, intent on arriving quickly, refused to waste any time on idle talk, figuring it would somehow slow them down. He kept just short of running the horses, and the pair rode at a fast canter. It was high noon when they finally arrived at Richardson's Inn. With the sun directly above him, John guided his horse toward the stable.

"Where are you off to now?" Keith demanded, his voice grating. He was clearly uneasy about losing John now that they had finally arrived.

"Heck, Keith ... you would think you owned me, and could order me around," John retorted.

Unabashed, Keith replied, "I am sorry, John. But Daddy is waiting."

John remained firm. "He can wait a few minutes more. I am puttin' Cornerstone in the stables. Go tell your daddy I am here and will be along shortly."

Keith dismounted, tied his horse to the hitching post, and leaped up the steps, vanishing inside.

John sighed heavily. *What is so damn important that I have to rush here like a race horse? Richardson better have a good explanation for this*, John thought, as he meandered slowly toward the barn.

After settling Cornerstone, John decided the horse required a quick brushing-down. John looked around for the stable hand but Ol' Riley was nowhere to be seen. John smiled. He would have to brush the horse down himself. This was another opportunity to stubbornly drag his feet.

When John finally arrived at the inn, Mr. Richardson was waiting for him. Terrance Richardson, an older man in his fifties, had gray, receding hair. The top of his scalp was already bald. His face remained youthful, though. If he had a full head of hair, John would have put him in his forties. Mr. Richardson had led a gentleman's life running the inn. Being wealthy, Mr. Richardson owned a dozen slaves who worked the inn for him, and his enterprising wife handled all the business transactions. Age had not stooped his shoulders, and the man stood straight and tall. Proud, Mr. Richardson was very conscientious about his attire. He wore a dark green suit, a lacy gray shirt, and French cuffs. Regardless of all the finery, the innkeeper appeared agitated. "Mr. Connolley, what took you so long? Keith said you were just going to put your horse in the stable. You should have been back here ten minutes ago."

John shrugged, offering no excuse.

Not waiting for one, Mr. Richardson hastily uttered, "Come in, come in." Grabbing John by the arm, Mr. Richardson rushed him up the steps. "I have a surprise waiting for you … one you are going to appreciate." Mr. Richardson's smile was so exaggerated, John could see why Keith described it as stretching all the way to Savannah. "Mr. Connolley," Mr. Richardson sighed, "I had no idea it was your birthday."

John grimaced. This was not a day he enjoyed celebrating. "Uh … yes, suh. It is." Mr. Richardson's comment had taken John aback. He preferred ignoring his birthday and surely had not told anyone about it. John would rather work than eat cake on his birthday, for the day truly troubled him.

Mr. Richardson beamed. "Well, Mr. Connolley, behind this door stands the greatest birthday gift of all."

John tried to back away; Mr. Richardson tightened his grip. "The ol' man said you would try to get away. In fact he instructed me to be cagey, but I never could keep a secret."

"The ol' man?" John queried. "What ol' man?" John suspected it was Mr. Barlow, and this was perturbing.

Mr. Richardson shrugged off John's concerns, knowing all would be fine. "Come inside and see for yourself!"

He dragged John through the door, which was no easy task—and without John's commitment to decorum, it would have been impossible. Within seconds John stood face-to-face with Mr. Jacob Barlow.

"Happy birthday, son!" Mr. Barlow's joyful expression was genuine. Flinging his arms around John, Mr. Barlow gave him a mighty bear hug. "Has it been three long months? I am happy to see you, son."

John stood unresponsive, frozen like a sculpture, as Mr. Barlow continued to hug him. "Yes, suh. It is good to see you, too, Mr. Barlow," John finally said with civility, rather than love.

"What is this 'Mr. Barlow' nonsense?" Mr. Barlow laughed. "I told you not to call me that anymore." His laugh was deep and rich, as he wrapped an arm around John's shoulder.

Instinctively John began to retreat, but stopped when he observed Mr. Richardson's shocked expression.

Mr. Barlow, ignoring John's body language, tightened his grip on the young man's shoulder and kept on as if nothing were wrong. "Let us put this 'Mr. Barlow' business to rest. You must return to calling me Uncle Jacob."

An awkward silence erupted. Detaching himself from Mr. Barlow, John turned his attention to the lobby, where a marble staircase, trimmed with a cherry railing, ascended to the second floor. John wished he could escape up that stairway and avoid all this nonsense. Turning his attention to the chandelier, he counted the candles that sparkled through the crystals. There were thirty-six altogether. John pondered the effort required to light the fixture. Mr. Richardson suddenly interrupted John's reverie of escape.

"This way, gentlemen." Mr. Richardson motioned them toward the dining hall. "My wife has prepared a birthday dinner y'all are not likely to forget. She also baked her famous chocolate cake for dessert. I wish I could say I tasted it, but she slapped my wrist every time I tried to look at it." Mr. Barlow joined Mr. Richardson in laughter at his fine joke. John smiled, too, knowing full well the tenacity of Paullina Richardson. Two inches taller than her husband, with icy eyes that sent shivers through the north wind, Paullina Richardson was not a woman to cross. No one, not even her husband, wondered who really ran the Richardson Inn and household.

Mr. Barlow entered the dining room, John following silently at his heels like a dog suffering from heat exhaustion.

"The best table in the house." Mr. Richardson said, beaming with pride as he motioned for the two men to sit. "Next to the window, so y'all can watch folk out on the street."

You mean so folk can see who y'all are entertaining, John thought cynically.

"You have yourself a mighty fine inn, Mr. Richardson," Mr. Barlow said. "As fine an inn as any in New York or Boston."

Mr. Richardson absorbed the compliment like a sponge. "Would y'all care for some wine with your meal?"

"Most definitely," Mr. Barlow responded, adding with emphasis and expertise, "Will red or white meat be served?"

Puffed up with pride, Mr. Richardson responded, "My wife is preparing a fine roast as we speak."

"Then it seems fitting we have a red wine to complement the main course." Although he spoke politely, Mr. Barlow still managed to make his request sound like a command. "Make it a fine wine … no matter the price. This here is a day of celebration, for it is John's thirtieth birthday."

"Indeed it is." Mr. Richardson, a true sycophant, hastily agreed with everything Mr. Barlow had to say.

Mr. Richardson's speedy acquiescence to Mr. Barlow's every whim sickened John Connolley, diminishing his respect for the innkeeper.

"I have the perfect wine," Mr. Richardson continued. "Allow me to fetch it for you." Knowing John's eyes would follow him, Mr. Richardson purposely turned to the left, directing John's attention to the right wall. There sat a small pianoforte … a piano John was intimately acquainted with.

Shocked and overwhelmed, John uttered, "My piano!" Looking up with surprised dismay, John queried, "What is it doin' here?"

Mr. Barlow, pleased by John's reaction, responded with a robust laugh. "I knew you would be happy seeing that ol' piano again."

The square piano was nothing fancy, but John remembered how its music rang sweet and true. He had spent the most pleasurable moments of his youth sitting before that very instrument, escaping the misfortunes of life. While others called it daily practice, John considered it a refuge and stronghold, but never a chore. Georgia's finest pianist, who always remarked that John's fingers were long and nimble, designed by God to dance across ivory keys, had trained John. Mastering Mozart and Haydn before age thirteen, John had even composed a few works of his own. He loved music—particularly the range of music the piano alone could create. He had dreamed of becoming a concert pianist—a dream shattered by Mr. Barlow's refusal to allow him to train in Europe, as his music teacher had suggested. Raymond Poitras, an influential trading baron, had recognized John's musical talents and offered to provide the necessary connections for John to study in both Vienna and Hamburg.

It was evident Mr. Barlow expected a concert from John today. John had performed for an audience on many occasions but had always known of the event well in advance. He had made it policy to be thoroughly prepared. To perform cold was like planing wood against the grain; John simply could not do it. Fudging or slurring over notes would degrade the very instrument he loved and insult the great composers who provided him with so much solace. To make matters worse, the piano was really the property of Mr. Jacob Barlow, not of John Connolley. It stood as a reminder of John's dependence on the man.

"What is it doin' here?" John demanded again.

Meanwhile the dining hall was filling up with folks expecting a concert. The door chimed, and Katherine MacPhearson and her family entered. *Good Lord*, John agonized. *Why Miss MacPhearson?* Mr. Richardson must have spread the word that a concert was going to take place. It had been months since John had practiced. His anxiety heightened as he realized he had very little choice but to play. Frantically his mind rehearsed Beethoven's Moonlight Sonata; his fingers tapped against the table.

Looking at Mr. Barlow, fighting back exposed panic, John whispered, "I am not prepared to play, suh."

Frustrated, Mr. Barlow barely maintained his smile against John's reluctance. "Nonsense," he replied. "You are a fine piano player. All you need to do is sit down at your instrument, and it will all flood back to you."

Pulling his eyes away from the piano, John looked Mr. Barlow directly in the eye. "Why did you bring it?"

Opening his hands, Mr. Barlow exclaimed, "It is your birthday present, son. Happy birthday!"

Clenching his fists, John restrained the desire to punch Mr. Barlow in the jaw. "I ain't your—" Catching himself midslur, John forced himself to resume the language of a gentleman. "I will accept no gifts from you!"

Mr. Barlow, looking at John with parental resolve, folded his hands and advised, "Now, John, a man of your talent should never be parted from his instrument."

"It is not my instrument, suh."

"It belongs to you now. I just gave it to you."

"I am givin' it back."

Mr. Barlow furrowed his brow and shook his head.

John shuddered. While he truly wanted to keep the piano, he did not want to be beholden to Mr. Barlow. Placing his palms on the table to remain calm, John tried reasoning with him. "Mr. Barlow, I appreciate everythin' you have done for me"—John lowered his voice into a harsh whisper—"but I shall accept no more gifts from you ... no more money. So keep your piano, suh. All I ask is that you leave me be."

"Don't talk that way, son," Mr. Barlow pleaded.

Without realizing it, John had raised his voice. "I am not your son!"

"Is everything all right?" Mr. Richardson inquired.

The question alerted John that the whole room had their eyes and ears locked upon him and Mr. Barlow.

Embarrassed, John lowered his voice and politely replied, "We are fine. Thank you, suh."

Brandishing his best wine, Mr. Richardson presented it to Mr. Barlow. "Would you do me the honor of tasting the wine, Mr. Barlow?"

Mr. Barlow nodded.

Mr. Richardson pulled the cork free and passed it to Mr. Barlow before pouring a small amount of wine into a glass.

Mr. Barlow pushed forward, sniffing the cork and swirling the wine in his glass. Although he sipped the wine, he did not taste it. The sting of John's rejection consumed him. With his mind reeling, Jacob Barlow wondered, *What do I have to do to get John to forgive me? Why should he? Will he ever forgive me? Can I forgive myself? If only I could undo what I have done. Even the Bible claims that love can cover over a multitude of sins. But,* he questioned, *are my sins forgivable?*

Seeing the vacant expression on Mr. Barlow's face, Mr. Richardson assumed the wine did not meet with the great man's approval. "Should I take it back, suh, and find one more to your liking?"

"By no means. This is as fine a wine as any I ever tasted." Mr. Barlow lifted his glass. "Pour away, my good man."

Mr. Barlow's approval swelled Mr. Richardson's pride, and a gigantic smile spread across the innkeeper's face.

"Terrance," shrilled a woman's voice from the kitchen. "Terrance, get in here. Their meal is done."

Mr. Richardson leaped like a spring colt into the kitchen, returning with two finely dressed meals. With great fanfare, he pushed the teacart into the room. These meals were so elaborate, Mr. Richardson would not risk carrying them. Murmurs of awe accompanied Mr. Richardson as he presented Jacob Barlow's meal. Trailing behind Mr. Richardson was his good wife, Paullina, carrying a bottle of very expensive brandy. Mr. Richardson took the bottle from his wife and liberally poured the liquor, knowing that the bigger the flame, the greater the impression made.

Mrs. Richardson looked around, enjoying the entire congregation's obvious awe at the spectacle of the flambé. *Just like the finest restaurants in New Orleans,* she thought to herself.

Mr. Richardson placed an arm around her shoulder and studied her admiringly, then spoke to Mr. Barlow. "My wife, suh, is a fine chef. Would you not agree?"

"Yes, suh, I do believe she is," Mr. Barlow said in concordance. He always felt it important to remain polite to those wanting to please—especially folk he knew could help him. Mr. Barlow was certain Mr. Richardson would be more than willing to keep an eye on John for him. The doctor's reports were good, but it always helped to have more than one perspective. "I swear, if this meal tastes as good as it smells," Mr. Barlow added, "I will instruct all my friends to stay at your inn."

Mrs. Richardson turned a proud smile toward her husband. Had they not been in public, she would have kissed him.

"Now leave us be, good people." Mr. Barlow waved them off as if they were flies. "John and I have some catching up to do."

The Richardsons, titillated by Mr. Barlow's weighty compliments, took no notice of the harsh dismissal. Bowing formally, they rushed off to the kitchen to chatter excitedly.

With all the weight and authority he could muster, Jacob Barlow looked John straight in the eye. "You are keeping the piano, son. I will not take it back to Savannah."

"Yes, suh, Mr. Barlow." John winced at how quickly he deferred to Mr. Barlow's dominance. The years spent with Mr. Barlow had made it habitual, and John acquiesced without even thinking. *So much for being my own man*, he thought grimly. Looking at his plate, John reckoned this was a fine meal. But Mr. Barlow's presence made every bite taste like sawdust.

"Must you still insist on calling me Mr. Barlow?" Mr. Barlow asked, discouraged. "I was hoping we could get beyond that."

John put down his fork, placed his knuckles on his forehead, breathed deeply, and exhaled audibly. "It is a sign of respect, suh," John responded correctly. Internally he screamed, *I ain't ever gonna call you Uncle Jacob again!*

"Now, son—" Mr. Barlow's voice had softened.

John looked directly at the old man. It was one of the traits Mr. Barlow loved about him—and hated: John was never afraid to look him in the eye.

John wanted to holler, but he kept his voice to a whisper: "Stop callin' me son!" His tone was harsh enough, though, to cause Mr. Barlow to lower his fork and cover his face with his hands. John was not about to give him any pity. "We both know I am not your son."

"You must know how I feel about you. You were always like a son—"

"Stop sayin' that," John ordered. No one ever made demands of Mr. Barlow, but at this moment, John's force and Mr. Barlow's insecurity (an insecurity seldom seen) allowed for it. Many folks' eyes turned their way. John hushed his voice but felt no pity. He wanted to hit hard. "If I were your son, you never would have—" John stopped short. His voice had risen again, and the last thing he wanted was to make a scene. Emotionally exhausted, both men looked down at their plates. John methodically pushed at the caramelized potatoes, which were arranged next to the beef. The silence between them was purgatory.

John turned his attention to the floor. *Mr. Richardson must have quite a bit of money*, he thought. The stone tiles were hand-painted blue with a green leaf in the center. For a fleeting moment, John reflected that hand-painted tiles were a bit extravagant for a floor.

"John."

Mr. Barlow's voice broke the silence, startling John. The younger man lifted his head, and for a moment, they were eye to eye.

"I have always regretted—"

"Stop!" John responded, his fists turning to stone. Planting his hands on his thighs, John pressed down to keep from swinging them.

"But, son—" Mr. Barlow stopped, shaking his head. "No, you are correct. Whatever we had ended that day."

Wrenching his eyes away, John glanced down to watch a black spider meander across the floor to the piano. Climbing up the back leg, the spider slipped under the lid. *It ought to have a fine time making its web in there*, he thought bitterly. *Lots of wire to latch onto, with no pounding of the hammers to wreck its home.*

Attempting to wrestle control back, Mr. Barlow changed the conversation. "I have heard some disturbing rumors, John. Folks have been telling me that you have failed to attend church … the last two Sundays, from what I can ascertain."

John straightened his back. "I have a garden to plant."

"No excuses, boy." Mr. Barlow was firm. "Reverence to the Lord is not an option. Sunday is the Lord's day, and his alone. Are you giving up your faith, too?"

"No, suh."

"Do you remember your Bible studies?"

John lowered his eyes in defeat. "Yes, suh."

"Do you remember what the good Lord said to the chosen people in the desert after he led them out of Egypt? Exodus twenty, verses eight through eleven?"

"Yes, suh."

Mr. Barlow's voice strengthened as he reveled in his renewed sense of control. "Then recite it for me."

John recited the passage word for word; the man had a powerful memory. "'Remember the Sabbath day, to keep it holy. Six days shalt thou labor, and do all thy work: But the seventh day is the Sabbath of the Lord thy God: in it thou shalt not do any work, thou, nor thy son, nor thy daughter, thy manservant, nor thy maidservant, nor thy cattle, nor thy stranger that is within thy gates: For in six days the Lord made heaven and earth, the sea, and all that in them is, and rested the seventh day: wherefore the Lord blessed the Sabbath day, and hallowed it.'"

"Good. So you do remember." Mr. Barlow smiled. He was not letting up. "Now, if the good Lord can rest on Sunday, so can you. You will attend church every Sunday from now on. Do you understand?"

Defiance flared in John. His eyes sparked with anger. "I cain't get all my work done in just six days. I need to be workin' every day."

Mr. Barlow's voice boomed, and everyone in the room turned to look at John. "'And the Lord spake unto Moses, saying, Speak thou also unto the children of Israel, saying, Verily my Sabbaths ye shall keep: for it is a sign between me and you throughout your generations; that ye may know that I am the Lord that doth sanctify you.'"

A voice from the crowd uttered, "Amen!"

Mr. Barlow was consumed by the fury of the Lord. His voice trembled like thunder approaching on the horizon. Many folk figured he should have been a preacher—he had the entire dining hall entranced with his every word. "'Ye shall keep the Sabbath therefore; for it is holy unto you: everyone that defileth it shall surely be put to death: for whosoever doeth any work therein, that soul shall be cut off from among his people.' Exodus thirty-one, verses thirteen through fourteen." Turning a burning eye on John, Mr. Barlow questioned him. "Do you desire to be cut off from God's people?"

John glanced around the room. He was being stared at, all right. It was as if folk were watching the purification of his soul. Katherine's look of horror bothered him the most. Sickened, he uttered the appropriate response: "No, suh. I do not wish to be shunned."

"Of course not, son. The good Lord forgives you, just as I do. The Lord our God expects us all to be of a forgiving nature. Do you remember his words in Isaiah one, verses eighteen through twenty?"

John sighed, then recited for Mr. Barlow. "'Come now, and let us reason together, saith the Lord: though your sins be as scarlet, they shall be white as snow; though they be red like crimson, they shall be as wool. If ye be willing and obedient, ye shall eat the good of the land: But if ye refuse and rebel, ye shall be devoured with the sword: for the mouth of the Lord has spoken.'"

Voices in the crowd erupted.

"Amen to that!"

"Praise the Lord!"

Mr. Barlow leaned back, triumphant. "There now. The light of the Lord is still within you." Mr. Barlow's voice softened, and with fatherly concern, he inquired, "Given you refused to take on a Negro, surely you have hired some help?"

John shook his head. "No, suh."

"Why not?" Mr. Barlow demanded. "When I left, you had more than enough money in the bank."

John's determination resurfaced. "I am not touchin' your money."

Mr. Barlow's face was red with anger. "That is not my money, boy. It is yours. You earned it, and I gave it to you."

John balked. "I gave it back!"

"Hush," Mr. Barlow hissed. "Quit acting like a fool!" He noticed John was looking around furtively. Folks were hanging on their every word. Automatically lowering his voice to a harsh whisper only John could hear, Mr. Barlow cautioned him. "Fine, if you want to play that way. Remember, this land of yours ... and the rhetoric of being your own man ... is a conditional agreement."

"Everything is conditional with you," John spat derisively.

"Conditional that you make it on your own. Not attending church, not taking on a hired hand, not using the financial resources at your disposal ... that all seems to demonstrate you might not be capable of becoming your own man."

Grasping at straws, John lowered his head. "What is wrong with me doin' it on my own?"

"But as of now, you have not done it on your own. Have you, son?"

John's harsh whisper shot each word like a bullet aimed directly at Mr. Barlow's heart. "I. Am. Not. Your. Son!"

"I raised you!"

John countered, "My mama raised me! You were my ..." He paused to avoid the ominous curse between them. "We both know what you were to me."

Mr. Barlow's whisper took on a threatening tone. "And I am going to be that again if you refuse to comply."

"I cain't afford help."

"Speak as I taught you!" Mr. Barlow ordered.

Sighing, John corrected himself. "I cannot afford help. I had to buy an ox, and it was more expensive than I expected."

"I heard that story." Shaking his head in disgust, Mr. Barlow added, "The whole town is laughing at you, John. You must stop making enemies, especially over some Negro child."

John, knowing his excuses were weak, forged ahead anyway. They were all he had. "I have to buy all my preserves until I can get a garden planted."

Mr. Barlow interjected, "That is why you need hired help."

Desperation filtered into John's resolve. "I cannot afford one right now. Why will you not accept that?"

"Then use that money to buy yourself a Negro," Mr. Barlow advised matter-of-factly.

"I ain't ownin' nobody nohow!"

"Speak like the gentleman you are supposed to be!" Mr. Barlow hissed.

John hissed back, "Well, I ain't no gentleman, an' we both knows it."

Mr. Barlow crossed his arms, determined to regain control. "The plantation market is competitive, boy. Nobody makes it alone. Everybody with a plantation owns at least one Negro."

"Well, I plan to be the first to make it on my own, Mr. Barlow."

Reaching across the table, pointing his finger in John's face, Mr. Barlow demanded, "Now you listen to me." He was no longer concerned whether anyone heard him; his voice boomed. "You shall take the Lord's day to rest and pray! I will see to it your preacher informs me if you ever miss another service. I do not care if you are flat on your back. You will be seen in church every Sunday! Do you understand?"

With eyes downcast, John responded, "Yes, suh."

Another voice uttered, "Hallelujah, brother."

"Now, I do not know why I should, but Christian charity demands I continue to help you." Before John could protest, Mr. Barlow shot him down. "You keep your mouth shut, boy." Then, in a tight whisper intended for John only, Mr. Barlow added, "I swear, if you forget yourself one more time, I will drag you back home behind my horse."

Beaten, John replied, "Yes, suh."

"Now. I will be leaving Mamadu behind. He is a hardworking Negro."

John stiffened, jerking his head toward Mr. Barlow. He growled, "No, suh! I will not have it!"

Mr. Barlow bellowed, "I said silence!" His voice echoed against the walls. All eyes turned their way.

Katherine gasped.

John reddened.

Mr. Barlow bore his eyes into John. With an angry, piercing whisper, he pronounced, "You will take Mamadu, or you will come back with me today. Do I make myself clear?"

John lowered his eyes to avoid Mr. Barlow's stare. His only recourse left was to plead with the man. "Mr. Barlow, suh … I just need more time, is all."

"Time I have given you. Now, I am giving you Mamadu."

"Did you bring Matthew?" John figured if he had to do this, he might as well try to help out a friend.

"Matthew?" Mr. Barlow scoffed. "You want Matthew? Of course you do. Matthew is a runner. That nigga dunce was born with the noose around his neck. Damned Ashanti! I never should have bought him in the first place. My daddy always said, 'When you buy a Negro off the boat, make sure it comes from the Gold Coast.' But I bought Matthew from a friend to help him repay a debt, without looking into that nigga's heritage." Mr. Barlow's face reddened. "Those damned Ashanti are too rebellious. Whenever there is a slave revolt, you can be sure an Ashanti is behind it. Vengeful, spiteful creatures, all of them." Mr. Barlow shook his head in disgust. "Matthew is Ashanti through and through. Did you know I had to brand him a second time?"

John grimaced. He knew Mr. Barlow's rules: "Run once, and I brand your shoulder. Run twice, and I brand your face. Run a third time, and you will rendezvous with the noose."

Mr. Barlow shrugged. "Branding his face was an improvement. That Matthew was one ugly little nigga. He is almost bearable to look at now." Mr. Barlow smiled grimly. "I keep him chained to his bed at night."

John was not shocked at this recitation but was disgusted nonetheless.

Noting John's reaction, Mr. Barlow justified his action. "I will be damned if I am going to hang him unnecessarily. Negroes are mighty expensive these days. Under your care, Matthew is likely to hightail it to the north. Then I will have to hang him. Do not prove yourself a fool, boy. If Matthew runs again, his neck will be on your conscience."

"Then you are goin' to give him to me?"

Mr. Barlow choked laughing. "You want to own a nigga, boy? Are you planning to be a slave owner, a trader of flesh? Whatever happened to 'I ain't never gonna own nobody?'" Mr. Barlow's sarcasm was as thick as his mockery of John's accent. "Besides," Mr. Barlow persisted, "you keep saying you want to grow rice. Well, Mamadu is Bango—"

"Baga," John corrected.

Mr. Barlow ignored his error. "Bangos grow rice in Africa. Mamadu taught me everything I know about the crop. That is one highly skilled piece of chattel. If you are serious about growing rice next year, you best be taking Mamadu."

"Just give me Matthew. Since I have to take someone on, let it be Matthew. If you insist on callin' me son, pretendin' like I am a blood relative, then treat me like one, and give me the man of my choice."

"Fine," Mr. Barlow said with a sneer. "You can have him … but there is a condition."

John rolled his eyes. *Everything with that man is conditional. Mr. Barlow don't give nothing for free.*

"Matthew is a loan, not a gift. You can buy him when you can afford twenty-seven bushels of tobacco." Mr. Barlow laughed sardonically. "You might want to make your profit first."

Deafening silence filled the room. Although folks' eyes were turned away, their ears were sharply focused on what these two men had to say. John opened his mouth to respond, but Mr. Barlow cut him off with a whisper as cold as ice. "If Matthew runs again, I will be taking you home as his replacement." Mr. Barlow paused to study John's demeanor. John was slumped over, a defeated man. Mr. Barlow had John where he wanted, doing as he was told. "Well, son, do you agree to these terms?"

"Yes, suh." It was hardly heartfelt compliance, but it was compliance nonetheless.

Smiling, Mr. Barlow leaned back in a relaxed fashion. "Now get on over to that instrument. I brought it, and I intend to hear you play it."

Fear pricked John's innards. He barely managed to stutter, "I-I would rather not play it in front of all these folks, suh, not having practiced for so long."

Once again Mr. Barlow dismissed John with his authoritative persona. "Nonsense. It was a trial getting that thing down here. Now, get on over there, and play me something."

"Yes, suh." Once again John caught himself deferring to the old man before he knew what he was doing. His fork dropped, clanging against the pewter plate, drawing the attention of the good folk around them. Cautious eyes followed as John slowly made his way over to the piano.

John felt no joy as he seated himself at the bench. Softly touching the ivory, he began with a slow Celtic tragedy. A voice called out for a jig, but John was in no mood for an upbeat melody. As the afternoon wore on, he played an old Floridian waltz, then sang them "Crazy Jane" and "Sweet is the Vale," before finishing off with "River Divides," a melody he wrote himself. By then the room was over-flowing with folk begging for more. John gave in. The music had transported him from the present and kept his mind away from the past. As for Mr. Barlow, the music spirited him back to the days before John turned fourteen.

CHAPTER 8

▼

FOURTEEN

John barely slept a wink in anticipation of his fourteenth birthday. Mr. Barlow always treated birthdays with the utmost joy and revelry. Expecting something special, John tossed and turned until he heard the creak of the door. Trying to feign sleep, John heard footfalls crossing the floor and the soft poof of the package landing on the dresser. After the footfalls receded, endless waiting ensued as John held out until enough light finally shone through the curtains to denote morning. With the sunshine finally in his eyes, John leaped from bed and reached for the gift deposited on his dresser. Tearing through blue paper, he unwrapped a pair of riding chaps. Without even waiting to put on trousers, John threw the chaps over his short breeches. They fit the child perfectly.

Running down to the kitchen, John hollered, "Mama! Uncle Jacob gave me ridin' chaps … the kind Montgomery used to wear."

John's mother chastised him, "Well, now. Don't be so high and mighty about it. You look ridiculous running around in your short breeches with those things slung over them. Get back upstairs, you hear, and put some clothes on. Hurry up now, before folks see you half-naked like you are."

Try as she might to be angry with her son, Evelyn could not help but laugh. Her life had not turned out as planned, but with Jacob Barlow's help, John's life would be better. She knew Mr. Barlow owned her and the boy, but Mr. Barlow loved John. He had practically adopted John, never having had a son of his own.

Mr. Barlow's good wife, Louise, God bless her soul, had died giving birth to Mr. Barlow's only child, Emily. As Emily was only two months younger than John, Evelyn had been Emily's wet nurse, treating her like her own child—much as Mr. Barlow saw John as his own.

Little Emily and John had grown up like brother and sister, but lately they had not been acting like siblings … well, they were not siblings. Still, they had grown up like blood relatives. Evelyn suspected Emily and John were sweet on each other. Just yesterday morning, she caught the two sneaking out to the barn to be alone. Evelyn had chastised Emily, warning her of the consequences that befell a wanton woman. Then she took the switch to her son, cautioning him most sternly not to ruin the girl.

Still, she suspected that Mr. Barlow, unlike her own father, would never do away with Emily. Mr. Barlow was not like Evelyn's father. The man, whose name she vowed never to say again, had abandoned her, murdered her lover, and sold her like a Negro into slavery.

Evelyn shuddered to think what her life would have been like if someone other than Jacob Barlow had purchased her. The day of her auctioning was seared into her soul. She recalled the faces of the men leering after her with lust as the bidding proceeded. Some of the men were even so bold as to grab for their private regions as they bid for the white whore. She remembered her father's smug smile when the sale had gone through. He saw the deal as a transaction that would forever wash her shame from his family.

When Evelyn's father turned to Mr. Barlow, the highest bidder, he adamantly warned him, "You may have purchased this harlot, son, but if you wish to retain the profitable business alliance we have forged over the years, you will ensure that I never have to lay eyes on that traitorous whore again!" Before abandoning his daughter to her new master, Evelyn's father walked over to her and spat in her face.

Standing there the day John turned fourteen, Evelyn shook her head in an attempt to pull herself away from painful memories. After all, it was her son's birthday, and a happy day it was turning out to be. Mr. Barlow had drummed it into John's head that this was the day John would become a man. And near enough to being a man he was, standing six feet two, towering head and shoulders over every other man on Mr. Barlow's plantation. It was evident, too, by the way he was still outgrowing his clothes, that he had not yet grown to his full height.

Mr. Barlow often bragged about the boy's stature: "I do declare, by the time he finishes springing upward, John will be as tall as Tomo-chi-chi. Yes, suh. That boy is going to be well over seven feet!" Still, John's weight belied his size. Weighing a mere one hundred and thirty-five pounds, John was tall, but far too lanky. "He will build the muscle when he gets older," Mr. Barlow would often say, to reassure the boy's mother as well as himself.

Evelyn often shuddered to think what would happen to her son if Mr. Barlow ever decided to work John in the fields. She knew he would not last two days out there. Mitch, the overseer, had a reputation for working men to their deaths. Mitch did not care if they were black or white; he delighted in working men harder than their bodies were designed to work. Evelyn was relieved that Mr. Barlow kept John in the stables. John loved the horses. For this Evelyn was grateful, and Mr. Barlow knew she would do anything to save her son from hard labor. This fact kept her on her knees and prostrated before Mr. Barlow. Mr. Barlow enjoyed the power he exercised over her—a power most satisfying, given she had come from a family grander and more powerful than his own.

John, bounding down the stairs three at a time, leaped in front of Mr. Barlow. "I am ready, Uncle Jacob. May I ride Cornerstone now?"

The boy's smile was intoxicating. He was beautiful and brimming with innocence. Mr. Barlow loved the child, but he kept the depth of that love in check by constantly reminding himself that John was property.

"Oh, no, you don't, young man." Evelyn's cry moved up from the kitchen stairs into the front foyer. She strode into view. "I am sorry, Mr. Barlow, but this here child"—John's chagrin caused his mother to smile—"I mean, young man, has not eaten his breakfast. I will not let him ride the likes of Cornerstone on an empty stomach."

John squirmed to free himself from his mother's grip. Her hands were clamped to his shoulders, and she would not let go until he did as he was told.

"Aw, Mama!"

"Your mama is right, son," Mr. Barlow said, ruffling the lad's curly red locks. "Eat your breakfast first, John. You can meet me at the stables when you are finished with your meal. By the time you arrive, Mitch will have Cornerstone saddled and ready."

"Yessuh!" John replied exuberantly.

"Yes, suh," Mr. Barlow corrected, separating the two words distinctly. "I do not want you talking like a nigga dunce."

"Yes, suh!" Nothing could deflate John at this moment. Grabbing his mother by the arm, he swung her back into the kitchen. "Hurry, Mama. I's finally gettin' ta ride Cornerstone. Don't make me wait all year!"

"I am finally," Jacob corrected. "Do not make me."

John parroted the appropriate words. "I am finally allowed to ride Cornerstone by myself, Mama. Please do not make me wait."

"Much better, son. It is bad enough your mama has learned to talk like a Negro slave. I suppose it cannot be helped since she works in the kitchen alongside them. Still," Mr. Barlow admonished the woman, "that does not mean John's speech has to suffer. Evelyn, I want you to censure your son's language from now on."

"Yes, suh, Mr. Barlow." Evelyn's promise was adamant.

Mr. Barlow ruffled John's hair one last time before leaving.

As soon as Mr. Barlow was out the door, John pushed his mother into the kitchen. "Hurry, Mama. I finally gets to ride Cornerstone, jes' like Montgomery."

Evelyn turned to her boy's will. "Montgomery, Montgomery. All I ever hear from you is Montgomery! The way you say his name, you'd think he were the good Lord himself." As she spoke, Evelyn set a plate of steak and eggs on the table.

John's eyes popped wide open.

"Mr. Barlow said to feed you a man's breakfast today." She kissed John and sighed. "Happy birthday, son." Evelyn could not help but laugh as she watched her son shovel down his man-sized meal.

This was no ordinary birthday for John. The dawn had risen on his entrance into manhood, for this was the day Uncle Jacob had told him he would be old enough to ride Cornerstone, the pride of Mr. Barlow's stock, on his own. Caught two years previously, Cornerstone had defeated five of Mr. Barlow's men in their attempt to break his spirit. In the end, Mr. Barlow brought in James Montgomery, a famous horse whisperer from North Carolina, to help tame the beast.

John had trailed after the man day and night, watching him work his magic. At first Mr. Montgomery merely walked the horse, speaking to him constantly, feeding him bits of carrot and apple. Mr. Barlow, an impatient man by nature, cursed Mr. Montgomery, but left him to his eccentric ways.

Mr. Montgomery did manage to train the animal over the course of many months. Cornerstone, for his part, retained many aspects of his free spirit.

"Breakin' the animal's spirit's not my way," Mr. Montgomery intoned in a deep but gentle baritone. "The horse needs ta know who's boss, but remain master of its own soul." John nodded thoughtfully. Though only a boy, he understood the man.

"Can I try ridin' 'im now you got 'im takin' the saddle?" John asked. He desperately wanted to be in charge of the wild beast that had whipped five men.

"'Fraid not, son," the giant began. "Cornerstone's only willin' ta let me ride him. I have ta work him ta take ta your daddy first."

"Oh, Uncle Jacob ain't my daddy."

"Sorry, son. I misunderstood."

"That's OK. Lotsa folks think that way. He acts like my daddy, an' I treat him like one, but I call him Uncle Jacob. He ain't my real uncle, neither. Mama works in his kitchen. She's the finest cook Uncle Jacob ever had. His wife died when Emily was born. Mama says since Uncle Jacob ain't got no son, so he treats me like one."

Mr. Montgomery smiled, wrapping an arm around John's shoulder. "Well, you're one lucky little fella, ain't you's?"

"I ain't little. I's twelve." Standing erect, John added, "An' near as tall as you."

Mr. Montgomery's laugh was rich and deep. "Y'are at that, lad! Y'are at that."

John sensed honesty in the man. It did not feel as if Mr. Montgomery were laughing at him, but rather as if they shared a special bond.

"I like you, Mr. Montgomery," John burst out.

The tall man smiled. "My friends call me James."

Thrilled at being equated with the man's friends, John inquired, "May I call you James, suh?"

"'Course you can."

"An' you can call me John."

Mr. Montgomery laughed. "John it is, then."

Two years had passed since Mr. Montgomery broke Cornerstone for Mr. Barlow. Uncle Jacob had promised John he could ride the mighty stallion to the east pasture all by himself this day, his fourteenth birthday. John, barely containing his glee, gobbled down the steak and eggs his mama had prepared.

"Slow down and eat proper," Evelyn chastised.

"But Mama," John protested over a mouthful of eggs, "I get to ride Cornerstone!"

Ever pragmatic, Evelyn intoned, "You rode him before."

"But never alone. An' never as far as the east pasture," John protested, spitting bits of egg as he spoke. "An' I don't gotta have Mitch followin' me or nothin' this time."

Evelyn laughed. "That sure is special, isn't it? Mr. Barlow trustin' you to ride his favorite horse."

"Yessum—"

"Watch your talk. That is 'yes, ma'am.'"

John rolled his eyes. "Yes, ma'am. Uncle Jacob trusts me, but he ain't gonna wait all day. He's a busy man, you know."

"Yes, child. I know."

Stifling indignation, John protested, "I ain't no child, Mama! Uncle Jacob said I'd be a man on my fourteenth birthday, and today I's fourteen."

"Yes, my young man, I know. But even men have to eat proper or suffer from indigestion, so slow down."

With little regard to his mother's advice, John continued to stuff food rapidly into his mouth.

John left the big house wearing his new leather chaps. As anxious as a mustang wanting to kick his heels up at the sky, he was ready to tackle the heavyweight.

Mitch had already saddled Cornerstone by the time John arrived at the stable, and Mr. Barlow waited there, holding the horse's reins. "Mornin', son," Mr. Barlow said, as he turned the horse to face John.

John sucked in his breath, giving away his excitement. After taking a moment to collect himself, he tipped his hat most gentlemanlike. "Mornin', Uncle Jacob."

Mr. Barlow beamed with pride. "You look mighty fine in your brand-new chaps, son. They make you look like a man. Are you pretending to be a man, son?"

John knew Mr. Barlow was only fooling, so he only pretended to be indignant. Straightening his back and lowering his voice as deep as he could, he replied, "No, suh! I am fourteen today."

"Fourteen? Well, bless my soul!" Jacob Barlow, toying with the lad, pretended to ignore John by rubbing Cornerstone's neck. "I plumb forgot today was your birthday."

"You did not, Uncle Jacob. You gave me these," John said, while proudly slapping his chaps.

"Did I now? Well, you might be right." Patting the horse, Mr. Barlow reminisced, "You know, John, I was fourteen when I got my first pair of chaps. That was the day my daddy told me I could finally call myself a man. Yes, suh ... every man needs a pair of chaps."

John's grin gave away his clinging youth.

"Being a man and all," Mr. Barlow continued, "I reckon it is time for you to tame the wild beast."

"Ah, Uncle Jacob, Cornerstone's not wild anymore. Montgomery tamed him two years ago." John was so anxious to get his feet inside the stirrups, he was dancing around as if he were barefoot on coals.

Sensing the boy's intensity, Mr. Barlow cautioned him. "Now, Cornerstone may be easygoing for me, but you just take care not to let him get spooked."

John's impatience burst out of him. "I know how to handle Cornerstone. I's ridden him before—"

Mr. Barlow took on a stern stance. "I have ridden him ..." Mr. Barlow corrected. Before John could parrot him, Mr. Barlow pushed ahead with his lecture. "... but never alone, son. You have always had Mitch or me sitting next to you. Still, I reckon you are old enough to handle him. Go no farther than the east pasture now, you hear?"

John leaped into the saddle. "I promise, Uncle Jacob." Taking the reins, John turned Cornerstone toward the stable entrance and cantered into the open.

Mr. Barlow followed close behind, adding concern to his chagrin. It was hard for him to let the boy ride Cornerstone—and especially hard for him to grant John some freedom. Still, John had earned the privilege. That did not stop Mr. Barlow from adding, "Mind the time now, John. I have some important business in Savannah today, and I plan to ride Cornerstone."

John rolled his eyes. "Uncle Jacob, you can trust me."

Mr. Barlow held the bridle to keep the boy from racing off. "I want that horse back in the stable in an hour and a half." Mr. Barlow pulled out his gold watch, the one his daddy gave him when he got married. It was attached to his vest pocket by a gold fob. "It is nine-thirty. That means—"

John cut the old man off. "—that means I have to have Cornerstone back in his stall by eleven o'clock. I can tell time, Uncle Jacob."

Mr. Barlow laughed.

"I will be back on time. I promise!" John vowed.

With that, Mr. Barlow watched as the boy and Cornerstone took off at a full run. Laughing to himself, Mr. Barlow thought the boy would have made a fine little jockey, if only he had been shorter.

That was the last Mr. Barlow saw of John until Mitch dragged him back in.

CHAPTER 9

▼

AN HONEST MISTAKE

It was almost noon. Jacob Barlow stood at the stable doors and frowned in the direction of the east pasture. It was not like John to be late. On the contrary—the lad was notorious for being early, always wanting to please his Uncle Jacob. Mr. Barlow furrowed his brow. John failing to return home when he said he would simply did not make any sense. Still, it was the boy's birthday, and excitement could get the best of a young fellow. Mr. Barlow decided to shrug it off and give John a few more minutes. Behind him Mitch was saddling Rusty. Now, Rusty was a good horse, and Mr. Barlow did not mind riding him into town. What worried him was John.

"Where do you suppose that boy got to?" Mr. Barlow spoke his mind without realizing it.

"You askin' me, suh?" Mitch queried. He knew the mood his boss was in, and he was not willing to volunteer anything unless it was asked for.

"Just wondering," Mr. Barlow muttered.

Mitch took that as a request. "Well, suh, I figure the boy run off on you's."

Turning his building anger on Mitch, Mr. Barlow hollered, "Why would you say such a thing?"

Mitch knew he had erred, but it was too late to retract, so he pushed ahead with his theory. "He knows what he is. Ya treat him well enough, suh, but he knows he's property. An', like your niggas, he'll run if given half a chance."

Mr. Barlow gave an agitated shrug. "John is not a Negro. He would never run." The idea of John betraying him was beyond belief. "He only got a little overzealous on his birthday. He will be back shortly. But I simply cannot wait any longer for him. Hand me Rusty."

Mitch complied, handing the old man Rusty's reins. Because Mr. Barlow was not chastising him too harshly for his opinion, Mitch asked, "You want I should go lookin' for 'im?"

Hunting runners was Mitch's favorite sport, and Mr. Barlow respected this skill. He had only lost one Negro since he hired Mitch as overseer, but Mr. Barlow did not want Mitch chasing after John. "No," Mr. Barlow responded. "He will likely ride up any minute now, probably as soon as I leave. I will talk to him about being late when I get back."

"Whatever you say, suh." Mitch donned his hat and went to saddle his own horse. Still he persisted. "I could have 'im back here in less 'n an hour, iffin ya give the word."

Mr. Barlow's voice hardened. "I trust the boy! He will come back on his own." Looking west, Mr. Barlow nodded toward the north field. "I need you out there. Those Negroes are working far too slow. Frank does not have the same gift with the whip as you."

Mitch smiled at the compliment. He enjoyed pacing the work of slaves almost as much as he relished hunting them. Mitch had a violent streak; working for Mr. Barlow was all that kept him on the right side of the law. Mr. Barlow granting Mitch a free hand with the whip had provided Mitch the very outlet his sadistic nature required. Mr. Barlow never once checked on how Mitch treated his slaves, as long as productivity and profits remained high.

After mounting Rusty, Mr. Barlow headed toward the south gate. Just as he was about to pass through, he turned back and hollered, "Mitch!"

Mitch wheeled around excitedly, figuring the boss had changed his mind, "Yes, suh?"

"When John shows up, make sure he gets sent to the fields to work. I want him sweating under the whip for a couple of hours. Mind you crack above his back; I do not want you hurting him. Just scare him a little. I want him to learn the importance of being punctual."

Mitch smiled. "Yes, suh."

At that both men turned toward their individual pursuits, one to battle the paper wars, the other to land a whip across the backs of men.

*   *   *   *

It was nearly four o'clock when Mr. Barlow returned. En route he had ridden alongside the south cotton field to see if John was working. Mr. Barlow's cotton fields were the envy of Savannah. He also cultivated indigo, sugar cane, tobacco, and rice. Mr. Barlow advocated agricultural diversification, especially since tobacco prices had become so volatile. Cotton was doing really well, thanks to Eli Whitney's cotton gin. Mr. Barlow had been among the first to invest in Whitney's recent invention—or rather a reproduction of it.

It was no secret that Ol' Eli Whitney was showing off his newfangled contraption to the ladies. Mr. Barlow, not willing to wait for the man to patent his invention, sent a spy dressed as a woman to learn the inner workings of the cotton gin. Although underhanded, Mr. Barlow's entrepreneurship paid off. The financial gains were staggering, even for a man of Mr. Barlow's economic standing. It did not bother Mr. Barlow in the least that Eli Whitney was left penniless. Cotton was the future, and Mr. Barlow wanted the future to arrive that instant. With such money to be made, he was seriously considering tilling up the east pasture to plant more cotton. The fields had always done better than his horses. Still, he loved racing horses more than farming. *That is why I hired Mitch*, he thought wryly, *to keep my fields running*.

Mr. Barlow's crops, spread across an entire township, only represented half of what he owned. Mr. Barlow didn't just raise horses; he also raised Negroes. Most worked his plantation, but some were bred for sale. He had numerous breeders; he expected each to produce a child every year. These nigga wenches, as Mr. Barlow liked to call them, were promised freedom after bearing fifteen children. Hannah was on her thirteenth. The last one, though, had been some kind of deformed monstrosity. Mr. Barlow had it put down like a wounded horse, as he only counted children that would bring a good dollar at the block. Hannah's wails reached such a feverish pitch that Mr. Barlow threatened to put her down, too, if she did not shut up.

Mr. Barlow rode over to Mitch and Frank. Both men were cracking whips over the backs of field slaves. There was no dissension. The coloreds were working as expected, if not a mite too slow. No slave could ever work fast enough for Mr. Barlow. He scanned the length of the field for one white back. He expected to find John working there, but saw no sign of him. Grimacing, he turned to Mitch. "Where is John?"

Taking off his hat, Mitch shook his head. "Don't know, suh." Mitch glanced toward the big house. "I left word wit' Ol' Henry that John were ta come ta the fields when he got home, but I haven't seen hide nor hair a him yet." Mitch spat at the ground, then looked Mr. Barlow straight in the eye. He made no bones about his feeling that Mr. Barlow was too soft on John. "If you want a servant ta be a servant, suh, ya gots ta treat 'im like one. Otherwise they takes advantage a' your good nature." *Today*, Mitch thought smugly, *proves me right.* "I hate ta say I told ya so, suh, but it looks ta me like you got yourself a runner."

Mr. Barlow's glare would have daunted any other, but Mitch was as bad as they came. Besides, Mitch was confident in his position. "Six hours has given him quite a lead, suh. 'Specially since he made off wit' your fastest stallion." Looking north for effect, Mitch added, "Heck, Mr. Barlow, that boy's likely halfway 'cross the Carolinas by now." Glancing back at Mr. Barlow, Mitch watched as the old man looked thoughtfully toward the east pasture. Now was the time for Mitch to play his card. "Iffin you're thinkin' ya shoulda let me go after 'im this mornin', you're right. I mighta had a better chance a' catchin' 'im." Mitch did well to keep his smile inside. Mr. Barlow simmered, on the verge of boiling. Mitch intended to keep Mr. Barlow's anger focused on the boy. "Still, I daresay I could haul 'im back iffin you were ta let me go now." Tossing another glance north, Mitch asked, "You want I should go after 'im, Mr. Barlow?"

Mr. Barlow glared at Mitch. "I intend to talk to his mother first."

Mitch shook his head. "Don't see what she's gonna tell ya. The boy's done run. She ain't gonna help ya none. Findin' 'im only means trouble for John … the kinda trouble a mama don't want for her youngun."

Turning toward the big house, Mr. Barlow paused. "You come with me," he said to Mitch.

"Yes, suh." Mitch knew what the old man was up to. Mitch was to play the bad man and scare the bejesus out of the woman, so she would speak. It was a role his temperament was well suited for. Following Mr. Barlow to the house, Mitch turned to speak to the other overseer. "Frank, you keep them niggas workin'. No slowdowns, ya hear?"

Frank nodded, waved, and cracked his whip for effect. As the two men rode off, they could hear Frank yelling, "Get on wit' you's."

At the big house, Mr. Barlow was first to enter the kitchen, with Mitch trailing behind. Evelyn was peeling potatoes. Turning red, swollen eyes toward them, she forced a smile to suggest nothing was wrong. Mr. Barlow was not fooled. "Where is your boy, Evelyn?"

Evelyn burst into tears. She had spent half the day running about, trying to find John. The hands had said Mr. Barlow planned to send John to the fields for not coming home on time. If that had been all, she would not have been too worried, but the rumor mill swirled like a tornado. John had run off, he was being whipped, he'd stolen Mr. Barlow's horse, he'd been strung up, Cornerstone had toppled over and crushed him, Mitch had dragged him back home behind his horse. By the time Mr. Barlow caught up with her, Evelyn was frantic with worry, not knowing whether her boy was alive or dead.

Mr. Barlow felt no sympathy. His only concern was for John and where he might have taken Cornerstone. Mr. Barlow's voice cut through Evelyn like a razor through flesh: "He left at nine-thirty this morning, and it is now four o'clock in the afternoon."

"I don't know where he is, suh," Evelyn blubbered. Desperate to exonerate John, she sank to her knees. "Please find him for me, Mr. Barlow. Something must have happened to him. Maybe he's lost."

Mitch snorted. "Lost! What a fool thing ta say." With a voice dripping with scorn, he added, "John's been ta the east pasture dozens a' times." Mitch spat on the floor for emphasis. He played his part well.

Evelyn wept.

Mr. Barlow reached out and jerked her face up, forcing her to look at him. "Mitch is right, Evelyn. I fail to see how John could get lost." Letting go of her chin, Mr. Barlow watched as she dropped in dejection. Mr. Barlow shook his head, his voice taking on an icy calm, "I trusted your boy."

Evelyn shivered. "Oh, Jacob—"

Raising an eyebrow, Mr. Barlow formed a fist and landed it against Evelyn's cheek. "I am Master Barlow to you, woman!"

Evelyn fell to the floor, crying. Jacob Barlow had never made her call him master before. "Master Barlow, please. You can trust John. I know you can."

Mitch was enjoying the show. Taking full advantage of Mr. Barlow's anger, he threw in his jab. "Iffin Mr. Barlow could trust 'im, he'd be here by now."

Fear seized Evelyn's bowels. Begging on her hands and knees, she cried, "He didn't run, suh, I swear he didn't run. You can't think that. You just can't. John loves you."

Mr. Barlow backhanded the woman.

Evelyn fell back.

Mr. Barlow hovered over her threateningly.

Evelyn's voice was almost indiscernible, with words competing with gasping sobs. "Maybe he's hurt."

Mr. Barlow turned his back on the woman. Part of him wanted to believe Evelyn was right. *She has to be right. Why would John run? But where is he? John never comes late. Never. He always tries to please me. Even still, he is property. He knows he is a slave, and every slave tries to run at least once. Damn! Everything points to a run. Lord knows if John did run, I will have no choice but to come down hard on the boy.*

Mr. Barlow knew letting John off easy would send the wrong message to his slaves. Keeping Negroes in line demanded ruthless discipline. John was not colored, but everyone knew him to be property. No, Mr. Barlow knew, he could not let the boy off easy. He truly hoped Cornerstone had thrown the boy, so he would not have to punish John too severely.

"Mitch will find John for me." Mr. Barlow fought to maintain the voice of an impartial owner. "He is the best there is at hunting down runners."

Evelyn screeched, "Please, Master Barlow, don't let him hurt my boy!" She knew only too well how Mitch brought in runners.

Mitch sneered, "He'll suffer the penalty a' every other runaway."

Crawling to Mr. Barlow, Evelyn latched onto his feet, her words a jumble of stuttering sobs. "But this is John, suh. He would never run on you. He looks to you as a father. You've always treated him like a son."

Mitch interrupted. "There's gratitude for ya. Ya treat 'im like a son, an' the boy done run off wit' your finest horse." Mitch grabbed the woman and dragged her to her feet. Pulling her face to face with him, he whispered threateningly, "Just pray Mr. Barlow here don't hang your boy for a horse thief."

Frantic, Evelyn struggled unsuccessfully to free herself. "No, Master Barlow. No, suh. Please don't hang my boy. John loves you. He didn't run. I swear."

Mr. Barlow turned and walked out of the room. As he departed, he gave Mitch his instructions. "Find me the boy! Bring him to me as soon as you get him back, you hear?" The kitchen door slammed shut behind him.

Mitch grinned as he let the woman fall to the floor in a heap of tears. Questioning her may have been a waste of time, but he was sure glad Mr. Barlow had insisted on it, as it was fun watching Evelyn squirm. It was hard to believe she was the daughter of the richest man in Georgia. Just the idea made him laugh. Kicking her out of his way, Mitch went to fetch his horse. He had him some hunting to do.

*   *   *   *

John galloped Cornerstone all the way to the east pasture. With only an hour and a half, he wanted to get to the river valley as soon as possible. The stallion had been conditioned to run hard, and John knew Cornerstone could take the punishment. They slowed to a canter as they neared the river valley. John loved the view of the rolling hills. Mr. Barlow often brought him there to fish or swim. This was the first time, though, that John had been allowed to come this far alone. In his excitement, John became lost in thought. At first he didn't notice when Cornerstone got edgy and began to dance. Finally the horse jostled John out of his trance. This agitated John. All he wanted to do was sit quietly with his eyes closed, feeling the sun and the moist breeze on his face.

"Whoa, calm down, boy. You're ruinin' it." But Cornerstone grew more restless as John pulled back on the reins. "What's wrong with you, boy? Shh, shh." But no soothing sounds would calm the stallion. Suddenly John knew why.

A bobcat leaped down at them from an outcropping of rocks. Cornerstone reared back, nearly throwing John off. Fortunately the boy had one hand wrapped around the reins, with the other gripping the saddle horn. He had learned a few tricks from Mr. Montgomery. The cat's claws made their mark, though, ripping deep into Cornerstone's flank. Flaring his nostrils, Cornerstone thrust forward into a full run. John just held on and let Cornerstone take the lead. He knew better than to try to control the animal at a time like this. Besides, John had no desire to slow down. The bobcat spooked him as much as it had Cornerstone.

When Cornerstone finally slowed to a trot, he was foaming at the mouth and dripping with sweat. John knew he needed to walk him for a bit. John had no idea whether Cornerstone had injured himself during that wild run, but he knew it was probable. After a brief rest, John took off his shirt and rubbed the stallion down. Glancing at the sky, John realized that his run-in with the bobcat would cause him to be late. It was already well past the hour Mr. Barlow expected him back. John knew Mr. Barlow would be angry. Having experienced the man's wrath before, John did not want to incur it again.

"He won't be mad at me, will he, boy?" John said this more to console himself than to reassure the horse. He continued talking to Cornerstone as he rubbed him down. "He'll understand. I'll jes' get you rubbed down, an' then I'll walk you's back."

That was when John noticed the wounds on Cornerstone's flank. "Holy moly, boy. Look at what that ol' bobcat did ta you's." The horse whinnied and reared away when John's shirt touched his wound. "We better do something about that. You're bleedin' real bad." John could hear water rushing in the distance. Thinking they were still close to the river, he led Cornerstone in the direction of the sound. When he got there, he only found a small creek rushing over rocks, not the Savannah River. John surveyed his surroundings, only to realize he had no idea where he was. He was not even sure if he was still on Mr. Barlow's land. Nothing around him looked familiar. John had no idea how far they had come … or even in what direction. Everything had happened so fast—it was all a blur.

"What're we gonna do, Cornerstone? I don't suppose you know the way home?" John paused, almost if he were expecting a reply. Practicality and concern for Cornerstone took precedence: "First we gotta do somethin' about your backside." John washed Cornerstone's wounds and sealed them shut with mud. Cornerstone was none too cooperative, but when the mud was finally in place, and the bleeding had slowed significantly, the horse became less agitated.

"Come on, boy," John encouraged. "We might as well start walkin' back." John tipped back his hat and scratched his head. "But which way is back?" The horse shook its head, which John took as an answer. "Yeah. Your guess is as good as mine." The sun was at dead center in the sky, giving John no clue which way was west. And John needed to head west … at least, he figured he did. To make his choice, he chanted, "Eenie, meenie, minie, moe, catch a nigga by the toe. If he hollers, let 'im go. Eenie, meenie, minie, moe." John set out in the direction his finger was pointing, saying with little conviction, "Guess we go this way, Cornerstone. Hopefully I'll get you home real soon."

Unfortunately, John traveled north, away from Mr. Barlow's land. Before he figured out he was going the wrong way, Mitch had caught up with him.

CHAPTER 10

▼

RASH CONCLUSIONS

Mitch kicked the flanks of his horse as he approached the big house. Riding in fast with a boy in tow always made for a good show. For added effect, Mitch took a sudden turn, tossing John directly at Mr. Barlow's feet. Grinning with satisfaction, speaking loud enough for all to hear, Mitch hollered, "I found 'im, Mr. Barlow."

Ignoring Mitch, Mr. Barlow glared down at John, bellowing in his ear. "Where the hell have you been, boy?"

It was not like Mr. Barlow to curse, and that frightened John. To make matters worse, John was in no condition to answer; Mitch had gagged him.

Mr. Barlow gave John a swift kick in the side, but the gag muffled his grunt.

Mitch let out a laugh. "He were runnin', suh. I found 'im headin' north, just like I said I would. Ya ought to string 'im up for stealin' your horse."

"Is that what I should do, boy?" Another boot landed in John's side. "String you up for a horse thief?"

John stared up in terror at the man who had just that morning called him son—the man he felt greater love for than his own mother.

Evelyn, standing at the front entrance of the big house, pleaded with Mr. Barlow. "No, suh! Please don't hang my boy. Don't hang him, please!" She would have thrown herself at Mr. Barlow's feet, had Geoffrey not held her back.

Mr. Barlow, turning his rage on the Negro, hollered, "Geoffrey, you take that crazed woman inside, you hear!"

Geoffrey, middle-aged and muscular from working in the fields, had a firm hold on Evelyn. Still, it was an effort for him to drag her inside. Whispering condolences, Geoffrey tried to reassure her that her son would be fine. But Geoffrey knew better, having run once himself.

"I got you a rope, suh," Mitch said sadistically, as he yanked at the rope tied to John's wrists. Gesturing toward the garden area, he added, "Shall we hang 'im from the ol' oak?"

John's eyes opened wide with fright.

"Shut up, Mitch," Mr. Barlow growled. "I do not intend to hang him. Not for his first run, even if he did steal my best horse." Grabbing John by his shirt, Mr. Barlow pulled him to his feet.

John was suspended in horror. He had never seen such anger and hate in Mr. Barlow's face. He barely recognized Mr. Barlow, as his features were so distorted.

"I treated you like a son, boy! Gave you a good education, taught you to ride, and fight ... let you sleep in my house and eat at my table! Hell, I even took you and your mama to church!" Shaking John, Mr. Barlow howled, "And is this how you repay my kindness? By running?"

John shook his head desperately. He wanted so much to tell Mr. Barlow what really happened, but the old man refused to give him any opportunity. *If only I could remove the gag*, he thought anxiously.

"Mitch!" Mr. Barlow's voice cracked like thunder. "Tie him to the whipping post!" Then he added as an afterthought, "And take that gag out of his mouth. I want him counting every stroke." With that Mr. Barlow thrust John into Mitch's rough grip.

"Yes, suh," Mitch replied enthusiastically. Dragging John across the yard by his hair, Mitch used the rope that bound John's wrists to tie him to the post. After tearing John's shirt off, Mitch removed the gag.

With his first breath, John desperately cried out, "Uncle Jacob, wait!"

The whip cracked.

John's scream reverberated through the kitchen to be joined by Evelyn's unceasing wail.

"What did you call me, boy?"

Gasping, John tried to explain. "Uncle Jacob, please!"

Crack!

Mr. Barlow refused to listen.

Crack!

"Count, boy!" Mr. Barlow's voice echoed in the silence.

Mere moments, which seemed like an eternity, transpired before John regained his senses. The whip delivered a searing pain John never realized existed. Shuddering, he muttered the word, "Three."

"Louder, boy!"

Again John muttered, "Three," but it was lost beneath the next crack of the whip.

"I said count!" Mr. Barlow hollered.

"F-four," John stuttered.

"Four who?" Mr. Barlow queried mercilessly.

"F-four, Uncle—"

Crack!

"Four, Master Barlow!" Mr. Barlow's voice grew dark and ominous. "You are my property, boy. It is time you realized that."

Crack!

"F-four, Master Barlow."

Mitch, standing off to the side, laughed. "So much for your educatin' 'im. The boy cain't even count." He was enjoying this far too much. He always figured John was uppity. Mitch never could stand the way John ordered him around. *Well,* Mitch figured, *this here's for all the times that boy figured himself superior.* The only way this show could be better was if Mr. Barlow had let Mitch handle the whip himself.

Crack!

Mr. Barlow was relentless. "That was six, boy. Count!"

"S-six, Master Barlow."

"Mitch, get the brand ready."

A new terror seized John, one that tore through him, as if the whip had ripped open his back and seized his heart. "Uncle Jacob, no!"

Crack!

"What did you call me, boy?"

"M-master Barlow, s-suh, p-please—"

"I said count!"

"S-seven, Master Barlow."

John continued to count until the whip hit thirty. By that point, he was hanging by his wrists like a wet rag.

Crossing over to him, Mr. Barlow lifted John to standing. John's emerging groan was cut short by a grunt as Mr. Barlow shoved him face-first into the whipping post. "Now," Mr. Barlow growled, "you will never forget yourself again, will you, boy?" Showing John the whip, he said, "The whip was for running, and the branding …" He paused to look around for Mitch. "Mitch, is that brand ready yet?"

John groaned, quaking in fear.

Mitch, just returning from the smithy, hollered, "Yes, suh."

"Well, then, give it to me," Mr. Barlow demanded.

John felt his innards turn to water as Mr. Barlow's arms shoved into his back. The red-hot iron, forming the letters *JB*, was barely an inch from his face, its intense heat drying his tears. John closed his eyes and clenched his teeth.

Mr. Barlow shook him hard. "Look at it, boy!"

Defeated, John complied.

"This brand is to remind you of what you are: my property." Mr. Barlow spat the last two words with vehemence, as he pushed the brand into John's left shoulder. The screams of mother and son joined to form a crescendo of agony that echoed across the plantation.

As soon as Mr. Barlow released his grip, John fell limp against the post.

"Untie him," Mr. Barlow barked.

Mitch obliged. He ripped his knife through the rope, making sure to take some of John's flesh along with it.

Once free John staggered and fell to the ground, dirt grinding into his wounds. He lay in a heap, wanting to cry, but he was too exhausted.

Pulling the boy to standing, Mr. Barlow brought John to within inches of his face. Tears formed in his eyes. "Why, John? Why would you run on me?"

John, wavering in Mr. Barlow's grip, heaved a heavy sob, keeping his head down.

"Answer me!"

"I-I did not run, Master Barlow," John muttered.

Mr. Barlow backhanded the boy across the face. "Do not lie to me, boy!"

John would have fallen had Mr. Barlow not been holding onto him. John hung like a limp rag in his hand. "I'm not lyin' Master Barlow, suh," John pleaded, fearful of another beating. He did not know if he could take any more.

Mr. Barlow backhanded him again then yanked John back to standing his fingers gripping like gator's teeth into the boy's wounds.

John tried again to tell his side of the story. "I-I was ridin' Cornerstone an' a bobcat jumped us. Cornerstone got spooked an' I lost control. We got lost, suh. We just got lost is all." John ended his account in a rush of tears.

Mr. Barlow stared incredulously. The boy's audacity to make up such a story angered him beyond belief. Raising his hand, he slammed another fist directly into young John's face.

John had tried raising his arm, but pain kept him from covering his face in time. Once again John was slung backwards, hanging limp in Mr. Barlow's grip. Once again Mr. Barlow yanked John to his feet.

"I told you not lie to me, boy!"

"I ain't lying, Uncle—" John winced, and expecting another blow, he quickly changed his salutation. "I ain't lyin', Master Barlow, suh. I ain't lyin', I swear. I didn't run, suh. A bobcat came after me an' Cornerstone!"

Shaking John to rattle the truth out of him, Mr. Barlow hollered, "Bobcats live in the mountains, boy. They never make their way down here!"

"It was a bobcat, suh, I swear." Remembering the evidence, he stammered, "Check Cornerstone's flank. The cat scratched him."

Momentarily Mr. Barlow stared at the boy. John's head hung in shame. Lifting John's face, he forced the boy to look him in the eye. "Mitch, bring me Cornerstone." Mr. Barlow's voice remained steady, his features unwaveringly hard. Beneath, a turbulent wave of guilt threatened to overwhelm him.

Mitch whispered, so no one else could hear. "Perhaps ya oughta look at the horse later, when there ain't so many niggas around."

Mr. Barlow turned on Mitch, hollering, "Bring me that horse, *now!*"

Shaking his head, the hand fetched Cornerstone, turning him so Mr. Barlow could inspect the wounds on its flank.

"Who did this?" Mr. Barlow stammered, struggling to retain authority in his voice.

"The bobcat scratched him," John replied, as he swayed in Mr. Barlow's grip.

"I mean tending to his wounds."

"I did, Master Barlow. I did not want Cornerstone goin' lame. I figured mud in the wounds might stop the bleedin'." John answered in a monotone fashion, no longer caring whether Mr. Barlow believed him.

"Good thinking." Mr. Barlow inspected the innocent child who hung limp in his arms. Today's events had destroyed something deep inside the lad, and Mr. Barlow felt the full weight of that responsibility. "Mitch, take Cornerstone to the barn, then ride into town and get the animal doctor." Looking at John, Mr. Barlow asked, "Are you OK to walk on your own, son?"

John nodded in assent, but the second he tried to stand on his own, he stumbled.

Mr. Barlow caught him, lifted him over his shoulder, and carried him into the big house. Before entering, Mr. Barlow turned, calling out, "And Mitch, fetch Dr. Haverton. John needs tending."

CHAPTER 11

▼

DR. PHILLIP HAVERTON

Dr. Phillip Haverton did not arrive until the following morning. All he had been told was that a slave needed tending. Mitch did point out that it was a particular favorite of Mr. Barlow's but went into no further detail. The good doctor assumed it was a wench, and he had no intention of losing a good night's sleep over some Negro whore, no matter how partial his old friend Mr. Barlow might be toward her. Dr. Haverton took great delight in imagining the many ways the girl might have displeased Mr. Barlow—or maybe she had not displeased him at all, and the beating was a part of the pleasuring. Whatever the case, the doctor was sure it could wait until morning.

When the doctor finally arrived, Mr. Barlow greeted him on the veranda. He had sat up all night, waiting. Guilt had ravaged Mr. Barlow fiercely. Too proud a man to admit fault, he had spent the night battling with that guilt, pounding it down deep inside.

"Phillip!" Mr. Barlow exclaimed. "Where in hell's name have you been? I have been waiting all night for you." Before the good doctor could answer, Mr. Barlow barked an order. "Moses, get the doctor's carriage and take it round back." Climbing down the steps with outstretched hands, Mr. Barlow continued, "The horse doctor got here hours ago, and he had farther to ride than you. Were you engaged in an emergency, suh?"

"Jacob, my old friend." Phillip Haverton's exasperation was evident. "I treasure your friendship, truly I do, but I will not lose a good night's sleep over some nigga whore." Before Mr. Barlow could interject, Dr. Haverton rattled on, "Well, I am here now. Lead me to the lusty wench. I will fix her up good as new, so you can have at her again tonight." The doctor added with a knowing laugh, "Be careful not to rough her up too much, as I will not be coming back tomorrow!" Slapping Mr. Barlow on the back, Phillip Haverton continued to laugh heartily.

Mr. Barlow exploded, incensed at the suggestion that he would lay down with a colored woman. "Now listen here, Haverton! I would never sell my soul for a black harlot. I am a man of honor!" Mr. Barlow's fists clenched tight.

The doctor backed away, fearing his old friend might commit an act of violence against him.

"I called you here today," Mr. Barlow harried on, "to take care of my boy, John!"

"John?" Dr. Haverton exclaimed. "Your cook's son? John?" Realization dawned. "You mean to tell me that boy is mulatto? Why, that is impossible. He is too white to have any colored blood. I heard tell of some of them being born light and all … but not like that. Why, John has the palest complexion of anyone I know."

Mr. Barlow's impatience got the better of him, and he pulled Dr. Haverton inside. "John is not colored, Phillip." Then, with a sigh, he added, "But I do own him."

It was Phillip Haverton's turn at indignation. "Owning a white man is wrong, unless he is indentured to you." He pulled his arm free of Mr. Barlow's grip. Eyeing Mr. Barlow suspiciously, Dr. Haverton demanded, "Well? Is his mama indentured to you?"

Mr. Barlow grimaced, releasing a long sigh. "No. I bought her at the block when her daddy sold her."

Phillip Haverton gasped. "In the name of all that is holy, why would a man sell his own daughter?"

Mr. Barlow's voice lowered. "Come upstairs. I will let the boy's mama explain it to you."

✳   ✳   ✳   ✳

John's room, small but comfortable, was sparsely furnished with a bed, dresser, night table, and reading lamp. A small bookshelf adorned the wall next to the window, where John was allowed to keep a few books from Mr. Barlow's library. A chair had been added to the room's decor, so John's mama could sit by his bedside and watch over him. John lay on his stomach, his arms draped over the edges of the bed. Every so often, a groan issued from his lips, but otherwise he remained silent. Milly, Geoffrey's wife, cleaned John's wounds, spreading balm over them. She refused to apply bandages, claiming the good Lord's air was best for healing. Bandages, she said, stuck to the wounds, making removal painful. Evelyn had agreed, not knowing what else to do.

John's face was turned toward his mama. His lashes fluttered as he hovered between agonizing consciousness and brutal nightmares. Evelyn constantly dabbed a cool cloth on his forehead—not that this was any real treatment, but it kept her occupied, offering her an outlet for her love and concern.

When the door finally opened, admitting the doctor, Evelyn leaped out of her chair to greet him. "Dr. Haverton!" she cried with mixed emotions of relief and agony. "Thank you for comin', suh. My boy, he's in a real bad way. He's been feverish, comin' in and out of consciousness all night. Please help him, suh!" Her pleas were slurred by gasping tears. It tore her heart to see John suffer so.

Dr. Haverton shoved Evelyn's extended hand away and looked upon her gravely. "First, you are going to explain to me how your son became a slave." With a lecherous leer, he added, "Did you rut with some light nigga to spawn a boy who only looks white?"

Evelyn's face blanched. She was taken aback by the doctor's bold accusation. "N-no, suh," she stuttered. "John is white, I swear to you." She turned to Mr. Barlow with pleading eyes. "Please, Mr. Barlow, tell him, suh. Tell him John is white."

Mr. Barlow turned his back on the woman. "I told him. It is up to you to explain the details." With that he left.

John groaned.

Why now, Evelyn thought miserably, *does John have to be conscious?*

▼

CHAPTER 12

RIGHTFUL DEFIANCE

John lay in bed on his stomach for three days before his wounds scabbed over enough to be considered healed. The *JB* branded on his left shoulder still puffed an angry red and was covered over with a thick, black crust. His mother insisted on lancing it to let the pus drain out. It was a painful procedure that left the rough scab flush against the wound. This was the day Mr. Barlow made his first visit.

"How is your boy doing, Evelyn?" he asked from the doorway.

"Fine, Mr. Barlow." Evelyn carefully smoothed her voice so as not to show any contempt. "He's healin' real fast, suh. John's strong as a bull even if he is lean."

Standing like a beam of wood against the door, Mr. Barlow tried to sound cheerful. "Good to hear," he grunted. "He will be working the fields come morning." Mitch had convinced him that even if the boy was telling the truth, Mr. Barlow could not back down. Going easy on the lad now would allow his slaves to perceive him as weak. Mr. Barlow, reckoning this to be true, was determined to push John even harder.

Evelyn gasped and cried, "Not the fields, Mr. Barlow ... No!" Mr. Barlow's glare brooked no opposition, but Evelyn's worry emboldened her. "Please, suh. He's just a child, and his back is not healed yet. Please put him back in the stables. He works well with the horses ... you said so yourself!"

Not even bothering to respond, Mr. Barlow grabbed Evelyn by the collar and threw her out of the room. Turning back to John, Mr. Barlow ordered, "Rest up now, boy. Tomorrow you work the fields under Mitch." With that, he left.

John's eyes closed. Images of the former Mr. Barlow, the man he had once loved, swirled inside his head. Now he felt only contempt for "Master Barlow." The sting of the lash and the burn of the iron were seared into his soul. It had all been a horrible mistake. When Mitch had caught up with him, the overseer was intent on seeing the boy beaten. He refused to listen. Being dragged back home had been the worst humiliation John had ever endured, but he had been confident Mr. Barlow would be enraged at the injustice and maltreatment John had received at the hands of the brutal overseer.

The torturous drag home was nothing compared to the horror he felt when he saw the rage in Mr. Barlow's eyes—a rage directed at him, not Mitch. Adding insult to injury, Mr. Barlow had forbidden him to use the endearment "Uncle Jacob" ever again. Mr. Barlow's status was made apparent as John's owner, his master—a reality John had always been aware of, but had never before felt. *Never again*, John vowed, *will I ever think of that man kindly! Never again will I live in his house.*

Tomorrow I work the fields, John thought bitterly. *Tonight I sleep with the rest of the slaves.*

*   *   *   *

The morning sky was checked gray with specks of orange and tawny red as the sun struggled to shine through heavy clouds. Inside the slave quarters, Negroes prayed for heavy rain to save them from another day of backbreaking labor. The room, though still dim, revealed an unwanted and clearly misplaced visitor. John had slipped out of the big house late in the night and claimed the empty cot at the back of the room. It was worn out, with a knotted old mattress (just slightly worse than the rest), and was only used as a spare. John had slipped in quietly enough so as not to wake any of the exhausted men, but his presence was made evident when the first dim rays of the morning sun illuminated his pale skin.

Moses, a stout little Negro, leaned close to Geoffrey's bed. "De white boy musta really come down low in de massa's 'pinion, bein' made ta sleep out here wit' us niggas."

Geoffrey whispered in reply, "Thought de massa'd forgive 'im after de whippin'. Weren't really his fault nohow, were it?"

Moses shrugged his shoulders. "Dunno." Scratching the stubble on the side of his face, he pondered the situation. Finally he came to his conclusion: "Sho don't look like de massa's forgivin' 'im iffin he's in here."

Both men were startled by the sound of Mr. Barlow's voice. "Where the hell is he?"

Moses leaned closer to Geoffrey and whispered, "He be lookin' for de white boy ag'in."

"How you know that?" Geoffrey asked.

"Cause he don't belong in here wit' us," Moses growled contemptuously. He hated stating the obvious. "John ain't no nigga."

Geoffrey's eyes opened wide with fear.

Moses continued, "One a' us best be tellin' 'im."

"De white boy?"

"No, ya fool … de massa." Moses rolled his eyes, frustrated at dealing with this buffoon. Fools like Geoffrey were always getting Moses beaten for their stupidity. "Now, get on out thar an' tell 'im."

Geoffrey shrank back. "Why me?"

Moses, definitely the smarter of the two, explained, "Lord knows what de massa'll do iffin he thinks your hidin' 'im."

"Me?" Once again Geoffrey's eyes widened in fear.

"Yeah, you." Moses nodded toward John Connolley. "He be sleepin' next ta your bed. Ya wanna get whipped 'cause a' him?"

Just as Geoffrey was about to stand, the door burst open, and Mitch screeched, "Get up, ya lazy, good-for-nothin' niggas. John's gone again. Anyone seen—"

Silencing Mitch by pushing him aside, Jacob Barlow walked into the slaves' quarters and stood in the doorway. Never once, in all his years as a slave, had Moses ever seen the master come into the slaves' house. Mr. Barlow had arrived with a scowl ripping across his lips and a heavy slant to his brows. It was evident his first visit was not going to be a good one. Mr. Barlow's pounding boots spat up dust and the wooden floor groaned with every step as he entered the room. He crossed to the back and towered over John's bunk. His voice took on an ominously low tone. "Get up, boy."

John shifted. He had heard Mr. Barlow, all right—heard him yelling outside for him, heard Mitch throw open the door, heard Mr. Barlow's methodical walk to his cot. John turned, and without rising, looked up at the old man. He angered Mr. Barlow even further by refusing to speak.

Growling like a ferocious bear, Mr. Barlow hollered, "I said, get up!" Mr. Barlow hated repeating himself, so when John refused to move, Mr. Barlow reached down, grabbed him by his hair, and hauled him to his feet.

John gritted his teeth to stifle a yelp.

"I gave you an order, boy." Mr. Barlow's face was so close that John was showered in spit. "When I say move, you move!"

John's eyes were filled with bitterness thinly veiled with subservience. His curt reply of "Yessuh" showed just how thin that veneer really was.

Mr. Barlow tossed John toward the door. "You say 'yes, suh' when speaking to me, boy. I taught you to speak proper English, not to slur your words like some nigga dunce."

"Yessuh, Massa Barlow."

Mr. Barlow's fist cracked across the back of John's head, causing him to stumble. "What the hell do you think you mean to prove sleeping out here, boy?"

That sent startled looks among the slaves. *De white boy come out here on his own? What kinda fool'd choose ta sleep in this here place?*

Continuing to push John toward the door, Mr. Barlow rambled on. "Your poor mama is worried sick, thinking you might have run again."

"I never ran!" John retorted, as he was shoved. John never took one step himself, only moving when Mr. Barlow pushed him.

Mr. Barlow whipped John around to face him, then backhanded him.

John did not defend himself.

"Do not talk back to me, boy. Your mama is in there, crying her eyes out—"

John had recoiled from the hit, but he maintained his balance. Looking Mr. Barlow directly in the eyes, John retaliated, "You told me to see myself for who I am: your property. You want me slavin' in the fields … well, this is where your field slaves sleep."

Once again Mr. Barlow's hand cracked down across John's face. "You are white, boy, and a white man does not sleep in the company of Negroes."

"Black, white … what difference does it make? A slave is still a slave."

"You are white. There is a difference."

"Not from where I'm standin'," John barked.

"These folk are Negro. You have no black blood in you."

"I's still your property, Massa Barlow. You said so yourself."

Mr. Barlow punched John so hard the boy spun round, landing face-first on the floor. Stepping forward, Mr. Barlow kicked John in the ribs to turn him over, then stomped his boot on John's chest. Mr. Barlow's voice growled, "You want to play slave, do you?"

John grunted and convulsed under the blow. "I ain't playing nothin'," he gasped. Vehemence shot like fire out of John's eyes. "You done tol' me I forgot myself. Well, Massa Barlow, I ain't forgettin' no mo!"

Mr. Barlow stepped back, giving John room to stand. While John rubbed sawdust off his legs, Mr. Barlow nodded in the direction of John's bunk. "Get your stuff back to the big house."

John stood his ground. "No!"

The room gasped.

"You ain't Uncle Jacob no mo," John said. "You's my massa." The two men locked eyes. John refused to back down.

"If you insist on playing nigga slave, so be it. Mitch, tie him to the whipping post."

Mitch eagerly complied, securing John's wrists tightly enough to cut off circulation.

At the whipping post, Mr. Barlow called for his whip. Mitch, cooperative as usual, produced one instantaneously.

"You will receive ten lashings for defiance, boy. And I can promise you an additional ten every morning you wake up in the niggas' shed. Now count."

"One."

This time John did not cry—

"Two."

—or beg for "Uncle Jacob" to stop.

"Three."

Never again would he love that man—

"Four."

—feel any regret—

"Five."

—or sorrow.

"Six."

John gritted his teeth.

"Seven."

The whipping continued—

"Eight."

—for three days.

"Nine."

In order to force John into submission—

"Ten."

—Mr. Barlow commanded John be worked twice as hard as any Negro in the field.

On the fifth night, John was unable to rise from bed. Pain and exhaustion restrained him inside the big house. Mr. Barlow believed he had won, and John had finally succumbed to his will. Two nights after his wounds began to heal, though, John stubbornly made his way back to the slave quarters. Finally Mr. Barlow assigned Ol' Henry to watch over John's door.

Ol' Henry had been Mr. Barlow's slave since before John was born. It seemed to John that Ol' Henry had always been old. His hands were gnarled with arthritis, and his shoulders stooped, keeping his face toward the floor. What was left of Ol' Henry's curly hair was gray. Caverns replaced sockets, sinking eyes deep into his skull. Ol' Henry sat there with his hands on his knees, praying. When he heard John open the door, Ol' Henry stood up to meet him.

"Massa John." Ol' Henry teetered on the verge of tears.

John was shocked at the sight of his old friend. "Henry? What you doin' here? It's late. Shouldn't you be in bed?" Ol' Henry no longer slept in the slave's cabin. Mr. Barlow had boarded up the space under the stairs and converted it into a room for the old man.

"Yessuh, Massa John. I's tired, all right. I sho could use me some sleep. I's too old ta be hangin' 'bout late like this."

"Please don't call me massa, Henry. You know what I am. We all do."

"Yessuh, John. I knows."

John glanced over at the chair. "Why you sittin' here?"

Henry glanced toward Mr. Barlow's room. "De massa, suh, he don't want ya leavin' de big house no mo." Ol' Henry closed his eyes. He found it difficult to face John as an equal, having spent the last fourteen years serving him. Ol' Henry coughed some before continuing. "De massa wants ya here wit' your own kind, not out thar wit' us niggas."

"An' you're supposed to keep me here?" John asked incredulously.

"I knows I ain't much of a guard, but de massa figures y'all won't let nothin' happen ta Ol' Henry. Please, John, don't let nothin' happen ta Ol' Henry."

"Happen to you?" John shivered in confusion. "What do you mean?"

"Well, Massa Barlow, he's figurin' iffin ya keep slippin' out on 'im, he's gonna hafta take drastic measures. Thems were his very words … 'drastic measures.' He says whippin' you's ain't doin' no good; you're a stubborn mule. So he says I's ta tell ya that iffin ya try sleepin' in de niggas' cabin again, he'll be whippin' me, instead a' you's."

The old man lowered his head as John sat down on the chair. Pleading with John, Ol' Henry lifted his eyes—eyes glossed over with the fog of cataracts. "Please don't let Massa Barlow whip me. I's too ol'." The old man's eyes filled with tears. Both men knew Mr. Barlow to be a man of his word; if he said he would whip Ol' Henry, he would.

John slid off the chair onto his knees. Ol' Henry stood before him, holding the young man's head gently in his hands. Pools of tears formed in the old man's palms. Ol' Henry saw this as a good sign—it meant John was relenting. "Massa John, please say your gonna stay in your own room from now on."

"Henry, please. I ain't your massa," John sobbed. "Don't be callin' me that no more."

"Yessuh, John."

"I ain't even a suh. I ain't even a man." Looking up through red eyes, John gestured to the furniture behind him. "I ain't no better'n this here chair."

"Yessu—John, I unda'stands."

In a wail of desperation, John cried out, "Barlow ain't never gonna let me be free, is he?"

Ol' Henry tried his best to comfort John. He knew only too well what John was feeling. "I reckon he might. You's white, after all. 'Sides that, de massa, he loves ya like a—"

John vehemently cut him off. "That man don't love me! Never say that again!"

"I's sorry, John." John's outburst rekindled Ol' Henry's fears of being whipped. "Please say you's goin' stay here, in de big house … that ya ain't goin' slip out on de massa no mo."

"It's OK, Henry," John reassured him. Then, in a voice dim of hope: "I won't let him whip you."

"You's a good boy, John. I knowed ya wouldn't let 'im flog Ol' Henry—no, suh! Now get up off your knees. It be time for you's ta get ta bed. Ya gots a long day ahead a' you's. Ain't so good workin' them fields, I knows. I remembers. A body don't never forget a thing like that."

John stood, allowing the old man to usher him back into his room. Through the dim moonlight, John studied the facade he was forced to live under. Although his mattress was stuffed with Spanish moss, its bed frame was carved oak, as were the dresser and night table. The fine porcelain basin and pitcher he used for washing had red roses painted on them. John shook his head. "I cain't live like this."

"What's wrong wit' ya, John?" Ol' Henry asked with a hint of irritation. "Ya got yourself a fine room, wit' a good bed that gots lotsa warm covers, even a real pillow. An' you gots this big room all ta yourself. It gives ya privacy, a place ta be alone, ta hide yourself from de world. Ya also gets ta eat in de kitchen, de same food your mama cooks for de massa, not that thar gruel they be servin' us niggas." Ol' Henry was actually angry. "Shoot, ya gots it good, boy. What's ya complainin' for?"

"Because it's all a lie."

Shaking his head, Ol' Henry berated the boy. "Well, I sho do wish I had me your lie."

"I suppose you do," John conceded, "but a cage is still a cage, no matter how fancy you make it."

"Well, I's gots ta live in my cage, an' I's right happy ta have a room a' my own, even iffin it is jes a li'l ol' hole." He added with resentment, "But I gots me a room and none a' them other niggas do. I's gon' die in my cage, boy, an' I sho wouldn't mind a li'l gold on it." With that, Ol' Henry shrugged before slowly turning and walking away. As soon as the door closed, it opened again.

John turned around. "You forget somethin', Henry?"

"I am not Henry."

John sat down on the bed to watch Jacob Barlow enter. "It pleases me you finally decided to come to your senses."

John studied the floor between his feet. "Yessuh, Massa Barlow."

"You say 'yes, suh' right now, or I will whip Ol' Henry this instant!"

"Yes, suh."

Sitting next to John, Mr. Barlow softened. "I hated having to beat you, son."

John refused to look up. "If you say so, suh."

"I have not enjoyed this, if that is what you are thinking." Mr. Barlow was incensed at the unspoken charge. "You have been like a son to me—"

John looked up and glared at him.

The sight of hate in the eyes of the child who once idolized him threw Mr. Barlow off balance. "Look, son—"

John cut him off. "I am not your son!" The word "son" stung like a rattler's strike. "I am your property."

"We have to come to some kind of truce here, boy."

"If you say so, suh."

"Hell, boy! You cannot keep challenging my authority. This all should have ended the day you ran—"

"I did not run!"

Ignoring John's interjection, Mr. Barlow barged on, "—but you refused to let it."

John stared intently at the rug beneath his feet. It had been made in India. Mr. Barlow brought it back with him after a yearlong honeymoon with his wife. In the center of the carpet was the image of a beautiful, brown woman seated cross-legged. On her forehead was a red dot. John wondered why anyone would paint a red dot on her forehead.

"What do you want from me, son?"

John looked the old man in the eyes. "I want my freedom."

"You are not ready."

"Who are you to say whether I am ready?"

"Your owner ..." Mr. Barlow, realizing the harshness of his words, softened his voice. "I am the man who raised you. You are like a son to me, John."

Staring into the brown eyes of the woman at his feet, John muttered, "I do not feel like much of a son."

"No, I reckon not." Mr. Barlow paused for a moment, then turned to look at John. "All right, then. You want your freedom? Here is the deal: you have to buy it from me."

"Buy it?" John asked incredulously. "With what?"

Mr. Barlow looked at John thoughtfully, then said, "Take a week to heal. When you get back out in the fields, I will pay you ten cents a day."

"You are goin' to pay me?" John queried skeptically.

"Ten cents a day. My word is my bond, boy." Mr. Barlow was insulted by John's sudden lack of trust. "I will put your wages in trust for you. When you have saved enough to buy your own place—"

John was already calculating in his head. "That should take—"

"Slow down, boy," Mr. Barlow said irritably. "You also have to save enough money to be able to make your way in the world. Only then will I consider setting you free."

"Consider?" This didn't sound like much of a deal to John.

"That is correct," Mr. Barlow said. "Consider. You are going to have to prove to me you can make it on your own. Once you can buy a section of land, and all the supplies you will need, then I will give you one year to make a profit. If you can do that, then you can buy your freedom, using your profits."

John slumped in recognition of the enormity of the task. "That is impossible."

"Do not sulk with me, boy. You have a chance here ... a chance none of your Negroes out there are ever going to see." The room was silent; the tension between the two men cracked like ice resisting spring heat. Mr. Barlow stood, crossed the room to exit, then turned and faced John. With disgust he uttered, "If you are the type to give up before you even try, then you do not deserve your freedom."

Dust drifted in a stream of light that pushed its way through a crack in the curtains. Dawn was being born. Standing up, John extended his hand. "I will do it, suh. You have my word."

Mr. Barlow shook his hand. Before John could release his grip, though, Mr. Barlow pulled him closer. "I want you to shake on one more thing, son."

"What?"

"You will never run on me."

"No, suh."

"Give me your word, boy."

"You have my word that I will never run."

"And you will live in the big house until you can afford to buy your own land."

"Yes, suh. You have my word."

Mr. Barlow, taking on an even sterner look, inquired, "Do you remember what you promised me when you were twelve?"

John looked confused at this sudden query.

"You promised me then you would never disobey me."

John lowered his eyes.

Mr. Barlow tightened his grip on John's hand. "I expect you to keep that promise, too."

"Yes, suh." Thinking it was finally over, John tried to release his hand, but Mr. Barlow refused to let go.

"Your routine will not change, except for the field work. We train in the morning, you work all day. After supper you continue with your studies and then practice on the piano for an hour before you go to bed. You get no free time until you are a free man ... except, of course, on Sundays, because that is the Lord's day. You and your mama will still attend church with me."

"Yes, suh."

Finally Mr. Barlow released his grip. He smiled and sat down on the bed, motioning for John to follow suit. "I have an idea on how you can make a little extra money."

John sat down. "How is that, suh?"

"We will get you fighting."

John's interest perked. Mr. Barlow had been teaching him to box since he was ten, and had trained him every morning for two years.

Mr. Barlow smiled. John's training had not gone as well as he had hoped, but now that the boy was motivated, Mr. Barlow was certain he could turn John into a champion boxer. It was time to offer a little more incentive. "You know, I have fighters circulating all over the union. My fighters earn five dollars a bout if they win. For you, I will add one percent of my take."

John saw a glimmer of hope. Fighting could mean earning money fast. "When can we start, suh?"

"Not before you are sixteen. I need to train you first."

"But you have been trainin' me for two years now," John protested. "I am ready."

"You are not big enough."

"I am six foot four. How much bigger do you want me to be?" John asked incredulously.

"I am not talking about height, boy. Right now you are still too skinny. You need to build up your muscle. You have the potential to be a champion boxer, son. You are taller than most but not clumsy. Your opponents will expect you to be slow, but I have ways to teach you how to dance fast. Besides that, you are smart, and it is a man's brains that will win him the fight more times than brawn. Give me another two years, and you will win every fight." For a brief moment, Mr. Barlow felt as if they were connecting again. He smiled briefly, but John's look of scorn wiped it away. Angered by the rejection, Mr. Barlow let out another warning. "If you forsake me, boy, I will have no mercy on you. I buy no stock with men who break their word."

"I have never broken my word, suh."

Mr. Barlow's brows raised incredulously. "Really now? What do you call refusing to obey me for the last ten days?"

John said nothing, knowing it was Mr. Barlow who had first broken their trust.

Mr. Barlow coined his own phrase: "A man is nothing if not his word, son."

"Yes, suh."

"You just remember that, boy."

"Yes, suh."

With that Mr. Barlow turned his back and left the room.

The door shut with a whisper that slammed inside John's head.

CHAPTER 13

▼

MATTHEW, LUKE, AND JOHN

It looked to be a fine day, though far too hot for comfort—unseasonably hot, like mid-July, even though it was only the first of May. Even at this early hour, the sun ran sweat down John's forehead, burning his eyes. There had been no rain for nearly two weeks, and John was getting worried. Of course it was going to rain … it always rained this time of year. As it was, though, the usually muddy streets of Laurel Creek were parched and cracking. Dust lifted behind every passing cart or horse, hanging in the air like a heavy fog before slowly descending back to earth. Even the darkest boots turned dirty beige, and most men wore scarves over their noses while riding.

John grabbed a cloth from inside his vest pocket to wipe the sweat from his face. The cloth was already damp and did little more than smear the newly formed beads. Even Amos, John's old coon dog, was not his usual spirited self; he had taken to the shade of the cart.

John had parked his horse and cart at the edge of town in front of the lumber-yard. Matthew and John were loading the cart with wood and supplies to fix the old barn. The framing was still sound, but most of the roof needed replacing, as did a good portion of the back wall. Just as they loaded the last of the supplies, Luke, one of Mr. Richardson's slaves, came running up. He was a tall lad for his age—four feet eight at age ten. He had dark brown hair, with curls snug to his head. The boy's eyes, too big for their sockets, combined with a miniscule nose, left him with a perpetual look of surprise. Adding oversized ears to the equation made him appear stunned. Now that Luke had arrived in a flurry of excitement, John could not help but laugh at how ridiculous the boy looked. Luke was so thrilled about the news he was sent to deliver, he let it all spill out in one rush of wind.

"Mista Connolley! Mista Connolley!" Luke blustered. "Mista Barlow's in town ... Mista Jacob Barlow! That's twice he's been ta town now. An' he's stayin' at Massa Richardson's inn again! He's thar wit' that grand lady, Mrs. Delilah Poitras. A Poitras ... right here in our li'l town! They say she used ta be an Ogelthorpe. An' they wants ta see ya. They's eatin' breakfast. Ordered ya some, too." Stopping briefly to eye Matthew suspiciously, Luke hurried on, "Mista Barlow says you's ta come right away, an' ya ain't ta bring no nigga wit' ya. 'Ya tells 'im,' he says, 'he ain't ta bring no nigga boy.' That thar were what he said, all right." Luke stared up at John, his neck craning upward so he could look into the big man's eyes. John Connolley was the tallest man to ever walk the streets of Laurel Creek. Standing six foot five, he was a giant sequoia, towering over everyone.

Luke's face split open in a grin. (He inherited that smile from his daddy—not that Mr. Richardson would ever admit to having sired the boy.) Luke clearly believed this invitation, though delivered as an order, was a great honor.

John turned his back on the boy and continued loading the wood stacked next to the cart.

Confused by John's blatant dismissal, Luke became more insistent. "Ain't ya comin', suh? They's waitin'. Them folks ain't de type ta be kept waitin'." Stuttering some, the boy added, "A-an' your grits is g-gettin' cold."

John shoved the last piece of wood violently into the cart, causing Matthew serious concern. Even Amos, curled listlessly below, lifted his head, cocked his ears, and gave a sudden jerk. Matthew shrugged, knowing better than to broach any topic with John when his dark mood came on.

Matthew knew there was no love lost between John and their master, but he did not know why. Especially dumbfounding, though, was the way Mr. Barlow let John strut around like a free man. Even more confounding was why John refused to take the opportunity to run. *Shoot, iffin it were me*, Matthew figured, *I'd head for de North before de dust settled beneaf my feet.* As it was, John insisted on remaining right where he was, living a farce, pretending to be free, while the old man still had his hooks in him. *That's jes de way them white folks think*, Matthew thought. *Sure don't make no sense, though.*

John grabbed the hatch and shoved it back in place, latching the edges shut. His hands gripped the back of the cart, knuckles turning white. What Matthew did not know was that John was tied to Mr. Barlow by bonds thicker than blood. Mr. Barlow had raised John like a son—for the first half of his life, at any rate.

Even without this knowledge, Matthew had to admit some understanding. *Shoot, I's in jes' as good a spot fer runnin' as Connolley,* Matthew mused, *bein' under his care an' all.* Yet he never tried to run—not anymore. Matthew's insistence that John was a damn fool never seemed to change the fact that Matthew, like John, stayed put. Matthew knew Mr. Barlow would rip John's one chance at freedom out from under him if Matthew ran.

Not that Matthew cared whether John remained a slave or not—*No, sir, I don't care less*—or at least so he kept telling himself … *but Connolley got that damn coon dawg.*

Matthew could still picture himself trapped in the front room, Amos standing sentinel. It was the middle of the night. He had a small blanket rolled and a sack filled with bread and cheese he had stolen from John's pantry … and that damn coon dog had heard him. *'Course the dawg heard me,* Matthew reminded himself, *he's a coon dawg … got them coon dawg ears.* But what Matthew could not figure out was why John called Amos off. That old dog would have ripped Matthew to shreds, given half a chance. Amos had stood there, haunches forward, all weight on his front paws, lips pulled back in a snarl. No man standing in front of that would have been fool enough to run. Amos definitely kept Matthew from running that night—but John Connolley called the dog off.

"Amos! Get over here!" The damn dog had looked as shocked as Matthew. The dog turned his muddy, red head toward John Connolley's room, then eyed Matthew askance. The damn dog growled. If Amos had been a man, Matthew thought, he would have grumbled.

John took no broke from his dog. He shouted, "Amos! Get in here! Now!"

With one last look at Matthew suggesting the slave would be torn to bits if only John Connolley would allow it, the dog retreated.

Matthew listened for some word from John but heard nothing. Stunned, he sat down on the bench next to the door and waited, all night, until the first rays of sun carried John Connolley out of his room. After rubbing sleep from his eyes, his hair disheveled, and still wearing short breeches, John blinked in surprise. "You still here? I figured you'd be halfway 'cross the Carolinas by now."

Matthew stood up to look the man in the eye. He knew what John was and felt no fear. "Why ain't you's try an' stop me? Your dawg … he coulda had me for lunch iffin ya'd let 'im."

"I know."

"Then why?"

John just stared at Matthew, not saying anything for the longest time. He searched for the right words. Then he came out with, "You're a man. You need to be free."

Matthew, dumbstruck, figured that was the most stupid thing he had ever heard coming from a white man. "Free?" Matthew scoffed. "Y'all heard Barlow. Iffin I run, he hauls ya back."

John merely nodded in response.

Matthew scratched the back of his head. "You ain't makin' no sense, Connolley."

John shrugged. "But you didn't run. You stayed. Now I owe you."

"What ya owe me?"

"Freedom."

"Freedom? Who d'ya think ya are, de good Lord? Or maybe ya reckon you're Ol' Moses, goin' part de Savannah an' lead us to de promise land. Shoot, boy, y'all ain't nothin' but a white nigga. What they call your kind, mulatto? You cain't give me freedom any more 'n you can give it to yourself."

"You're right there," John muttered, "but Barlow says I can buy you if I make a big enough profit. With your help, maybe I can make this little plantation work. Then we can both be free, and my debt to you'll be repaid."

"So ya figures ya gots me on some point a' honor?" Matthew laughed.

John shook his head. "I don't got you at all. Barlow does. You's his nigga. You know if you try to run, he'll hunt you down. Mitch brings 'em back nine times outta ten. Paine makes sure a' that." Paine was Amos's daddy—named after Thomas Paine, the man Mr. Barlow both admired and hated. Mr. Barlow liked the irony of Paine chasing down Negro slaves. Even at nine years of age, that old dog could tree a runaway faster than it could tree a raccoon. Most folks credited Mitch for his winning streak, but anyone who knew the dog knew it was Paine who brought them back. John continued, "Hell, Matthew, you oughta know that better 'n anyone."

Matthew rubbed unconsciously at the *R* brand on his left cheek.

John never skipped a beat. "He brought you back three times already. Damn surprisin' you never had your neck in the noose. Hell, why don't I jes' build you a gallows, so you can throw the rope over your neck yourself! Here at least you can live and work, with nobody givin' you orders ... just two men, workin' side by side. Cain't do nothin' 'bout the ways of the town, mind you, but I'll treat you right. Hell, maybe we can even buy you someday. Then no one can hunt you down and bring you back."

"Grand promises." Matthew scoffed again.

"No promises," John countered. "Just a dream."

A dream ... now that was something Matthew could relate to: hopes and dreams.

"How long ya reckon that'll take?"

John shrugged. "Don't rightly know. Shoot, don't even know if I can make enough to buy myself. But as long as I pull a profit, even just one dollar, Barlow'll let me keep tryin'. After I'm paid for, then it'll be maybe another two or three years for you. In the meantime, you can live here with me. No more Barlow, no more whippin', no more brandin', no more watchin' your women bein' raped and beat. But the minute you run, we both ends up back wit' Barlow. Me right away, you after Mitch brings ya in ... then you'll be hangin' from the noose for sure."

That was the longest stretch of words Matthew had ever heard John utter. He knew John meant every word of it—and he knew, too, John would do nothing if he ran. Somehow he felt tied to the man. Matthew did not owe John anything, nor did John owe him. Still, John was willing to let him run. Knowing the odds, and Mitch's reputation as a "nigga hunter," Matthew was not even sure he would live long enough to make it to the noose. John Connolley was plumb crazy, but Matthew believed him when John said he would treat him right. Even with all this knowing going on, why he chose to stay was still a mystery to Matthew.

Shaking his head at his memory, Matthew grunted, "Nevah shoulda shook your hand."

"What you say?"

Matthew, stunned at John's inquiry, responded, "Nothin'." John's mood was intolerable, and Matthew had not realized he had verbalized his thoughts. "Jes' thinkin' 'bout what ya said, is all."

"What's that?"

"Somethin' 'bout no mo Barlow. Seems ta me you's wrong 'bout that."

"I meant no more Barlow for you."

Luke, who had been sent to fetch John, waited impatiently for the two men to finish their conversation. He was stunned by what he heard. All this talk about no more Mr. Barlow made no sense to him. Why would anyone say no more Mr. Barlow? Surely they knew what an important man he was—the owner of Georgia's biggest plantation. Add to that his connection with Raymond Poitras, and Jacob Barlow was the most powerful man known in Laurel Creek. Luke became nervous. Dust swirled around his feet as they shifted from side to side. "Mista Connolley? Ya gots ta come, suh. Massa Richardson done sent me ta bring you's. Mista Barlow an' de Lady Poitras, they's a waitin'."

"Run along, Luke," John replied curtly.

Luke gasped and began to stammer, clearly stunned at this unexpected turn of events. "B-but-but … I were s-sent ta bring you's, suh. I-I cain't go back alone. Massa Richardson, he'd whip me for sho."

John's grip on the wagon became tighter, something Matthew had not thought possible. John was a muscular man, with arms built like corded wood. Matthew swore if John Connolley gripped the hatch any harder, he would split it in half. Amos twitched beneath the cart, expecting to have to attack at any moment.

"Run along, Luke," John growled. "I know the way."

"W-will ya be c-comin' s-soon, suh?"

John let go of the wagon and spun on the lad. "I. Said. Run. Along!" Each word slammed emphatically into the boy. "I'll come when I's finished!"

Young Luke squeaked and turned on his heels so fast, small dust devils lifted from his heels.

John, knowing the boy really would get whipped, grabbed Luke by the shoulders and knelt by his side. "Look, son, I'm sorry."

Tears streamed down the boy's face.

"You wait here an' come along with me. Mr. Richardson won't beat you. I'll tell him it were all my fault."

Luke, choked by his fears, was unable to reply. He knew his master would beat him anyway. It was always "that little nigga's" fault!

Matthew edged his way around the two. "Ya want I should stay here?"

"No," John replied. "You come along, too."

"I … ah … I don't think that be a good idea," Matthew reminded him as gently as he could. "Y'all heard what Massa Barlow done said: 'Ya ain't ta bring that thar nigga wit' ya.'"

John nodded but persisted. "We'll go through the back. You can at least sit in the kitchen and eat somethin' while you wait."

"That be real nice. Thank ya, Massa Connolley." John's irritation over the title was evident, but he said nothing, because they were in town. They had agreed Matthew was to call him Massa Connolley there. Matthew hedged another bet and ventured a comment: "Iffin ya don't mind my sayin' so, suh, ya looks none too pleased 'bout …"

John cut him off with a sharp turn and headed toward the inn. It was evident by John's gait that he had no intention of discussing anything. Matthew was wasting his time attempting to engage John Connolley in conversation!

CHAPTER 14

▼

MRS. DELILAH POITRAS

After Matthew and Luke stowed themselves safely away in the kitchen, John returned to the front of the inn to enter the building, as Mr. Barlow expected. Mr. Barlow had seen him coming. Matthew, Luke, and John had walked past the front of the inn to get to the alleyway.

Being the type of people who needed to be noticed, Mr. Barlow and Mrs. Poitras had chosen a window seat. Mr. Barlow watched as John and his companions turned into the alley. His eyes bored into John's back as he walked past. As evidenced by his glower, Mr. Barlow was unimpressed with John's choice to set Matthew up before making his way directly to his master. Any other day, he would have dealt with John, but there was too much at stake with Mrs. Poitras. Knowing that made him smile.

The door chimed as John entered the inn. Removing his hat, he paused briefly to count the candles in Mr. Richardson's prized chandelier. Thirty-six ... it was always thirty-six. He lowered his eyes, glancing over the richly tiled marble floor. Again it crossed John's mind that the Richardsons were well-to-do. But all this was avoidance. He knew Mr. Barlow was waiting, had heard John enter, had heard the chimes. Exhaling slowly, John moved toward the dining hall. The door behind him chimed again. John turned and lost his breath at the sight of Miss Katherine MacPhearson.

Entering with her sister Shannon, smiling and looking like an angel, Katherine curtsied slightly in greeting. Judging from her blushing cheeks and fluttering lashes, she was more than pleased with this chance encounter.

John, thinking he must look a mess, quickly ran his fingers through his hair—his hat, he was sure, had matted it. Hoping the sweat had not smeared dust into his face, he tried wiping it off again. Embarrassed, he tried to lower his eyes, but they were drawn to Katherine's beauty as if to a magnet.

Katherine MacPhearson, although tall for a woman, was a slight girl in John's eyes. He could envision cradling her head protectively and lovingly against his chest. He saw himself bending to rest his head on top of hers, as well as lifting her a good foot off the ground to rest her head against his shoulder. He blushed to think of her so. Her beauty shone like wild magnolias in dawn's first light, the sun sparkling in their dew. The forget-me-not flowers spotted over the bodice of her pale pink gown accented her bosom. Her rich red hair curled naturally over her shoulders like ripples of water under the caress of the wind's fingertips. And her eyes … hers were the biggest eyes John had ever seen. Thick lashes flashed around emerald jewels, revealing an innocent honesty.

The two ladies giggled and curtsied.

John, feeling foolish, blushed in return. Ogling women was no way for a proper man to behave. He bowed awkwardly. "Ladies."

Katherine smiled mischievously. "Mr. Connolley, may we pass? My sister has kindly invited me to tea."

All John could do was clear his throat and step out of the way. Their continued laughter convinced him he appeared a dunce. Why did he have to turn into a tongue-tied fool every time he saw the woman? No one else ever seemed lost for words around her. He gave them a moment to pass so he wouldn't follow at their heels like a lost hound. Still, he heard Katherine say, "Is not he the sweetest man? And tall! Why, Shannon, I have never seen so tall a man in all my life."

Shannon readily agreed. "And sturdy, too. Why, he looks stronger than three oxen put together."

"Oh, Shannon!" Katherine gasped, as if her sister had just said something terribly naughty.

Following their voices, John smiled at the knowledge that Katherine did not think him a fool—and at the knowledge that she, too, was interested. John knew wanting Katherine MacPhearson was folly; that day at her father's plantation had reaffirmed that. Still, a part of John really did want Katherine to like him. His mind fought to quell those feelings, but his heart refused to listen. Standing in the entrance of the dining hall, John watched the two women settle themselves at a table against the far wall. Watching and wishing and hoping—no, not hoping, dreaming—entertaining the idea of marrying Katherine MacPhearson was a fool's fantasy.

A loud clearing of the throat pulled John out of his reverie. Mr. Barlow was summoning him. John looked over to the table next to the window and grimaced. Avoiding eye contact with Mrs. Poitras left only Mr. Barlow to look at. Mr. Barlow's angry eyes glared at John, even though he masked his expression with a smile. His face clearly showed him to be a hard man; its etched lines suggested he was a man experienced at doling out judgment. A thin, straight nose protruded forward above sharp, sculptured cheeks, giving the impression that Mr. Barlow was not a man to be crossed. His mustache covered thin, hard lips, and his goatee was trimmed neatly to a point. Mr. Barlow's wife once told him his goatee was his finest feature, and he groomed it daily.

"Ah, my boy." Regardless of his chagrin, Mr. Barlow managed to make his voice sound friendly. "So, you finally decided to grace us with your presence." Still, John could detect an edge of displeasure. "I am afraid your eggs are cold, but still good, no doubt, as nobody cooks a finer meal than Mrs. Richardson. Come, sit down and eat. We must not dishonor her by leaving any food behind." Mr. Barlow did not stand to greet John. He simply motioned for the young man to sit next to Mrs. Poitras.

John did as he was told. He edged his chair as far away as possible from Mrs. Poitras, though, and concentrated on studying the table. Mrs. Richardson had set it with her finest china. Crystal goblets held the drinking water. The table was dressed with fine, white lace and a delicate red cloth. A porcelain vase filled with flowers from Mrs. Richardson's garden sat prestigiously in the center. Mrs. Richardson had probably picked every last blossom for this event.

John used his fork to pick mechanically at his eggs. Noticing Mr. Barlow eyeing him, he lifted a piece of food off the plate. It crumbled into dust in his mouth. Food always tasted like ash when John ate with that man.

"So," Mr. Barlow continued. "I see you are taking good care of my Negro. Fattened him up some, you did. I fail to see how you can make a profit if you spend all your money feeding your slave like a pig for slaughter."

"I work him hard, suh."

"Oh, I am sure you do. I imagine you expect no less from him than what you do yourself."

"Yes, suh."

"Still, I should take him home and hang him."

John's eyes shot up to confront Mr. Barlow. He knew where the man was going with this threat. Mrs. Poitras's presence made that perfectly clear.

"He has not tried to run, suh. You said I could keep him as long as he behaves himself."

"I did, at that. But still … he is a three-time runner. I really should hang him as a deterrent to the others."

"He only ran twice," John retorted. "You said you had been keepin' him chained, so he could not run again."

"That was the situation. But after I got back from visiting you last month, well … Mitch had dragged him in again." Mr. Barlow smiled, remembering Mitch's disappointment. "He was none too pleased when I said he could not string him up." Mr. Barlow laughed. "I appeased him, though, by letting him hang the fool who freed Matthew. You remember Ol' Moses?"

John nodded. Moses had been a good man.

"Damn fool snuck into my study and stole the keys to Matthew's shackles. I never would have suspected it of Ol' Moses. He said he figured running or a hanging was better than living in chains." Mr. Barlow sighed. "I had trusted Ol' Moses … even gave him Ol' Henry's room." Mr. Barlow shook his head.

Suddenly Mr. Barlow noticed the look of distress in Mrs. Poitras's eyes. With a look of feigned concern, he turned to Mrs. Poitras and professed his deepest regrets. "Oh, Delilah, do forgive me. We should not be discussing such things in front of a lady."

"Take no mind of me, Jacob," Mrs. Poitras said beneath batting eyelids. "I have had to discipline a few slaves myself. I know what needs to be done with such creatures. Still"—she clicked open a small fan to express vexation, as well as cool herself—"proper etiquette does dictate that we not discuss such things at the dinner table." Then, quick as lightning, Mrs. Poitras shifted her mood and smiled her sweetest smile, focusing all her attention on John. "Surely, gentlemen, we can find a more pleasant topic of conversation."

Basking in the woman's delight, Mr. Barlow leaned back in his chair. "Delilah has been waiting for you, son. A man should never keep a lady waiting."

Mrs. Poitras's eyes twinkled mischievously. She was a stunning woman. Age had graced her face, not with wrinkles, but with a beautiful maturity. As with a fine wine, the years had enhanced her flavor. Her dark brown eyes were like pools that could drown a man. Her lips, full and pouty, were carefully dabbed with a light tinge of red. A hint of rouge accented her cheeks. Only wealth and aristocratic connections kept Delilah Poitras from being considered scandalous. Her long, brown hair, streaked elegantly with gray, was brought up into a bun at the back, with long strands of curls released and dangling. Her blue dress was lined with red lace, accenting a prominent and scandalous cleavage.

Mrs. Poitras's hand slipped discreetly under the table to secretly caress John's leg. His hand immediately arrested her efforts. As his flush of embarrassment became evident, Mrs. Poitras released a satisfied giggle. Her hand was firmly entrenched on John's leg, but she did cease her caresses.

"My goodness, Jacob, how the boy has grown!" Mrs. Poitras exclaimed. "Why, the last time I saw him, he was only sixteen."

"Eighteen." Mr. Barlow's smile for Mrs. Poitras, although genuine, was coated thickly with lust. "Back in seventeen ninety-eight."

"Seventeen ninety-eight!" Mrs. Poitras giggled. "That was a fine year. Was it not, gentlemen?" All her attention was on John. "Such capital times we had."

John grimaced, and Mr. Barlow chuckled. Mr. Barlow knew why the woman had asked to join him on this visit, and he approved. It was a daddy's duty to see to the boy's education. Of course, he was not the boy's daddy—and if Mr. Barlow had a son, he would never have educated him in this manner. Still, he could justify it. A man needed experience in all walks of life, and John, being who he was, had not been in any position to gain that experience. Besides, when a woman like Delilah Poitras was willing to offer the education, well ... what better gift could he offer the boy?

Mr. Barlow's smile widened. "John here had been fighting for two years when you met him." He gazed at John, and the two men locked eyes in epic battle. "Do you remember that fight, boy? You took that little Negro down as if he were a mouse, and you the eagle. Everyone said Watkins could not be beat, but you did it. And he was twice your age, at that. That fight established your reputation, it did. I sure would like to get you back in the ring." Eyeing John circumspectly, Mr. Barlow added, "Though that can wait until we see how things go for you this year." After a long pause, Mr. Barlow queried, "Are you keeping up with your training, boy?"

"Yes, suh."

"Every morning?" Mr. Barlow had insisted on this, in case things went badly for John. He wanted John Connolley in prime condition for fighting.

"Yes, suh."

"Two hours, before dawn?"

"Two hours, suh."

"Of course you would. You always were a good boy. You gave me your word, and I believe you. A man is nothing if not his word, right, John?"

"Yes, suh."

Throughout this dialogue, Mrs. Poitras's hand caressed John's leg again, moving precariously higher. John resumed his grip against her fingers.

"My, my, you are a strong one. I do so appreciate strength in a man." Her smile bordered on malice. "I remember that fight, too." Her voice became sultry. "Your body was covered in sweat." She reached with her other hand to caress his chest.

With one hand chained to his fork, the other holding back Mrs. Poitras's other wandering fingers, John froze.

Her smile widened; there was no stopping the woman. "I remember that nasty little Negro left a few welts." Her fingers etched a small circle above his heart. "One here …" Then she slowly dangled them to just below his stomach. "And one here …"

John winced. "Please, Mrs. Poi—"

Her finger quickly slipped in front of his lips. "Delilah, *mon cherie.* Call me Delilah."

In a strangled whisper, John pleaded with the woman. "Delilah, ma'am, we are in the public eye." John's eyes darted quickly toward Katherine's table; he was relieved to see her preoccupied in conversation.

The twinkle in Mrs. Poitras's eye became more mischievous. Her giggle held several possible meanings. "You always were a shy boy."

Mr. Barlow smiled knowingly. "Well, my boy, I am sure you are wondering why we are here."

John knew exactly why Mr. Barlow brought Mrs. Poitras.

"You have been more than adequate with your reports, and from the sounds of things, that little plantation of ours"—John winced, for he had paid for that land in full—Majestic Beauty was his!—"will likely produce enough tobacco to bring a profit. You might want to consider rice for next year, though … more of a market for it these days."

John grimaced at that. Mr. Barlow knew right well John had wanted to plant rice this year, but the old man would not allow it.

"Who knows, though … the way things are going for you, you may even have enough to purchase Matthew in a few years." Winking, Mr. Barlow added, "Possibly even this year. You never know … a windfall may land in your lap." Mr. Barlow, swirling his water as if he were drinking brandy, smiled knowingly, leering once more at Mrs. Poitras.

The fool woman giggled, and more effort was required for John to keep her hand down.

Mr. Barlow's smile was devious. "So, we came here today to see how you are doing. We would like a tour of your place. Perhaps Matthew can show me the fields while you entertain Mrs.—"

Before Mr. Barlow could finish, Katherine MacPhearson and her sister approached their table.

Mrs. Poitras's hand burned.

John blushed.

Katherine misinterpreted John's blush, and she, too, turned red. Her sweet scent mingled with the softness of her voice. "Mr. Connolley, I see you are at breakfast with esteemed company."

John attempted to stand in greeting, but Mrs. Poitras's hand gripped his leg, fingers biting with jealousy.

Her smile for the young girl, though, was motherly. "John, dear. Do introduce us to your lady friends."

John cleared his throat and firmly removed Mrs. Poitras's hand, taking the introductions as an opportunity to stand. "Ah … Miss Katherine MacPhearson, allow me to introduce you to Mr. Jacob Barlow and Mrs. Raymond Poitras." John directed his attention on Katherine's sister. "And her sister, Mrs. Shawn Willson."

Shannon was a beauty, much like her little sister, but marriage had added worry lines to her face. Shannon curtsied in return and extended her apologies: "My husband is waiting on me. We are heading back to Savannah today. Mr. Wilson wants to be well on our way before it gets late."

Jacob Barlow stood, responding appropriately. "Apology accepted, Mrs. Wilson."

Shannon giggled as she curtsied. She quickly departed, the chimes of the door whisking her away. Mr. Barlow, turning his attention to Katherine, kissed her hand and bowed respectfully.

Releasing a childish giggle, Katherine was thrilled that a man as important as Mr. Jacob Barlow would treat her so regally.

Mrs. Poitras rose from her chair and brushed past John, careful to ensure her bosom rubbed his arm. Placing herself firmly between John and Katherine MacPhearson, she took Katherine's hand and smiled her sweetest smile. "Such a pretty girl."

Katherine blushed, hearing only a compliment. Her eyes glanced down demurely, then back up toward John.

"Mr. Connolley," Katherine asked shyly, "would you consider bringing your esteemed guests to my daddy's house for tea?"

Mrs. Poitras answered, "Oh, my dear, such a lovely invitation … but I am afraid we will have to decline. We are only in town for the day, and Mr. Barlow has come to inspect Mr. Connolley's land."

At this Mr. Barlow laughed—a deep rumble. "Now, now, Delilah. You make it sound like I own John's land."

John's eyes lowered to the floor, but Katherine took no notice.

Directing his words toward Katherine, Mr. Barlow added, "John bought Majestic Beauty with his own money. He worked hard saving every penny. Did you not, son?"

"Yes, suh."

Katherine giggled. Her laughter was like a soft breeze rippling through leaves, gently wrapping itself around John's heart. "Oh, Mr. Barlow, you do not need to explain. Everyone knows you treat Mr. Connolley like a son. It is only natural for a daddy to check on his son's progress … or in your case, for a beloved patron."

"Why, Miss MacPhearson, you are a delightful child. I can only hope that John has designs to make you his wife someday."

John looked up in time to see a flush rise up the nape of Katherine's neck, painting her cheeks. She smiled so beautifully but quickly lowered her eyes.

Mr. Barlow's deep laugh and sudden grasp of her waist caused the poor girl to gasp with embarrassed laughter. "Perhaps we can find time to have tea with this young lady's family before we make our way over to John's plantation. Only it would have to be this morning. Does that suit you?"

Katherine's smile widened, enhancing her beauty. "Why, of course, Mr. Barlow. My Sarah's a fine girl. She could get things ready without a moment's notice."

Mr. Barlow's pleasure sounded sincere. "Now, that will be just fine, Miss MacPhearson." Mr. Barlow glanced warily at Mrs. Poitras. "Well, then. What say you, Mrs. Poitras?"

Only a slight tightening of Mrs. Poitras's eyes suggested any disapproval; her smile and lilting voice responded with complete agreement. "Why, yes, that sounds delightful." Turning to face John, Mrs. Poitras took advantage of the blocked view, gently strumming her fingers against him. "John, I am sure, has a few things to get ready in order to properly impress Mr. Barlow. You will not likely join us, will you?"

John glanced over Mrs. Poitras's shoulder and noted the look of disappointment in Katherine's eyes. John looked back at Mrs. Poitras and responded appropriately. "No, ma'am," John whispered, "I suspect not."

"I was afraid not. That is too bad." She turned back to face Katherine. "We will join you for tea after all, Miss MacPhearson. But remember, Jacob, we will need most of the afternoon to inspect this young man."

"Of course, Delilah. There is plenty of time for what needs to be done." Mr. Barlow suddenly shifted to a commanding tone as he instructed, "Fetch Matthew, son, and head on home. We should be there around ..."—with a pause to feign confusion—"... now, what time is it?" He pulled his gold pocket watch from his vest pocket. "Eight-thirty." He showed the watch to Katherine. "This pocket watch belonged to my great-granddaddy. It is a family heirloom. My daddy gave it to me when I married my sweet Louise. Perhaps I will have the opportunity to give it to John someday."

Blushing at the unspoken suggestion, Katherine lowered her head.

Mr. Barlow took Katherine's chin in his hand. In a gentle, fatherly tone, he inquired, "How long will it take to ride to your daddy's estate, my dear?"

Katherine answered in an embarrassed whisper, "Twenty minutes at most, suh."

"Ah, good ... and would you know how long from there to John's humble plantation?"

Katherine stammered, "I-I am not sure, suh. Perhaps a half hour, Mr. Connolley?"

John cleared his throat. The whole situation was far too uncomfortable. It was unbearable having to watch Katherine suffer. "Thirty minutes or thereabout."

"Well, then, John, we should be arriving at your place in time for lunch. Is that not so, Delilah?"

"Why, I will prepare lunch for the three of us," Mrs. Poitras responded. "That is, if you do not mind my working in your kitchen, John?" She faced John, once again taking advantage.

Knowing any attempt to stop Mrs. Poitras would publicly announce her actions, John just stood there, hands behind his back, grateful at least that the broad scope of her gown hid what she was doing. Struggling to keep composure, John somehow managed to make his voice sound level. "No, ma'am." He cleared his throat. "I would like that very much."

Latching onto him tightly with her eyes, Mrs. Poitras smiled devilishly. "I know you will. I am a very good cook. Not one to rival Mrs. Richardson, of course, but I can prepare a fine meal." She stopped her secret actions abruptly, turning back to Mr. Barlow and Katherine. "Shall we go?"

The sudden expiration of her movement caused John to stumble some—a disjointed jerk that was fortunately masked by Mrs. Poitras's gown.

Katherine bowed and responded, "I am truly honored."

Mrs. Poitras's smile radiated innocence. "Of course you are, child."

Mr. Barlow held out the crook of his arm for Katherine MacPhearson, and he and the young woman followed Mrs. Poitras out.

CHAPTER 15

▼

A POIGNANT MEMORY

John slumped into his chair as soon as he was alone. The dining room was finally empty, save for a young black girl clearing tables. Judith wore a starched gray dress with a magnolia cross-stitched over the left breast, the livery of Richardson's Inn. Her dark, curly hair had been cropped short. She was unusually plump for a slave—but Judith did, after all, work in a kitchen and was probably always nibbling on scraps. Crossing over to John, Judith tapped him on the shoulder.

"Sorry, suh, but are ya finished here? May I clear your table, suh?"

John looked down at his plate and noticed some grits remaining. Remembering what Mr. Barlow had said about dishonoring Mrs. Richardson, he picked up his fork and finished the scraps. "Just one moment, Judith," he mumbled over a mouthful of food.

"Lost in your thoughts, were ya, Mista Connolley?"

"Yessum." After a slight pause to collect himself, John passed her his plate, then added, "Could you please tell Matthew I's finished? We needs ta be gettin' back."

Judith nodded. "Yessuh, Mista Connolley. An' iffin I may say so, suh, it be quite de honor, ya havin' Mista Barlow visit again."

"Huh?"

"I were jes' sayin' what an honor it be for you's, havin' Mista Barlow come again. De Richardsons are jes' tickled, what wit' 'im stayin' at de inn again."

Distantly John responded, "I suppose they are." Then, with more urgency: "Please, Judith, get Matthew for me."

"Yessuh, Mista Connolley. Yessuh."

*   *   *   *

Alone again, John let his head drop to the table. Today was not a day he looked forward to. Yet his body contradicted that very thought. The desires of the flesh always betrayed him. He too remembered that fight. It was one of many down in New Orleans. Billy Watkins was said to be unbeatable—until he stepped into the ring with John Connolley. John's strength proved the advantage. One of the ways Mr. Barlow had trained the boy was to have his biggest Negroes hit him in the stomach repeatedly, so John could handle a whupping.

Billy was fast and he hit with lightning speed, but his fists made little impact on the mighty bulk Mr. Barlow had forced John to build. Billy, considered average height at five feet six, looked small and scrawny next to the giant John Connolley.

Billy took full advantage of his speed to dart in and out, taking jabs at John. John, though, was just as adept at landing punches, and his packed more weight than anything Billy dished out. John might have been big, and he might have appeared lumbering, but he had been trained to dance on his feet; Mr. Barlow had prepared John to fight by ordering Mitch to strike at John's feet with a whip to keep him moving. John might not have had Billy's lightning speed, but he could avoid most of the scrawny man's punches while landing just the right number of hits against his opponent. By the end of round one, Billy was the worse for wear. He did not stand a chance in round two; by then the skinny little man was staggering. All John had to do was aim and strike. Billy Watkins had been thoroughly pummeled by the end of round two, and John Connolley had beaten the unbeatable.

Mr. Barlow, thrilled with the boy's win, had booked him a room at L'hotel Louisiana, in the heart of the French Quarter. Upon entering his room, John was stunned at its size. There had been a couch, chair, and a coffee table off to the left … and next to it sat a concert grand piano. The first thing John did was pull out the bench and treat himself to a little Haydn. He was in the mood for something robust, and Haydn fit the bill. Playing a few bars from Haydn's Andante in D major, John stopped. "Not that," he muttered. Upping the ante, he switched over to Haydn's Allegro assai in F sharp minor. It had been written for woodwind, but John had arranged it for the piano a few years back.

Even the lure of Haydn's music could not hold John for long—not when the real prize sat smack dab in the middle of the room. Hot water sent steam rising from the shiny copper tub. Set on heavy carpet, it patiently waited for John's sore, aching muscles. This was the first time John had even seen a bath inside a bedroom. Still, Mr. Barlow was eccentric, and John had learned long ago not to question the man's oddities.

After undressing, John folded his clothes and placed them neatly on the edge of the bed, a four-poster big enough to fit three people with room to spare. This room was elaborate. The bedcover was draped with lace, and the pillows were the plumpest John had ever seen. He pressed down on the mattress to discover it was stuffed thick with feathers instead of Spanish moss. Goose down, he figured. He could not wait to lay down on it.

Mr. Barlow must truly have been pleased by the win. He had never treated John so royally before. *Best to enjoy it while it lasts,* John thought. On that note, he slowly lowered himself into the copper tub and luxuriated in the steaming, hot water. He laughed when the sweet scent of lavender wafted across his nostrils. Mr. Barlow truly was eccentric.

Lord, John thought, *but this bath feels good.* His body always felt like a crippled old man's after a fight, and the hot water slowly melted away the aches and pains delivered by small, bony fists.

Regardless of the perks, John took no joy in the win. Billy Watkins had stood little chance against him. Mr. Barlow was happy ... but this win would just mean tougher opponents. John would fight even bigger and stronger men. Mr. Barlow had even joked about pitting John against two men at once, to even the odds for the other side. No, the fighting had not ended—it had just begun. John closed his eyes and tried to forget everything but the hot water and steam. Unfortunately, that moment of respite was not meant to be.

The creaking of the door announced Mr. Barlow. The most beautiful woman John had ever seen entered the room with him. She was truly regal. Her dark brown hair hung down in curls, and her dress was by far the most elaborate piece of jewelry John had ever seen. Real pearls were sewn into the bodice. Soft pink embroidered apple blossoms floated across the light blue background of the gown. John was so taken by her elegant grace that, for a moment, he forgot he was naked. The sudden realization caused him to lower himself deeper into the tub.

The lady giggled mischievously. "I do so love a shy man. Jacob, please have him stand for me."

Mr. Barlow's laugh rumbled deep. It always had, but now there was a lusty quality to it. "You heard the lady, boy. Stand up and give her a look."

Aghast, John begged, "Mr. Barlow, please ..." He could not believe the order he had been given.

"Do not be foolish, boy," Mr. Barlow harrumphed. "Get out of the tub. Now!"

John simply could not do it. The idea of standing naked in front of a woman was too much. He slumped deeper into the tub.

Mr. Barlow grimaced—it was just as he had expected. "You cannot blame the boy for modesty, now can you, Delilah?"

"By no means. In fact, I find it quite tantalizing." The tip of her tongue slowly slipped across her upper lip. "But please, Jacob ... make him stand."

Mr. Barlow sighed and shrugged. "He is a stubborn youth. It is nigh on impossible to push him when he means to resist."

Mrs. Poitras rolled her eyes. "Oh, Jacob, really." She was not taken in. "Clearly you have pushed him this far."

"Yes, indeed ... but it is mighty hard work."

"I see what you are up to, Mr. Barlow." Mrs. Poitras opened her purse and produced a thick wad of bills. "Will an extra hundred inspire you to push your boy harder?"

Mr. Barlow smiled. "Why, Mrs. Poitras! You are a generous woman."

John's ears burned. He was being sold. He almost uttered unforgivable words. "Uncle Ja—Mr. Barlow, suh, don't sell me. You cain't!" He nearly lifted himself out of the tub. "You promised I could work ... I could ..." Realizing he had nearly exposed himself, John dropped back into the tub, splashing water over the floor. "Please do not sell me, suh, I beg you."

Delighted by John's outburst, Mr. Barlow crossed over and placed his hands on the boy's shoulders. "Of course not, my boy. I have no intention of selling you. You are like a son to me. I have always said that, have I not?"

John flushed with indignation. "Yes, suh."

"And you always called me Uncle Jacob, remember?"

"Yes, suh."

"Then why would you think I would ever want to sell you?"

"I ... you were ... that lady, suh, just offered you money for me."

Mr. Barlow laughed, shaking the wad of bills Mrs. Poitras had handed him. "Oh, my boy, you are worth more than a mere two hundred dollars. After the way you fought this afternoon, I would not let you go for less than five thousand dollars. Today's fight alone made me that much."

John sank lower. Five thousand dollars! He could never hope to save that much money.

"No, son. Delilah does not want to buy you. She just wants to rent you for an hour."

By the time Mr. Barlow had finished his speech, Mrs. Poitras had made her way to the bath. Placing her fingers on John's chest, she began walking them into the water. John grabbed her hand. Without thinking he pushed his back against the tub. Suddenly the room spun all around him. Its lavish appearance came into perspective; the lavender scent soured in his nostrils.

"You mean to whore me, suh?"

Mr. Barlow scoffed at John. "Men do not get whored, boy. Only women do. I am offering you a great opportunity to lay with a woman as fine as Mrs. Poitras. Men envy your position." Mr. Barlow shook the bills in John's face. "And she is willing to pay good money, too. With the fighting, you get one percent. With Delilah here ... well, she talked me into giving you ten."

"But will he participate?" Mrs. Poitras chimed. "The boy is restraining himself. I want to be pleasured, Jacob ... not fought with."

"Oh, he will participate." With a greasy laugh, Mr. Barlow added, "Any man would."

Mrs. Poitras assumed a pouty frown that made her even more beautiful. "But he refuses to stand for me."

"Fear not, my duckling." Mr. Barlow laughed again. "As you said ... I have managed to push him this far."

Mrs. Poitras's eyes twinkled in excitement. "Do tell me your secret, please."

Mr. Barlow barked, "Mitch, bring her in."

The door swung open. Mitch entered, dragging a small black girl. She could not have been more than ten years old. Her hair was tightly curled and pulled into pigtails. She wore a plain beige dress. Her eyes bulged with fear as Mitch towered over her, whip in hand.

"No!" John yelled. He slowly stood, hands covering his shame. He could hear Mitch's menacing laugh. Mrs. Poitras's sigh was a mixture of satisfaction and delight.

Mr. Barlow smiled. "You see, it is really quite easy. Turn around and show her your back, boy."

John complied.

The sigh released from Delilah Poitras's lips sent shivers down every man's back. "Oh, my. He is so tall."

"Six foot five," Mr. Barlow replied.

"An anomaly."

"Rare indeed," Mr. Barlow agreed.

"Such a sculptured body. You have certainly done well with him, Jacob."

"Now." Mr. Barlow placed his index finger lightly under Mrs. Poitras's chin and lifted her gaze. "If you will just look up ever so slightly, you will notice all the scarring."

"Oh, my." Her fingers feathered the rubberized tissue. "You have whipped him considerably." She touched the scar on his shoulder. "JB." Her tsk held more amusement than scorn. "Jacob, you branded him."

Mr. Barlow shrugged. "He tried to run."

John grimaced. *I never ran!* Mr. Barlow maintained the story to justify what he had done.

Continuing with his litany, Mr. Barlow added, "You see, I am a fair man. After the first run, I brand my slaves to remind them to whom they belong … and give them a whipping, of course."

"Of course," Mrs. Poitras chimed.

"After the second run, they get the letter *R* branded on their faces."

Mrs. Poitras uttered her disgust. "Oh, that is so horrible. But … if they insist on running, what can you do? My Raymond has had to brand a few on the face, too."

Mr. Barlow continued, "I have only ever done that twice. If they run a third time … well, then there's nothing left to do but hang them. Fortunately, I have yet to do that. But John here … he only tried running once. After that he gave me his word he would never run again. He is a man of his word, Delilah. Once given, he will keep it. A man is nothing if not his word. Is that not right, son?"

John strangled the reply he wanted to give, saying instead, "Yes, suh."

This conversation was more than John could handle. It was bad enough being spoken of in the third person … but Mr. Barlow's persistence with the lie truly curdled John. Bile spoiled his tongue. It took all his strength not to turn on the man and kill him. But murder was not part of John's makeup. As much as he wanted the man dead, he knew he could never bring himself to kill.

"That is very interesting, Jacob," Mrs. Poitras simpered, "but please, explain how this little girl is going to make him do as I ask."

"Quite simple, really," Mr. Barlow uttered with confidence.

"You keep saying that, Jacob." Mrs. Poitras maintained her composure, keeping most of her impatience out of her voice.

"As I was saying, all that scarring taught me John can handle pain, so I had to try a different tactic with him. You see, there was one time when he absolutely refused to mind me, and I simply cannot tolerate that."

Mrs. Poitras feigned horror. "By no means. One must have order."

"So, when whippings did not work, I had to promise to make Ol' Henry, a gnarly ol' Negro, John's personal whipping boy. Ol' Henry was terrified. He begged John not to make me whip him. It worked. John can take pain, but he cannot take causing it, or inflicting it on others. So I had Mitch here hunt out the oldest or youngest Negro working in this fine establishment. It seems to be this little girl here. Mitch tends to like them young." In a curt tone, Mr. Barlow ordered John, "Turn around and look at the girl, boy." After John complied, Mr. Barlow softened his voice for Mrs. Poitras. "One word from me, and Mitch will start switching her."

The suggested threat caused the little girl to wail. John closed his eyes.

"Oh, Jacob, he is not mulatto, is he? Is that why he feels such sympathy for these people?"

"No." Mr. Barlow stretched out the vowel for emphasis. "There is not a drop of colored blood in the boy. In fact, he is nobly born, if you can believe it."

John opened his eyes and locked horns with the old man.

Delilah Poitras's sigh drew John's eyes to hers. Her eyes, wide like those of a doe, gave the suggestion of innocence John knew could not possibly exist. She was schooled in her expressions. "Oh, this is just so wonderful!" Mrs. Poitras squealed. "Do tell the story."

Mr. Barlow was eager to oblige. "His mama was the daughter of a man you know quite well."

The intrigue was too much for her; her voice bubbled over in delight. "Oh, do tell, Jacob, do tell."

Mr. Barlow's deep laugh rumbled and shook. "Ah, my pretty little bird, some confidences must be kept. His granddaddy and I still do business. He would not take kindly to this bit of family history being revealed."

With a look of disappointment, belied by the twinkle in her eyes, Mrs. Poitras giggled, "Jacob Barlow, you are such a tease." She tickled the old man's goatee. "Please continue with your narrative."

Mr. Barlow puffed himself into great importance and lowered his voice to suggest that even these tawdry details were best kept secret. "Well, the lad's grandfather, though he would never admit to being John's grandfather at all, was one of the most prosperous men in the new United States ... lives here in New Orleans now." Mr. Barlow's drawl transformed the word into "Norleens." "Why, he was even at the games. Bet against the boy. Lost himself a bundle, he did."

John's glare met Mrs. Poitras's eyes and watched as hers danced in delight. "Oh, Jacob, this is too wicked."

Mr. Barlow, pleased with the effect of his storytelling, continued on with pompous flair. "At that time, he was a patriot living up in Savannah. Having had his house and business burned to the ground by the British, like many a good folk did in those days, he was quick to join the rebel army." Mr. Barlow paused, allowing for Mrs. Poitras's sigh of disbelief. "His daughter was of marrying age, and her daddy had hoped I would take her hand ... but the silly little girl had fallen in love with a colonel in the British army."

Mrs. Poitras's disdain burst forth. "No! How horrible. The traitorous whore!"

Mr. Barlow laughed at the anticipated response. "That is exactly what John's granddaddy said."

John burned indignantly. He ground his teeth. This woman dared refer to his mama as a whore! He hated this story and despised Mr. Barlow for retelling it.

"Actually," Mr. Barlow continued, "I do believe his exact wording was 'trollop,' or 'strumpet.' No, I think it was 'wench.' Well, either way, it all adds up to a whore."

Mrs. Poitras was hooked. "Continue, continue."

"In all fairness," Mr. Barlow added, "the young lady was truly in love."

Aghast that Mr. Barlow would support such a horrible woman, Delilah Poitras burst out, "But, Jacob ... she was your intended!"

"I was her daddy's choice. She was never mine, nor I hers. In fact, I was already married to my sweet Louise by the time all this occurred. Her daddy planned our union during our childhood. Even still, John's mama and I remained friends."

Mrs. Poitras tsked. "You are far too generous a man."

"As I was saying, the young woman was truly in love, and it was wartime. Passions ran high, and there was always the threat of never seeing her loved one again. Not that I approved of her affair, mind you ... there is never a call for a lady to act like that."

Mrs. Poitras agreed wholeheartedly. "Indeed."

John silently scoffed. Could they not hear the irony?

Mrs. Poitras was too wrapped up in the intrigue to see herself. "How did her daddy find out?"

"The young couple were circumspect. Yet he, being an officer in the British army, was under the eye of the patriots. He was followed, and word of their tawdry affair reached her daddy. It was alleged that she was sharing tactical information with the young man."

Mrs. Poitras was about to explode in indignation when Mr. Barlow put a finger to her lips. "Now, now, Delilah. I do not believe she was traitorous in that way. She was a silly little thing, easily swept up by passion. She gave very little thought, really, to much beyond a pretty dress and the smile of a handsome man. I doubt she ever once thought about the war or any of its stratagems."

John burned. He could say nothing in his mama's defense. Any protest would land a whip to the back of that little Negro girl.

Unhindered, Mr. Barlow continued. "Had she considered it, surely she would have thought about the consequences of lying down with a British officer."

Mrs. Poitras nodded. "Then what happened?"

"Well, the boy's granddaddy made his way to a small inn on the outskirts of Savannah, where he found the two of them, wrapped together, flesh on flesh." Mr. Barlow paused to allow Mrs. Poitras to flush and release a long, staccato sigh. "Outraged at seeing his daughter partaking lustily of the enemy, he hauled the young man out of bed and shot him before her very eyes."

Mrs. Poitras gasped.

John kept his eyes lowered. Too many times, he had been forced to hear his family's history spouted in this manner.

Mr. Barlow completely ignored John. He was too caught in the ecstasy of storytelling to give him any notice. "He took his daughter, naked as the day she was born, and dragged her to the block to be sold."

Mrs. Poitras feigned horror. "Oh, Jacob, that is just awful! How did she come to be in your possession?"

"Why, I bought her, you silly little goose. She was an acquaintance of mine, and I felt sorry for her."

Mrs. Poitras giggled. "Oh, you! You had me going there. How could you have possibly known she was to be sold that day?"

Mr. Barlow shook his head and smiled wryly. "I had no previous knowledge. It just happened I was at the block that very afternoon. I bought thirteen Negroes that day … and one young white woman who, unbeknownst to anyone at the time, was pregnant with this young man." For a brief moment, John's presence was acknowledged—and immediately forgotten.

"It was so kind of you to buy her." Mrs. Poitras flushed with admiration for the older man.

"Well, my little sparrow," Mr. Barlow replied as humbly as he could, "I wanted to help her find a comfortable life, considering her dire circumstances."

"Your generosity astounds me."

"Miss Delilah, you are too kind."

Their mutual admiration so sickened John that he could feel the bile rising in his throat.

"Please, continue," Mrs. Poitras chimed sweetly.

"Well, the poor woman, knowing there was no future outside my charity, begged me to keep her for life ... which, of course, made her unborn child my possession, too." With a tsk and a mournful shake of his head, Mr. Barlow added, "Had she only known she was pregnant ... a pity, really. Indentured servants are seldom held for life, being they only have a debt to repay." Responding to Mrs. Poitras's dumbfounded expression, Mr. Barlow explained, "I had offered the woman the opportunity to repay me, which would have made her an indentured servant instead of a slave, but she refused my generous offer. John's mama knew that even if she paid back all the money I spent buying her, she would have no decent life once she left my service."

"Of course not!" Mrs. Poitras vehemently agreed.

"So," Mr. Barlow continued, "when she begged me to keep her for life, I agreed. I felt sorry for her. After all, she had no hope for a proper marriage ... not after being sold as a traitor and a whore."

"But what about the boy?" Mrs. Poitras inquired, clearly distressed that an innocent child should suffer such an abominable fate.

"Well, you see, I had legal papers drawn up stating that his mama was to become my property ... a slave for life, in essence. She signed them readily in front of witnesses. I insisted on that, so no one could call me into account for owning a white woman. Not that complexion really matters, with so many mulattos passing for white these days. Still, I thought it prudent. It was shortly after all legal affairs were finalized that she began to show with the boy here."

"I am sorry, Jacob ... but I simply do not understand. Why did he become a slave, too?"

"You need to study up on your slave law, my little chickadee. The child takes on the status of the mama if the mama is a slave. So John became my slave for life, just like his mama was." Then, to soften her distress, he added, "It does not matter that the boy is white. The law, after all, is the law. The day his mama signed, sealed, and delivered me her fate, she delivered me his fate as well."

"Such a sad life ... and such a rarity." Mrs. Poitras's sudden shift from sympathy to mischief belied her previous look of concern. "Oh, Jacob, make him lift his arms for me." Motioning with elegant grace, Mrs. Poitras lifted her arms like a ballerina.

John flushed with humiliation and fear at the thought of exposing himself this way. "Mr. Barlow, please … I beg of you, do not make me do this."

Mr. Barlow's reply was curt: "Mitch." The willing hand swung his whip and lashed the little Negro girl.

Her screams tore through John like a hurricane ripping through a shanty. It only took one hit.

Compliance.

Delilah Poitras walked closer, her fingers gently strumming against him.

John shook.

"Oh, please," she said. "Do not tell me we have to have that man and child in here with us."

Could he experience even greater mortification? John shook his head.

"Then kiss me, and we will let these three go."

Compliance.

Mrs. Poitras smiled. It was a winning smile, charming and delicate enough to set a man's heart on fire. But for John, it only served to fan the flames of humiliation.

"You may leave us now, Jacob. I do believe I am upputting the boy."

Mr. Barlow left the room with a chuckle. Mitch followed with a sinister laugh, dragging the sniffling Negro girl behind, leaving John alone with Mrs. Poitras.

*   *   *   *

Those words drifted through John's memory. "I do believe I am upputting the boy." The conflict between body and soul raged inside him. No, John was not looking forward to this day at all. He lifted his head and hollered, "Matthew, get in here. Now!"

Hearing John holler caused Matthew to leap through the kitchen door. "Sorry, suh. I were jes' visitin' wit' Judith is all." He should have known John would be riled up. Mr. Barlow always left him in a foul mood.

John sighed. "No, Matthew … I'm the one who's sorry." John regretted shouting. He softened his voice some, trying not to blame Matthew for his own downfall. "None a' this is your fault. It's just that we gotta go."

"I unda'stand."

Downcast, the two men made their way back to the cart and horse. Amos leaped out from under the cart when he heard them coming. John stroked the dog behind his ears. Then, leaping up on the cart, he barely waited for Matthew to join him. Even before Matthew was seated, John lashed at the reins and shouted "Hiyah," tossing Matthew back so hard he bruised his tailbone. The cart rumbled back toward John's—Mr. Barlow's, conditionally speaking—plantation. John whipped the reins and pushed the horse harder. Matthew lowered his hat to cover his eyes. There was no point in even trying to look at John Connolley in this mood.

CHAPTER 16

▼

TANGLED FLESH

John's barn had an ordinary look to it. Against the left wall were three stalls. The first was for his milking cow; the second was for Gator, his ox; and the last housed John's horse, Cornerstone. Even at twenty years of age, the stallion was still proud, beautiful—and faster than most mustangs half his age. John hung his tack and saddles next to the back entrance. Above and to the right was the hayloft, with spillage dripping off the edge and matting the ground.

Where John's barn differed from the standard was on the right side, where all of the stalls were torn out. John used this space for training. Mr. Barlow made it very clear that John was to stay in shape, in case he failed to make his plantation work. In such an event, Mr. Barlow had plans to put John back in the ring. It was the last place John wanted to be, but if he ended up there again, he certainly did not want a year's softness endangering him. Boxing was illegal in most states, and the fighting was cutthroat.

Swinging open the barn doors, John went directly to his punching bag, where he fought the turmoil inside him. With every blow against the heavy burlap sack, John pounded out his frustration—and his need. He wanted Delilah Poitras. He had even believed he loved her for a time, but it was mostly her warmth, the softness of her skin, her moist, tender lips ... the way she inhaled him. To be devoured so heartily by a woman was enough to light any man's heart on fire.

John had filled the sack that hung in front of him (the sack that was a good third his height and nearly matched his waist in girth) full of Spanish moss. He had stuffed it so tightly that his fists barely made a dent when he pounded it. Punching the bag couldn't take away the hurt that clenched John's heart. Being sold—"rented," as Mr. Barlow put it, to be whored—and to desire the very woman who whored him—agonized John to no end. Delilah Poitras was as vivacious as she was beautiful. Her passions always brought John to a boil. She had made him a man, schooled him, and seared his soul. She had branded him, as surely as Mr. Barlow had branded his shoulder.

Try as he might, denying Mrs. Poitras was impossible. Mr. Barlow's threat to hang Matthew if John did not comply was unnecessary. With her first touch, and the suggestive, knowing look in her eyes, John had given himself over to her. His struggle, backward as it might be, was all a part of her game. She needed his resistance. It gave her power, and he relinquished it willingly. He hated her for it, desired her more powerfully, wished she could love him, and felt eternal gratitude that she was incapable of such feelings.

John left the punching bag and moved to the center of the barn, where, hanging from the central beam, was a bar installed for chin-ups. He had worked up quite a sweat hitting the bag, so, heedless of the danger, he tore off his shirt before leaping up. He wasn't likely to have any unexpected visitors today. Most folk knew he was entertaining Mr. Barlow and Lady Poitras. News like that traveled through a small town fast. *Besides,* John figured, *them who's coming already knows.*

He dangled with his toes barely touching the ground. With a grunt, John lifted himself up. Huffing, he repeated the lift ten more times before he felt her presence. John never heard her enter. She was far too delicate and graceful to make ungainly noise, treading lightly, as if on gossamer's threads—a line he remembered from *Romeo and Juliet.* (Mr. Barlow also loved teaching Shakespeare.) But John and Delilah Poitras were no Romeo and Juliet. He doubted Shakespeare ever dreamed of the possibility of their existence. They were not "star-cross'd lovers" thrown together by fate. Mrs. Poitras was just a woman who bought the services of a man. *What does that make me,* John wondered. *A man-whore?* Was there even a name for that?

It was her scent that first registered. A waft of powdered lavender tickled his nostrils, and he dropped down. Mrs. Poitras glided toward him. As she drew nearer, shivery shocks tingled up and down John's spine. Her fingers did their usual dance across his scars. Mrs. Poitras's fascination with his scars never diminished. If given half a chance, she would caress and kiss every one fifty times over and still feel the need to continue … especially with that damn brand. John turned to face her, and she pressed her face tight against his sternum. Her nails, gently scratching his chest, separated the hair there. She giggled at the feel of him.

John's response was uncontrollable. If he could, he would turn his body off. Her touch was more powerful than his will. Her sigh sent another wave of shivers up his spine; her lips and breath caressed him.

"Oh, John. You looked so strong when you were pulling yourself up against that bar. When you were hanging there, I wanted to tie you to it."

Oh God, he groaned inwardly. *Only the good Lord knows what sordid plans that woman has for me this time.* He fought to keep his composure. He forced the essence of reason into his voice. "How can I be of any use to you like that?"

Mrs. Poitras's giggle was more than mischievous. "You just let me worry about that." She bit his nipple. No pain, just flashes of ecstasy. "Please cooperate with me." Although she worded it as a request, her voice was commanding.

John sputtered. He was trying to resist—trying to say something to convince her that this idea of hers was ridiculous and depraved. But she continued to nibble relentlessly. She even caressed his sides with her nails. Partly to escape the physical taunt of her touch, partly because he really did want to acquiesce, John leaped for the bar and held himself suspended, toes swinging slightly against the ground, swishing the dirt and hay into a jumble to match the mulch that had become his brain.

Mrs. Poitras's hands remained attached to his body and were now embracing his buttocks. Her face nestled against his chest, breathing hot air against him. Her sudden jerk away startled John, and he shook. "Do not move, *mon cherie.*" Mrs. Poitras giggled as she strolled with casual grace, rotating rotund hips—not more plump than the average woman, but with just enough flesh to give her backside definition.

John's eyes were transfixed. Once again he feared what she had planned for him—feared and anticipated it.

Mrs. Poitras retrieved his milking stool, swinging it gently at her side as she made her way back to him. She planted it directly in front of him and used its extra height to her advantage. Almost eye to eye with John, she held him in her gaze as she slowly removed the soft blue taffeta sash she had delicately draped over her shoulders. Even atop the milking stool, she could barely reach his hands, so she stood on her toes as she tied them in place.

John grunted his disapproval as she tightened the sash more harshly than necessary. She seemed to enjoy the idea of his being truly fixed in place. Taffeta was a tough fabric; John knew he could not simply rip it away. It would take time for him to free himself from this restraint.

There was no time to think about freedom, though, as Mrs. Poitras went to work as soon as she knew John was secure. Her lips caressed his eyes and ears, finally gripping his mouth in a lasting kiss. With saliva dripping, she took the time to wet his neck and chest. Stepping off the stool and kicking it aside, Mrs. Poitras began her descent. Suddenly the buttons loosened on John's trousers.

John's release from his trousers and Mrs. Poitras's subsequent acts left him gasping for air, like a catfish tossed onto the bank. John's whole body tensed. He could not believe what she was doing. He hadn't known women did things like this. Never in his wildest dreams had he ever imagined something like this. John could barely contain himself. Groans welled up inside—groans he fought to keep from releasing. Mr. Barlow and Matthew were out there somewhere, and the barn doors were slung open. At any moment, either one of them—or both— might hear him, might enter the barn and see what was happening. This woman was beyond insane. The risks she loved to take were intoxicating.

John's toes flexed, his body arched, his head flung back. Holding in the desire, muting the sounds so desperately wanting to be released, only enhanced the sensations Mrs. Poitras was creating. He might be a whore, he thought, but at this moment, there was no reality crashing down on him. Pleasure was welling inside, tossing him like waves crashing against the shore: a storm battering against the rocks of his resistance. John could no longer remain mute, and with his release came a moan so satisfying that Mrs. Poitras held on to him until he was no longer able to keep his strength. John's body hung limp, and his knees sagged beneath him.

Mrs. Poitras stood up and casually smoothed the skirt of her dress, whipping away bits of dirt and hay. Sagging forward as he was, Mrs. Poitras was able to reach John's lips with little effort, but she did have to stand on tiptoe. She kissed John, delighting in his fervor.

The taste of himself on her lips caused John to tremble.

With a giggle, Mrs. Poitras lifted his trousers and redid the buttons. The sudden containment brought a groan of displeasure from John and elicited a wicked grin from the lady. *Lady*, he thought wryly.

With a sudden turn, Mrs. Poitras walked away.

She had already disappeared outside the barn doors when John came to his senses, calling her back. "Delilah? Delilah, get in here. Delilah?"

Her only response was a distant laugh.

"Delilah! You cannot leave me like this." Not even her distant laughter remained to keep him company. John struggled like a fish against the hook, trying to reach under the bar with his fingers. She had known all along what she was doing. Tying the fabric under the bar made it nigh on impossible for John to free himself. He pulled with his arms to try to loosen the grip she had so adeptly created. The more he struggled, the more the taffeta cut off his circulation. "Delilah! Damn you, woman, get in here!"

He heard footsteps. He closed his eyes and lowered his head. The flush of humiliation flooded over him. *Damn her all to hell!* If it had been Mrs. Poitras, he would never have heard her coming. He knew only too well.

With a deep, rumbling laugh, Mr. Barlow blurted out, "My, my, my! What has that fool woman done to you? Why, she has you tied up like a pig ready for slaughter. No doubt she has committed some form of treachery." He paused to circle John and peruse him up and down, looking for some sign of evidence, a clue—anything that might reveal what Mrs. Poitras had done. Once more his laughter erupted. "Well, Delilah is in the kitchen. I would say 'cooking in the kitchen,' but that woman never cooked a meal in her life. She is unpacking the basket Miss MacPhearson had her Negro girl make up for us."

The mention of Katherine sent waves of guilt pulsating through John.

"She also had Matthew draw you a bath. Had him drop lavender oil in the water. I figured it was because she likes her men clean … but it appears she likes her men sweaty and dirty, too. Still, the bath is waiting, so come on now. Get yourself free. Untie those knots, and jump down."

John wanted to look up at the man incredulously, but the shame embedded in him kept his eyes cast downward.

Mr. Barlow waited an unforgivingly long time before offering aid. "I suppose you need me to do it for you. Not willing to ask, though, are you? Stubborn fool. That is something I always admired about you … humph … hated, too." Adding a pause for effect, Mr. Barlow continued, "Go on, ask me for help."

John's head remained bent. He could not look the man in the eyes—not after what had happened, not with the knowing quality of Mr. Barlow's voice. Knowing he would hang there for hours without aid, John muttered a plea. "Mr. Barlow …" A heavy sigh ensued before John continued. "I ne—" No, he would not word it that way. Telling the man he needed him was more than John could bear. "Would you untie me, suh?" Another hellish moment ensued until John added, "Please."

Mr. Barlow drew himself up like a judge ready to pronounce the sentence. "Well, that is a fine request from a young fellow in quite the pickle. But it seems to me you might want to think of me a little more kindly. When you were a boy, you used to call me Uncle Jacob. I would be more inclined to help family out of a mess like this. Slaves, strangers, acquaintances and the like … they call me Mr. Barlow. Well, quite frankly, boy, they can all stew in their own pots, for all I care." Mr. Barlow turned and began a slow, agonizing walk to the door. "Try not to take too long freeing yourself, now," he tossed back offhandedly. "Delilah is not a lady to be kept waiting."

John felt his throat tighten, and his breath stopped inside his chest. He thought his heart might explode from pounding so hard. "Mr. Barlow, suh ... wait ..." But the man just kept right on walking, slow and steadylike. The last of John's dignity and self-respect were torn away from him as he begged, "Uncle Jacob, please untie me." He swallowed a nearly expressed "suh" and hastily continued with, "I need ... I need your help."

Mr. Barlow stopped in his tracks and slowly turned. He eyed John gravely. "Look up at me, boy. Do not stare at the ground between your feet."

John complied. Tears fought to break through red eyes, but he held them back.

Mr. Barlow smiled. He was his fatherly self again. Suddenly his walk became brisk, and he was in front of John in less than a breath. Picking up the stool, he undid Mrs. Poitras's work. With a bit of a grunt, he expressed in tones of surprise and slight admiration, "My word, that woman can certainly tie a knot." It took a few tries before Mr. Barlow was able to loosen the fabric enough for John to let go of the bar.

John's first impulse was to rub at the welts on his wrists. He refused to look up, though, and muttered a strangled "thank you" to the ground. It took another sigh before he could let out, "Uncle Jacob."

Mr. Barlow laughed. "Any time, son. Any time." He slapped John on the shoulder and gave him a friendly shake. "You know I am always here for you." Mr. Barlow stood between John and the door. Before John could veer around him, Mr. Barlow latched onto his arm. "You must tell me why that woman hung you like that." John pulled his arm free and pushed his way past the man, escaping through the barn doors. Mr. Barlow's knowing laugh proved no explanation was required.

*　　　*　　　*　　　*

John and Mrs. Poitras lay in a tangle of flesh. Sweat glistened off their bodies. Mrs. Poitras's skin seemed to glow in the rays of the sun that shone through John's bedroom window. She looked so scintillating, with eyes closed and long lashes fluttering gently. John never ceased to admire the woman's intense beauty. No line etched her face, even though she was something of an age over forty. A man never asked a woman her age, especially not Delilah Poitras's. He gently brushed aside the curls dangling over her face and neck. He wanted a pure picture of her. Lying like this, she always seemed so fragile, so meek. The contrast between appearance and reality was stunning. John knew Mrs. Poitras took advantage of that disparity with every man she had ever met. Her guile most certainly worked on him. Even knowing this, John still believed in her innocence in moments like this.

His fingers caressed her cheeks, and Mrs. Poitras woke. Again John felt himself drowning in the deep pool of her brown eyes. With throat clenched, he barely managed to utter, "You are so beautiful." Her smile fluttered against his heart.

"Why, thank you, *mon cherie.*"

Unable to stop himself, he added, "And such a formidable woman."

She lifted up onto her elbow, tilted her head, and readied her lips for a kiss. John complied.

She sighed, "That is the nicest thing any man has ever said to me."

Her feel suggested honesty, and John believed her.

She inhaled his scent and murmured, "I do so love being in your arms."

John wanted her. He wanted to take her kindly. Wanted to hold her as a man. In that moment, he truly felt what they shared was real. *If I were to take you now,* he thought, *it would be proper. Not as a whore, but as a man.* His kiss was passionate and suggestive.

Mrs. Poitras drew back.

John sat up, amazed. She had never denied herself a piece of him before. Why now? Why this time?

Her genuine smile was gone. Her eyes sparkled with their usual mischievous flare. "As much as I would love to, *mon cherie,*" she said in a tantalizingly seductive voice, "I have had all I have paid for. Your good uncle would not stand for my taking more than my due. I swear the old fool is sitting out there in the other room, just listening to hear if we moan."

John growled as he flung the covers off. He leaped from the bed and stormed across the room. His fists planted against the wall as he hunched forward. With one leg bent, the other stretched, he looked as if he might be able to force the wall from the room.

Mrs. Poitras was all a-titter. "Oh, John, you are truly a magnificent specimen. I swear there is no finer man than you."

He whirled on her, fire in his eyes. "You dare call me a man? I am no man. I am your whore!" He spat the word with vehemence and disgust.

She took on a look of worry and dismay.

Could he believe her?

Her voice carried hurt and displeasure. "I do not think of you that way, *mon cherie*."

Incredulously he shot back, "How can you not? You pay for me every time!"

Her smile was mischievous. "I should think you would appreciate our encounters, when ten percent of all the money I pay Barlow goes to you. All that money is to help you pay for—"

John spat, "You think I touch that money? It sickens me. It sits in the bank and can rot there, for all I care. I am never going to use it. I am a man, Delilah, not a whore, and I despise every moment you use me like one."

An impish smile bloomed across her face. "You certainly did not feel like you were despising it today."

John's anger burned. His fists clenched. "I could just—"

Mrs. Poitras squirmed, her voice provocative. "Just what, John? Hit me?"

John flushed.

"I truly do wish I could, John, but my husband has been keeping a tight hold of my purse strings these days. I think he might suspect something." She paused a moment to admire him in the flesh. A girlish giggle bubbled up from inside, like a spring trickling over rocks. "Just look at you, standing there naked. Why, I remember the first time we met. You could barely bring yourself to get out of your bath."

John could take no more. He ripped his trousers from the floor and threw them on. Buttoning up as he went out, he stormed through the door, Mrs. Poitras's laughter pushing against his back. When he reached the front door, he kicked it off its hinges to get outside. Engulfed by rage, John missed seeing Mr. Barlow sitting by the front window.

Unimpressed with John's behavior, Mr. Barlow hurried outside after him. "What in tarnation do you think you are up to, boy? I will not have you offending—"

Before Mr. Barlow could finish, Mrs. Poitras's voice danced against his. "Oh, Jacob, leave the boy alone."

John turned on them, hollering from the depth of his soul, "Do not call me boy!" When the fury left his eyes, John saw before him Mrs. Poitras, wearing only a shift. The wind pressed the cream silk snug against her body, its opacity adding even greater definition. He was mortified. The woman had no shame, exposing herself, more naked than if she were standing in the flesh. It was not just for him, either. Mr. Barlow's lips were moist, and his tongue was flicking out to lick them. No wonder Mr. Barlow had not chastised John for his outburst—he was too busy leering at Mrs. Poitras.

John's rage exploded. Fuming, he rushed toward Mrs. Poitras, lifting and flinging her over his shoulder. He smacked her bottom so hard, he was certain she would suffer from a welt. He surely did hope so. She yelped, but did not struggle.

Mr. Barlow leaped forward. "You put her down this—" Mr. Barlow had no chance to finish, but this was not because John turned on him, or because Mrs. Poitras said anything in his defense. She merely raised her head and gave it a slight shake. It was enough to stop the old man in his tracks. Befuddled, Mr. Barlow turned and walked toward the barn, where Matthew was working. Not knowing what else to do, he stood there, watching the Negro work.

When John got Mrs. Poitras back into the bedroom, he slung her down onto the bed. John's voice was commanding. There was nothing meek or complying about him. "I intend to make love to you, woman," he said. "Make love to you as a man. Not one penny, you hear"—he raised his voice, so Mr. Barlow could make out every word—"not one damnable penny is to change hands."

At the barn, Matthew made sure to turn his back, so as not look at Mr. Barlow's face. He had learned the hard way a slave never pointed out a master's predicament. Help him save face, and you may just save yourself from suffering the wrath of his disgrace.

Looking down, John saw a frightened doe shiver beneath him. He slowly lowered himself. Before bending in for a kiss, John whispered a barely audible request. "May I?"

Mrs. Poitras responded with a kiss.

*   *   *   *

The sun was well past its zenith. Hanging low to the west, it flickered through leaves, scattering diamonds across the room. When John released Mrs. Poitras she looked up at him. He tried to lie at her side, but she held him in her arms. He rested gently against her. His voice, brushing against her eyelids, made them flutter. "I do not want to squash you."

There were tears in her eyes. "Do not leave me, John. Not yet."

He smiled and gently kissed her lips.

Her voice quivered. "I want to feel the full weight of you. I want my breath caught beneath you. I want ..."

John rested his full weight atop her for a brief moment.

When he rolled off, she shivered. "I will never leave my husband."

Silence tore between them.

John nodded. "I know." His eyes studied the ceiling. A crack ran along it to the far wall. *I'll have to fix that*, he thought. Still looking up, he added in a hollow voice, "This can never happen again."

Mrs. Poitras stifled a cry. After an endless pause, neither wanting to end what was already over, she rose and slowly dressed. John could not bear to watch her. Instead he rested his arm over his eyes, listening to the rustle of taffeta. She did not even bother to ask him to button her up. This time he heard her move, but still gracefully—he suspected she added sound as a way of saying good-bye. In a voice softer than gentle rain, she said, "I will talk to Jacob for you." Shutting the door behind her, she left.

As John lay there, he could hear their muffled voices. Every now and then, a snippet would emerge from the murmur. Delilah Poitras had changed. No longer sounding authoritative, she merely stated facts. "He is a man … he has paid his due … a thousand times over … breaking point …" And then, most clearly: "Jacob Barlow, you are a fool."

The only expressions that rang clear from Mr. Barlow's voice were "handshake," "gave me his word," and "when he has earned it." John lay there, no longer in endless shame, but trapped all the same.

The following day, Mr. Barlow deposited fifty dollars into John's account.

CHAPTER 17

▼

COFFIN KELLY

It was another sweltering day. The sun nearing the horizon did little to cool the sweat produced by its rays. No cool breeze eased the clamp of the heat. It was definitely the dog days of summer; old Amos lay sprawled out under the front porch. When he heard John climbing up on the cart, though, he sprang into action, refusing to be left behind. John sat next to Matthew, who was ready to chauffeur him to the MacPhearsons'. Amos howled, and John ordered him back to the house. Amos backed up a few paces, but fearful of missing out, he howled again. John turned to look at the old dog and then did what he always did—gave in.

"All right, Amos, come along if ya want." He waved a hand, and Amos danced toward the cart, his wagging tail like a flag flapping wildly in the wind. "Stay close, ya hear?" John hollered. "I ain't runnin' round any swamps lookin' for ya." The dog barked as if he understood, standing ready.

John was dressed in black. He was not attending a funeral; it just happened to be the only good suit he owned. Mr. Barlow had given it to John on his thirtieth birthday. The old man had showered John with far too many gifts that day. It was as if Mr. Barlow were trying to make up for sixteen years of hell in one lavish spray of gift giving. Still, John was glad to have the suit. He could not have gone for dinner at the MacPhearsons' dressed in work clothes. He eyed Matthew, growling displeasure at being chauffeured. "I feel like a damn fool havin' you drive me."

Matthew laughed and put on his best subservient attitude. "Yessuh, Massa John," he said, tipping his hat. "Iffin ya don't mind my sayin' so, suh, a man a' your stature oughtn't be goin' ta no affair wit'out a proper attendant."

John scoffed, refusing to see the humor in the situation. "Get on with it, then. You're makin' me late."

"Don't be takin' it out on me," Matthew quipped back. Unconsciously rubbing at the *R* branded on his left cheek, Matthew added, "Shoot, ain't like you's able ta leave me behin'. Folks be wonderin' who be watchin your runaway nigga."

"I know, Matthew. I'm sorry." John truly did feel bad. He hated taking his anxiety out on others. "I's jes' nervous, is all."

Matthew clicked his tongue to get the horse moving. As soon as they were on the road, Amos lit off on his own. John growled, "That damn dog better not get lost again, 'cause I ain't goin' lookin' for him."

Matthew laughed at that. "'Course ya ain't, John."

"I mean it this time!" John tried to sound determined, but he loved that dog too much to let him go missing. Amos was the first creature that had ever listened to him. Knowing he had a friend in Amos, John trusted that dog with his life. Besides, Amos was a fine hunting dog. He had helped keep John fed over the winter months.

It did not take John long to forget about Amos; he had this fancy dinner to attend and was as nervous as a mouse surrounded by corn snakes. He kept picking at his jacket and running his hand through his rusty red hair, leaving a mass of curls that looked like the Savannah when ravaged by a hurricane.

Matthew eyed him warily. "Settle yourself, John. You're all jumpity, like you's sittin' on coals. Jes' like them li'l ol' flies that bounce up an' down ag'in de water. Ya keep this up, an' your gonna make de horse skittish."

"Sorry, Matthew. I jes' … I ain't comfortable about tonight. My stomach is tied in knots worse'n a noose ready for a hangin'." Suddenly jerking around in fright, John howled out, "Where's my sheet music?"

Matthew rolled his eyes and tugged at the papers underneath John.

John heaved a sigh of relief. "Thank the good Lord. Leastwise whilst I's playin', I don't have ta talk ta folks."

Eyeing him askance, Matthew had to ask, "Ya means ta tell me ya ain't never been ta one a' them fancy dinnas before?"

John shook his head. "Barlow used to make me play at 'em, but I were never asked to sit at the table. Shoot, Matthew, I don't know what ta say."

Matthew simply shrugged. It was not as if he had ever been to one of these fancy to-dos. "I reckon ya don't say nothin', then."

John nodded. "Sounds like fine advice. But what if someone were ta ask me a question?"

This was truly dumbfounding. *What's de man doin' askin' me for?* Matthew wondered. "Shoot, John, I dunno … answer 'em, I guess."

John shook his head. "I sure hope I don't go makin' a fool a myself in front a' Miss—"

John never got a chance to finish. Matthew scowled at him good. "Ya jes' better watch yourself, John." Matthew was used to talking to John as if he were an equal. He still thought John was mulatto. "It be mighty obvious that li'l missy got eyes for ya. Ya knows ya ain't in no position ta marry no uppity white woman. How's ya gonna explain your back and that *brand* ta de likes a' her?"

John slumped. "I cain't."

"No, suh! Ya cain't! An' it ain't jes' your life you's riskin' here." Matthew was worried, all right. If anything were to happen to John, he would be back at Mr. Barlow's with his neck tight in a noose.

"I know, Matthew." John sighed. "I won't ruin it for you. I promise."

"You's branded, boy. Don't ya never forget it!"

"How the hell can I?" John barked. "Damnation, Matthew! I ain't never called you boy, so don't be callin' me one!"

Matthew was taking no broke, though. "Iffin them folks get a whiff a' you's bein' mulatto … why, they'd have you's on the gibbet swingin' beneath de trap before ya even knows it."

"I ain't mulatto, Matthew. How many times do I have ta tell you that? My daddy were in the British army, an'—"

Matthew cut him off. "Tell yourself whatever ya like, boy."

Trying to speak over him, John hollered, "It's the truth!"

It did not matter what John said. *Facts be facts*, Matthew thought, so he kept right on talking. "Believe whatever ya wants, but Barlow don't treat no white man de way he treats you. Ya gots to be colored. Thar ain't no way round it."

John nearly hit Matthew but held his fists tight against his legs. "Look at my eyes. Have you ever seen a colored man with blue eyes?"

Matthew shrugged. "They looks gray ta me."

John looked at him incredulously. "Stone gray, ocean blue … who cares? You ever see that on a colored man?"

"No, suh, ya got me thar, but …" Before John could cut him off, Matthew countered, "… but thar be an awful lotta mixed blood. Them massas been thinnin' us out. 'Sides, we all knows it only takes a drop a colored blood ta make you's a nigga in thar eyes."

"Damnation, Matthew! Do you really think Barlow be lettin' a nigga live free?"

"Ya got me thar," Matthew admitted. "Maybe ya ain't colored. But ya sho as hell been treated like one. An' de way ya act ... hell, ya ain't like no indentured servant I ever seen. Them white folks stick ta themselves. I reckon they knows they's gonna go free someday." Matthew eyed John suspiciously. "So, iffin you's white, why ain't ya jes' paid off your debt? Ya gots de money."

"We were never in debt. Leastwise I don't think we were."

"We?"

"Me and my mama."

Matthew looked at John quizzically. He had never met Evelyn, as she had passed away long before Mr. Barlow purchased him.

John answered in a clipped manner. "Her daddy done sold her when he caught her with my daddy. He shot my daddy and sold my mama. He claimed she were a traitor an' a whore. She done gave herself ta Barlow for life before she even knew she were carryin' me."

This piece of intelligence left Matthew stunned. "Why in de name a' all that's good an' holy would anyone do that?"

John shrugged. "I dunno. She didn't see no hope. All chances for a good marriage were done away with, what with her havin' been sold an' all. So Barlow had the papers writ up, an' Mama signed 'em. There were even witnesses. Barlow made sure it was all done legal-like. When Mama started ta show, she couldn't take it back ag'in. Barlow always said the law's the law, so I's a slave for life, just like she'd been."

"Your mama dead?"

"She died when I was sixteen. Yellow fever."

"That's hard."

"Barlow wouldn't even let me attend her funeral. Had me fightin' that day."

"Ya win that one?"

"Naw, I lost ... partly outta spite, partly 'cause it was my first time in the ring." After a long pause and a sigh that shuddered on the verge of tears, John added, "He should've let me say good-bye."

It was evident John was reliving the loss of his mama, so Matthew waited awhile before asking, "Barlow lay wit' her?"

John responded by hanging his head in shame, his face between two monstrous hands that could have gripped Mr. Barlow's skull easily. Those hands were strong enough to squash the life out of that man, if he would only try.

Matthew murmured, "Yessuh, thems de hardest, I reckon … havin' ta watch your womens get raped … that and bein' sep'rated from 'em. Not sho what burns a man mo.'"

John replied, "Watchin' 'em get beat."

"You got that right. Watchin' a whippin' is jes' as hard as them other two." Then, after a short pause: "Ya ever seen your mama get beat?"

"Naw. I thank the good Lord for that. But she had ta watch Barlow whip me … too many times, I suppose. She pleaded with me, begged me to keep my oath."

Once again Matthew was befuddled. "Your oath?"

"Ta never lie ta Barlow or disobey the man."

Now this was truly beyond comprehension. A man obeyed because he had to, not by choice—and Matthew told him so. "Why in de name a' all that's good an' holy would your mama ever ask that a' you's?"

"He saved her life, she'd always say."

"How'd he do that?"

"By buyin' her."

Matthew just shook his head and muttered, "Ya gots ta be white ta think like that. No nigga'd ever be that stupid. Not lessen he be threatened wit' a hangin' or somethin'."

John could not help but agree. "Yeah, I reckon you got the right a' that. But Mama always said only the good Lord knows what would've happened ta us iffin Mr. Barlow hadn't showed up like he did. She said doin' what she had ta were a small price ta pay for his helpin' us out."

Matthew nearly choked.

John sighed. "I know that sounds strange, but he did raise me right." Then, as an afterthought, he added, "'Til I turned fourteen."

Matthew's curiosity was peaked. "What happened then?"

"Barlow'd given me lotsa freedom back then. Let me go ridin' on my own … but I got lost, an' he assumed I'd run."

"Nothin' burns that man mo' than a runner."

"You got that right."

Matthew was not one to give up hope. Most folks called him a fool. He suspected they were right. He had the *R* brand on his left cheek to prove it. Still, he had to point out that at least one runner had made it.

John grunted in agreement.

Both men grinned and whispered the name simultaneously, uttering it with expressions of awe: "Coffin Kelly!"

Matthew broke their silent reverence with a laugh. "Coffin Kelly … sounds like de man had 'imself a cold."

John laughed at that. "That there is one stupid joke."

"Yeah, well, ya laughed, didn't ya?" Matthew retorted victoriously.

"Yeah, you got me there." John resumed the narrative. "Good ol' Coffin Kelly had some set a' nerves, didn't he, ta be sealed up in a coffin for Lord knows how many days?" Both men shuddered.

Matthew picked up the story from there. "Didn't Barlow rent Kelly's services ta de cabinetmaker in Savannah?"

"Naw," John replied. "It were the undertaker."

"I thought it were de cabinetmaker next door ta de undertaker."

"Naw, it were the undertaker. That were in ninety-four. Had a rash a yellow fever that year. The undertaker were doin' real well, and he needed a hand, or so he told Barlow."

Both men laughed.

"Yeah," Matthew quipped. "Sure wish I were one a' them skilled artisans."

"Yessuh, they got it better, that's for sure. An' ol' Kelly had it real sweet. Outta Barlow's grip and inta the arms of a Quaker."

"Still, it damn near kilt de man."

"Shoot, yeah … being sealed inside a coffin for Lord knows how many days, riding in the belly of a ship north ta Canada. Crazy ol' fool."

"Still," Matthew countered, "he made it!"

"But inside a coffin?"

Both men shuddered.

"What you figure, Matthew? Would you be able to stow away in a coffin like that jes' ta escape?"

"Yessuh, I reckon I might, iffin de opportunity ever come my way." Matthew shuddered at the thought. "Still, it be a mite scary." After a moment's contemplation, he added, "But it be like you's always sayin' … it be de chance for a new dawn rising, a li'l hope shinin' light on all a' this here darkness an' despair." Looking at his companion, he asked, "What 'bout ya, John? Could ya hide out in a coffin like that?"

"Don't know. My coffin'd be mighty suspicious, with its size."

Matthew laughed. "Yessuh. They's gonna have ta nip ya at de knees ta fit you's inside a box."

John blanched. He had never once thought about having to fit inside a coffin before, and the thought of his body being desecrated just to fit into one made his throat tighten.

Matthew noted his discomfort and immediately apologized. "Sorry, John. I reckon that weren't too pleasant a thought." Pausing only long enough for John to nod that all was well between them, Matthew persisted with his inquiry. "But would you's, iffin ya could, I mean, stuff yourself inta a coffin jes' ta escape?"

"Naw, I cain't," John replied, shaking his head. Sighing, he closed his eyes. "I gave my word, remember?"

This time only Matthew shuddered.

▼

CHAPTER 18

ON THE DEATH OF
THOMAS PAINE

The MacPhearsons' estate was as John remembered. His first visit there—and up until now, his only visit there—had been dumbfounding, to say the least. Katherine MacPhearson had practically thrown herself into his arms, angering her daddy in the process. John had been so befuddled by the experience that he had purposely avoided any contact with the MacPhearsons for over a month.

Mrs. Angus MacPhearson and Gertrude Atwell were seated in the teak plantation chairs next to the door on the veranda, drinking cool lemonade. Mrs. MacPhearson rose gracefully from her seat as Matthew pulled the cart up to the front of the house. Smiling as she crossed over to the stairs, Mary MacPhearson chimed a greeting. "Why, Mr. Connolley. I am so pleased you decided to join us this evenin'."

Taking a moment to collect his thoughts, John paused before stepping down from the cart. He knew he was about to enter high society and that every word out of his mouth would rank him as either a welcome guest or a lowly field hand. He heard Mr. Barlow admonishing him, "You talk like the gentleman I raised you to be!" John knew he was no gentleman but he was resolved not to spout his words out like some field hand. John ascended the left staircase to the veranda to greet his hostess. He took her hand in his and kissed it. "It is indeed an honor to be invited to your home, ma'am."

Mrs. MacPhearson smiled. "I hope you do not think we lack proper etiquette in our home, Mr. Connolley. We do have house servants to answer the door and present our guests. It is just that Mrs. Atwell and I were enjoying the fine summer breeze out on the veranda whilst the other ladies take a stroll in the gardens."

"I assure you," John replied, smiling, "I am not one to stand upon ceremony. I would much rather be greeted by two lovely ladies than by a stuffy servant."

Mrs. MacPhearson giggled at the compliment. "He certainly is a charmer. Is he not, Gertrude?"

Mrs. Atwell, who had remained seated, took a moment to scorn John with her eyes. Mr. Barlow may have made a sizable deposit in the man's name, but that did not change the fact that John Connolley himself had not deposited a single penny on his own. The rest of the town might be fooled by his connection to Mr. Barlow, but he was no gentleman as far as Gertrude Atwell was concerned. Sniffing loudly, she pointedly looked toward the garden.

Mrs. MacPhearson quickly guided John's attention away from Mrs. Atwell's condescending demeanor. Smiling, she glanced at the papers in John's hand and ventured a request. "Will you be playing the piano for us tonight?"

John bowed slightly. "I would be delighted to play for you and your guests."

Matthew had to hold back laughter. All this came from the man who claimed he had no idea what to say!

John, oblivious to Matthew's snickering, continued. "In fact, I took the liberty of bringin' some sheet music … a few of the great German composers." A little embarrassed for having presupposed too much, John added quickly, "I figured y'all might ask me to play. I do hope that is all right."

Mrs. MacPhearson smiled genially. "Of course, Mr. Connolley. I am sure your choices will be more than acceptable for tonight's guests." With a brief glance at Matthew still parked in front of the house, she suggested that John instruct his Negro to drive the cart around back. "When he is done putting your horse and cart away," she continued, "he can join the rest of the Negroes in the kitchen for a bite to eat."

John turned to Matthew. "You heard the lady, Matthew." The old coon dog had trailed John up the stairs. He shooed him off. "And keep Amos with you."

Matthew nodded. "Yessuh, Massa Connolley, suh."

Matthew called the dog, but Amos would not budge until John ordered, "Amos, get!" The dog actually whined before turning to follow Matthew.

Prior to taking John by the arm and leading him into the house, Mrs. MacPhearson encouraged him to take a drink from a glass resting on the silver tray Abraham was holding. Mrs. MacPhearson had rung the bell as soon as she saw John's wagon approaching.

John picked up the heavy crystal glass. "Thank you, Abraham."

Abraham's look of surprise turned into a wide grin. "You're welcome, Mista Connolley, suh."

Mrs. MacPhearson laughed and gently patted John on the arm. "Why, Mr. Connolley. You are a delight." Then, over her shoulder, she added as an afterthought, "Abraham, go serve the men in the smoking room."

Abraham bowed. "Yessum, Mrs. MacPhearson." With that, the old Negro became invisible.

When John and Mrs. MacPhearson entered the manor, John could not help but admire the French chandelier hanging in the center of the great foyer. He grinned, remembering thinking that his whole house could fit inside this one room. Instinctively he looked to the left to see if the ballroom doors were open. Through them he could see the MacPhearsons' concert grand piano. It was one of the most beautiful instruments John had ever seen. From the first moment he had set eyes on it, his fingers had itched to play it. Tonight he would finally be granted the opportunity. Supper could not come fast enough for him. As he walked over to the shiny black instrument, he noticed how it gleamed against the marble flooring, its reflection stretching beneath his feet. Setting his music on the stand above the keys, John brushed his fingers over the cover and sighed in anticipation.

Mrs. MacPhearson tapped John's arm, the one she held wrapped tightly around her own. "There will be time enough for you to play after dinner, Mr. Connolley. Perhaps you would care to join the rest of the men in the smoking room?"

John looked up, slightly stunned. "Yes, ma'am."

Mrs. MacPhearson tugged gently on John's arm. "Come with me." She led him across the great hall and gestured toward two large oak doors. Pulling them open, John noted their great weight and saw they were a good three inches thick.

John took a moment to study Angus MacPhearson's smoking room. A huge fireplace decorated the back wall. The metal doors were shut, as the early summer heat made fire unnecessary. Above the fireplace, as in the smoking rooms of most men of wealth and social standing who had fought in the revolution, hung a large painting depicting patriots at battle. This particular painting was of the British siege of Savannah. People seemed to forget that Savannah had been a British stronghold for over two years. For these men, that was a moot point. For them the siege of Savannah meant that fateful day of October 9, 1779, when over a thousand men were slaughtered. That was when they made their stand. That was when they lost friend and battled foe. The men in that room were bound together by the ties of having fought in and survived one of the bloodiest battles of the revolution.

Against the right wall sat three tables with games cut into the square marble tops. Chess pieces made of ebony and ivory were arrayed on one board; round marble pieces of dark brown and light beige were placed, ready for backgammon, on the second; and the third board was too strange for John to recognize. It was divided into eight bowls each with its own signet. Shiny blues stones and a deck of playing cards were placed neatly in the center. John had no idea what game that could possibly be, or how one might play it.

Two card tables ran along the left wall. Several men stood around the table nearest the door. Their attention was focused on Frank Crawford, as he was reading them a news editorial. They were clearly enjoying the sarcastic slurring he made of the article's account; a great many of the men were laughing.

"Indeed," Mr. Crawford drawled, "it says here that the man did little good and much harm." He slapped his hand down on the paper in a triumphant clap, pleased to have his position vindicated in print. "Not that I think much of these northern rags, but this time they have something decent to say." Turning to the men surrounding him, Mr. Crawford raised his glass. "Gentlemen."

Mr. Atwell, Mr. Hodson, and Mr. Richardson, along with Mr. Richardson's eldest son, Keith, and Junior, all raised their glasses to clink against Mr. Crawford's, shouting, "Hear, hear!"

Mr. Crawford turned to his host. "Angus?"

"Now, Frank," Angus MacPhearson countered, "you know I would never drink to a thing like that, even if I disagreed with most of the man's policies."

Mr. Crawford laughed. "You are too soft, my old friend."

"I suppose I am," Mr. MacPhearson replied. Turning, he noticed his son's anxious expression. Patrick MacPhearson, the youngest man in the room (having just turned sixteen and gained the privilege of socializing with the men for the first time), was eager to speak his piece. He looked to his daddy for permission.

Angus MacPhearson smiled at his son. He knew Patrick was looking for his approval before speaking, so he gave it to him by asking, "Well, Patrick, what say you to this editorial? Do you agree with the account made of Thomas Paine?"

Patrick grinned widely, thrilled at being asked his opinion—especially since his daddy knew he was not in full agreement with him or his friends. He began by clearing his throat, trying to make his voice as deep as those of the other men. "Well, Daddy, I find it fascinating how y'all hold such animosity toward the man, yet every one of you was influenced by him when y'all ran off as boys to be a part of the revolution."

Mr. MacPhearson's laugh rumbled deep; it shook his mighty bulk. "Point well made, son. Point well made."

Patrick blushed at his daddy's positive reinforcement. He took a ginger sip at the amber liquid in his glass.

John smiled. He liked the young man. Patrick had strength enough to hold the sail of his convictions against the tide of general belief. John stepped into the room and added his own comment: "I agree with young Patrick here."

Eyes looked forward to take in the man behind the voice.

Mr. MacPhearson smiled and raised his glass. "Welcome, Mr. Connolley. Join us."

John nodded, stepping closer to the table to stand next to Patrick.

Mr. Richardson smiled at John, reached across the table, and extended his hand. "Hello, John. Good to see you again. Have you heard from Mr. Barlow lately? Is he planning another surprise visit?"

John forced a smile. "He talked about coming back in August last time he was here. I am afraid I have not heard from him since, suh."

Mr. Richardson beamed. Mr. Barlow was the finest man to ever stay at his inn—and on his third visit he had brought Delilah Poitras, the wife of Raymond Poitras, with him. *Raymond Poitras … now there is a man of truly fine lineage*, Mr. Richardson thought. *Why, the man owns the largest shipping and trading company in New Orleans.* As Raymond Poitras's franchise extended as far north as Boston, Mr. Richardson was hoping beyond hope that John's connections might bring the great man himself to Laurel Creek some day. He desperately wanted the great man to stay at his inn, believing Mr. Poitras would spread the word about his hospitality throughout the nation. *That would be the very thing*, he believed, *to solidify my reputation as the owner of the premiere inn along the Savannah … why, in all of Georgia, for that matter.*

So scintillated with his fantasy was Mr. Richardson that he blurted out, "You have yourself a mighty fine connection with Mr. Barlow, John. He certainly speaks highly of you every time he is in town."

John nodded, struggling to hide his unease. "Yes, suh. Mr. Barlow is a fine man." Eager to change the subject, John took the men back to their original topic. "Y'all were talking about Thomas Paine." Turning to Patrick, John smiled. "I heard a story about the man you might find fascinating."

"What is that, suh?" Patrick asked, clearly interested.

"As you might know," John replied, "Thomas Paine was in France, supporting their revolution. Unfortunately the French turned feral and started beheading the monarchy, as well as most of the nobility." A disappointed shudder rippled across the room. Most Americans—everyone in the room, in fact—had supported the French Revolution until the brutal executions began.

John pushed on with his story in an attempt to cover over the discomfort he had created. "Well, Thomas Paine opposed the French Revolutionists' plan to execute Louis XVI."

"As well he should have," Mr. Richardson muttered.

"At least the man did something right," Junior grumbled begrudgingly. It irritated him that he agreed with John Connolley, even on such a small point.

"What happened next, Mr. Connolley?" Patrick asked, truly interested in the story.

"Well, the French retaliated by throwing Thomas Paine in jail and sentencing him to death."

Amazed at this outcome, Patrick blurted out, "However did he escape?"

"Luck and providence," John replied. "The night before Thomas Paine was to be executed, he was visited by a doctor. Paine's cell door was left open while the doctor was checking him for some sort of ailment."

"What ailment?" Patrick inquired.

"Well, I am not sure, Patrick, but it really makes no difference for the story. All we really need to know is that Thomas Paine's cell door was left open while the doctor was inside."

"Why is that so important?" Patrick had suddenly turned into a querist.

"Now, son, you are asking too many questions and not letting Mr. Connolley get on with his story." Mr. MacPhearson, too, found the tale intriguing, and Patrick's inquisitive nature was beginning to irritate him and a few of his guests.

Abashed, Patrick muttered an apology.

"No worries, Patrick," John said to ease the boy's guilt. "You are just curious. Anyway, as I was saying, while the doctor was visiting Thomas Paine, the prison guard assigned to mark all the doors of the cells housing condemned prisoners was making his rounds."

"Did he forget to mark Thomas Paine's door?" Patrick asked excitedly, having already forgotten his father's admonition.

"Paine's jail cell was marked, but as the cell door was opened wide, the cell guard made his mark on the inside of the door. After the doctor left and the door was shut again, the mark was no longer visible."

"So when they came to collect the condemned men, they passed by Thomas Paine's cell!" Patrick shouted excitedly.

"That is correct," John said.

Patrick whooped at having made the right guess, and all but the Crawfords laughed.

Junior scoffed, "I heard me another good story about ol' Thomas Paine. They say he was tarred and feathered in New Jersey."

That story, too, brought forth laughter—this time by all but Patrick and John.

"There is no proof of that," John countered.

"Well, I for one, do not need any proof," Junior sneered. "I like the sound of it. Besides, it makes no difference now that the man is dead."

John's shock at the news of Thomas Paine's death added an edge of delight to the young man's sneer. Junior hated John Connolley, not only for his height, which accented the fact that Junior was the shortest man in town, but for the attention he received from all the ladies—most specifically from his own intended, Katherine MacPhearson. John Connolley was a thorn stuck between Junior and Katherine, and Junior was going to pluck him out somehow.

John gripped the edge of the table with his free hand. "Thomas Paine is dead?"

Junior delighted in John's dismay. He could not keep the derisive laugh out of his voice. "Yes, suh. He died on June 8. Mr. Hodson brought us last week's editorial from the *New York Post*, and we are having ourselves a celebration." Junior, lifting his glass toward John, added, "Care to drink to the death of Thomas Paine, Mr. Connolley?"

John's grip tightened on the table, and Mr. MacPhearson grimaced, thinking the big man might just rip the wood off. "No, suh," John replied in a most contumely voice, "I most certainly do not. I admired Thomas Paine's writing. I would have liked to have met the man."

Patrick looked up at the giant in surprise and delight; before him stood a man who had the nerve to disagree with the Crawfords. Finally there was someone besides himself who was not interested in playing the sycophant.

"As I see it," John continued, "Thomas Paine was a man of reason and principle."

"Hear, hear!" Patrick chanted, mimicking the way the others had toasted earlier before taking another gingerly sip of his drink.

John smiled and clinked glasses with the boy, but he never raised his to his lips. "He served our country well, most influentially in his editorial *Common Sense*. If what young Patrick said here is true"—Patrick beamed at being included—"who among you can deny that his words helped inspire an alliance among the colonies?"

"Not one of you," Patrick added with emphasis.

John paused briefly, knowing his next point would have considerable impact. "Many a Loyalist changed perspectives upon reading Paine's work … Mr. Jacob Barlow being but one such man."

"Indeed, Mr. Connolley, you have the right of it." Mr. MacPhearson appreciated political discussions and looked forward to debating this issue with a learned man of opposition. "Why,"—he patted his son on the shoulder—"that is exactly what my Paddy was just saying. Is that not right, son?"

"Yes, suh, Daddy." Taking over the argument, Patrick added, "The numbers of patriots swelled after Thomas Paine's editorials, and—" Patrick grunted as his daddy cut him off.

"However, one simply cannot deny the harm caused by such a man," Mr. MacPhearson countered.

"If you are referring to his attitude toward slavery, suh," John said in variance, "many a man in the union stands by that position, including our recent president, Thomas Jefferson."

Mr. Crawford sneered. He despised any who did not see things his way. With clenched fists, he expostulated, "Jefferson is a fool! That man did not belong in office."

"Do you believe Madison will do a better job?" John asked.

"Hell, yes!" Frank Crawford's reply was a bit more emphatic than necessary, but his distrust of John Connolley led him to suspect the man's inquiry. "James Madison is from Virginia. He knows where his allegiance lies: with strong, independent states."

"That was Jefferson's policy as well, suh," John responded. "Everyone knows he was a vigilant proponent for the rights of the states. He did what he could, which was considerable, despite all the Federalists he had in his cabinet. Fortunately he has removed them all, so now James Madison can act unimpeded." John studied Mr. Crawford curiously. "I am somewhat confused as to why you so dislike the man, since you seem to hold many of the same beliefs." Tension tightened like the knots on a noose.

Mr. Crawford was barely able to restrain himself. "Because, as you just pointed out, the man was a hypocrite. The man calls for the emancipation of nig-gas, whilst he himself owns slaves."

Mr. MacPhearson, knowing the temper of his old friend, turned to placate him. "Indeed, Frank, Jefferson has contradicted himself on occasion." Raising a finger to silence Mr. Crawford, Angus MacPhearson continued, "Particularly on the issue of slavery. But it is not Thomas Jefferson we are debating here." Jefferson was one issue Mr. MacPhearson did not agree with his longtime friend on. As far as Mr. MacPhearson was concerned, John Connolley was right. Thomas Jefferson could only do so much with a cabinet of Federalists impeding him. Mr. Crawford had placed unrealistic expectations on the man, insisting he should have removed all of Hamilton's policies. The Crawford family had lost considerable money as a result of Hamilton's tariff proposal. Any discussion that touched on any of Hamilton's work as Washington's Secretary of the Treasury always angered Frank Crawford beyond reason. Mr. MacPhearson was determined not to allow such a heated debate at his wife's party. He steered their conversation back to an area the majority agreed on. "It is the service of Thomas Paine to the united colonies we are discussing."

Mr. Crawford leaped at this opportunity to shoot down the new upright. "Indeed, and when looking at what Paine did for our country, one cannot forget that he was removed from government office for giving out state secrets." Mr. Crawford's eyes bored into John like red-hot pokers. "What say you to that?" After a pause ample enough to stratify his sarcasm, he rounded it off with, "Suh?"

John smiled. "Quite simply, suh ..." He successfully kept the contempt out of his voice (years of practice talking with Mr. Barlow had taught him that trick). "... Thomas Paine believed that government needed to remain simple. Otherwise the complexity of the machinery would cause it to become corrupt." Patrick was smiling like a child being handed his first bag of candy. John placed a hand on the lad's shoulder. "For Thomas Paine, a government designed for the people and by the people would have no need for secrets. Thus he would tell you he had betrayed nothing."

Mr. MacPhearson's laugh was deep and rich, matching his bulky weight and nearly shaking the room entire. "You are right, Mr. Connolley. I do believe Thomas Paine would have thought himself most correct." Mr. MacPhearson was enjoying this debate. "Still," he added with stern admonition, "that does not make Paine's actions appropriate." The other gentlemen nodded and muttered agreements as Mr. MacPhearson continued, "Government secrets are essential for national security. You might be able to explain why Paine committed such a heinous act, but that most certainly does not exonerate the man from the crime."

Mr. Crawford, seeing Mr. MacPhearson's statement as a summative triumph, lifted his glass, shouting, "Hear, hear!" The other men joined in on the toast.

John, noting the tension and general mood, chose to drop the argument.

Mr. MacPhearson acknowledged John's gesture by placing an arm around the man's shoulder, cajoling, "Come, my good man. You hold a drink, but it does not touch your lips."

John looked down at the crystal glass, slowly swirling the fine, amber liquid. There was a touch of unease in his bearing.

"I am afraid I am not a drinker, suh."

Mr. Crawford sneered.

Mr. Richardson and Mr. Hodson laughed.

Junior was unable to resist. "Why, he is a bloody shakin' Quaker!"

Frank Crawford whirled on his son. "You watch your language!"

"Sorry, Daddy." Junior always cowered when his father admonished him. "But it fits. Connolley refuses to drink. He is a nigga lover and a hypocrite, like Thomas Jefferson … both men own slaves. Everyone knows Jefferson beds a nigga wench like she was his wife." Junior turned toward John. "Are you planning to bed a nigga wench yourself, Mr. Connolley?"

John took deliberate steps around the table, his full height looming over Junior.

Mr. MacPhearson and Frank Crawford stepped between the two men to stop any potential brawl.

Taking John by the arm, Mr. MacPhearson led him to the fireplace.

Mr. Richardson and his son followed, but the Crawfords remained at the poker table. Mr. Atwell stood firmly by the Crawfords.

Mr. Hodson seemed to teeter on the edge, not sure with which side to align himself. He ended up standing close to the second card table.

Angus MacPhearson ignored the building rift. "I am sure Mr. Connolley has good reason for not drinking. Even if," he added with emphasis, "the Scotch you are holding just happens to be single malt, over one hundred years old, and sent over by my granddaddy from Scotland. There is no finer whiskey, suh." Winking, he added, "As smooth as a woman's inner thigh quivering from a man's touch." Mr. MacPhearson placed special emphasis on the word 'inner' to accent his meaning.

All the men chuckled as John blushed. From his experiences with Delilah Poitras, he did indeed know exactly what his host meant. John cleared his throat; he was not quite sure how to word what he was about to say. "I, uh, did a little fighting for Mr. Barlow."

"Fighting?" Mr. Richardson was intrigued. He had thought he knew everything there was to know about John Connolley. Jacob Barlow always stayed at his inn, and John Connolley was the man's favorite topic of conversation. Mr. Barlow always asked questions about John and spoke freely about John Connolley's youth. He had never once mentioned John fighting. "What kind of fighting, suh?"

"Bare-knuckle boxing."

Mr. Hodson let out a hoot. "Ooowee. That explains how you took down Junior and his two men without so much as a scratch."

Junior scowled.

The poker table suddenly perked the interest of the store owner, who appeared desperate to pretend he hadn't said anything at all.

Junior turned the heat of his gaze on John Connolley. He had not liked the stories that spread around as a result of that fight. Junior and two cohorts had tried to jump John in the alley next to Richardson's Inn. They had tossed a hood over John's head, but before they knew what had happened, all three men were laid out cold. When Junior tried to claim they had been the ones attacked, Mr. Richardson brought his boy, Luke, to the jailhouse to speak as a witness to the event. Luke had seen how Willie tossed the hood over John's head and watched as the three men tried to take the giant down.

The failed attack occurred on a late Sunday afternoon, shortly after John finished playing the piano Mr. Barlow had brought up from Savannah—the one presented to John on his thirtieth birthday. John's house was too small for the piano, so Mr. Barlow had asked Mr. Richardson if he could store it in the inn. They had set the piano up in the dining hall, and John had taken to playing it every Sunday after church. Mr. Richardson was pleased at this particular turn of events, as it brought in regular business. Even the minister frequented his establishment now. John Connolley could spin a tune on the piano like no other; his fingers danced across the keys.

What had angered Junior that day was John Connolley's attention toward Katherine MacPhearson. Junior had invited the lady to join him for tea after services, and she had reluctantly agreed.

Their mothers had pushed for their union since Katherine was an infant. Junior remembered the first time he ever saw Katherine. He was only five and looking down on her in her crib. "Frank," his mama said, "that little girl is going to be your wife someday." It was a promise Junior intended to fulfill. It had been Mary MacPhearson's influence that put Katherine arm in arm with Junior that afternoon. Junior was certainly glad he had Mrs. MacPhearson in his camp. She was a formidable woman, not one to be denied. He knew Katherine did not love him, but neither had his mama loved his daddy when they married. *It may take Katherine a long time to love me,* he figured, *but she will be my wife.* It tired him that she continued to put him off. He yearned for her and was unsure how much longer he could wait. She had grown into a beautiful woman with an abundant bosom. Her rich, full lips always seemed to beckon him. An afternoon spent with Katherine excited him so much, he often had to end the day with a visit to Margarette's whorehouse.

Katherine had been dressed in green on that day—a color that accented her beauty and highlighted her auburn hair. Tiny peach blossoms had been embroidered across the bodice, and a white lace shawl was draped over her shoulders. Auburn locks delicately caressed her neck, and her eyes twinkled with the gleam of the morning sun sparkling on the Savannah. Junior was proud to present her to the public. Everyone knew she was his—or would be someday—and this afternoon was to help reinforce that fact. No other man would dare court Katherine MacPhearson.

Shortly after sitting down, Katherine focused her attention on the piano—or rather on the man playing the piano. She, too, played, but claimed she could never hope to match the excellence of John Connolley. On that particular day, John was playing Irish ballads. His voice had all the ladies titillated, Katherine included. Many of the songs he played that day were love songs; Mrs. Richardson had admonished him for singing songs like "All for Me Grog," though the men had certainly enjoyed that one. On that day, there was not a lady in the room, single or married, who did not have a hint of flush running up her neck to her cheeks. Most men were annoyed, but no one so much as Junior. Never once had Katherine blushed for him, and now she was eyeing another man. And not just any man—Mr. John Connolley, the man who had had the audacity to stop him from disciplining one of his Negroes. As he looked across the table, Junior noticed that Katherine's startling green eyes were on fire … on fire for John Connolley.

When John Connolley sang "My Sweet Bonnie Kate," Katherine's delighted giggle resembled the rushing waters of a spring bubbling up between rocks. She was so taken that she left Junior's table and sat down beside John Connolley on the piano bench. John smiled and blushed, clearly pleased at her presence. Katherine smiled radiantly as John finished singing the song directly to her.

Junior had determined, then and there, to teach that man a lesson. He convinced Willie and Harrison to lie in wait with him. When John left the hotel, Harrison beckoned him. As soon as John entered the alley, Willie tossed a burlap sack over the giant's head. Willie and Harrison, grabbing the big man's arms, tried to hold him back. Before Junior could deliver a punch, though, John had the two men shoved against the brick wall. Bracing against Willie and Harrison, John swiftly kicked his attacker in the chest. In mere seconds, all three men were splayed out cold. John removed the burlap sack, tossed it on the ground, and spat in disgust.

Shortly after John arrived at the stables, the sheriff came to arrest him. He locked up both John and Matthew—John for attacking peaceful men, Matthew because a nigga couldn't run loose, especially one with the letter *R* branded on his face. The sheriff, figuring John to be dangerous, cuffed his hands around the bars.

Matthew sat on the wood bench, which doubled as a bed. "Ya sho gots us in a fine mess," Matthew chastised him.

"Be quiet, Matthew," John grumbled back.

"Didja really jump them men?" That was hard for even Matthew to believe. "I know you's big an' all, but ain't that a li'l foolish?"

John was clearly irritated. "I never jumped nobody. They jumped me."

Matthew rolled his eyes and smirked. "Iffin ya say so, suh." Matthew knew he was pushing John, but because John's hands were chained to the bars, he was not likely to turn on Matthew. Besides, Matthew wanted to know what had really transpired.

John turned as best he could to look Matthew in the eye. "I don't need you doubtin' me, too, Matthew. Shoot, the whole town's gone half crazy thinkin' I beat Junior. The man's half my size. They must think me some kind a monster."

Matthew actually felt sorry for John at that point. He softened his tone. "Well, iffin ya say ya didn't do it, John, then I believes ya."

"Thank you, Matthew. I appreciate that."

Matthew simply could not contain himself, though; he let all his vehemence against Junior spill out. "He's a mealy mouthed li'l bastard. I daresay he deserved a whuppin'."

John did not even bother to check Matthew on his language, which suggested John felt the same. All he did was question Matthew. "How you come to think that about Junior?"

"We niggas talk from time ta time. Shoot, I had ta sit in that thar stable for nigh on three hours today. What else were I to do? Peter were in thar tendin' Crawford's horses, an' he told me how Junior likes ta beat his niggas. I reckon it makes 'im feel like a man, bein' such a li'l un an' all."

John laughed outright. Junior really was the kind of man who needed to prove himself superior by hurting others. That was not a humorous thought, by any means, but Matthew was right, and John silently agreed with his assessment of the little man.

Fortunately John did not have to stand chained to the bars for long. Mr. Richardson had come by the sheriff's office with his boy Luke. Luke had seen the whole fight, and the truth came out. Old Artemus Sprague did not like the idea of letting John go; he was married to Junior's sister, after all, and had a personal interest in seeing justice done. Still, the sheriff was an honest man. When presented with the evidence, he agreed to free John. It took some convincing, though. He kept arguing that one nigga's word against three men was not enough. Mr. Richardson had to encourage the sheriff to see reason by threatening to involve Mr. Jacob Barlow if John were not released immediately. John was rubbing his wrists and thanking Mr. Richardson in no time.

It did not take long, either, for Luke to spread the story. It flew through town like flame through a haystack. All the talk made Junior look like quite a fool. Folks still enjoyed snickering behind Junior's back. All the gossip had built a powerful hatred and vindictiveness inside Junior. Youth already had its passions running wild. Those passions coupled with a fiery temper and constant rejection from his lady to make Junior like a stallion, caught fresh and ready to buck any man who got in his way. His was a consuming hatred directed entirely at John Connolley.

Now, in Mr. MacPhearson's smoking room, Junior pushed his way past his daddy and grabbed John's arm, turning the man to face him. Junior stood a short five feet four. Until John Connolley had moved to Laurel Creek, his slight stature had not caused much concern. But now the fact that Junior was the shortest man in town was accentuated by John Connolley's height—especially when the two stood face to face like this. Junior had to crane his neck upward to stare into John's eyes. "I do not like you, Mr. Connolley. You come waltzing into our little town and start spreading your Northern sentiments."

The Crawfords did not intimidate John Connolley, though the family had that effect on most Laurel Creek residents. That was another aspect of the man that annoyed Junior.

"I am not from the North, Junior." John's refusal to address Junior formally added even greater insult. "I come from Savannah."

"We know where you come from, boy," Junior sneered. "But that does not make you Southern. You and your ideas do not belong here."

John glared down at the little man. "I belong where I choose to belong."

Before their confrontation could go any further, Mrs. Angus MacPhearson entered the room. "My, my gentlemen. What a ruckus is being heard … and all the way into the drawing room! We ladies are trying to have a pleasant conversation, and it is nigh on impossible against this uproar. Now, Angus, I know you do not like me meddling in your political conversations, and you can toss me over your knee tonight after everyone has gone, but I am insisting now that this barroom brawl of yours come to a halt."

Angus MacPhearson was delighted by his wife's interruption. It saved him from having to stop the younger men from actually coming to blows. Junior was foolish to think he could take on a man like John Connolley, especially after John had successfully fended off Junior and two other men with little effort. John Connolley's recently revealed bare-knuckle fighting experience lent credence to the idea that one should not try to agitate the man. Mr. MacPhearson, stepping between the two men, crossed over to his wife. His smile belied his words. "My dear, I may just take you over my knee right now for interrupting us. But, as you say, we are here tonight for pleasant conversation, not a bullyrag. I will forgive you your intrusion for now." Then, in a more mischievous manner that caused his wife to blush, he added, "But perhaps I will take you over my knee later."

Mary MacPhearson was saved any further embarrassment by the arrival of Sarah. Timorously the girl announced that dinner was ready. Mrs. MacPhearson turned and expressed her gratitude while simultaneously shooing the Negro girl away. She rounded on the men, issuing a stern order for them to head to the dining room. "Be sure y'all sit down where I placed your name card. I did not go to all the trouble to seat you proper just to have you changing things around."

The gentlemen laughed politely, following Angus MacPhearson and his wife out of the smoking room.

CHAPTER 19

▼

A PEAL OF THUNDER

The MacPhearsons' dining room was the most elaborate room John had ever seen—even more regal than Mr. Barlow's. A large cherry table that seated thirty stretched the length of the room, set with fine porcelain china. Each place setting was decorated with tiny, pink flowers and odd-looking green leaves. The elegantly carved Chippendale chairs were made of the same wood as the table. Each seat was upholstered with a soft pink cushion that matched the colors of the tableware—a design clearly chosen by the lady of the house. There were more forks and knives than John knew what to do with. He decided to watch his neighbors so he would know which utensil to use. High above the table hung a chandelier imported from France. Although more modest than the great lighting fixture that hung in the grand foyer, the fixture matched the grandeur of the room.

Dinner passed without incident. Mrs. MacPhearson had wisely separated John and Junior, facing them the same direction and at opposite ends of the table to lessen the chances of their making eye contact. As a result, conversation was as tender as the ham they consumed with sweet corn cakes served alongside. Grilled catfish was delicately sautéed in lemon and pepper. This was a meal meant to tantalize the eyes as well as the taste buds. Sweet yams, carrots, and okra were served as complementary vegetables. The meal made John think kindly on his mother. She had prepared many a fine meal for Mr. Barlow's guests, always saving a plate for John.

A rosé wine was served with the meal. During dessert, the guests' taste buds danced to the tune of rice pudding with raisins soaked in rum. John ate slowly, careful not to gulp his food down like an old coon dog, hoping to match the proper graces exhibited by the other gentlemen.

After dinner, folks moved into the grand ballroom. Mrs. MacPhearson had had her Negroes set up chairs auditorium-style, with the concert grand piano sitting majestically up front for all to see. John knew Mrs. MacPhearson had only invited him so he could play for her guests, but he never thought she would set the room up like a concert hall. Sweat beaded his forehead. Although only a select few had been asked to dine with the MacPhearsons, it appeared the entire town had been invited to hear John Connolley play.

John always got the jitters before playing, and he had never performed before such a large audience. He was particularly nervous that night because of the style of music he had chosen to share. Mozart and Haydn were commercially well accepted in Europe, but his finale number was a controversial piece by a new composer, one Ludwig van Beethoven. Mr. Raymond Poitras had brought Beethoven's sheet music back from Germany. Beethoven was making quite a stir over there. John found the man's music both compelling and passionate. Although John looked forward to sharing this fine composition with the citizens of Laurel Creek, these folk were used to hearing him play ballads and jigs. Determined to pursue the concert as originally planned, John sat down, flipping out the tails of his morning suit.

Seeing John Connolley seated, folks hurried to take their seats. An insufficient number of chairs were available, so these men of good breeding gave up their chairs to the womenfolk whilst they stood along the sidewalls. Junior was among them. All the while, John concentrated on the concert he was about to play. He flipped through his sheet music and settled on Haydn's *Surprise* Symphony.

Before beginning, John took a moment to explain how Mr. Raymond Poitras, having been in Europe last summer, brought him back the sheet music. This little bit of intelligence caused quite a stir in the crowd. John Connolley might own the smallest plantation in Laurel Creek, but with his connections, the fine folk of Laurel Creek automatically elevated him to the status of high society. The Crawfords were the least accepting, but even they could not boast of associations like Jacob Barlow and Raymond Poitras.

John explained how the piece was written for a variety of instruments, mostly woodwind: "I had to arrange it for the piano." He apologized, saying he hoped he had not destroyed the intent of the man's work.

Mrs. Richardson piped up. "Do not fret, Mr. Connolley. Terrance and I have been listening to you practice your music for nigh on three weeks. I can assure y'all here that if this Mr. Haydn could hear Mr. Connolley play his music, he would be well pleased."

John bowed his head. "Thank you, ma'am. I appreciate the vote of confidence." He went on to explain a little bit about Haydn—how the man had been taken from his home at an early age to sing in a church choir but was cast into the streets when his voice cracked. "Franz Joseph Haydn raised himself out of poverty to become one of the most renowned composers of our time." There was a murmur of approval from the audience.

Before beginning, John asked for a volunteer to turn the sheet music for him while he played. Katherine MacPhearson was out of her seat and standing at John's right side before any other lady had a chance to volunteer. John coughed slightly. He could see the animosity in Junior's eyes, but he was pleased nonetheless. Junior, resembling a dog moving in to mark his territory, left his place along the wall to stand next to Katherine at the piano.

"Thank you, Miss MacPhearson," John said. "I will nod every time I need you to turn the page for me."

Katherine giggled. "My pleasure, suh."

John smiled. Katherine MacPhearson was clearly in the public eye; that was not her normal laugh.

When John finally began playing, a hush fell over the room. His fingers danced across the keys. Folks were used to John playing the piano at Richardson's Inn, where he played mostly Irish ballads and jigs. This music had depth and passion beyond anything most of those folks had ever heard. A silent awe cradled everyone, including the Crawfords. Junior, having caught himself enjoying the music, scowled, but it was not long before he was swept up by the passion of John's playing, as well as by the incredible depth of Haydn's music.

When John finished the piece, the small crowd leaped to their feet, applauding with as much vigor as John had given to performing. They were far from sated, though, and insisted John play more. In response, John offered up one of Mozart's romantic pieces, Piano Concerto no. 21. Katherine smiled at John when he spoke the word "romantic." She took the choice as a gift in her favor. John blushed. She was right. He tried not to look her way and found the lapse caused by folks returning to their seats most awkward.

When the audience finally settled down, John resumed playing. The piece started softly, with single notation slowly building to a series of high-pitched trills, accompanied by lower notes keeping rhythm. Katherine became so fixed on the movement of John's fingers that she forgot to turn the page for him, and he found himself having to improvise a few bars until he could get her attention. Junior helped by slapping her behind. Katherine blushed, focusing back on her work. Only a true connoisseur of Mozart's work would have caught the disruption to the piece; John kept the melody clean while he waited on Katherine.

When he finished the piece, Katherine MacPhearson dropped down on the piano bench next to him. "Oh, Mr. Connolley, that was just lovely. Do play us another."

John shrugged an apology. "That is the only piece of Mozart's I have with me, Miss MacPhearson. I am truly sorry. But I did bring a piece from a new composer, Ludwig van Beethoven. Mr. Poitras reports him as making quite the stir all over Europe. His music is stunning."

Katherine's smile was a ray of sunshine breaking through the clouds, bestowing grace and divinity. She was truly the most beautiful woman John had ever seen. "Why, then ... please, Mr. Connolley, play us this Ludvan fellow."

John could not help but laugh at her mistake. "Ludwig van Beethoven, Miss MacPhearson."

A small titter rippled through the crowd, and Katherine blushed.

Junior, on the other hand, scowled. His face was redder than a burning coal. Mrs. Crawford glared at her son and, with one glance, encouraged him to restrain himself. He pulled his anger inward, and his color shifted to ashen gray. Anyone who knew the young man was not fooled. His limpid pallor did little to mask a burning anger that was soon white-hot. John and Katherine were too enamored with each other to take notice.

Junior, managing to hide his anger, uttered, "Perhaps you should commence playing, Mr. Connolley."

John, clearing his throat, introduced the final piece. "This is a part of Beethoven's Piano Concerto no. 4. It was just written a few years ago. Mr. Raymond Poitras and his lovely wife, Delilah, had the good fortune to see the debut performance. Mr. Poitras had himself introduced to Ludwig van Beethoven and purchased a copy of the music for me." Once again gasps and expressions of awe were audible among the listeners.

The piano trilled as John hit a series of crescendos. Outside, thunder rolled in the background. It seemed nature had chosen to match its rhythms to the third crescendo. The electricity in the air raised the hair on the backs of the listeners' necks. *Allegro moderato* swelled and settled, only to swell again. The wind seemed to lift in time, and once again thunder crashed as John's fingers raced across the keys. As in the eye of the storm, the piece settled into a delicate trickle, only to build and lift again. Heavy weight hit the lower keys, and a lightning flash shot through the front window. A few ladies gasped. A moment of almost imperceptible sound led to a slow building of musical momentum that whipped into a frenzy, like the wind swirling around the trees. A few smaller branches cracked and were ripped off. High keys trilled while a few lower notes played in opposition. Thunder crashed again as John hit the final crescendo. The audience erupted, leaping to their feet. Within moments everyone was huddled around the piano as close to John Connolley as possible.

Mr. MacPhearson smiled and patted John on the back. "It sounded like you were playing to that storm we are about to have, Mr. Connolley."

John chuckled. "It added a nice flavor."

"It nearly scared the wits out of half the ladies, myself included," Mrs. MacPhearson added.

John looked abashed. "I-I am truly sorry, ma'am. I did not mean to frighten y'all."

Mary MacPhearson laughed. "Not at all, Mr. Connolley. It is the brewing storm that is frightening. And eerie, too … the way it seemed to be playing right along with you."

Katherine MacPhearson sat down beside John. "Mr. Connolley, I have never before heard such beautiful music played … never in all my life."

John cleared his throat. He could not help but blush at the compliment from the young lady. "Thank you, Miss MacPhearson."

"Please, call me Katherine."

There was a slight titter from the crowd.

Junior growled.

John ignored the younger man and addressed Miss MacPhearson. "All right, Miss Katherine … as long as you agree to call me John."

Her smile widened. "Not Jonathan?"

John rubbed his hand behind his head, pondering that for a second. "My name has always been John. I never saw my birth certificate, but I think that is what is written on it."

Katherine giggled. "Then John it is."

Little Amanda Hodson pushed her way to the front of the crowd and plopped herself down on the other side of John. She was not going to let Katherine MacPhearson monopolize John Connolley—not when she had designs on him herself. She was nearly fourteen years old, and that was the age at which her sister Penelope had married. Amanda Hodson was determined to marry at fourteen, too, and she had her heart set on John Connolley. Somewhat out of breath from shoving her way through the crowd, she gasped, "Mr. Connolley, may I call you John, too?" That caused another titter among the crowd.

John smiled down at the child. "Of course you may, Miss Hodson ... as long as I may call you Amanda."

Amanda beamed and nodded vigorously. "I'm almost fourteen, John."

"Is that so? Why, Miss Amanda, you are almost all grown up."

"My birthday's in August. My sister Penelope got married when she was fourteen. I reckon that means I'll be old enough to marry, too. What say you to that, John?" Amanda asked, placing her hand on John's thigh.

John tugged slightly at his collar. Suddenly his shirt felt too tight. "Well." He coughed, clearing his throat. "Miss Amanda, I think you ought to consider waiting a few years."

Just the image of the great man turned tongue-tied by a little girl had the ladies tittering and many of the men laughing outright. Even Katherine was enjoying the show.

John struggled to maintain composure. "You are still pretty young."

Miss Amanda was not even listening; she had become fascinated by the feel of John's leg. "Why, John! You are as hard as Ol' Man Adley's anvil."

Once again, the men erupted in laughter. A few ladies gasped, and whisperings began as those who understood explained to those who feigned to be, or truly were, ignorant. The number of belated gasps caused even further laughter.

John turned crimson.

Amanda, completely oblivious to the double entendre, kept right on talking. "Ol' Man Adley says the best way to temper steel is to heat it." To make matters worse, she giggled along with the laughter and added, "I think I can temper you, John Connolley."

It had taken her daddy that long to push his way through the crowd. He stared down at his daughter, fuming like the fires of Old Man Adley's forge.

Amanda gasped. She knew she was in trouble, but the why of it was beyond her understanding. She almost uttered, "Daddy," but Mr. Hodson never let the poor girl get a word in edgewise. Instead, he lifted her off the piano bench, slinging Amanda over his shoulder. With one loud crack that rivaled the thunder, he smacked her behind, turned, and walked through the crowd. Folks spread as the Red Sea had parted for Moses.

Mrs. Hodson, concerned about departing without saying good-bye, turned and curtsied quickly before running out after her husband.

The Hodsons' departure encouraged another raucous outburst from the men. Junior decided to use the moment of humor to push John Connolley into the arms of another woman. "That is one fiery little lady you got yourself, Mr. Connolley. A man needs to be careful how he stokes the coals of such an impetuous wench before he is legally wed."

John eyed Junior askance but said nothing. He felt sorry for the little girl. She had given him a sad, bleary-eyed look before being hauled out by her father. He uttered his concerns. "The poor little thing had no idea what she was sayin'."

Seizing the opportunity, Junior replied, "Yes, suh, but you could teach her quick enough how to temper a man's steel. Shoot, you ought to marry that little girl. Then you could give her a proper whupping. Mind you, a man would need to suffer from satyriasis in order to keep up with a wench as lusty as her."

A few men chucked; ladies gasped in disgust. John stood with such force that Katherine was required to rise as well to avoid falling with the piano bench. With fists clenched, John growled, "You are a vulgarian, suh! That is a thirteen year ol' girl you are talkin' about. She may not have known what she was sayin', but you most certainly do!"

Angus MacPhearson stepped between the two men and addressed Junior. "Mr. Connolley is right, son. This is hardly the place for a bullyrag."

John's anger bested him, and he shot a pointed finger toward Junior, over Mr. MacPhearson's shoulder. "In case you have failed to notice, suh, there are ladies present."

Junior leaped at John like a mousing hawk trying to take down a pedigreed falcon. "How dare you get high and mighty with me!"

Mr. MacPhearson held the young man back. Angered by the lad's stupidity, he threw Junior into the arms of his daddy. "That is enough! This party is a pleasant gathering among ladies. There will be no brawling in my house."

Junior began to argue, but his daddy pulled him back. Speaking into the young man's ear, Frank Crawford managed to calm Junior down. "Do not fret, son," he said. "Connolley will get what is coming to him."

Junior pulled himself free but made no more attempts to attack John.

Mr. Crawford turned to his old friend and extended his apologies. He called to his wife and made his way to the door. Junior stood there scowling at John, but his daddy refused to waste any more time. Calling his son like a dog, Mr. Crawford hollered, "Junior, come."

Junior delayed, angrily eyeing the massive John Connolley. He sneered and laughed under his breath. "I will be seeing you real soon."

Frank Crawford growled, "Junior. I said come."

Junior turned and left.

Picking up the piano bench, John inspected it for scratches before putting it back in place. Crossing over to Mrs. MacPhearson, he bowed. "Mrs. MacPhearson, I am truly sorry for upsettin' your party."

Mary MacPhearson, ever the social diplomat, smiled genially. "Why, Mr. Connolley. You did no such thing. A man defending a lady's honor is always acceptable etiquette."

Katherine crossed over and wrapped her arms around John's. "It was mighty fine the way you stood up to Junior. He is rude, crude, and socially undesirable."

John bowed, thanked the ladies, and politely excused himself. "If someone could fetch Matthew for me, I would be much obliged."

Katherine responded by calling her girl. "Sarah, fetch Matthew. Tell him to get his master's wagon hitched and bring it round front."

Sarah smiled, pleased to finally have an excuse to approach the dangerous young rebel that her mama had warned her about. With a quick curtsy, she ran off toward the kitchen.

The crowd milled about, with folks getting ready to depart. Most saw fit to leave rather than stay and gossip. A great deal of bowing and apologizing went on until John, at least, was ready to leave.

The instant Matthew pulled up front, John stepped outside. Ever faithful, Amos leaped up on John as soon as he saw him, front paws on the great man's waist, struggling to reach his face. John bent a little so the dog could get a lick, and then he shoved Amos off. Leaping up onto the cart, John nodded for Matthew to head off. The old coon dog trailed after.

CHAPTER 20

▼

THE BREWING STORM

With a click of the tongue, Matthew got the horse moving and steered the cart down the road. John lit a lantern. It cast a weak light against the darkness and fought a futile battle against the wind. Distant bolts of lightning helped them navigate their journey. After each strike, John counted the seconds until the thunder rolled. He doubted they would make it home before the storm hit; he hoped it was not a hurricane brewing.

John called for Amos. That damn dog was always running off to find game, and John was worried he might get lost with a storm coming. There was no answer. Before John could even wonder where Amos had gotten to, another lightning flash revealed two men approaching on horseback. As quickly as the lightning had exposed them, the returning darkness hid them from view.

A gunshot spooked the horse, causing the cart to jar. Matthew reined Cornerstone in, bringing them to a stop. The two men brought their horses in closer. Burlap sacks hid their faces. The lead man pointed a pistol at John's head.

"You an' that nigga get outta that cart."

Attempting diplomacy, John responded. "We ain't got much, but y'all are welcome ta whatever we have."

"What I want," the lead man said menacingly, "is for you an' that nigga ta get outta de cart before I shoots you."

The burlap sack on the right laughed. John had heard that laugh before. The lightning crack was a grim reminder of their precarious situation. "We better do as he says, Matthew."

Before anyone knew what happened, another lightning flash exposed Amos leaping out of the bushes, howling and lunging at the lead man, who calmly turned and shot the dog.

There was a yelp, and John howled, "Amos!" Dropping to his knees, John cradled the limp dog. His eyes burned as he fought back tears. Gently resting Amos's head on the ground, John whispered a quick prayer before leaping up to his feet.

He raged on the man who shot his dog. "Damn you all to hell!" Before John could take more than a step or two toward him, a shot rang out, burning a bullet into John's thigh. Knocked back off his feet, falling face-first on the ground, John instinctively rolled over and grabbed for the wound, trying to keep blood from gushing out. Hot pain seared his flesh, causing his vision to blur. Matthew instantly dropped to John's side. John attempted to speak, but was unable to, as all of his energy was directed toward breathing. His body was so racked with piercing pain, he could barely make out what the lead man was saying.

Feigning a slave accent, the lead man barked out a warning. "Let that be a lesson in respect. You better watch your language round me, or I'll shoots you ag'in."

John, gritting his teeth, forced himself to speak. Pain emphasized each word. "What. Do. You. Want?"

The burlap sack to the right laughed. "Ain't that obvious?"

John tried to glare at him, but his face was so contorted in pain that all he could manage was a grimace. John knew that hidden voice. The stupid fool had not even tried to disguise it. In order to ensure vengeance John knew he had to survive.

The lead man growled at the younger man. "That be enough outta you." He then turned his attention to Matthew, tossing a rope his way. "Nigga! Tie your massa's hands, good an' tight."

Matthew looked at John. Seeing no options, John nodded. "Do as he says, Matthew." He tried to keep his eyes on the lead man, but his vision kept flashing in and out.

Matthew let go of John and picked up the rope.

Pulling his bloody hands away from his wound, John held them together in front for Matthew to bind.

The lead man growled out further instructions. "Use de end a' the rope ... we needs lots left over for de tree."

When he said that, though, Matthew panicked and threw his body over John's protectively. "Don't hang 'im, suh, please don't hang my massa!" Matthew was terrified those men were planning to murder John.

The younger voice cackled. "Oh, we's gonna hang him, all right … just not by the neck." He finished off with his high-pitched, raucous laugh.

John's breathing became erratic. "It's all right, Matthew," he muttered. "Just do as they say, and no harm'll come to you." It was more of a hope than a promise, and Matthew knew it.

As Matthew wrapped one end of the rope tightly around John's wrist, the lead man let out a heavy laugh. "That's a mighty fine promise for you ta be makin'."

John tried not to wince, but his eyes squeezed shut as the ropes tightened.

Matthew felt guilt for his complicity.

John forced his eyes open to look directly at the lead man. "Y'all ain't got nothin' ag'in him."

Matthew was stunned. Even with a potential lynching, John was trying to protect him.

The man's laughter growled against the night sky like a thunder burst. "He's a nigga. We's gonna treat him as we sees fit."

As Matthew finished tying the knots, John struggled to sit up. Matthew put an arm around his shoulder to help him. John's voice was raspy from the effort. "Y'all leave Matthew be."

"Nigga," the lead man ordered Matthew, "get up and toss de rope over that thar branch."

When Matthew hesitated, the lead man shouted, "Now!"

Leaping to his feet, Matthew did as he was told.

Turning to the younger man, the lead man issued another command. "Grab de rope an' secure him." His voice was rough and devoid of conscience.

Quick to respond, the younger man grabbed the rope dangling from the branch, wrapping it around his saddle horn. As the horse walked forward, John slowly rose into the air. He grunted as his arms jerked upward. It was not long before he was hanging a good two feet above the ground.

"Toss de nigga your rope," the lead man ordered his accomplice. Turning his burlap gaze on John, he added, "I don't want your legs free ta do any kickin'."

The younger man laughed. "That ain't likely to happen with a bullet in his leg."

Impatience grated in the older man's voice. "Just do as I say, an' toss de nigga your rope." Glaring at Matthew, he added, "Once his feets is tied, you secure 'em to this here tree." He pointed to the base of the tree John was suspended from.

The younger man laughed. "You get ta hog-tie your massa. That ought ta be any nigga's dream."

Seeing no other recourse, Matthew bent down to tie John's feet. He looked up apologetically, but John failed to notice; he was forcing himself to focus on the lead man. It took every ounce of concentration the giant had. Suddenly a bullet struck the ground near Matthew.

"Now get runnin', nigga," the lead man growled. "We's givin' you a ten-minute lead." Another shot hit the ground, leaving Matthew no choice but to abandon John. Turning to run back up the road, he heard the lead man shout, "That's about all de time we'll be needin' to finish up here."

After Matthew departed, the younger man jumped off his horse. He flexed his hands, cracked his knuckles, and formed fists.

John braced himself for the punch.

The young man's fist hit hard flesh, causing the villain to grunt. That John had not even winced angered the scoundrel, and he growled beneath his sack.

John readied himself for another blow. This time the younger man threw a round of punches at John's middle. They only made a little dent—not enough for John to worry over. He had taken worse beatings in the ring and walked away. After tightening his stomach muscles for a third assault, John released them to watch the young man curse, shaking his hand in pain.

"What's the problem?" the lead man growled. Before the younger man could answer, he rumbled on, "Hell, son, I cain't make this any easier for you."

Desperate to exonerate himself, the smaller man explained, "I swear, Daddy, that little girl had the right of it. He is harder than Old Man Adley's anvil."

Scowling beneath the burlap, Frank Crawford hollered, "Jes' hush, an' hit de bastard!"

Another fist slammed into John's ribs, causing the attacker to grunt and bend over. Cradling his swollen fist, Junior frantically rubbed it with his other hand. If John could have seen beneath Junior's sack, he would have seen a face riddled in pain. Even though the blow hurt, John held back a grunt, refusing them the satisfaction of hearing him cry out.

"You're wastin' time," the lead man growled in disgust. "If you cain't make a dent with your hands ..." He reached behind him and pulled out his musket. Tossing it down, he finished, "... then use this as a hammer. You only got ten minutes ta beat de shit outta this here man. We gots us a nigga ta hunt."

John's tormentor grabbed the musket and let out a high-pitched cackle. Admiring his daddy's musket, a shiny smoothbore used during the siege of Savannah, he exclaimed, "This here will do the trick." The young man sighed happily. His father's smoothbore weighed heavily in his hands—a good twenty-five pounds. "Yes, suh," he remarked. "This'll break a few ribs for me."

John readied himself for blows he knew he could not withstand. Expecting a hit to his stomach, he was taken aback by a blow to the wound in his left leg. John had hoped to keep all screaming inside, but he found himself yelling out. The unexpected pain caused him to release the grip he held on his stomach muscles, leaving him vulnerable. The younger man took advantage, slamming the musket butt into John's abdomen. It was more than a grunt that John let out; it was the forced expulsion of air, combined with a cry of pain. He jerked forward to cave in under the pressure, but the ropes held him taut.

Before John could even hope to suck air back into his lungs, a stream of blows rained down against him. Ribs cracked. John jerked back and forth with every blow, his body convulsing, causing muscles to rip in response to the brutally savage onslaught of the musket. John felt like a slab of beef being tenderized. His screams muted into groans as the unending beating made it impossible for him to catch his breath.

Finally, in some dim distance, as if blood had clogged his ears, John heard the lead man call out, "That's enough. Knock him out." A blow to the back of the head snapped John's face forward into darkness.

CHAPTER 21

▼

LOYALTY

The wind picked up and the smell of rain was in the air. John's body swayed in a continuous series of reverberating jerks, constricted in its movement by the taut ropes. A lightning flash illuminated John's image, and was followed instantly by a peal of thunder. Junior nearly leaped out of his saddle. He wobbled slightly in his seat and wrapped the reins tightly around his wrists, as if expecting the beast to buck. The horse skittered and danced beneath Junior's anxiety, its eyes rolling white and wild. With a few soothing clicks and a "Whoa, Tenet," Junior steadied his horse. Smiling at his father, he nodded toward John Connolley. "He sho got his what-for. Didn't he, Daddy?"

Junior tended to end his statements with a question when talking to the older man. Never sure how his father would respond, Junior was always desperate to say the right thing—the end result being a never-pleased Frank Crawford Sr.

Frank Crawford rolled his eyes. "You can stop talking like a nigga dunce. The man is out cold. He can no longer hear you."

"Sorry, Daddy." Another clap of thunder hit, and Junior again nearly leaped out of his saddle, causing his horse to become skittish once more. Frank Crawford looked at his son and shook his head disapprovingly.

Junior had not grown up to be what Mr. Crawford wanted in a son. He was all show and no substance. It did not take much for a daddy to see deep inside. Beneath the veneer, his son was a coward, terrified of even his own shadow. It made Mr. Crawford sick to his stomach. He blamed his wife; she had always coddled Junior. Every time he went to discipline the child, his mama would come running and Junior would hide behind her skirts. That was why the boy was no fighter. That was why one hit to a man's belly made him whimper. He had no steel. Mr. Crawford glanced over to the man hanging by his wrists. Hell, he would rather have a man like John Connolley for a son, even if John's nigga-loving ways sickened him. At least John could fight. The fact that they had to tie him to a tree just so Junior could beat him was testament enough. Still, Junior was blood, and that meant standing by him.

Looking up warily, Junior saw another lightning spike flash against black, swirling clouds. "Damn, Daddy. That storm is getting close." Removing his burlap sack and tossing it to the ground, Junior twisted to look off in the direction Matthew had run. "Are you sure we have enough time to catch that nigga?"

Clenching his fists, Mr. Crawford hollered, "Hell, yes!" He shouted partly to carry his voice over the wind, and partly because he wanted to yell at Junior. Frank Crawford growled at his son. Lifting the burlap sack from his face, he stuffed it into his saddlebag and watched Junior fidget. *Damn*, he thought. *Junior's afraid of running the chase. My own son is willing to let a nigga go free to avoid a little wind and rain.* Mr. Crawford could have hit him. "That storm has a good hour or two yet before it hits. We will have that nigga swinging from a tree long before then."

Junior tried to sit up tall in his saddle, but his shoulders, hunched against the wind, exposed his fear. "Which way do you figure he went?"

Frank Crawford scoffed at his son. "Did you not see him running?"

Awkwardly pointing to John Connolley as his excuse, Junior started to stammer, "Ah ... n-no, suh ... I was ... uh ..."

Before Junior could finish, Mr. Crawford roared, "Connolley's nigga ran back toward the MacPhearsons'." He stared incredulously at his son. "So, what does that tell you?"

Junior shrugged.

Junior annoyed Frank Crawford to no end. He barked at the lad, "He would have turned northeast in order to hide out in the swamps."

Junior laughed; the tittering edge failed to hide his unease. "You figure he plans to cross the Savannah and make his way north through South Carolina?"

"Of course he wants to head north, you fool! But he will not get that far, will he." Even though his answer was worded as a question, there was no query in Mr. Crawford's voice. Frank Crawford was rough, demanding, and to the point.

Junior, used to being addressed so by his father, took it for a question anyway. "No, suh, Daddy. He surely will not."

"Well, then, stop your fidgeting. We have to hurry, or the gators will get him before we can string him up."

"Yes, suh!" Junior, desperate for his father's approval, was willing to brave even the worst of storms if it meant Frank Crawford would clap an arm around his shoulder.

He did not. Mr. Crawford only sneered and rode past his son. His indifference stung.

Mr. Crawford led them back to the MacPhearsons'. Veering off the road, they made their way toward the swamps.

*   *   *   *

Guided only by the thought of saving John, Matthew ran straight for the MacPhearson manor. Pushed by the wind at his back, Matthew ran faster than he could run on his own. When he reached the plantation house, he started pounding his fists against the door, shouting for someone to answer.

A voice called out, "Abraham, go see who is doing all that clamoring."

When Abraham opened the door, Matthew leaped at him, grabbing his lapels. "Get your massa! John an' me, we's been bushwhacked. Highway men gots 'im tied up, an' they's beatin' on 'im." Abraham stood dumbfounded. Matthew started yelling. "Mista MacPhearson! Ya gots ta help 'im!"

Abraham woke up from his shock as Matthew tried to push past him. It took all his strength to hold the crazed Negro back. Abraham was not sure what to make of Matthew and his story. *If they really was jumped, how did Matthew get free, an' what's he doin' here instead a' runnin'? Lordy, did he jes' call his massa John?* None of it made any sense to Abraham.

The entire household was roused by Matthew's screaming. Mr. MacPhearson and Patrick were the first to make it to the entrance; they only had to come from the smoking room. Katherine and her mother descended the stairs, having been in Katherine's room talking about the evening. Mary MacPhearson had not been impressed by Katherine's flirting with Mr. Connolley. The impropriety of her asking him to call her by her first name in front of all her guests—Junior being one of them!—was too much to bear. She had admonished the girl sternly, so Katherine was grateful for Matthew's disruption. Her mother simply refused to understand why she did not want to marry Junior. Katherine took the distraction as an opportunity to escape the continuous, searing lecture on morals and proper marriages.

Even before they were halfway to the landing, Katherine was first to speak—partly because she was curious, but mostly to keep her mama from dragging her back to her room. "What is all this ruckus about?"

"You quiet down, little girl," Mr. MacPhearson ordered. "I am about to find out." Katherine and her mother stood midstair as Angus MacPhearson turned a hard eye on Matthew. "This better be good, boy."

Matthew shoved Abraham aside and ran to Mr. MacPhearson. "It be John, suh. Highwaymen bushwhacked us. Theys got 'im tied, an' thar beatin' on 'im. Ya gots ta help 'im. Please, suh, ya gots ta help 'im!"

Katherine screamed. She ran down the stairs and leaped at Matthew. "Where is he?"

"Tied ta that big ol' oak y'all gots at de end a' your land."

Katherine shoved past him, hiked up her gown, and rushed out of the house. She knew exactly what tree Matthew was talking about. She and Paddy used to climb that old tree when they were children.

Mr. MacPhearson swallowed back a curse and turned to his son. "Patrick, get after your sister. Make sure she does not hurt herself."

"Yes, suh, Daddy," Patrick said, as he rushed out the door after Katherine.

Mr. MacPhearson turned to grab his wife, who had frantically followed her daughter. He held her tightly by the waist and issued another stern order. "Mary, do not worry about the girl. She will be fine."

Mrs. MacPhearson interjected, "But, Angus, a storm is brewing—"

Before she could finish, her husband countered, "Patrick will fetch her."

"Oh, Angus …"

Mr. MacPhearson took his wife in his arms and held her tight. "Katherine will be fine, Mary." Rubbing a few tears from his wife's eyes, he added, "Besides, there is work to be done. You have to get one of our spare rooms ready for a patient."

Mary MacPhearson looked longingly at the door before leaping into action. Calling Sarah, she issued orders: "Get on upstairs, and fetch some fresh sheets and pillows for the spare room." Sarah entered from the dining room. A dozen slaves stood in the doorway, listening to all the commotion. Mrs. MacPhearson turned on them sternly. "The rest of you, get back to work. This is none of your business." Turning to Sarah, she shouted, "Move it, girl!" Sarah quickened her pace and followed her mistress up the stairs.

Angus MacPhearson smiled in admiration. His wife sure could run an effective household.

Matthew grabbed ahold of Mr. MacPhearson's arm, bringing himself back to the man's attention. "Please, suh, we ain't gots no time. Ya gots ta help John, now, ya jes' gots ta help 'im."

Mr. MacPhearson released Matthew's grip and held him by the wrists. "Calm yourself, boy. We are going to help." Turning to his own slave, he ordered, "Abraham, fetch Lucas. Tell him to get the wagon hitched."

Abraham ran to the stables.

Matthew tried to argue. "We ain't gots no time for a—"

"Think, boy." Mr. MacPhearson grabbed Matthew by the shoulders and gave him a shake. "Your master has been tied and beat. He will not be walking or riding a horse, now will he?"

Matthew sagged. "No, suh. You's right, suh. I's sorry, suh. I's sorry."

The plantation owner continued. "It is more likely, with the condition we will find him in, that Mr. Connolley will be better off laid down than tossed over a horse's back."

"Yes, suh, I knows that, suh ... but what if they means ta kill 'im?"

Mr. MacPhearson was taken aback by the stark fear in Matthew's eyes. The slave was honestly afraid for his master's life. Although he didn't want to be cruel, Angus MacPhearson knew a rational stance had to be taken. "If they mean to kill him, Matthew, then your master is already dead."

Matthew dropped to his knees, wailing, "Oh, Lordy, please don't let 'im be kilt! Please, Lord."

Mr. MacPhearson's eyes rolled. *Lord, I do not need a hysterical Negro on my hands.* Grabbing Matthew by the shirt and lifting him up, he commanded, "Listen here, boy. We are going to help." Mr. MacPhearson held tight to his grip until Matthew nodded. "Now," Mr. MacPhearson ordered, "I want you to go into the kitchen. Ruth is in there. She will take good care of you while Lucas and I fetch your master."

Matthew, dry washing his hands, pleaded with the man. "No, suh—" He caught himself. "I means, please, suh, please lemme go wit' y'all. I can help. I wants ta help. Ya gots ta let me help."

Mr. MacPhearson eyed Matthew carefully, then nodded. "As long as you keep your wits about you."

"Yes, suh. I promise, suh. I will."

"All right, then. While we are waiting on Lucas, I want you to tell me a few things."

"Yes, suh, Mista MacPhearson. Anythin', suh ... anythin' that can help."

"Did you see what these men looked like?"

"No, suh." Matthew shook his head. "They was wearin' sacks. Eyeholes, though, wit' glarin' hate shootin' outta them."

Mr. MacPhearson considered this for a moment. "What kind of sacks?"

"Burlap, suh."

"Hmmm." Mr. MacPhearson raised a bushy eyebrow.

Matthew sensed something wrong. "Suh?"

"Nothing, Matthew," he muttered. "A burlap sack is no real evidence." Then, more deliberately: "How big were they?"

Matthew concentrated best he could. "They sat on horses de whole time I were thar, suh … but one man, he were definitely older. Had 'imself big shoulders, he did. De other one, he were kinda skinnylike … looked a lot shorter, he did. Had 'imself a real high-pitched laugh, too."

Mr. MacPhearson considered this a moment, then inquired as to the attackers' clothing.

"They was wearin' fancy suits, but was talkin' like field slaves. De older man, he were wearin' gray, an' de li'l un, he were wearin' blue."

Angus MacPhearson grimaced. They had not even bothered to change; Frank Crawford was always so sure of himself. Rubbing the stubble on his chin, Mr. MacPhearson frowned. It was insufficient evidence, especially with Sprague as sheriff. "What else can you tell me about them?"

Matthew scratched the back of his head. "I ain't rightly sho. They made me tie 'im up. Got 'im hangin' by his wrists, an' his feets is tied ta de trunk. They's a good two feet off de groun'. They's plannin' ta beat John senseless." Matthew paused for a moment before adding, "Iffin ya don't mind my sayin' so, suh, they's cowards."

Mr. MacPhearson patted the man on the back. "It is all right, Matthew. I have to agree with you. A man has no chance of defending himself if he is strung up like that."

"There's one mo thing, suh."

"What is that, Matthew?"

"They shot John's dawg. Iffin he lives, thar'll be hell ta pay for that. John loved that dawg."

Mr. MacPhearson believed everything Matthew had been saying, but he still had to ask: "How is it you got free?"

"They's plannin' ta hunt me, suh. They gived me a ten-minute head start. Then they shot bullets at my feet ta gets me runnin'."

Still scratching his chin, not even noticing whether it was itchy, Angus MacPhearson said, "But you never ran. You came here instead. Why?"

Matthew looked dumbfounded. That was a very good question. He had not even considered the option of running. All he could think of was getting to the MacPhearsons and finding help for John. "'Cause ... John needs me, suh. They's gonna kill 'im."

Mr. MacPhearson looked at Matthew thoughtfully. "You keep calling Mr. Connolley John. Why are you not calling him Master Connolley?"

"I ... ah ..." Matthew knew he had erred. "I ... ah ... I's sorry, suh ... I's ... I's jes' so worried, an' ... uh, Massa Connolley, suh, he ... uh ... well, suh, when we's alone, he prefers ta be called by his Christian name. He don't like Massa Connolley much. Says at home a man don't hafta be so formal."

Mr. MacPhearson grunted. "Hmph. Sounds like the man, all right." Scratching his chin again, he muttered, "What the hell is taking Lucas so long?"

As if Lucas had heard his name, the cart creaked as it pulled up front. Mr. MacPhearson put his hand on Matthew's shoulder. "All right, then. Shall we fetch your master?"

Matthew did not even wait to respond; he just dashed out the front door and leaped into the back of the cart. Mr. MacPhearson shook his head in wonder at John Connolley's slave before grabbing his coat and hat. Within moments—seconds that stretched into eternity for Matthew—Mr. MacPhearson stepped onto the cart and motioned for Lucas to head out.

Matthew crouched in the back, his hands gripped in prayer. True, John's death would mean a one-way ticket back to Mr. Barlow and the noose, but that was not the only reason Matthew wanted to help. He had thrown his lot in with John Connolley ... but it was more than that. John never once yelled at him, never once hit or whipped him, never once forced him to work. The man even paid him—cash! Ten cents a day ... money Matthew was saving. Money he would use to purchase his freedom. John swore, on the Bible, that he would help Matthew buy his freedom. John was no overseer. A couple of weeks back, when Matthew was sick, John had ordered him to stay in bed, refusing to let him get up to work. Matthew had never experienced kindness like that before. Under Mr. Barlow's service, he was ordered to the fields and beaten if he attempted to stay in bed. John was not like any master he had ever known; the man showed him respect. Matthew counted John Connolley a friend.

*   *   *   *

Patrick had not run after Katherine. Instead, he headed straight for the stables, shouting at Lucas to get his horse ready. Within minutes he was racing down the road on Glenora, the fastest horse in his father's stables. Katherine was on foot; he knew it would only take seconds to catch up with her. She was a good enough runner when they were children, but tonight she was in a fancy gown and running like a love-crazed fool. Soon enough he had swept her up into his arms and seated her sidesaddle in front of him.

Katherine pounded his chest until she realized Patrick was still riding in the direction of John Connolley. Then she pressed her face into his chest instead, crying, begging him to hurry. Patrick did not bother to say anything. Glenora was galloping as fast as she could against the wind, what with carrying two of them. They would get to John Connolley as soon as they could. Patrick noticed the mess his sister was in. Running in an evening gown could not have been easy. Her skirt was ripped and covered in dirt, while the palms of her hands were scratched and bloody. She must have fallen a few times. Her shiny red curls were in disarray, with strands clinging to her eyes and mouth. She was so frantic she had not even noticed.

Patrick knew his sister loved John Connolley, because she had confided in him. Even if his mother did not approve, Patrick liked the gentle giant. He would much rather have John Connolley as a brother-in-law than that loudmouth Junior.

Patrick had never liked Junior. The younger Crawford had been a bully when younger ... and still was, as far as Patrick was concerned. Patrick knew firsthand what Junior was capable of, having been the brunt of many a cruel joke during his youth. Too many times he had been locked inside the outhouse, Junior tipping the thing over with Patrick still sitting inside. Patrick had learned to get his pants up really fast, before the older boy could roar in laughter. It was a stupid joke, played over and over again. Junior lacked imagination. Junior was the last man alive Patrick ever wanted to see his sister married to, and Patrick made no bones about telling his mama that! Thank the Lord his daddy saw reason and was letting Katherine make up her own mind. Although the marriage would provide Katherine with fine social connections, no amount of money could make up for Junior's mean nature. It was a testament to Katherine that she could see that.

As soon as they rounded the bend, the siblings saw him. Katherine gasped in horror. "Oh, Paddy, what have they done to him?" Patrick carefully lowered his sister—a lot slower than she would have liked—and then leaped to the ground after her. Katherine ran straight for John and tried to wrap her arms around him. Patrick caught her just in time.

"Careful, girl. We have no idea what they did to him. You could make his injuries worse."

Tears blurred her eyes. "Help me get him down, Paddy."

Patrick went to work immediately. "Steady him, Katie. Hold him careful, mind you. I shall attempt to lower him slowly." Katherine braced herself, then placed her arms carefully around John's waist. Patrick dropped into a crouch and worked on the knots around John's feet. "Bloody hell!"

That Katherine did not sanction Patrick on his language showed the magnitude of her concern. "Hurry, Paddy. Please!"

"I am doing my best. These knots are tight." He pulled at the ropes, and John's body jerked.

"Try not to shake him so, Paddy. You might hurt him."

"You just leave me be and hold him steady." Patrick did not want to admonish his sister, knowing how racked she was with worry, but he could not afford her breaking his concentration either. The knots were tight. After a few attempts, he finally got John's legs free. Patrick dropped the rope and looked up to study how John was suspended. Patrick muttered another curse. "It is too high for me to reach. I am going to have to cut him down." Patrick jumped back up on Glenora and then turned to warn his sister, "Get out of the way, Katie. Mr. Connolley is about to drop." Patrick stood up in the stirrups and, using his pocketknife, sliced through the rope.

Katherine refused to move. If her man was going to fall, she was going to catch him. Suddenly John came tumbling down, landing on top of Katherine. Patrick raced to his sister's side, grunting as he pushed the heavy man off her. Katherine could barely breathe as Patrick lifted her up to sitting. "Why did you not get out of the way?" he demanded.

Katherine gasped. "I ... I simply could not let him fall." She stopped to catch her breath. "He is just too badly hurt. Look at him, Paddy. They shot him."

"Something tells me that is not the worst of it," Patrick hissed. He crossed over to John and felt his ribs. "They beat him real bad, Katie. Feels like at least six ribs have been broken." He checked behind John's head and brought his hand out to expose blood. "Bandage him as best you can. I am heading into town to fetch Dr. Odland."

Katherine looked to the sky. The thunder and lightning were relentless, and the wind continued to pick up. "Be careful, Paddy. Please."

Patrick nodded and leaped onto his horse. "I will be fine, Katie. You just watch over Mr. Connolley here. Daddy is coming with the wagon."

Katherine started ripping strips off her chemise for bandages. She wrapped a strip around John's leg, tying it tightly to stop the bleeding. She folded up another strip, placing the pad on the wound behind his head, and wrapped it in place. After she was done, Katherine lifted John's head and gently rested it in her lap. Softly running her fingers through his hair, she rocked back and forth, muttering prayers to the good Lord to save her man.

*   *   *   *

An eternity passed before the cart arrived. John was so pale that when lightning flashed, his image jumped out at Katherine like a specter. Clinging desperately to him, Katherine tried rubbing his face, hoping to bring color back. His skin was clammy and cold. Katherine whimpered, terrified he would die. Lightning flashed continuously now, and the thunder rolls were the heartbeat of the sky. The wind continued to pick up. If Katherine had not been holding on to John Connolley, it would have picked her up and carried her off.

When the cart finally rolled up, Katherine shouted, "Daddy, hurry! I think he might be dying." The wind swallowed her voice. Not that it mattered; her father and Matthew were moving as fast as they could.

Fat raindrops splashed down, picking up speed as they were whipped about by the wind. Angus MacPhearson shouted at Katherine, but she could not hear a word. She tried to read his lips, but her eyes blurred with tears and rain. Frustrated, Mr. MacPhearson began to untie the ropes around John's hands. When he had to struggle to get them loose, he gave his daughter a sympathetic look. He had wondered why she left the man tied up, and now he knew. The ropes were almost too tight even for him.

Katherine surmised what her father had been shouting and felt a stab of guilt. Patrick had untied John's feet and must have assumed she would untie his hands. Overwhelmed by the situation, she had not even thought about it. She had left the poor man tied. Her tears grew hot against the rain.

After Mr. MacPhearson untied John, he felt the man's ribs for breaks. He noted the bandages tied to his leg and head, having no trouble figuring out the nature of the wounds underneath. He motioned for his daughter to get out of the way, and then to Matthew to help lift John Connolley. Matthew shouted something, but his voice was lost in the wind.

Seeing that Mr. MacPhearson could not hear him, Matthew ran up to the man and shouted in his ear, "We gots ta get John back ta his house."

Mr. MacPhearson, shocked and angered by the suggestion, boxed Matthew across the ear. "Come to your senses, boy!" Matthew could barely hear, what with the storm and the ringing in his ears, so Mr. MacPhearson leaned in to shout in his other ear, "With this storm and riding against the wind, it will take hours for us to get to Mr. Connolley's place, assuming we even make it. If we do not get him inside real soon, he will die."

Matthew, resigning himself to reality, nodded and took his place at John's feet. The two men lifted John and half carried, half dragged the big man to the wagon. Katherine, following behind, opened the latch for them. John was sprawled across the wagon cart with knees bent over the edge. Katherine leaped into the back and resumed cradling John's head on her lap. Matthew joined her and lifted John's knees up onto his legs to keep his master's feet from dragging behind the cart. As soon as Mr. MacPhearson was in his seat, Lucas whipped the reins to get the horse in motion. The horse was more than anxious to obey, wanting desperately to get away from that storm.

The storm hindered them in more than one way. The wind blew at their backs with such force that the cart wobbled and nearly overturned several times. The road was fast turning into a river of mud, sucking the wheels into deep ruts. Twice they got stuck, and Lucas and Matthew had to get out and push.

Once they arrived at the plantation house, Mr. MacPhearson and Matthew carried John inside. They found it a trial to lift the big man up the stairs, so Abraham was solicited to help. Matthew figured they were lifting a good two hundred and fifty pounds of dead weight—and not one ounce of it fat. When John was finally laid out on a bed, desperation made Matthew try to take charge: "Iffin y'all jes' leaves me now, I'll be tendin' ta my massa." The look of consternation on Mr. MacPhearson's and his daughter's faces pushed Matthew into an even more desperate explanation. "Massa Connolley's a mighty private man … ah … he wouldn't want nobody else in here … ah … I gots ta remove his clothes an' all."

"Nonsense!" Katherine burst out. Under no circumstances was she to be kept from John's side. "It is foolish to take a man's sensibilities into account at a time like this."

Matthew was practically on his knees—in fact they bent deep into the mattress as he pleaded over John's body. "Please, Missy Katherine. De man cares for ya. He'd be mortified iffin he knowed you's in here seein' 'im like this." He knew he was pushing things way too far, but he could not help himself. "Worse, iffin ya see's 'im wit' his shirt off—"

Katherine smiled slightly before cutting Matthew off. "It is comforting to know Mr. Connolley cares for me, but that is all the more reason for me to stay by his side." She turned to her father. "Daddy, I can tend to him. You know I can. I worked with Dr. Odland for three years before Mama made me quit. I know what to do." Barely waiting for her daddy's nod of approval, Katherine turned back to Matthew. "It could be hours, maybe even days, before the doctor arrives, what with this storm and all. I am staying with Mr. Connolley, and that is that."

Matthew lowered his eyes in defeat.

Katherine persisted. "The question here, Matthew, is whether or not I am willing to let you stay and help."

Matthew paled, his face a ghostly gray, his eyes opening wide. "Please, Missy Katherine ... please let me stay an' help. Please!"

"Of course I will let you stay. Your loyalty toward your master is commendable." Then she added with stern admonition, "Just do not presume you can be giving orders around here."

Matthew shook his head vigorously. "Naw, Missy Katherine. I's sorry, Missy. I'll do as ya says. I's jes' worried, is all. I'll do as ya says, I promise, jes' ..." Matthew looked up sheepishly, terrified she would deny him his request. "Jes', please, ma'am ... let it be de two a' us ... jes' de two a' us?"

"I can accept that," Katherine said warmly. Now that her authority was established, Katherine turned to face the folk crammed into the doorway. There were far too many people in the room for her liking anyway. Most of the house servants were crammed in behind her daddy. Pushing through them all was her mother, followed closely by Sarah. Katherine was not going to let her mother pull her from that room. Mary MacPhearson had lectured her daughter sternly for showing Mr. Connolley affection and allowing him to call her by her Christian name.

"All right," Katherine said to them all. "Y'all leave Matthew and I alone. We have work to do."

Mary MacPhearson stood there, tossing her glare between Matthew and her daughter, hands positioned angrily upon her hips.

Sarah stood behind her mistress, wide-eyed and stunned at Matthew's audacity. She held a basin of hot water, and bandage strips were wrapped around each elbow.

Angus MacPhearson rubbed his chin thoughtfully, trying to figure out this strange little Negro. He certainly did not act like a runaway slave with an *R* branded on his face. This was a mystery Mr. MacPhearson intended to solve. In the meantime, he would give his daughter the lead and let her tend to John Connolley. She was right about one thing: it could be days before Dr. Odland made it out there. Even after the rain ceased, the roads would be knee-deep in mud. He turned to the milling mass. "Y'all heard the lady. Get on out of here."

Sarah tried to be the first to run out of the room, but Mary MacPhearson grabbed her arm, causing her to spill some of the water in her basin. "Hold off there, girl." Turning her glare onto her daughter, she pointed to the items Sarah carried. "You will be needing these. Will you not, Katherine?"

Katherine, noting her mother's discontent, smiled sweetly. Daddy had put her in charge, and Mama was not happy. "Thank you, Mama. Sarah, put the water and the bandages on the dressing table next to the scissors, please."

"Yessum, Missy Katherine." Sarah gingerly made her way through the small crowd, pushing past the slaves, bowing and excusing herself to her master and mistress. After placing the basin and bandages on the table, Sarah turned to leave.

Katherine called her back. "Sarah, wait." Turning to face Matthew, Katherine used every woman's prerogative: "Matthew, I have changed my mind."

Matthew grimaced.

"Mr. Connolley will simply have to live with the indignity of two women taking care of him. Sarah," Katherine said, "I will need your help."

Matthew groaned.

Angus MacPhearson added that to his mental notes. With one gruff swing of his arm and a growl to his voice, he swept everyone else out of the room.

Before her father could leave, though, Katherine called him back. "Daddy, I am going to need some of your whiskey to clean the gun wound."

"I will bring you some." Mr. MacPhearson paused a moment and considered the situation. "Have you figured out how you are going to get the bullet out? Or were you planning to leave that for the doctor?"

Katherine looked worried. "I am not sure, Daddy. I might have to dig it out. The wound could get infected if the bullet stays in there too long. Bring me a sharp knife, too, just in case I have to go in."

"And if the bullet is stuck in the bone?"

Katherine sighed. "You are asking all the hard questions, Daddy."

"They have to be asked, little girl."

"I know." With a deep breath and a loud exhale, she decided, "First I will tend to the broken ribs ... then I will look to the gun wound."

"I will fetch the whiskey and a knife."

"Thank you, Daddy."

As soon as the room was empty, and the door shut on the voice of Mary MacPhearson arguing with her husband about the consequences of Katherine attending to Mr. Connolley, Matthew lunged forward, laying his body across John's. Katherine stared, dumbfounded, at the man. When she came to her senses, she had to bite back the kind of curses she heard her father and brother mutter from time to time. For a brief instant, she understood why they would sometimes use such language. "What do you think you are doing, boy?"

Matthew knew he was likely to end up swinging from the end of a rope, but he had to try. "Please, Missy Katherine … do ya loves de man?"

"What in tar—da—" Katherine groped for polite words. "You are making me want to curse here, boy. Now get off of Mister Connolley." Katherine moved to the dresser table and picked up the scissors. "I mean to get his clothes stripped, so we can tend to him."

Matthew persisted with this strange act of defiance, his eyes a fiery storm of fear. "Do ya loves 'im, missy?"

Katherine was befuddled. Her confusion dampened her anger somewhat, but her anxiety for John was building worse than the storm. She needed to tend to his wounds before his injuries took him into the great unknown. "Of course I love him. Now get off of him, before I call my daddy back and have him strip the hide off of you."

What Matthew said next shocked and dismayed both Katherine and Sarah. "He can whip me, missy, but y'all gots ta promise that ya ain't gonna say nothin' 'bout what ya sees here today. Promise me ya ain't gonna tell nobody 'bout John."

Katherine sputtered, "John? You mean Master Connolley, do you not?"

"Yessum," Matthew said quite calmly, almost as if he were talking to an equal. "I means my massa. An' before I's movin', y'all gots ta promise ta be keepin' what ya sees here a secret." Katherine was incensed by Matthew's upright attitude, but before she could say anything, he continued, "Iffin ya loves 'im like ya says ya do, y'all be willin' ta promise anythin' for 'im."

Katherine's mouth dropped open, as did Sarah's. Sarah looked to the floor. She did not want to see the man hung, but he was walking right into the noose. She understood now why her mama called him dangerous.

Katherine stammered on in an attempt to remain in control. "I-I … Now, you listen here, boy. Your loyalty toward your master is commendable. In fact, it is the only thing keeping your neck out of the noose right now. But if you do not move—"

Matthew hit them both between the eyes with his next words. "Ya can hang me iffin ya wants, missy, but ya gots ta promise first, 'cause I ain't budgin'."

Dumbfounded, Katherine nodded and agreed. "All right, Matthew, I promise."

"Ain't good enough!" Matthew pronounced.

Sarah clasped her hand to her mouth to stifle a cry.

Katherine glared indignantly. "I beg your pardon!" This was no question. It was a demand.

Matthew was running on stark fear and adrenaline. "I's sorry, missy, but ya gots ta promise on de Bible, ag'in your immortal soul."

Katherine, coming back to her senses, responded curtly, "Well, I am truly sorry, boy, but there is no Bible in this room. Now, we have wasted enough time. I must tend Mr. Connolley's wounds before he dies!"

"He'll die anyways iffin ya don't promise."

Katherine frowned. Clearly this foolish Negro was not going to budge, and getting men to pull him off would likely cause further injures. She placed her hand on her heart and swore. "I swear to the Lord our God, on pain of death and the eternal suffering of my soul, to never speak of what I see here today." Then, with a shake of her head, she asked, "Good enough?"

"Yessum. Now Sarah."

Sarah stammered and looked to Katherine, who commanded, "Say it, Sarah, or we will never get any work done." Sarah repeated verbatim what Katherine had said, and Matthew finally stood, so Katherine could start cutting John's shirt.

Matthew crouched at the side of the bed with his hands behind his head, eyes squeezed tightly shut.

Before Katherine could slice the shirt open, there was a knock at the door. Katherine stiffened and shot a curt order to Sarah. "Answer it!"

Sarah rushed to the door, revealing Mr. MacPhearson.

"I brought the whiskey and knife you asked for, little darling."

Without turning to look, Katherine asked, "Why did you bring it yourself, instead of sending it with one of the Negroes?"

Her father grumbled, "I wanted to see how you were making out."

Katherine turned to face her father. "As you can see, we are doing fine." Turning to Sarah without so much as a nod to her father, she said, "Get the whiskey and the knife, please." Sarah crossed quickly to the door and grabbed the bottle and knife from her master. She curtsied slightly, then ran back to Katherine's side. "Set them down on the table, girl. You are not going to be much help with your hands full."

Sarah looked startled to see she still held the bottle and knife in her hands. Her eyes held the wide-eyed stare a doe gives just before the bullet whizzes between its eyes. Quickly setting the items down, she muttered, "Yessum."

Angus MacPhearson rubbed his chin thoughtfully. The room was filled with tension, and not just the worrying kind. Something strange was going on, but now was not the time to try to figure things out—not when a man's life was on the line. "All right, little girl. But you be sure to call me if you need anything."

"I will, Daddy." Katherine remained focused on John, holding the scissors midair, waiting for her father to leave. Matthew was hiding something, and whatever it was, it was underneath John's shirt. Katherine was not sure what she would find, but she knew she did not want her daddy in the room when she discovered it. Something was making that boy act worse than a coon treed by redbones.

As soon as the door closed, Katherine cut John's shirt, exposing welts across his chest. Gasping, Katherine cried, "Oh, Sarah, look."

Matthew groaned.

Sarah responded, "Yessum, Missy Katherine. It be terrible what they done ta him."

"They beat him like a slave."

Matthew winced.

Katherine looked down at him. "Get up, Matthew!" she commanded. "We need your help. We have to lift him up, so we can pull his shirt out from under him."

Matthew, still crouching, hands gripping the edge of the mattress, begged, "Couldn't ya jes' tend his wounds like that?"

Katherine's shock turned to instant rage. "Get up this instant, boy, and help Sarah lift him!"

Matthew stood as ordered, gently cradling John's shoulder.

Katherine's voice softened as she expressed her concern for John Connolley, "Careful, now."

Sarah held the other side, and they lifted him slightly, so Katherine could pull John's shirt out. Sarah gasped when his shoulders were lifted and nearly released her hold on John.

Katherine admonished her, "Watch yourself, girl. We are trying to help the man, not make his injuries worse."

Automatically Sarah adjusted her body angle to help hide John's brand from Katherine's eyes. "Sorry, Missy Katherine. I's sorry. I's ... I ..." Even though her apology was addressed to Katherine, her eyes were firmly fixed on Matthew. Anger, surprise, and stark fear fought for control over them. *What de hell has that dimwitted nigga got me into? He done made me swear ta something that could get me lynched. If Missy Katherine sees this, she ain't gonna keep quiet nohow. We be tending one of them white niggas.* Gasping, Sarah remembered Katherine's declaration. *Missy Katherine be in love wit' him! When she finds out, I sho don't want to be in de room for that!* Sarah cleared her throat. "Ah ... Missy Katherine, Matthew here is right. We oughts ta leave tendin' Mr. Connolley ta him ... Matthew bein' his man an' all. Sho'ly he knows best …" Sarah's voice petered out under the daunt-ing glare of her mistress.

Katherine was not taking any more nonsense. "What has gotten into you, Sarah? I will not leave Mr. Connolley's care in anyone's hands but my own. Now, if either of you says one more fool word, I swear I will send you both to the whip-ping post. Is that understood?" She glared at Matthew for the last word.

Matthew and Sarah both replied meekly. "Yessum."

With a commanding voice that could rival Major General Nathaniel Greene, one of the most trusted generals of the American Revolution, Katherine barked orders. "Lay him down! Gently." Roughly shoving Sarah aside, Katherine contin-ued, "Now, get out of my way. Both of you! I have to feel for broken ribs." After a moment, Katherine announced, "It looks like Paddy was right. He has at least six broken ribs, far as I can tell." Her anxiety quelled her burning anger. Chewing her thumbnail, Katherine sucked in a deep breath. As she exhaled, she questioned her skill: "I sure do hope I can remember how to set them." She shook her head slightly. "Dr. Odland showed me a few years back, but Mama … damn her for having made me quit!" Suddenly catching herself cursing, she looked up to Sarah. "You will say nothing about my cursing, you hear?"

"Naw, Missy Katherine," Sarah stammered. She had been muttering more than a few curses herself.

Katherine went straight to work. "Thank the Lord he is out cold, as this would hurt like the dickens if he were awake."

As Katherine nursed John, both Matthew and Sarah tried to work out in their minds how they might keep her from seeing John Connolley's back. They were lucky she had not noticed anything when they were holding him up … but soon she would want him lifted again to wrap bandages around his chest.

Matthew worried even more than Sarah. *Lordy*, he prayed, *forgive me. I's been playin' de man's slave. Thar ain't no good in lyin'. I should'a jes' run and jes' kept right on runnin'. Massa Barlow done lent me to 'im, but who's gonna think about that when they learns de truth? Shoot, even if he is white, like he's always sayin', de only proof we got is what's on his back. Oh Lordy, Lordy, help us. Please get Missy MacPhearson ta keep her promise. What white woman gonna keep that secret? Dear Lord, could she love 'im that much? How much she gonna love 'im after she sees that?* Matthew's mind continued to whirl around, his thoughts like tornadoes, until Katherine made her announcement.

"All right," Katherine said. "I am ready for the compression wrap. Lift him up."

Desperate, Matthew remembered something his mama said the one time his daddy had his ribs broken. "Are ya sho ya wants ta be wrappin' his chest? He could end up wit' pneumonia or somethin' iffin he cain't breathe proper."

Katherine nodded thoughtfully. "Hmmm. Dr. Odland mentioned the like ... deep breaths are real important for healin'."

Matthew held his breath, and Sarah said a quiet prayer, both hoping beyond hope Matthew's suggestion worked.

Katherine continued, "But, he also said if the breaks were bad, and there were lots of injuries, a compression wrap was necessary, especially during the first forty-eight hours."

"But iffin he's out cold like this, he ain't gonna feel noth—"

Katherine would not let Matthew finish. "I made my decision, boy." Taking a moment to tap her finger to her lips and closing her eyes slightly, Katherine pondered what to do next. "If I recall correctly, Dr. Odland also said it would be best if the patient slept sitting up, so we will need more pillows."

Sarah leaped at the opportunity to escape the room. "I'll gets 'em for ya, Missy Katherine."

Before she could turn to run for the door, Katherine grabbed her arm and hauled her back. "You can get the pillows later, Sarah. Right now I need you to help Matthew lift Mr. Connolley again, so I can wrap his chest."

Sarah piped up, "Ya looks a mite tired, Missy Katherine. How's 'bout I do de wrappin'?" She fought hard to keep her voice calm, and her expression void of worry.

Katherine smiled. "Why, that is real nice of you, Sarah, but I had better do the work. Besides, it will take the two of you just to hold Mr. Connolley upright for me."

Matthew followed Sarah's lead. "That be OK, Missy Katherine. I can hold Massa Connolley by myself. He ain't that heavy, an' Sarah here be right ... ya looks a mite tired."

"I am fine," Katherine insisted. "Now leave me do my duty."

Sarah and Matthew looked dejected. Sarah even quivered a sigh. They cradled John in their arms and lifted him, so Katherine could begin wrapping bandages around his chest.

When Katherine saw his brand, there was a slight pause and a sudden intake of breath.

Both Matthew and Sarah held theirs.

Katherine said nothing. She continued to wrap the bandages around John's chest. When she was finished, she ordered, "Sarah, give me your side. I will help hold him while you get the extra pillows." After Katherine took hold of John's shoulder, Sarah stood with eyes fixed like magnets to the floor. Katherine's eyes bored into Matthew's. He started to sweat, as if the heat of her gaze were penetrating him. "Sarah!" Her voice snapped like a whip, and the poor girl leaped like a frightened rabbit. "Get the pillows. Now!" Sarah curtsied and dashed out of the room without even a "yessum."

The pause that ensued was excruciating. Matthew felt as if hot pins were slowly being pushed into his eyeballs. Katherine waited until sweat dripped down his forehead.

"All right, Matthew. Start talking."

Katherine's curt command caused Matthew to stammer some. He had no idea how to explain this. "Ah, I's ... uh ... Massa Connolley, here ... ah ..."

Katherine sneered. "Master Connolley, indeed!" Her scowling look analyzed Matthew. "I see why you have been calling him John now."

Matthew was shaking—partly from having to hold John's weight for so long, but mostly from fear. He did what his folk did best in desperate situations: he started to plead with the woman. "Missy Katherine, please. It ain't what it looks like ..."

Before he could finish Katherine piped in, "I know what it *looks* like! I suppose he is Barlow's son after all. All this talk of him being his cook's son and being raised by him is probably true. Tell me, Matthew, does Barlow like the taste of sweet molasses?"

Matthew stammered. "I's ... ah ... ain't never heard tell a' Massa Barlow doin' no such thing."

"Servant, indeed!" Katherine scoffed. "Can you feel the noose tightening around your neck, boy?"

Instinctively Matthew cracked his neck. Sweat stung his eyes. As begging was not working, he figured he might as well try reason. "Missy Katherine, why would Massa Barlow lie?"

"The boy looks white, that is why." She looked down at John and sighed. "Barlow said it himself: he always wanted a son. I reckon John here was the closest thing to it. Maybe this was his only way, hmm? Spawn a mulatto and hope he comes out white, like this one did."

Matthew became bold. He had no choice. It was the only way left to keep the rope off him and John Connolley. "Do he even look like Barlow?" Even more forcibly than he ought to, he repeated, "Do he?" Noting Katherine's consternation, Matthew added an apology. "I's sorry, Missy Katherine, but his mama were white, an' so were his daddy. I don't knows de whole story, or de whys an' de hows, but they say his mama were sold 'cause she done laid wit' a British solider."

Katherine scoffed, "There is no law against marrying a British soldier."

"Pardon me for sayin' so, missy, but she weren't married. From what I's been told, her daddy were a patriot, an' ... uh ... it were war an' all." In desperation, Matthew pleaded, "Please, Missy Katherine. I don't know de whole story, but Massa Barlow wouldn't lie. Please wait an' ask 'im before ya goes an' does anythin'"—he paused for emphasis—"anythin' that might hurt de man ya loves." The edge was getting real slippery, but Matthew took another step anyway. "Ya did say ya loves 'im, didn't ya?"

Katherine's eyes revealed a combination of hurt and anger. "Yes, Matthew, I did." With a sharpness that could cut through iron, Katherine commanded, "You are not to tell a soul I said that either, you hear?"

"Yessum. No one, missy."

"No one!" Katherine reiterated. With her eyes fixed on Matthew, she added, "I will keep Mr. Connolley's secret for now. I did give my word, though I do not rightly think it would be a sin to break it. The good Lord would not expect me to hold back on the truth, now would he?"

Matthew winced and lowered his eyes, avoiding her stare.

"If he is passing for white, he will pay for his lying. And you will pay with your life for helping him lie."

In a voice near to inaudible, Matthew persisted, "Massa Barlow wouldn't a' lied. Everyone knows 'im ta be a man a' his word."

Katherine glared at Matthew with sullen hate. "You better hope he is." There was a timorous tap at the door. Katherine shouted, "Get in here, Sarah."

The door creaked. Sarah entered with her arms cradling four pillows. She held them tight to her chest, as if they could protect her from Katherine's wrath.

"Bring them over here, girl. Now! We cannot keep holding him up forever."

Sarah darted to the bed and placed the pillows behind John's back. Slowly Katherine and Matthew laid the man down. Released of her burden, Katherine motioned to Sarah to bring her a chair. Sarah placed it right next to John's bed, and Katherine sat in it. Looking at the two slaves as if she were looking at dirty cats, she muttered her discontent. "Now get out of here, both of you." Looking directly at Matthew, she added, "I cannot stand to look at you."

Matthew crossed the room and hurried out the door without another word. Sarah followed at his heels.

Katherine seated herself next to John, hot tears burning her eyes.

CHAPTER 22

▼

A CHANGE OF HEART

Abraham led Jacob Barlow to Mr. MacPhearson's study. He pushed open the great doors and bowed. Waving his white glove, he announced, "Massa MacPhearson, Mr. Jacob Barlow has arrived."

Angus MacPhearson stood from his desk, extending his hand as he walked over to the gentleman. "Welcome, suh. It is an honor to have you abide with us." With a dismissive glance from his master, Abraham backed away and pulled the doors closed behind him. "Come, suh, please sit down." Mr. MacPhearson gestured toward two large wing chairs. Between them stood a small round table with a box of cigars and a crystal ashtray. Once seated, Mr. MacPhearson offered Mr. Barlow a cigar. The man accepted readily, and, for a moment, the two men sat in silence, enjoying the luxury of the smoke, both lost in their own contemplations.

For Mr. Barlow, all worries rested on the state of John Connolley. He had been assured that Dr. Odland was confident of John's recovery. John Connolley would come out of his coma with all his wits intact ... but apparently, Dr. Odland had not said when. It bothered Mr. Barlow that John had not woken since his attack two nights ago. *John should have come around by now*, he thought. *What did those men do to him? Why did they attack him so brutally? Who were they? How am I to exact my revenge? If they are men of business, I will destroy them. Much better*, Mr. Barlow figured, *than getting my hands dirty.*

While John Connolley's health was definitely a concern, Mr. MacPhearson's thoughts ran along a completely different vein. It always bothered him when someone was brutally attacked. The doctor had confided to him that he was unsure whether John Connolley would ever wake. Even Katherine was under the impression that John just needed a few more days' rest before coming to. For all Dr. Odland knew, John Connolley could snap out of it any minute … or remain in a coma indefinitely. An even more looming uncertainty for Mr. MacPhearson was his daughter's odd behavior. If she truly believed John Connolley was healing, why was she in such a somber mood? There was more to it, he could tell, than concern over a loved one's health. In her, anger battled with concern.

Mr. Barlow interrupted their reveries. "I thank you, suh, for your generous hospitality. Your family has kindly tended to John these past few days, at great expense and inconvenience. Your daughter Katherine nurses my boy, and I have been told your son, Patrick, is tending to his plantation as well as overseeing Matthew. Y'all have been very kind."

"There have been no expenses, suh, beyond minor necessities like bandages and such." Mr. MacPhearson dismissed it with a wave. "Inconsequental. Dr. Odland said he would wait on his fees until your arrival."

"I will settle up with him when next he comes," Mr. Barlow determined. "Even still, you have tended to my boy in his time of need."

Angus MacPhearson arched an eyebrow at what seemed to him to be a confession.

"And you are kindly offering me hospitality to make my sitting at John's sickbed easier. I am truly grateful. If ever I can assist you and your family, be assured, suh, I intend to wield all my influence in your favor."

"I thank you, suh, for your generous offer," Mr. MacPhearson replied most diplomatically. "But that is not why my family has chosen to aid Mr. Connolley. It is, suh, I believe, the duty of every citizen to help those in need. We certainly do not offer aid for material advantage." Mr. MacPhearson, not wanting to exploit the man, changed the subject. "Surely, suh, you are here today to see your son …" Stumbling over the word *son,* Angus quickly changed it to "Mr. Connolley."

"I am truly sorry, suh," said an embarrassed Mr. MacPhearson.

Mr. Barlow smiled at the error. "No apology necessary, my good man. John is like a son to me. I have often called him *son* myself. And you are quite right. My main purpose is to check on the condition of Mr. Connolley. Would he were my son!"

Mr. MacPhearson smiled, believing more than ever that John Connolley was indeed Jacob Barlow's illegitimate offspring. Why else would the man come all this way in the middle of the night, arrive in a state worse than a field slave, and drop important business on such short notice, if John Connolley was only the cook's son?

Before Angus MacPhearson could stand, Mr. Barlow gestured for him to remain seated. "But first, I wish to discuss the brutal circumstances of John's attack." Mr. Barlow's eyes narrowed, and his voice took on a grave tone. "Who were these men? What possible motive did they have? What condition was John in when y'all found him?"

Mr. MacPhearson sighed. Having expected such questions, he determined to tell the man the truth. He began the long and arduous story with an emphatic reminder that there was no proof.

"Your son offended the sensibilities of a few folk the night of my wife's dinner party."

✳   ✳   ✳   ✳

The storm had raged for hours after John was cut down from the tree. It was well past noon the following day before Patrick and the doctor could depart Laurel Creek for the MacPhearson home. The roads, slopped over with mud, made their travel difficult. Even riding horseback was slow going. A horse could easily break a leg in all the hidden ruts. It was nearly five o'clock by the time they had arrived and the doctor was cleaned up enough to tend to John.

Dr. Odland's response upon seeing his patient was to praise Katherine for her fine nursing. He credited her for saving John Connolley's life. "I do miss your assistance," he sighed regretfully. "It is most unfortunate that a lady of esteem cannot pursue talents beyond that of art, music, and beauty." Katherine blushed at the compliment.

Apart from removing the bullet from John's leg, Dr. Odland spent very little time with John; Katherine had done all that he would have in circumstances such as these. Now it was up to the body … and given time, it would heal. Dr. Odland encouraged Katherine to get some food into John. "Rice and black beans cooked soft and ground into a mush can be liquefied with milk or water." Noting her sour reaction, he added, "Taste is inconsequential. It is just important to get food into him. His body is going to need all the help it can get." He warned her, though, of the dangers: "He could easily choke if you are not careful." Still, he insisted she try.

Katherine agreed and immediately instructed Sarah to prepare the mixture.

"You did a fine job here, Miss Katherine … a fine job," Dr. Odland said as he inspected the constriction bandage Katherine had applied. "It is necessary for him to wear this for a time, until we can be sure he will not move around too much in his sleep … but the sooner we get it off him, the better. It will help his ribs heal, but it is none too good for his lungs. His breathing is shallow, and I am a little worried about lung infection. We do not want him coughing. That will only cause further damage. Be sure you keep him warm."

"Yes, suh," Katherine replied, making mental notes of everything the doctor said.

"It is good you have him sitting up," Dr. Odland continued. "You must keep him upright. Lying down in this condition could lead to bronchitis or pneumonia. If he catches either, he will likely die. Also, make sure he does not jerk around too much. Nightmares are common in cases such as these. Victims often relive the attack in their sleep."

Katherine shuddered. *How am I to keep such a big man still if he starts to thrash about?*

Dr. Odland noted her concern. "Not to worry, little lady. You have done a fine job. I have no doubt you can nurse Mr. Connolley back to health. He is a lucky man to have you by his side. It would be best, however, if he were to have someone sit up with him all night."

Katherine readily agreed. She was determined to be the one. Only she and Sarah knew about John's brand and back lashings. No one else must ever find out.

"I will drop by again in a few days to see how he is progressing. Be sure to send for me if he wakes."

Katherine nodded.

"I will leave you this." Dr. Odland handed her a small bottle of clear liquid and a needle. "It is for the pain. Be sure to give him an injection as soon as he wakes. He is going to be mighty sore indeed." He eyed her sternly; it had been a while since she worked with him. "Do you remember how to administer it?"

"Yes, suh," Katherine replied with confidence, "directly into the vein. First, I must pull up a little blood, and then slowly—"

"Very slowly," Dr. Odland reminded her.

Katherine nodded. "—very slowly inject the morphine."

"Good." Dr. Odland nodded. "Be sure you clean the needle after every use. It can get mighty dirty after a time."

Katherine muttered a thank you and saw the doctor to the bedroom door. Before leaving, though, the doctor had a few words to say … something he had been avoiding. His hand paused on the door handle. "Miss Katherine …"

His distress was all Katherine needed. "I am aware, suh, of Mr. Connolley's ... brand."

The doctor sighed. "You have not acted rashly, which is good. Few would have had your patience given the circumstances."

"As you are aware," Katherine inquired, "why have you not acted upon it?"

Dr. Odland pondered for a moment, then replied, "It would be best if Mr. Barlow explained." With that he closed the door quietly and departed.

Yes, Katherine thought bitterly. *Mr. Barlow shall explain.*

*   *   *   *

John, racked by frightening dreams, jerked and moaned all night. Katherine, terrified he would injure himself further, gave him an injection of morphine, hoping it would calm him down. Rather than stop his dreams, the drug intensified them. Had she known that the drug was named after Morpheus, the god of dreams, she never would have administered it to him at such a time. She sat down on the bed but was unable to hold John still, so she rang for Sarah. Together they sat up all night, holding onto John, trying to keep him still. Sarah suggested asking a man for assistance, because it was nigh on impossible for the two women to hold such a big man down, but Katherine refused. Too many folk already knew John's secret. Katherine was not going to take the risk of anyone else finding out.

Sarah left early that morning when Abraham came to fetch her. Apparently Ruth needed her in the kitchen. Mr. Jacob Barlow was coming, and Mrs. MacPhearson had ordered a fine breakfast for his arrival. Then there was dinner and supper to consider, and all meals were to be prepared carefully—intended, of course, to impress the great man. Abraham was not sure whether Sarah could be spared again.

Although it annoyed Katherine that Mr. Barlow's meals should take precedence over Mr. Connolley's health, she reconciled herself to remaining at John's bedside without a break until Mr. Barlow was ready to sit with him. Abraham encouraged Katherine to let him find someone to relieve her, but she ardently refused. She dismissed Sarah and Abraham by saying she was not to be disturbed, except in an emergency. She eased their minds, though, by promising to call for help if any was needed.

Once alone with John, Katherine's exhaustion burst forth into tears. She cried over his injuries, cried over his back ... and, most fervently, cried over Matthew's claim. *Is it true? How could any man treat a beloved child this way? Or is John mulatto? If so, why would the good doctor not take any action against him? In any* event, Mr. Jacob Barlow would arrive shortly, providing her with all the intelligence she needed. His side of the story would determine for her what she would do. That was the last thought to enter Katherine's head before it dropped onto John's shoulder. She was in such a deep sleep that she did not hear her father or Mr. Barlow enter the room.

"Katherine!" Angus MacPhearson shouted, giving his daughter a few good shakes. "Wake up this instant, girl! Explain yourself."

Katherine stuttered a few times before registering her father's presence. It took her a moment to remember she was lying on the bed next to John Connolley. Her father helped her stand. Katherine took a moment to straighten her dress in order to compile her thoughts before presenting her defense. Straightening her back, she began, "Dr. Odland told me it was important to keep Mr. Connolley sitting up at all times. He also said to make sure Mr. Connolley does not move around, so his bones can heal proper. The only way to accomplish that was to sit beside him. He was racked with frightful dreams, and if I had not sat next to him, he surely would have done further injury to himself. Now, I am sorry I fell asleep. I understand the impropriety, but it was purely unintentional. The gentleman requires twenty-four-hour attention."

Katherine's father, sympathizing with his daughter's dilemma, decided not to be angry. "You have taken on too much tending to Mr. Connolley. Allow me to fetch Maggie ..."

"No, suh, I will not have this room overrun with incompetents. Dr. Odland was adamant on Mr. Connolley receiving the best possible care. Since I am the only one with medical experience, I shall be the one attending to his needs."

"You cannot attend to his needs if you fall sick from exhaustion, now can you?" Angus MacPhearson kindly pointed out.

"You are correct. But the only person I would feel comfortable leaving Mr. Connolley with is Sarah. I have shown her most of what needs to be done. Unfortunately, her aid was removed from me, so she could work in the kitchen to help prepare food for Mr. Barlow."

Mr. Barlow interjected, "Why, there is no need to worry over my keep. I would much prefer this Sarah be here with John. His needs are paramount, and mine secondary."

Mr. MacPhearson nodded. "I will arrange for Sarah to relieve you, Katherine."

"Thank you, Daddy. I would appreciate that. But wait half an hour, please. I have private concerns I wish to address with Mr. Barlow." She added to her icy tone: "Alone."

Jacob Barlow smiled kindly on the girl. "Miss MacPhearson, I would dearly love a private conference with you, but first I wish to sit with John."

As he attempted to sit, Katherine placed a not-too-gentle hand on his arm, gesturing for him to remain standing.

Her father found this most curious. This puzzle was getting more complex every minute. It was not like his daughter to be so rude.

"Mr. Barlow," she said most curtly. "You will talk with me." She only added the honorific "suh" as an afterthought.

This was the most confounding thing Mr. MacPhearson had ever witnessed. Not only had his daughter acted in a most unbecoming manner, but Mr. Jacob Barlow seemed to shrink at her glance, acquiescing without argument. His daughter was ordering the mighty Jacob Barlow around like a common household servant, and he was obeying her command. Angus MacPhearson decided to hold off on his reprimand at that moment. But he was determined, more than ever, to figure out what was really transpiring.

*   *   *   *

The messenger had arrived at Jacob Barlow's manor just past three in the morning. He was to talk to Mr. Barlow upon arrival. It was not an easy task to summon the great man. Mr. MacPhearson's messenger had arrived covered in mud, as the road had been washed out by the storm. His horse broke a leg in a pothole, and after putting it down, he had continued on foot. His late arrival, coupled with his dirty appearance, led to suspicion. He persisted, though, and insisted that he carried a message of great importance concerning Mr. John Connolley. That got the attention of the old Negro, and he rushed to Mr. Barlow's room to wake him.

Upon hearing the news of John's attack and uncertain condition, Mr. Barlow immediately ordered his carriage brought forth. The messenger warned him of travel conditions and convinced Mr. Barlow that the only alternative was to ride horseback. Conditions were perilous, though, so they had to be careful. Riding too fast could mean the death of another horse. Mr. Barlow had a saddlebag packed with one change of clothes. He ordered a wardrobe be sent as soon as conditions warranted. By the time he arrived at the MacPhearsons', Jacob Barlow looked like a disheveled slave returning from a full day's work digging canals.

Mrs. MacPhearson instructed her Negroes to see to Mr. Barlow's immediate needs. Abraham ushered him to the room next to John Connolley's, where a hot bath was waiting. His clothes were laundered, the outfit in his saddlebag pressed.

Food and coffee were brought to his room, so he could eat before meeting with Mr. MacPhearson.

Asked if he wished to rest, Jacob Barlow refused, insisting he meet with Mr. MacPhearson forthwith. Abraham quickly escorted him to his master's study. By this point, Jacob Barlow, being well into his sixties, was harried and exhausted. His mind was also racked with worry over John's condition. He knew doctors expressed only the most favorable hopes and downplayed obvious dangers. As a boxing trainer, Mr. Barlow knew how serious head injuries could be. When finally confronted by Katherine's knowing eyes, Mr. Barlow's insecurities and guilt over what he had done to John Connolley surfaced. He found himself complying with her demands, like a wayward boy being called to account by his mama.

$$*\qquad*\qquad*\qquad*$$

"I have seen Mr. Connolley's brand, suh." No niceties. No allowing for Mr. Barlow to ask how John was doing. Just a cold, frank address.

Mr. Barlow was so shocked by the girl's harshness that he dropped into the chair with a thump.

"Well, suh, what say you to that?"

Mr. Barlow was so stunned, all he could do was watch dust motes float past his eyes.

Katherine pressed on mercilessly. "You had best explain yourself to me, suh, before I feel obliged to take what I know to Artemus Sprague."

The threat of insurrection brought Mr. Barlow back to attention. "There is no need for such drastic measures, Miss Katherine. I assure you, John Connolley is as white as you or I."

"Then how came he to bear the mark of a Negro slave, suh?" The word "suh" hissed out of Katherine with such contempt, Mr. Barlow shivered. Her eyes were sharp needles piercing into Mr. Barlow. Katherine pressed on. "Explain it to me!"

Suddenly it all poured out of the old man—thirty years of truth without the usual flair of fancy storytelling. It came forth without embellishments. Mr. Barlow related everything about Evelyn's fate, her love affair with a British officer, their rash engagements, how her father had caught them. He spoke of legal transactions that led to his owning Evelyn, of her willingly signing away her freedom, unaware that she was pregnant. When he explained about slave law regarding the children of female slaves, Katherine cut him off.

"A law you took full advantage of," she scoffed, refusing to add the honorific "suh." "Surely you could have seen it in your heart to grant the child his freedom … a child you claimed to raise and love like a son!"

"Indeed," Mr. Barlow admitted. He had not been required to hold to the letter of the law, but he had. His guilt was so overwhelming that he found himself crying through the rest of his confession. Opening the blackness of his soul, Mr. Barlow told of the day the boy got lost, whipped, and branded. He spoke of rightful defiance that his pride rode like a wild bronc, leading to a scar that would last a lifetime. He even found himself confessing to the renting of the man, though he never mentioned the lady in question's name.

Katherine blanched. How could anyone—a woman—commit such a heinous act? She speculated: Mr. Barlow had, after all, brought a most powerful and wealthy lady to Laurel Creek to visit John Connolley … no doubt for tawdry business.

Mr. Barlow sat bent over, face cradled in wrinkled hands.

Katherine stood towering over the broken man, assuring him of her confidence. "Mr. Connolley's secret is safe with me." With a sigh, she turned and left the room, abandoning Mr. Barlow to his misery. She knew now what she had to do.

*   *   *   *

"Mama," Katherine called as she descended the stairs. "Mama?"

"Here I am." Mary MacPhearson entered from the sunroom. "What is all the hollering about? Is Mr. Connolley failing?"

"Mr. Connolley's condition remains stable," Katherine replied curtly. "I am not calling on you to discuss him."

"Well, then, what is it?" Mrs. MacPhearson had remained cold with her daughter ever since the night of the party. Katherine had behaved improperly, shunning Junior. Junior had not come by to visit her once since that night. Mrs. MacPhearson was convinced Junior was angered by Katherine's blatant flirtations with John Connolley.

"I would like you to accompany me to Pine Grove."

"Pine Grove?" Mrs. MacPhearson's heart surged with joy. Hopeful, she asked, "Are you hoping to sit awhile with Junior?"

"If he wishes to sit with me."

Startled, Mary MacPhearson could not help but ask, "Why this sudden change of heart?"

"Junior has always wanted to marry me. I am twenty years of age. I do want babies. And no other man would consider me. Junior has made sure of that."

"Only because he loves you, dear. You cannot blame a gentleman for discouraging the competition."

"Indeed. He has done that."

Mary MacPhearson eyed her daughter suspiciously. "I thought you were hoping for a proposal from Mr. Connolley?"

"Mr. Connolley is a confirmed bachelor, Mama. He shall never marry."

"My dear Katie, I am so pleased you have finally come to your senses. Wait here … I must fetch your father. We shall make this momentous occasion a family affair."

"No!" Katherine paused to collect herself. "I mean, Daddy is busy. We need not bother him with trivial affairs."

"His daughter's impending marriage is hardly trivial."

"Let us visit Junior first and determine whether he still desires a union."

"You are correct. After all your colting and gallivanting with Mr. Connolley, Junior may have lost all interest."

"This afternoon shall determine that."

CHAPTER 23

▼

STUDYING PAINE

Knowing everything had been his fault, Mr. Barlow fervently scolded and blamed himself for the attack on John. Mr. MacPhearson had explained to him about the night of the party and the heated debate about Thomas Paine. Although no clear accusation was made, it was obvious the attack had been sparked by John's controversial views.

Rather than see the injustice of the world, Mr. Barlow chose to blame Thomas Paine for his writings, himself for sharing the man's work, and a boy who had stubbornly read what he had been ordered not to. All this, as Mr. Barlow saw it, was the reason John lay in bed, unable to wake. Rather than suffer the blows of self-recrimination, Mr. Barlow chose to dwell on a lesson taught eighteen years ago.

*   *   *   *

"John!" Mr. Barlow's voice cracked like a whip.

John quickly turned back to the table where he and Emily Barlow were studying Thomas Paine's pamphlet *Common Sense*.

"Are you paying attention, son, or lost again in some foolish daydream?"

"Sorry, suh. I were just lookin' out the window."

"Was looking out the window, John." Mr. Barlow admonished. "Speak proper English, young man."

Mr. Barlow's library was a large room with two huge windows that stretched the height of the room and were nearly half as wide. Swagged brocade curtains hung open to show the glow of the sun setting behind the stables. Low, billowing clouds shimmered a fiery orange. Bookshelves paneled the other three walls, with sliding ladders attached.

Mr. Barlow's library was considered the finest in all of Savannah. Having studied business at Cambridge in England, graduating at the top of his class, Mr. Barlow was accounted a scholar in social circles. After arriving in the colonies, he used his hard-earned money to build, over time, one of the largest plantations on the river's bank, just north of the burgeoning Savannah. His plantation grew cotton, tobacco, sugar cane, indigo, and rice. He always believed in diversification. Mr. Barlow did little work on his plantation, short of tending his horses. He left running things to Mitch, who was more than adept at overseeing the day-to-day operations. Mitch kept the slaves in line and always ensured a profit. With Mitch holding the whip, there was never any trouble … none he had ever had to bring to Mr. Barlow, at any rate. At his ease, Mr. Barlow was content to breed horses and educate his children.

Mr. Barlow smiled fondly at John. He was not the boy's father, but he loved him like a son. Mr. Barlow surveyed the large pine table next to the window, where Emily and John sat. Mr. Barlow felt a surge of pride at the sight of four high-backed chairs with ornately carved scenes of the revolution on the back panels. He reminisced about the role he had played as a soldier with the patriots.

Both Emily and John squirmed often on the hard pine chairs; they were made for show, not practical use. Emily always sat on the chair depicting Paul Revere's famous midnight ride, while John preferred the one with the scene commemorating the battle Mr. Barlow fought in: the October 9 siege of Savannah in 1779. This had been Mr. Barlow's first taste of war, and sitting in that chair always made John feel proud the man was raising him.

As much as Mr. Barlow appreciated the memories produced by the chairs, the real reason he made the children sit in them was to keep them from getting too comfortable or drifting off. Unfortunately, very little seemed to keep John's mind focused since James Montgomery had come to Mr. Barlow's plantation, known far and wide as Heartland.

Emily, Mr. Barlow's only child, snickered at John's explanation. "You mean you were looking for Montgomery." Only two months younger than John and wet-nursed by his mama, Emily acted like John's sister.

John's hackles rose. "I weren't! I were just—"

"Enough!" barked Mr. Barlow. He slowly circled the table until he was towering over the lad. "If you do not pay attention to your lessons tonight, you will not be helping Montgomery break Cornerstone tomorrow."

That threat was sufficient to bring John back to his senses. Quick to comply, he blustered, "Yes, suh, Uncle Jacob. I's sorry, suh. I'll listen, I promise."

"I am sorry," Mr. Barlow admonished. "I will listen. We are not nigga dunces in this room. And it is 'I was,' not 'I weren't.'"

John corrected himself. "I am sorry, Uncle Jacob."

At twelve years of age, John had come to idolize James Montgomery, the hired hand Mr. Barlow brought in from North Carolina to break his wild stallion, Cornerstone. Not even Mitch had been able to tame that magnificent mustang. Mr. Montgomery had a reputation for being able to break any wild horse, and, even though Cornerstone still would not take the saddle, he now let the quiet man put a bit in his mouth and lead him around the stable yard. Mr. Montgomery's methods were slower than Mr. Barlow would have liked—the man spent more time whispering to the beast and grooming it than anything else—but Mr. Barlow decided to trust the man, since trying to break the beast had failed. Three of Mr. Barlow's best hands were laid up with broken ribs, and Mitch had dislocated his left shoulder in the bargain. If Mitch could not tame the beast, then something else had to be done.

Mr. Montgomery was a giant of a man—the only man on Mr. Barlow's plantation who stood taller than John. Already six feet tall, John towered over everyone. To actually have to look up to a man was powerfully hypnotic for John. But it was not just the man's height that appealed to him. Mr. Montgomery's disposition was like nothing John had encountered, except among the Negroes. Mr. Montgomery seldom spoke except for quiet whisperings to Cornerstone, or when John asked a question. He usually kept his answers short and circumspect, since John was quite nosy, but when asked about horses, Mr. Montgomery's eyes lit up, and the man became a running narrative.

John grinned wildly as he remembered Mr. Montgomery recounting how he had tamed a black stallion. He had said the stallion taught him he didn't want to break the animal so much as encourage the horse to accept working with him.

"We gots ta do much de same wit' Cornerstone, here," he added. "Keep de animal's spirit intact, John, an' you'll have yourself a lifelong companion an' loyal mount." Mr. Montgomery's voice had a soothing quality.

Someday, John thought, *I's gonna tame wild horses like Mr. Montgomery.*

"You most certainly shall not!" Mr. Barlow's deep voice shocked John. "I am not schooling you to become someone's hired hand. And what did I say about I's?"

John had not realized he had verbalized his last thought aloud.

Emily giggled. She thought John's fascination over Mr. Montgomery quite amusing. For the life of her, she could not understand why John admired him so much. As far as she was concerned, James Montgomery was scruffier than a mangy dog—unshaven, uncouth, and unmannerly—and reeked like a barn nigga. His uncivil nature was evident, as he never once tipped his hat to her or said good morning. She might as well have been invisible as far as James Montgomery was concerned. All he ever did was walk around with that stupid horse, whispering in its ear, or talk to John when the boy was making a pest of himself.

"I's sorry, Uncle Jacob … I mean, I am sorry. I am listenin' … I am …" John stammered out but was unable to finish, as Mr. Barlow had interrupted.

"You will be spending tomorrow running errands for Mitch." Mr. Barlow raised a hand to stop John from protesting. "If your attention improves, I may reconsider allowing you to run errands for Montgomery come Wednesday."

John slumped in his chair. "Yes, suh."

In a commanding tone, Mr. Barlow resumed his lesson. "Now, John, how does Thomas Paine use scripture to prove that a monarchy is essentially an evil form of government?"

John, assuming a studious pose, began his memorized erudition. "Didn't he say them Jews were askin' for a king, and God was mad at 'em for it?"

"Very good!" Mr. Barlow was truly impressed. The boy had a powerful memory. "What scriptures did he use to show this?"

John, biting his tongue and screwing up his lips, arched his eyebrows in a desperate attempt to remember.

Emily took advantage of his pause. Puffing up like a hen, she answered, "The one about the children of Israel being oppressed by the Midianites."

John scowled; it had been his turn. Emily was awful about giving him a chance to answer. If he failed to answer instantly, she would jump in to earn extra marks. Indignantly he burst out, "I was goin' to say that!"

"Word for word?" she replied smugly.

"Uncle Jacob never said we had to memorize it … just understand it. Right, Uncle Jacob?"

"That is correct, my boy, but you should know better by now: you have to have the information on the tip of your tongue if you are to beat my Emily at the track." Racing metaphors were among Mr. Barlow's favorites. Next to boxing, horses were the man's greatest passion. "Now, John, you answer this time. Emily, you wait for him to answer, you hear?"

Emily muttered begrudgingly, "Yes, suh, Daddy," but the icy gleam in her deep blue eyes suggested she would do no such thing.

"Now, John. What was God's response to the Jews' pleas for a king?"

John practically leaped from his chair. "The Lord shall rule over you!" He smiled victoriously, shooting Emily a triumphant glance before continuing, "God said only he could be king, not them fools."

Emily sniffed. "That was just plain easy."

"I ain't finished. Them Jews refused to give up. They went and asked Samuel for a king. When Samuel said no, they got mighty upset. I guess they must've scared Ol' Samuel 'cause he asked God for a king."

The boy's proper tongue had slipped some, but Mr. Barlow overlooked it because of John's answer and the excitement John felt over his lesson. Mr. Barlow decided to turn the tables at this point. "And Emily, how did God respond to the Jews' request for a king?"

John jumped in immediately with the answer. "God said his people had forsaken him and Samuel told them Jews they were sinners."

When it was evident John had said all he could, Emily, swelling with feelings of superiority, recited Thomas Paine word for word: "'That the Almighty hath here entered his—his—?"

Mr. Barlow, hearing the girl's query, helped her along, "protest."

Emily smiled sweetly, "'—protest against monarchial government is true, or the scripture is false.'"

Mr. Barlow passed over John's accomplishments and showered his daughter with compliments. "Very good, little darling. You remembered that perfectly. I am so proud of you."

Emily, shaking her golden locks, shot John a condescending glare. "Thank you, Daddy."

Mr. Barlow's voice had softened substantially with his pleasure at Emily's success. "Let us continue then. Which of you can tell me what other evil Thomas Paine identifies with a monarchial government?"

The two children, desperate to outdo each other, shouted their responses at the same time: "Hereditary succession!"

Mr. Barlow nodded, pleased with their enthusiasm. He encouraged competition between the two, as it made Emily study harder. "And why did Thomas Paine consider hereditary succession to be evil?"

John stood up from his chair, so excited that he knocked it over, his arm raised high in the air. "I know this one, Uncle Jacob. I know this one."

"Then answer, John. But pick up your chair first."

John spoke while he put his chair back in place, but he did not sit down. He stood there staring at Emily, intending her to take every word as an insult. "You can never tell what the child of a king might be like. Why, just because you are born rich doesn't mean you are goin' to be smart. With hereditary succession, you could end up with a simpleton runnin' things."

Emily jumped to her feet, angered by the obvious suggestion. "Are you calling me a simpleton?" Her chair, too, fell by the wayside.

Mr. Barlow had no intention of letting his lesson turn into another brawl between these two hotheads. Competition was one thing, but out and out fighting was unacceptable. "Enough!" His bellowing voice subdued the brewing storm. "Now," he said, quietly but firmly, "pick up your chair, Emily, and both of you sit down."

They did as they were told as fast as foxes ran from hounds.

In a much softer tone, Mr. Barlow addressed his daughter. "Emily, dear, John was not calling you down, now. He was just answering the question, and everything he said was correct."

It was John's turn to feign innocence. "Thank you, Uncle Jacob." He spoke to Mr. Barlow, but his stone gray eyes were firmly set upon Emily.

"But he was looking right at me, Daddy … right at me when he said the word 'simpleton'!" She was so indignant, tears welled in her eyes.

Mr. Barlow, melting at the sight of her tears, gently took her head in his hand, stroking her golden locks. "My poor, sweet Emily. Would it make you feel better if John apologized?"

Emily sniffed and whimpered, "Yes, Daddy." And then, in a more maniacal tone, she added, "And make him say it like he means it." She batted wet eyelashes at Mr. Barlow.

John knew Emily had won this round. He extended her his most sincere insincere apology. "Why, Miss Emily, I am sorry I hurt your feelings by giving Uncle Jacob the right answer." He smiled, and the girl frowned. It was as flattering an apology as one could make, given the situation, while managing to get in yet another jab.

Uncle Jacob was placated and immediately moved forward with the lesson. "Which of you can tell me how *Common Sense* impacted the revolution?"

It was Emily's turn to boast an answer. "Thomas Paine proved how evil the monarchy really was."

Mr. Barlow successfully held back his disappointment. "Yes, my little darling, that is true, but there is so much more to it than that. John?"

"He also told us how mean King George was being to the colonies. He said the British armies were burnin' homes, killin' good folk, and leavin' behind widows and orphans, proving the British will never be fair."

Mr. Barlow, beaming with pleasure, exclaimed, "Excellent, my boy! But there is still more."

"Yes, suh. He said we needed a declaration of independence. Told us how to get it, too. Once folks knew they could be free, they began fightin'."

"Splendid, my boy, absolutely splendid."

John went for the ultimate pleaser. "And that's why you became a patriot. You said you couldn't serve no king who didn't like us so you started fightin' the British in Savannah."

Mr. Barlow beamed with pride. "Right you are, my boy, right you are."

Emily, hoping to bask in some of the acclaim, piped up. "Daddy, didn't Uncle Gabriel die at Lexington? Isn't that is why Thomas Paine's words meant so much to you?"

Mr. Barlow clapped his hands together and announced joyfully, "Splendid! You are both right. John, my boy, you have exonerated yourself. You may run errands for James Montgomery tomorrow."

Jumping out of his chair, John let out a whoop and ran over to hug the man.

Mr. Barlow's laugh reverberated so deeply it actually shook the boy. He ran a rough hand over John's head, tousling his already messed-up curly red hair. "All right, son. That is enough." Even though his words seemed to indicate admonition, his voice was not stern. "Get back to your seat. Lessons are not over yet."

John was more than eager to please the old man now. "That Thomas Paine sure is smart. Right, Uncle Jacob?"

Jacob Barlow grimaced slightly. "He did some good with *Common Sense*, as it helped the patriots by swaying public opinion, but ..."

Emily leaped at the chance to outshine John. "... but he wasn't the only reason people changed their minds, was he, Daddy?"

Mr. Barlow smiled. "No, little darling, he was not. What was the political event that impacted folks here in Georgia?"

Emily smiled sweetly. "The Olive Branch Petition, Daddy."

"That is correct." He patted his daughter on the back. "And do you know why the Olive Branch Petition swayed public opinion?"

Emily twisted her brows in concentration, desperately trying to find the answer in the recesses of her mind. John bounced up and down on his chair, desperate to answer.

"Go ahead, John, as Emily does not seem to know."

"The king wouldn't talk to the man with the petition. Why, he wouldn't even look at him. That really made the colonists mad, didn't it Uncle Jacob?" Jacob Barlow smiled and patted the boy on the back. John laughed in delight at having beaten Emily once more.

Emily, offended, decided to take him down a notch or two. She knew something John was not allowed to know. Daddy had hinted at it earlier. She took on her most studious pose, venturing, "I was thinking, Daddy."

"Yes, little darling?" Mr. Barlow inquired, hoping his daughter would provide another insight they had missed.

"Thomas Paine is not such a good man after all. Is he, Daddy?"

John was confused. "I do not understand."

Emily smirked. "It is simple, stupid—"

"Emily!" Mr. Barlow barked at the girl.

"Sorry, Daddy." She blushed moderately, blinking her eyes to accentuate her lashes.

"Do not apologize to me," Mr. Barlow demanded.

Rolling her eyes, Emily forced out the words, "Sorry, John."

Smirking, John released a satisfied giggle.

Emily's blue eyes smoked with indignation. "As I was saying, Thomas Paine is not a very good man. He wrote a lot of awful awful things, didn't he Daddy?"

"What inflammatory work did the man write, Emily?"

"That awful piece called 'African Slavery in America.'"

"And what did he have to say in that?"

"He said we are sinners for owning niggas."

"Negroes, little girl. We do not speak crudely in this household."

"Sorry, Daddy. He said we are buying folk who had been stolen."

"Ridiculous!" Mr. Barlow growled. "Those Negroes were living like animals back in Africa. They were hunted down the same way we hunt for game."

"And we all know Negroes are not equal to us white folk. Why, they are all stupid. Thomas Jefferson said so."

Here John protested. "But Jefferson said slavery was wrong. He said we ought to free the slaves."

"Yes," Mr. Barlow agreed, with an edge of agitation to his voice. He noted the boy had grouped himself in with the Barlow family, not the slaves. John was getting a bit too above himself because of these lessons. Mr. Barlow might have to work him harder with chores so he would not forget his station in life. "Jefferson did say owning slaves was wrong, but he contradicted himself when he said Negroes are not equal. If Negroes are not equal, then it cannot be a sin to own them, now, can it?"

John could not quite grasp Mr. Barlow's logic, but he responded accordingly. "No, suh." He did not want to risk losing running errands for Mr. Montgomery. "Not if you say so, suh." John blurted his next question out before even thinking; the temptation to read more Thomas Paine was too strong. "Can I read Thomas Paine's essay on African slavery, Uncle Jacob?"

"No, John, you may not."

"Why not?"

"Because I said so."

"But … I just want to understand what y'all are talkin' about."

Mr. Barlow's eyes darkened. "My saying no should be enough for you, John."

John pouted. "But you let Emily read it."

Mr. Barlow's tone became grave, causing John to shrink back in his chair. "Now, boy, you hear me good: you are not to read any more Thomas Paine! Is that understood?"

In a soft whisper, John acquiesced. "Yes, suh." But deep inside, he swore he would find "African Slavery in America" and read it. He might not be colored, but he knew Mr. Barlow owned him and his mama. He never felt like a slave, but his mama often reminded him that they were not like other white folk. He wanted to know what Thomas Paine had to say about slavery. Mr. Barlow had an extensive library, and somewhere along those walls was a forbidden article. Just the fact that he was not allowed made his desire to read it even more powerful.

During lunch the following day, John took his chance. Mr. Barlow was out back, working with Mr. Montgomery. James Montgomery insisted Mr. Barlow learn to talk to the horse, get it comfortable with him before sitting in the saddle. John peeked out the window to make sure Mr. Barlow was occupied before sneaking over to the bookshelf. Emily had told him he would find Thomas Paine's article in the March 1775 *Pennsylvania Journal*. Sure enough, it was right where she had said it would be. Opening the cover, John sat on the floor and immediately began reading.

The opening lines latched themselves to John's eyes, pulling him deep into a world of new beliefs.

"That some desperate wretches should be willing to steal and enslave men by violence and murder for gain," wrote Thomas Paine, "is rather lamentable than strange. But that many civilized, nay, Christianized people should approve, and be concerned in the savage practice, is surprising." Surprising, indeed! Mr. Barlow was a Christian. They attended church every Sunday. Mr. Barlow also insisted on Bible studies as a regular part of John and Emily's learning, yet he disagreed with Paine's notion that slavery was evil. Contradiction swirled inside John. He could not make out what to think.

Suddenly he heard the library door slam open. John leaped to his feet and swung around to see a disgruntled Mr. Barlow.

"What are you up to, boy?"

John stammered, "I's ... ah ..."

Mr. Barlow was in no mood for explanations or excuses. He was too busy for this nonsense—he was planning to race Cornerstone next season, and he still could not sit in the saddle. He had only come to confirm that Emily's report was true. He swore he would whop Emily if she had lied to him. Mr. Barlow grabbed the magazine from John's hand. The title of the article confirmed Emily's accusation. Mr. Barlow growled, "I told you not to read any more Thomas Paine ... did I not?"

"Y-y-yes, s-suh."

Mr. Barlow shook the magazine at John accusingly. "*And what is this?*"

John, taken aback by the man's aggressive tone, remained silent.

Mr. Barlow's voice dropped in volume, but not in its menacing tone. "Answer me when I speak to you, boy!"

Gasping like a fish out of water, John struggled to respond. "A-A-Afri ... A-A-Afri ..." Tears welled, his cheeks burned, and his heart pounded so hard, he thought it would burst through his chest. "U-Uncle Jacob, suh ... I's ... I's ... I's sorry, s-suh."

Mr. Barlow's bellowing voice stormed down on the boy. "Did I ask for an apology, boy?"

"N-no, s-suh."

Punctuating each word like a blow to the stomach, Mr. Barlow continued, "I. Asked. You. What. This. Is!"

Try as he might to control his tears, John started to bawl.

Showing no mercy, Mr. Barlow walked over to the study table and slammed the magazine down.

The subsequent hollow boom made John leap.

With eyes of fury, Mr. Barlow turned to confront the boy. "Run outside and cut me a switch."

John's eyes bulged with fear.

Mr. Barlow took one slow, definitive step. "Now!"

John ran outside as quickly as his feet could take him, grabbing a knife from the kitchen on his way out. Not even stopping to notice the look of concern on his mama's face, John raced out the back door, running for the nearest bush. Studying the branches, John searched for one that was thin and supple enough for Mr. Barlow's purposes. He knew it had to whiz like a whip and inflict welts. John made his selection, hoping it would meet with Mr. Barlow's approval. If it failed inspection, Mr. Barlow might resort to using his fists. John had seen the way the man punched the bag he had hanging in the barn. That scared John more than anything. He shivered in the wind as he stared back toward the big house. John could see the old man's back in the window. So much anger seemed to ripple there. Although he feared going back inside, John knew the repercussions of trying to hide would be worse. With grim determination muddied by fear, John quickly made his way back into the big house.

His mother, standing by the back door, was a blend of consternation and concern. "What did you do, John? What did you do to anger the man so? I haven't seen him so mad since Ol' Henry tried runnin' away ten years ago. We heard him yellin' all the way into the kitchen."

"I were just readin', Mama. Honest." His eyes pleaded with her. It was bad enough Mr. Barlow was mad. He could not bear to have her angry, too.

Mr. Barlow's voice thundered. "Get in here, boy."

John leaped at the sound. "I gotta go, Mama."

Evelyn Connolley shooed her son off. "You run now. Don't you keep him waitin'."

John raced into the library, coming to a sudden stop to avoid running into Mr. Barlow.

Mr. Barlow snatched the switch out of John's hand, motioning with it to the window. Reaching inside his jacket pocket, he took out a small knife. Slowly, methodically, he stripped the branch of twigs and leaves. His eyes, constantly glaring, shoved John's back against the window. By now most folks working round the house had heard John was getting a whopping. More than a dozen eyes watched through the library window. Mr. Barlow took no note of them. "You take one big step back from that window, boy, then drop your drawers and bend over. Hold on to the windowsill to steady yourself."

John sucked back the tears and replied meekly, "Yes, suh." He closed his eyes, so he would not have to see the snickers of all the folks looking in on him. He leaned forward, clutching his fingers tightly around the sill.

"Count off every switch, son." There was a hint of regret in Mr. Barlow's voice, but he kept a tight rein on it. Discipline always came first.

John shouted a number for every switch until he reached twenty. His buttocks and thighs were reddened with welts, his eyes swollen from crying.

Emily snickered. She had watched the whole thing.

John slowly bent down to pull up his trousers. The rough cotton stung his behind.

Mr. Barlow's voice remained firm. "You hurry and do up your trousers, boy. I am giving you over to Mitch to work you for the rest of the week. There will be no more working with Mr. Montgomery for you."

John turned to face Mr. Barlow. New tears sprang from disappointment. "Uncle Jacob, please don't make me work with Mitch. He's real mean, an' I's got so much ta learn from Mr. Montgomery. Please! Uncle Jacob, please!"

Mr. Barlow stiffened, swung John around, and smacked a hard hand against his bottom.

John howled at the harsh hit against an already swollen and sensitive backside.

"You get out there and start running errands for Mitch this instant, you hear?"

John, stumbling as he ran, bumped into Emily on his way out.

"Watch where you are going, you unmannerly lout. Daddy, did you see ..."

That was all John heard of Emily's ranting. He ran as hard as he could to find Mitch. He knew the chances of locating the man were nearly impossible, but if he did not try, Mr. Barlow would switch him again.

Ol' Henry, grabbing John's arm as he headed out, whispered quickly into his ear, "Mitch be workin' de nawth field."

John did not even take the time to thank the old Negro. He just raced around the house, running like a wild colt. The north field meant digging rice canals. He was going to have to do this all week. It was hard, muddy work. Mud weighed a man down and brought him to the door of exhaustion. Maybe, if he were good, though, Mr. Barlow might forgive him and let him come back to the stables.

Tears spilled from John's eyes over not getting to work with James Montgomery. John wiped away the tears, trying to hold his head high. If Mitch saw him bawling, he would work John even harder. For some reason John could never figure out, the overseer did not like him much.

*　　　*　　　*　　　*

That night, as he lay in bed, John's mama came into his room for a visit. Her voice was soft and cautious. "John, you asleep?"

"No, Mama."

"I want to talk to you."

"Yes, Mama."

Sitting by his side, Evelyn ran her fingers through John's curly red hair. "Mr. Barlow didn't say anythin' to me about what happened."

"I were just readin', Mama. I swear."

Annoyed, Evelyn slapped her boy across the head. "Do you think I'm a fool? Mr. Barlow wouldn't give you no whuppin' over readin'. He's been teachin' you to read since you were two years old."

"I know, Mama."

"Then why'd he beat you?"

"I disobeyed 'im."

Evelyn frowned.

"I were readin' somethin' he told me not to."

"Why'd you disobey him like that?" Evelyn was cross. Initially she believed it had all been some misunderstanding, and now her son was telling her he was at fault.

"Him an' Emily were talkin' about it, an' I wanted to read it, is all."

"But he told you not to read it, didn't he?"

"Yes, Mama."

"Then that meant you ought not to have read it."

"I know, Mama."

"Why'd you read it then?"

"I wanted to know what it said, is all."

"Know what?"

"Why Thomas Paine don't like slavery."

Sucking air through tightly drawn lips, Evelyn clasped her hands in prayer. "Those are dangerous ideas, John." She grabbed her boy and shook him vigorously. "You are never to touch that article again, you hear?"

"I's sorry, Mama."

"An' if Uncle Jacob tells you that you are not to read somethin', then you are not to read it!"

"Yes, Mama."

"I sure hope that whuppin' taught you a lesson."

"Yes, Mama." John could not help himself. He needed to know why he was denied knowledge Emily was allowed to possess. "But why is it wrong, Mama?"

"You know Mr. Barlow owns us."

"Yes, Mama. I know."

"You know you are his property."

"Yes."

"You know that man saved my life."

"Yes, Mama. I know."

"And yours, too."

"Yes, Mama."

"Only the good Lord knows where we'd be if he hadn't purchased me."

"I know, Mama."

"Your granddaddy had me up for sale like I were a stinkin' nigga."

"I know, Mama."

"Naked as a bird plucked and ready for cookin'. Oh, John, it was a horrible thing."

"I know, Mama. I's sorry … truly I am." John, feeling her anguish, cried along with her. The poor boy was riddled with guilt. Although there was no explaining it, he felt responsible for her downfall.

"There were men leerin' at me, John. If it hadn't been for Mr. Barlow …" She looked down at John as if she were revealing the story for the first time. "Did you know Mr. Barlow scolded my daddy an' told him he was wrong to sell me?"

"Yes, Mama."

Evelyn held John in a swaying hug. "Oh, John. We cain't be makin' that man angry. We've got to do what we's told."

"I know, Mama. I know."

"Promise me, son … promise me you will never disobey Mr. Barlow again."

"Mama, I cain't …"

Desperate, Evelyn tightened her grip. "John, you gotta promise ta always do as Mr. Barlow says. Promise me you will never lie ta him. Promise me you will keep your word." Evelyn demanded, "Promise me!"

Struggling for breath, John muttered words that would haunt him forever: "I promise, Mama."

Refusing to release John, Evelyn insisted, "Say the words for me, John. I've gotta hear you say 'em."

"I promise to obey Uncle Jacob, Mama."

"And?"

John sighed, "to never lie ta him."

"And?" His mother was relentless.

"An' to keep my word."

Evelyn was crying outright now. She loosened her grip but continued hugging John. "You are a good boy, John. I love you."

"I love you, too, Mama."

The door creaked open. Mr. Barlow smiled down at the pair. "Did I hear y'all correctly, Evelyn? Did our boy just promise to never disobey me again?"

Evelyn looked up with hopeful eyes. "Yes, suh, Mr. Barlow. He sure did."

Mr. Barlow's laugh rumbled like thunder on the horizon. "Evelyn, my dear, you are free to call me Jacob when we are alone." Mr. Barlow strolled casually over to the bed. He placed a hand gently on Evelyn's shoulder. His fingers squeezed her muscles. Even though he was speaking to John, he was looking down at the woman. "John, I will take you at your word ... and if you work hard all week, I will let you work with James Montgomery on his last day."

John gulped back the tears and muttered, "Thank you, Uncle Jacob." There was something about the way Uncle Jacob's eyes leered over John's mama that bothered him.

"Evelyn, I think it is time we let the boy sleep. He has a long day ahead of him tomorrow. And if I know Mitch, he will work John hard."

Although sad, Evelyn allowed Mr. Barlow to lead her out of the room. John watched them depart. He noticed Mr. Barlow's hand slipping around his mama's waist as the door closed. John had seen Mr. Barlow touch his mama before, but not in this manner. Something was wrong, but he did not know what.

Within seconds the door squeaked open, announcing Emily. "Hello, John." Her drawl dragged the salutation out to sarcastic proportions.

John did not want to talk to her now ... not after her snickering while he got switched. He gave her his worst scowl.

Emily was not taking any hints. "Do you know why Daddy beat you?"

John grunted, "I know."

"You know he owns you, right?"

"I know!"

"You know why your granddaddy sold your mama?"

John shot her a scornful look. "I know. Now leave me alone!"

Laughing, Emily continued with her taunting. "Your mama done laid with a nigga. You's a nigga, boy. Daddy beat you cause you's a nigga." Her mockery of a slave's accent added even greater insult.

"Ain't true!" John threw his head under the pillow and started crying. "Leave me be."

Emily was having way too much fun to stop now. "All the slaves say your granddaddy caught your mama with a nigga." Emily luxuriated over each word, adding to John's shame. "Your mama an' a nigga dog. When your granddaddy caught 'em, he shot the blackie in the head an' sold your mama." Emily swayed with victory. "You know what they do ta white women who have nigga babies? They turns them into slaves. Your mama's a slave, 'cause she had a nigga baby. Your mama's a slave 'cause she had you!" Turning to leave, Emily made sure to get in one final blow. "You's a mulatto, boy. D'ya knows what a mulatto is? Part human, part nigga."

"Shut up! Shut up!"

Emily's chin lifted. Staring down at John, she punched hard with her words. "You are a mulatto, and someday I am going to own you." The door closed, cutting off Emily's taunting laugh.

John shook under the covers. He knew his mama's story—some of it, anyway. Evelyn had fallen in love with a British soldier named John Connolley. She had even named her son after him. John's thoughts swirled in indignation. *Emily were lying, not Mama! Mama wouldn't lie. She wouldn't! Even Uncle Jacob told the same story. Granddaddy shot Daddy 'cause he were the enemy, and it were war. Daddy had been a lieutenant in the British army. Granddaddy sold Mama 'cause he thought she were a traitor. But she weren't no traitor. No, suh! Mama never shared no military secrets. She were in love, that's all.*

John's understanding of the story, though simple, was true. Evelyn had even taken John Connolley's name after she was sold. Mr. Barlow let her change it, and her father made no complaint—it broke the ties of blood that bound them. She would have, if it had been possible, married John Connolley. They had planned to go back to England after the war. Evelyn always said her and John's life would have been different if her father had not found her and Colonel Connolley together.

No, suh! John scoffed. *My daddy weren't no nigga. I ain't no nigga neither.* John knew he was not mulatto, but the accusation still shamed him to the core.

It was not just being called colored that worried John. He remembered Mr. Barlow's hand slipping around his mama's waist. What Emily had said brought back memories … memories that stirred his discomfort. He had forgotten this; it happened when he was little, on the first night he was made to sleep alone.

Mama had said he was too big to be sleeping with her. "Uncle Jacob has made you up a room of your own," she had announced proudly. But John had not wanted to be alone. His new room was big and dark and cold. He wanted his mama. He wanted to crawl into bed and be warmed by her. But when he snuck into her room, he saw Mr. Barlow on top of her. His mama's hand was clutching the bed board, and Mr. Barlow was rocking back and forth, grunting and moaning.

Frightened, John had yelled out, "Mama!" Evelyn and Mr. Barlow looked up at him. Mr. Barlow's eyes were wild and full of fire; John's mama looked frightened.

Mr. Barlow had growled, "Get out of here, boy!"

His mama's voice had quivered as if she were about to cry. "Back to your room, John."

"Now!" Mr. Barlow had roared.

John had turned on his heels and run. Having leaped into his new, foreign bed, John hid himself under the covers, much as he was doing now. It did not help knowing what Mr. Barlow was up to. His mind swirled with too many images: Thomas Paine's words, Mama's sad eyes, Mr. Barlow's lustful rocking, the switching, Emily's teasing laugh, and the face of a man who, according to his mama, looked just like him being shot in the head.

CHAPTER 24

▼

SILENT WHISPER

John woke with a start. Mr. Barlow was seated beside him. Before he could utter a word, pain shot through him, searing his chest. It felt as if a dozen knives were stabbing him. Agony distorted his features. Mr. Barlow leaned forward, putting his hands on John's shoulders to still him. "Relax, son. It is going to hurt, but you need to breathe slow and easy."

John tried to control his breathing, but the pain and the constriction bandage made it difficult. Slowly he managed some semblance of control.

"There you go. Nice and easy, son. Nice, easy breaths. You wait here. I will fetch Miss Katherine. She has some morphine for you." Mr. Barlow got up and left the room.

John took a moment to get his bearings. He was not sure where he was or what had transpired. *Miss Katherine?* He must be at the MacPhearsons'. *Morphine? No!* Images of a past addiction haunted him. Trying to sit up caused pain to slash through his head and chest. *What happened? Why am I here? What caused all this pain?* John muttered an oath and grunted. The memory of the attack returned so suddenly, it caused him to spasm. It was as if the blows were still raining down upon him.

Miss Katherine arrived and immediately administered morphine.

John tried to stop her, but he was too weak. Before passing out, John looked up into her eyes. As his hand gently caressed her cheek, he whispered, "So beautiful."

Katherine touched her cheek. She was stunned by the gesture and the passion of John's words.

"He is a good man, Miss Katherine."

Mr. Barlow's words startled Katherine. She turned to face the man, her voice a hiss: "You ruined him." Tears burned, and she quickly turned her back to Jacob Barlow. "Well, at least he has finally come to." Katherine fought for composure. "That is a good sign." Looking at the needle in her hand, she added, "The doctor said the morphine would likely put him out again … but that is also good. He needs rest. Next time, though, we are going to have to get some broth or rice gruel in him first. I will take over watching him, suh. You may return to your room now." That suggestion was issued so sternly that Mr. Barlow quietly turned and left the room without a word. As soon as he departed, Katherine sat down to study John's face.

CHAPTER 25

▼

JOHN'S PRAYER

"Lord, help me. I am so full of anger and hatred right now. It is uncontrollable. I fear I may do something untoward. Help me learn forgiveness like you had on the cross. How did you do it, Lord? How could you forgive them men, Lord? The ones who beat you, who whipped you, who deliberately hung you on the cross to die? You suffered for all of us. You died to forgive our sins ... but my sins are great, Lord. I cannot forgive. I hate Junior for what he has done to me. I hate him for taking Katherine. I hate him for his arrogance and mean-spirited nature. I don't care that his daddy ridicules him, or that he was promised to Katherine since birth. I hate him, Lord! I hate him, and I want him dead. Yet you did not wish death on the man who nailed you to the cross. Even as you were dying, you extended forgiveness to the thief who hung next to you. Where, Lord? Where did you get your strength?

"God our Father, help me.

"Lord, Uncle Jacob asked for forgiveness today. He begged for the love we once shared, but I refused to listen. I refused to grant him a single wish. When he left the room, he looked older than I had ever seen him. I felt no pity, no remorse. How can I reignite those feelings of love after all he has said and done?

"I cain't, Lord. I just cain't.

"In Genesis, God our Father says 'Forgive, I pray thee now, the trespass of thy brethren, and their sin; for they did unto thee evil.' But how, Lord? How can I learn to forgive?

"I hear you reply in Exodus, 'Yet now, if thou wilt forgive their sin—; and if not, blot me, I pray thee, out of thy book which thou hast written.'"

John shook his head. "Mark spoke wisely when he said, 'And when you stand praying, forgive, if ye have ought against any: that your father also which is in heaven may forgive you your trespasses.'"

John wept. And through his tears came the remembrance of a young boy sitting on a gentleman's lap, listening to tales of glory and patriotism and the birth of a nation. He recalled the days of fishing and horseback riding. Every night his Uncle Jacob had knelt by his bed and prayed with him. That image shone brightest in John's mind. Prior to John's fourteenth birthday, Mr. Barlow had never missed a single night's prayer. Regardless of all he had done, deep inside, in his heart of hearts, John knew Mr. Barlow loved him. He knew the old man was truly remorseful.

"Perhaps over time, Lord, I can learn to forgive. I can learn to love again. But not now, Lord. Don't ask it of me now."

CHAPTER 26

▼

THE GAMES WE PLAY

A day of games had been established, ostensibly in honor of Mr. Barlow's visit. Mr. Richardson was invited, of course, due to his long-standing relationship with the great man. All the gentlemen who had attended Mrs. MacPhearson's dinner party were also on the list, as well as a few others, so as not to suggest the true motive of the event. No one suspected, though, as it was a fine opportunity for the gentlemen of Laurel Creek to entertain themselves with poker, chess, and the like. Angus MacPhearson always had the finest Scotch whiskey to offer, and the sweetest cigars. Even Mr. Barlow, who was used to refined society, said as much. A slight haze had already formed in the room from all the smoke.

Minds were matched evenly at the various tables, but Jacob Barlow and Mr. Crawford played the game that inspired the most interest, at the chess table. A small ring of onlookers was intent on the diversion of these two gentlemen. Although his opponent was an adept player, Mr. Barlow took full opportunity to explain the most basic of rules to Frank Crawford when he nearly blundered.

Mr. Barlow smiled. The opportunity presented to him was too good to be true. "No, suh," he loudly pronounced, ensuring all in the room could hear. "The king may not advance against a player that is defended. Note, suh, how my rook is defended by my bishop." A great deal of laughter was shared over this. Mr. Crawford was a man to boast; to see him so easily deposed proved to be the delight of all.

Mr. Crawford cursed at having missed such an obvious detail.

"A king need always be careful of his attack," Mr. Barlow went on. "Without knowing it, you may just as well be constructing your own demise."

Mr. Crawford took a moment to study the man before him. Mr. Barlow's eyes suggested a lecture beyond the rudimentary skills of chess. There was something about him that looked ready for attack. "I assure, you, suh," Mr. Crawford replied most congenially, deciding then and there not to lose. "I shall not make such an error again."

"Without warning, good suh, you surely would have lost." There was a slight pause before, and an emphasis placed on, the word "lost."

"Indeed, suh," Mr. Crawford conceded. "You are a formidable opponent."

"Remember that," Mr. Barlow added most pointedly. "To be sure," he continued quite loudly, "the same should be said to the renegades who attacked my son ... for a son I do consider him. He may not be of my blood, but he is of my heart." Mr. Barlow's eyes locked horns with Frank Crawford's. "I intend," he warned, "to exact revenge in the most ruthless fashion."

Mr. Crawford blanched, shot back the last of his whiskey, resigned the game, and excused himself in order to join his son at cards.

"Games of chance, Mr. Crawford," Mr. Barlow added as Mr. Crawford walked away, "are the deadliest games of all."

Although Frank Crawford's step skipped slightly, he did not stop moving. Only the most discerning eye caught the slight inaction. Angus MacPhearson shook his head. His friend Mr. Crawford had gone too far this time. He disapproved entirely, but still he knew he must save him ... for his daughter's sake.

CHAPTER 27

▼

MAINTAINING DECORUM

John struggled to hold his composure; it was a difficult task when set against Miss Katherine MacPhearson's temper. Anger clenched John's chest and made even the shallowest breath agonizing. Regardless of the fury he felt, he was still astounded by Katherine's beauty. Anger had not disfigured her features the way it did most women's. Every lineament was highlighted against the fiery aspect of her eyes. As she whipped around, her loose hair leaped and swirled like flames. A strand caught in her mouth caused John's heart to skip a beat. Katherine noticed the intensity in his eyes—ocean blue swirling around stone gray. She turned away to hide her blush.

"At least allow me to inject you with some morphine to help make travel more comfortable." John's refusal caused her to spin back. "You are insufferable, suh! You cannot convince me that you are not in throes. You have six broken ribs and can barely draw your breath! Your head still has a bump the size of ... of ..."— she shook it in his face—"of my fist."

"I assure you, Miss MacPhearson, you might as well hit me with your fist, as your yellin' does little to assist the pain." Katherine lifted her hands in the air and screamed. John winced. He was in considerable pain, and her yelling was like a sledgehammer against his head. On top of that, his ribs ached, and the bullet wound still burned. Some relief would be gratifying, but John knew from past experience that too much morphine was dangerous. It felt too good, required more every time he used it, and soon became essential. The agony that had ensued when he was forced to taper off the last time was not something he wanted to experience again.

Still, that old desire had crept inside him, making his intestines shake. It was harder to deny morphine than anything else. That and Katherine's explosive refusal to accept his decision made maintaining decorum extremely difficult.

"You are absolutely impossible!" Katherine shouted. "Have you no common sense? Have you not listened to one word the doctor said? If you will not take morphine, then you will not leave today!"

John chose a point on the wall at which to direct his attention. "Miss MacPhearson, my decision is made. Matthew and Mr. Barlow will arrive shortly. Please, leave me rest until then."

"You foolish man!" Katherine turned, slamming the door behind her. She stormed down the stairs, pounding each foot to call forth her father long before her shrill voice cried out, "Daddy!"

Angus MacPhearson was already in the lobby, greeting Mr. Barlow. Matthew bowed to him and turned to head upstairs.

Katherine slammed a finger against Matthew's chest and commanded, "You hold it right there."

Matthew looked to Mr. Barlow for permission. "Go along, Matthew," Mr. Barlow insisted.

Avoiding eye contact with Katherine, Matthew darted past her on his way upstairs. Her wrath was something he knew to avoid.

Wheeling all her temper against Mr. Barlow, Katherine chided, "You, suh, are not responsible for Mr. Connolley's health. That is my duty! Your dear son, as you claim him to be, has only rested four days, an insufficient number to allow for arduous travel. The roads are gutted by the storm, and Mr. Connolley will only suffer further injury by such a hazardous journey. I cannot even convince him to take relief to make the trip less grievous. Do not take him home, suh."

Angus MacPhearson turned to gently reprimand his daughter. "Katherine, you cannot expect the man to remain here now. Not after your announcement."

Katherine persisted, "A man's sensibilities—"

Mr. Barlow cut her off. "Miss MacPhearson, we must look to the man's dignity at a time like this."

"The man's dignity!" Katherine replied incredulously. "Now there is something which you have taken great care to preserve, have you not, Mr. Barlow?" Jacob Barlow reddened at her accusation.

The tone of her voice, so clearly caustic, caused Mr. MacPhearson to flush. "Katherine! How dare you speak to Mr. Barlow in that fashion! He is a guest in my home."

Regardless of her father's censure, Katherine continued to glare at Mr. Barlow in stern judgment.

"Apologize this instant!" Mr. MacPhearson demanded.

Before Katherine was given opportunity to obey, John called out, "Mr. Barlow." He stood at the head of the stairwell, using Matthew as a crutch.

Jacob Barlow, forgetting every insult, turned to John. Pleased to see him standing and looking almost healthy, he called up, "Son." Gesturing, he issued an order. "Bring him down, Matthew. Slowly now … there is no need to rush."

Pain etched into John's face as he descended. Unable to bear the sight, Katherine turned, swishing her skirt and slamming the dining hall door behind her.

Angus MacPhearson flushed with embarrassment over his daughter's coarse behavior. "Mr. Barlow, I am truly sorry for what my daughter said. I have never before heard her utter such atrocities or seen her act in so vulgar a manner."

"Please, do not fret yourself, Mr. MacPhearson," Mr. Barlow replied most amicably. "The young lady is clearly distressed over Mr. Connolley's sudden departure. She is quite correct: travel at such an early stage in his recovery is dangerous."

John remained quiet on the subject. He had heard Katherine's admonitions against Mr. Barlow, and she was right. Yet recent events had shown Mr. Barlow in a different light. He had sat at John's bedside constantly, and John saw in his actions the man he once loved as a child.

Yesterday evening had been most astonishing. Mr. Barlow had repented. His expression of guilt was overwhelming. Through honest tears, he insisted all debts between them were paid. John believed Mr. Barlow had finally come to accept him as a man, not property. When Mr. Barlow first saw John, he had feared the worst. Katherine's admonition coupled that revelation with waves of guilt. Mr. Barlow sent a letter by messenger to his lawyer, requesting he draw up all the necessary papers to grant John's freedom. Mr. Barlow pressed the urgency of the situation, and the papers had arrived the very next day. Before Mr. Barlow presented them to John, though, he made one request.

"Another condition, suh?" John's sarcasm was biting. "Is that truly freedom?"

Mr. Barlow flushed. "I ask only that you call me Uncle Jacob again."

"If I refuse?"

"We sign anyway."

"Then we sign," was all John would say.

After all documents were complete, John expressed his gratitude but still refused to call the man Uncle Jacob. He was free, a fact he could appreciate, but too much had happened between the two men. The harsh treatment he had suffered under Mr. Barlow was something he would never forget.

When John inquired as to the old man's change of heart, Mr. Barlow said it was the fear of losing his boy, the fear that he had let a good man live and die in chains. John mused over how many good men, and women, Mr. Barlow continued to let live and die in chains, but he knew there was little he could do for them. *Matthew*, he thought. *At least I can help free Matthew.*

John turned to Mr. MacPhearson and bowed slightly, grunting in the attempt. "Your kind hospitality is truly appreciated. I will send Patrick home to you upon my return."

The two men shook hands. "That is not necessary, Mr. Connolley. Patrick tells me how much he enjoys working your land. He says Matthew here is one of the finest field Negroes he has ever had the pleasure to oversee. I am afraid Matthew has made Patrick's job far too easy for him."

Matthew kept his head low so as not to show any reaction, though he felt the weight of the compliment.

John, too, smiled at Mr. MacPhearson's praise and extended it. "Matthew is a good man."

Mr. Barlow raised a brow over that and wondered at such a change in a man whom he had nearly hung.

John continued, "I do appreciate your son's assistance. It is kindness indeed, beyond expectation. If there is anything I can do in return, please ask it of me."

"Indeed, Mr. Connolley." Angus MacPhearson looked grave, not wanting to bring up such a tender subject—one that had rushed the man out of his home—but the need was too great. "There is one favor I wish to impose on you."

"No imposition, I am sure," John replied amicably.

"As you know," Mr. MacPhearson began, "my daughter is to wed Frank Crawford Jr."

John closed his eyes and lowered his head. He knew only too well. As the reason for Katherine's choice burned inside his mind, he fought back all the old hatred. As good as it felt to be free from the bonds of slavery, he knew he would always suffer from its consequences. "Yes, suh, I am aware."

"I am sensible of your feelings for my daughter, suh. Recent events have shown me you are the better man, regardless of your legitimacy."

Mr. Barlow reddened, unsure how much Mr. MacPhearson knew. Katherine MacPhearson had promised to keep their secret, but the topic of discussion was precariously close to the truth. *Miss Katherine would not have revealed the truth,* Barlow assured himself. *Mr. MacPhearson must think John is my illegitimate offspring.*

"Still, my daughter has made her choice, and as unsound as it may be, I gave her my solemn word she would be free to marry the man of her choosing."

"I understand, suh. I never supposed myself proper enough to marry such a lady."

"Nonsense!" Jacob Barlow bellowed. "Why, the girl is a fool not to—"

Before he could finish his tirade against Katherine, John cut him off. "Mr. Barlow, please."

"I agree my daughter has made a foolish choice," Angus MacPhearson interjected, "but it is her choice to make." With a sigh of regret, Mr. MacPhearson pursued his expectation. "Mr. Connolley, I wish to ask you to exert your influence over Mr. Barlow here. Beg him not to pursue his act of vengeance against the Crawford family."

"That will not do!" Mr. Barlow replied. "No legal course of action can be taken, so I shall exact my own revenge."

"It is understandable, suh, that you should wish retribution … as would I, had it been Patrick." Mr. MacPhearson turned back to John. "But Mr. Connolley, surely you do not wish to see my daughter live a life of penury, which is what Mr. Barlow will reduce her to through the fate of her future husband."

"Indeed, suh." John nodded. "I wish no such fate for your daughter. No action will be taken against the Crawford family."

"Do not presume to speak for me!" Mr. Barlow's autocratic sensibility had returned.

John, having already lost too much to Mr. Barlow's control and experiencing a new sense of confidence as a result of his freedom, returned Mr. Barlow's glare. "It is you, suh, who presumes to speak for me. You wish to act on my behalf by cutting off all trade available to the Crawfords. Although I care little for the fate of the men who attacked me in so cowardly a fashion, I do care for the fate of Mr. MacPhearson's daughter."

Angus MacPhearson sighed audibly. "Thank you, Mr. Connolley."

"But is there no recourse to be had!" Mr. Barlow cried. "We cannot go to the law, for there is no tangible evidence. Mrs. Crawford swears the two men rode back to Pine Grove with her, and all three retired early. If you forbid my taking action in the business world, what recourse will there be?"

"Perhaps," said Mr. MacPhearson, "you could beat Junior on a playing field dear to his heart. Every year he races his gelding, Tenet, in the fall derby, and every year he wins. I have seen your stallion, Mr. Connolley. It is a fine horse, and with it, you could easily beat Junior."

"An excellent idea!" Mr. Barlow was pleased. Outside of boxing, horse racing was his favorite hobby. "Why, I will even place a bet in your favor, John. I know Cornerstone's worth better than Mr. MacPhearson here, and daresay he could still win against any horse."

John shook his head. "Mr. Barlow, you know Cornerstone is too old to race anymore. That is why you retired him two years ago. Besides, my size and weight would only further hinder him."

"Pshaw!" cried Mr. Barlow. "Cornerstone is only twenty … and ten times stronger than most horses half his age. He will beat young Junior's gelding, even with you on top. Or," Mr. Barlow added with a smile, "I could bring you Cornerstone the third. I just started racing that young stallion, and he has proven his worth in gold."

John remained adamant. "No, suh, that will not do."

Both Mr. MacPhearson and Mr. Barlow responded, "Why not?"

"Early this spring, the day I bought the ol' ox from you, suh—"

Mr. MacPhearson blushed at having taken advantage of one he now counted as a friend.

"—I overheard Mr. Crawford threaten a small, black child with hanging if Junior failed to win that race. His threat was sincere, suh. I will not enter that race."

Jacob Barlow grunted and was about to speak.

John politely cut him off by adding, "Even if I were persuaded to race against my better judgment, I would purposely lose."

"Indeed, I believe you would," agreed Mr. MacPhearson. He knew his old friend Frank Crawford too well to doubt Mr. Crawford's word in such a circumstance. "Such a loss," added Angus MacPhearson, "would be a worthy accomplishment. Such a loss I would celebrate more so than a win."

"They killed your dog," Jacob Barlow added, hoping to play upon John's strong attachment to the creature.

"Indeed, Amos meant a great deal to me, and I would like very much to crush the man who shot him. However, the importance of my dog does not outweigh Miss Katherine's future. Her comfort must be seen to."

"Is there to be no recourse?" Mr. Barlow lamented.

"None, suh," John replied.

"If I must." Suddenly the old man smiled. A thought had dawned on him. "There is still one way ... and surely you cannot counter this prospect."

"And what might that be?" John inquired.

"Fight Junior in the ring."

"A capital idea," Mr. MacPhearson replied.

"I swore I would never step into the ring again, suh, and I will not."

"But why?" Mr. Barlow demanded. "Your stubborn persistence is angering me beyond reason."

"I took no joy in that life. I fought too many men who were no match for me. And Junior, you must both agree, would have no chance against me. It would not be a fair fight, suh."

Angus MacPhearson smiled. More and more, he liked this young man. More and more, he felt the folly of his daughter's rash decision. *Why*, he asked himself for the hundredth time, *did Katie make such a foolish choice? If she only knew Junior's role in the attack on Mr. Connolley's person ... but the good man has refused her that confidence.* Angus MacPhearson agreed to the secret, as Katherine could never be happy in her marriage if she knew what Junior had done.

"Fair?" Mr. Barlow ejaculated. "Fair? Was the brutal attack against you fair?"

"No, suh, it was not. I, however, do not wish to stoop to their level. To challenge Junior, to step into the ring with him, would only dishonor me. Folks would look on me as monstrous and cruel. Where is a man's vengeance in that?"

"Surely you want retribution?" Mr. Barlow insisted.

"I thought long and hard upon retribution, suh, as I lay confined to my bed. Without a doubt, I would like to see Junior suffer for what he has done to me, but I can see no honorable way to procure it, short of your attack in trade. At least in the business world, Mr. Crawford, who is your equal, would have a chance."

"You are a more than generous man, Mr. Connolley," Angus MacPhearson replied. "And wise. It is an honor to call you friend."

"Thank you, suh." John's gratitude was earnest. "I should, however, take my leave. I have imposed upon you too long."

"Be sure, Mr. Connolley, you are always welcome in my home."

After the gentlemen left, Angus MacPhearson turned and made his way into the dining room, where he found his daughter waiting patiently for him. "My girl," he said sternly, "I am not impressed with you." He studied her gravely. "Have you anything to say in your defense?"

Her only reply was, "No, suh, Daddy." She could not defend herself without revealing Mr. Connolley's secret. Katherine turned to face her father with eyes that were red and swollen.

Mr. MacPhearson fought back the urge to comfort her.

Katherine lowered her head in shame.

Sighing as he sat down in the hard pine chair at the head of the table, Mr. MacPhearson proceeded to lecture his daughter. "You behaved like a child in there, Katherine."

Katherine's chest clenched, and tears welled in her eyes. Her father never called her Katherine … except when disappointed.

"If you were still the child you were acting like, I would take you over my knee this instant. But you are too old to be punished like a baby."

Katherine, bewildered, stammered, "Daddy, I …"

"I what? No, do not say a word. You have let me down, Katherine. Your mama and I taught you better than that."

"But Daddy," Katherine protested. "He is an awful man."

"I do not care what you may think of Mr. Barlow. He was a guest in our home, and we treat our guests with respect."

"I know, suh." Katherine was truly embarrassed.

"No, Katherine, you are a lady now, and I cannot spank away an adult's disgrace. The fact is, Katherine, you have to live with what you have done. Your shame must be your punishment." Mr. MacPhearson stood and studied his daughter gravely before abandoning her to her thoughts.

Tears flooded Katherine's eyes. Her harsh words, though true, had shamed her father. His disappointment in her was punishment enough.

CHAPTER 28

▼

A BATTLE OF WILLS ENSUES

The journey to John's plantation was arduous. By the time the carriage pulled up in front of John's home, he had passed out from pain. His gray complexion was so disconcerting that, as soon as John was settled into bed, Patrick was sent racing to town to fetch Dr. Odland.

The doctor's arrival did little to satisfy Mr. Barlow's concerns. Seated on the bed next to John, Dr. Odland reiterated all of Katherine's arguments for leaving John at the MacPhearsons' and upbraided Mr. Barlow severely for moving the man. He understood John's reasons for not wanting the morphine but insisted John take the medication until his ribs had a chance to heal. Mr. Barlow was put in charge of ensuring John took his alleviate as ordered.

"He is not to be given a choice in the matter, suh. This comes straight from his doctor. You make sure and tell him that." Because they no longer had Katherine to administer the drug by needle, Dr. Odland gave Mr. Barlow a bottle of pills. "It takes longer for the drug to work this way, but it will eventually take effect. Mr. Connolley needs to let his chest relax if he plans to breathe deep. A chest infection is the last thing he needs right now." Eyeing Mr. Barlow with more censure that even Katherine could muster, Dr. Odland added, "It is up to you now to nurse this man back to health." The doctor sighed as he wiped the sweat off John's forehead, then removed the thermometer from his mouth. "He has a fever now. I was afraid of that." Tsking slightly, he ordered Mr. Barlow, "Keep him cool, keep him sitting up, and most of all, keep him still. Do not let him jerk or move around. If you have to, get in bed with him like Miss MacPhearson did." Responding to Mr. Barlow's shock, Dr. Odland continued, "Yes, suh, I know what Miss MacPhearson did, and I applaud her for it. It is ridiculous to put stock in morals when a man's life is at stake. That woman would make a fine nurse if her mama would only let her."

The doctor looked back down at John and shook his head. "He was a fool, moving like that." Attacking Mr. Barlow, he added, "You see to it he refrains from any more foolish action!"

"Yes, suh," Mr. Barlow agreed most regretfully. "He will not behave rashly again. You have my word."

"Well," Dr. Odland sighed, "there is nothing more I can do here. Just watch him, and if he takes a turn for the worse, you send Patrick to come get me right away." Dr. Odland started to depart but turned on an afterthought. "And under no circumstances is he to move from that bed until he is better. I do not care if you have to empty his bedpan yourself. Is that understood?"

Dr. Odland actually had his finger pointed at Mr. Barlow's nose. Mr. Barlow moved it aside before responding, "You have my word, suh."

"Hmph," Dr. Odland replied. "I guess that will have to do."

Mr. Barlow nearly cursed. He formed fists but kept his hands at his sides. He could put up with all kinds of insolence from a doctor ... but to doubt his word? That was plain offensive.

After the doctor left, Patrick came into John's room. "Mr. Barlow, suh, I heard what the doctor is expecting of you. That is too much to expect of a man of your stature, suh. You ought not be working like a common household servant. Let me go home and fetch our Sarah. Her main job is tending to my sister. I have no doubt Katie would give her up for a week or two to help Mr. Connolley here."

"Why, Patrick, that is mighty fine of you. I do appreciate that, and I know John will, too. This ol' man is not much of a nurse. That kind of job requires a woman's touch."

Matthew was in the parlor, listening. When he heard Mr. Barlow agree to Sarah staying with them, he could not help but smile. Right now she was angry with him ... but he knew anger, being right close to passion, could work in a man's favor if played right.

"You know, Patrick," Mr. Barlow added, "if it is all right with you, once this Sarah arrives, I will just go make myself comfortable at Richardson's Inn. I will be spending the days here, of course, but we would all be more comfortable if I slept elsewhere. This little house just is not big enough to accommodate three men and two Negroes." He looked around John's room as if that would help him figure things out. "I feel right bad, you having to sleep in that small side room. It is clearly meant for a servant."

Patrick interjected, "I do not mind, suh. I am comfortable enough."

It was almost as if Mr. Barlow had not heard him. "Matthew is fine in the hayloft … but that Sarah girl. Where is that little Negro girl going to sleep?"

Patrick was quick to reply. "I have already thought of that, suh. I was thinking of hauling a mattress back with us and placing it on the floor at the foot of Mr. Connolley's bed. There would be no impropriety in that, and Sarah would be right close if he needs anything."

Mr. Barlow was pleased with the young man's foresight. "Why, that is a fine idea, Patrick. I must remember to commend you to your daddy."

Patrick smiled at the compliment, bowed to Mr. Barlow, and took his leave to fetch Sarah.

*   *   *   *

When it came to Mr. Barlow enforcing the doctor's rule about morphine, a battle of wills ensued. Mr. Barlow shouted, ordered, insinuated … and failed with every attempt. "God's truth, son, you anger me beyond reason!" Pacing up and down the room at the foot of John's bed, Mr. Barlow stopped to count to ten. "I gave the doctor my word you would take this medication. He wants your chest relaxed, so you can breathe proper."

"No, suh," was John's only reply.

"You would have me go back on my word?" Mr. Barlow demanded.

"You should have only promised to try," John replied. He worked hard to keep his voice composed.

"Why are you being so stubborn?" Mr. Barlow shook the pills. "This is the doctor's order. Am I going to have to crush them and hide them in your food?"

"That will not do, suh. From this point on, I will not eat."

"I beg your pardon?" Mr. Barlow asked incredulously. "Do you mean to refuse food now?"

"As long as there is a chance you will put that drug in it, I do." John softened some and used the words he knew would pacify the old man. "Uncle Jacob, please give me your word that you will not put morphine in my food. Without your promise, I will not be able to eat."

Jacob Barlow was losing control, and he knew it. That did not stop him from trying to hold on to the reins, though. "Son, I only wish to help you do as the doctor ordered."

"I know." John smiled. "And I am grateful for all your help. I could not get through this trying time without you, but I will get through it without morphine."

Mr. Barlow shook his head. With so many compliments coming from John, so many suggestions that John was his son, he had to give in. John had called him Uncle Jacob. "I will not force you to take your medicine. Nor will I hide it in your food or drink. You have my word on that."

"Thank you, suh. I know you are good for it. A man is nothing if not his word. Is that not right, suh?" Both men laughed. Mr. Barlow knew he had been had. John winced, though, as the laughter painfully rattled his ribs.

Mr. Barlow admonished John sternly, "You be careful now, son! You cannot afford to shake or move around too much, especially if you are refusing sedatives."

John took a shallow breath and muttered his agreement. "You are right about that, suh."

Mr. Barlow sat down on the bed next to John. "Will you at least explain to me why you are so adamant against taking morphine?"

"Do you remember my first fight?"

Mr. Barlow shook his head in regret. "That was a bloody mess." He sighed, remembering the fractures to John's cheeks and nose. The memory angered him, and he lectured John as if John were sixteen again. "You were not focused on that fight. I swear, if you had only kept your mind straight, you would have won."

"My mama had just died!" The curt reminder of Evelyn silenced Mr. Barlow. "I was fighting a strange man instead of attending her funeral. If that had been your mama, or your sweet Louise, could you have kept your mind straight?"

"No, son. You are right." Mr. Barlow sighed. "I am truly sorry."

"What is done is done, suh. We cannot go back and change it. We only have today and tomorrow to live for. But we can learn from the past ... and I learned something real important from that fight." John grimaced at the memory.

"And what was that, son?" Mr. Barlow asked.

"You remember how Dr. Haverton put me on morphine for the pain?"

Mr. Barlow grunted and nodded his head.

"Well, suh, it did more than ease the body's pain. It eased my heart's pain as well."

Jacob nodded.

"I kept taking it after my face had healed." John rubbed his cheekbones. "I thought it would be OK … just until after I got over my sorrow. Dr. Haverton seemed to think it all right, too … but then he ran out and was unable to get me more. That was when I got sick."

"You were laid up for weeks … feverish, vomiting. Dr. Haverton said the drug did that if you come off it too fast. He got you more, though. He tapered you off."

"It was hell, Uncle Jacob. Pardon my cursin', but it was sheer hell. I will never go through that again. I would rather endure this pain for two or three months than to have to taper off morphine again." John closed his eyes; he was shaking inside. "You have no idea how hard it is, suh, to refuse that drug. My body remembers. My mind is half convinced that I need it, and I need lots of it. I want you to give me it so badly." John's eyes were pleading. "Please do not ask me again. Please do not try to make me take it … for I know if I start, I will never stop."

Mr. Barlow noticed John's hands were shaking. He felt a pang of pity for the lad. Mr. Barlow had no idea what it was like to suffer from such an affliction, but he was able to empathize. "I swear, John, I will not pursue this matter again, no matter what the doctor says."

John's sigh of relief was audible.

"Now close your eyes, son," Mr. Barlow whispered. "You need your sleep."

John acquiesced.

"I will get Sarah in here to sit up with you, so you do not move around much."

John drifted off before he could even mutter a thank you.

CHAPTER 29

▼

THE TASTE OF FREEDOM

John had been laid up for two weeks before Dr. Odland would allow him to take short walks. Three more weeks had to pass before the doctor would consent to John's first visit into town. John was as ornery as a half-starved alligator and as restless as a housebound dog. Having been confined so long, he looked forward to seeing something other than his bedroom or front yard. John had nothing against Patrick or Matthew, and he certainly meant no slight against Sarah—she had done well caring for him—but he longed to see some new faces, talk to other folk.

John was so desperate, he was even willing to entertain Terrance Richardson with talk of Mr. Barlow. He looked forward to one of Mrs. Richardson's finely cooked meals, and his fingers itched for the piano. The digitorium Mr. Barlow had sent him helped keep his fingers nimble, and he could imagine the sounds he should be making, but he missed the music and the feel of real keys. A slab of wood with dead keys was no substitute for a hammer against wire. His fingers itched for a real piano.

Matthew escorted him to town and promised to look after the horse and cart while John wandered about and visited. John felt bad leaving Matthew stuck in the stable all day, but Matthew had no desire to meet with white folks—he would just be looked down upon. They would have to play slave and master the whole while, and John did not enjoy that either. "'Sides," Matthew said, "Ol' Riley's a great talker. He'll keep me well entertained."

"All right, Matthew," John agreed. "I'll be back around three o'clock. You make sure you have the horse and cart ready for me."

"Whatever ya says, Massa Connolley," Matthew said with a flourish and a bow. John winced as Matthew kept up his mimicking charade. "Yessuh, Massa Connolley, whatever ya says."

"All right, Matthew, point made. I'll be back at three, and we can get things hitched together."

"Don't ya fret, John. I'll have it ready for ya." Matthew laughed. "It'll give me somethin' ta do whiles I's waitin'. 'Sides, ol' Doc Odland would strip the hide offa me iffin he thought ya did any work. Ya gots ta wait 'til he gives de go-ahead before ya does any labor."

"That man is goin' ta drive me half crazy," John lamented. He hated having to sit back while Patrick and Matthew worked his land. What he would not give to feel dirt beneath his nails again.

"Well, ya took quite de beatin' thar in June," Matthew reminded him. "For a while thar, we weren't sure you's gonna make it. Broken ribs need lotsa time ta heal."

"All right, Matthew. I'll behave." John shook his head. "Shoot, it's bad enough I gotta listen ta all that from Odland an' Mr. Barlow … now you gotta be lecturin' me, too."

"Get on outta here. Go enjoy yer fancy meal." Before John could leave, Matthew tossed in a request: "Say hi ta Judith for me. She's a ripe, juicy thing, that girl is."

This bothered John some. "I thought you was sweet on Sarah?" He figured Sarah worthy of Matthew's attentions.

"I is, but a man's gotta keep his options open. Sarah's playin' things real cold. Didn't like de way I acted all uppity wit' her missy. She's too content bein' Missy Katherine's little nigga girl for my likin'."

"What do you expect? It's been her entire life. She was born and raised on that plantation. Lived her whole life in that big house, servin' Miss Katherine. What you want from the girl, to get her cheek branded to match yours?"

Matthew was annoyed at that. "I thought ya had a fancy meal ta eat an' fine folks ta visit?"

John turned and left. He had no intention of apologizing. *Too bad if Matthew's offended! That man expects everyone ta think like he does. Well, the world just don't work that way. If other slaves ain't chompin' at the bit ta run, then they're cowards, as far as Matthew's concerned.* John did not think that line of thinking was fair. *It ain't so easy gettin' away. Shoot … Matthew, of all people, ought ta know that. Not everyone wants ta risk swingin' from an old oak tree.*

Inside Richardson's Inn, John took a moment to count the crystals in the chandelier. He always counted thirty-six, but the size of it and its sheer beauty always awed John.

Junior's cackle pulled John out of his reverie. "What are you doing, Mr. Connolley, counting candles?" Turning to his fiancée, Katherine MacPhearson, he added, "You would think he had never seen a chandelier in all his life." Looking back at John, Junior continued to laugh. "Surely you cleaned a few light fixtures for Mr. Barlow. You were his cook's son, after all."

Junior's laugh was a mix of a high-pitched squeal and a wheeze. He had been drinking some, and alcohol always seemed to do that to him. He took Katherine by the arm and led her past John. She kept her eyes downcast so as not to have to look at Mr. Connolley. Just as they approached the door, opening it for the chimes, Junior turned around and called to John. "Oh, Mr. Connolley, I was thinking. As you know, my sweet bonnie Kate and I are to be married next June. We were wondering if you would be willing to play some of that fancy piano of yours at our fine solemnity. That romantic Mozart fellow you were playing awhile back … before your unfortunate incident."

Junior smiled smugly. "What say you to that, Mr. Connolley? Would you be up to playing some at our solemnity?" Junior did not even bother to wait for an answer. "No? I figured not." Then, turning to his future wife, he feigned a consoling manner. "Do not fret, my sweet. There are pianists enough in Savannah to entertain us at our wedding feast."

Katherine, mortified by the whole affair, turned and left the inn without a word.

John tried to ignore Junior as he walked past and entered the dining hall, but Junior's laugh pushed hard against his back. He did not order a meal. He just sat at the piano and started playing slow, sorrowful instrumentals.

Mr. Richardson came over and asked John if he could get him anything. John ordered a whiskey.

"I did not think you drank, suh."

"I do now," John answered curtly.

"We do not normally serve alcohol here unless folks are eating. We do not consider our establishment a saloon. Y'all got Baily's for that."

"Bring me a meal then, too," John replied. He did not care what it was, since he had no intention of eating it. Running into Junior and Katherine had killed his appetite. "Just bring me whatever you have on special. But wait awhile. I want to play the piano some."

"I will get you a whiskey, Mr. Connolley." Terrance Richardson looked at the young man in concern. "Are you feeling all right, Mr. Connolley? Did the doctor say it was OK for you to come to town?"

"Yes, suh. He gave me his OK. I am still sore but have been up and about these past few days. The good doctor said a visit to town would do me good. I need a change of environment. Besides, that whiskey you bring me will help numb the pain."

Of course John was not thinking about his ribs. His agony was even deeper inside. He thought about the sweet ease of morphine. *Damn the doctor for having given me some. No,* he reminded himself, *it wasn't Dr. Odland's fault.*

"Could you bring me that whiskey?" John asked a little too harshly. Noticing Mr. Richardson's reaction, John softened his tone and added, "Please, suh."

"I will get it for you right away, Mr. Connolley, and instruct Paullina to cook you up some catfish." Terrance Richardson stood, looking over John, wanting to express his concern but not knowing what to say.

"Much obliged to you, suh." John just wanted to be left alone to drink and play. The tightness of his voice suggested as much. Mr. Richardson turned and walked back into the kitchen, taking a moment to look back at John. He whispered his concern to his wife as the door closed behind him.

Three whiskeys later, John was playing jigs. Mr. Richardson was not thrilled at having a drunken man in his establishment but it was John Connolley, and at least he was not making a ruckus. Three whiskeys for most men would not have had such an effect, but John Connolley was not a drinker, and he had refused to touch his meal. He was not too ginger about the way he was tossing his drinks back, either. Mr. Richardson reluctantly brought the man another.

A few folk had entered the inn when they had heard John Connolley playing. Among them was Miss Amanda Hodson. She was a brazen young lady and tickled at finally being old enough to call herself a woman. It was high time, she decided, to find herself a good man of fortune … and that good man, as she saw it, was John Connolley. After John had finished a fast little ditty that suggested dancing was more than just a turn on the floor, Amanda sat on the piano bench beside him and drew his attention toward her.

"Why, Miss Amanda," John exclaimed. "How are you, little girl?"

"I'm not so little anymore, Mr. Connolley."

"I thought you had decided to call me John."

Amanda blushed at the remembrance of those circumstances. She stuttered, something quite unusual for her, "I-I am … real embarrassed about that, Mr. Conn … John. My daddy, he explained … well, after he switched me … ah …"

John softened. "Don't be feelin' bad, little lady. It's all forgot."

"I sure wish it were," Amanda sighed, "but my mama won't ever let me forget it. She keeps tellin' me I have to marry soon, because folks are callin' me a hussy." With bleary eyes, Amanda looked up into John's. "You don't think me a hussy, do you, John?"

"No." John wiped the tears from her eyes. "That was all an unfortunate mistake. It was pure innocence on your part." He gently ran his fingers along her cheek. "Innocence is always charmin'." He noticed for the first time her raven dark hair and rich brown eyes. He drew his hand away, coughed slightly, and reminded himself that, even if her mama was now looking to get her married, she was still only fourteen. Although her age was not a worry for most men, it was for John. Sixteen years, as he saw it, was a long span. A little girl like that ought to wait a few years before marrying … and then to someone closer to her own age. Delilah Poitras, John recalled, had been only fourteen when she married Mr. Raymond Poitras, and he was near forty when he took her as a wife. It reminded him of a line from Shakespeare: "And too soon marr'd are those so early made." *No, suh*, John thought. *Little girls need a chance to grow up some before they go and get spoiled.*

John's eyes settled softly on Amanda's features. He could not help but admire her beauty. Without thought, he started to diddle on the piano and make up a song about a dark-haired maiden with eyes of piercing glass. Amanda flushed with joy at being singled out. After fiddling around with a few lines, John stopped playing. "I think your mama is being unfair, Miss Amanda. You shouldn't rush into matrimony to assuage her fears. You ain't no hussy, and folks don't think a' you that way."

Amanda bowed her head demurely, trying desperately to play the part John had cast for her.

Mr. Richardson delivered John another whiskey, and Amanda's presence—the smell of her, the touch of her thigh against his, her eyes sparkling with tears, and her slight trembling smile—urged him to toss the drink back. Bringing his head back up caused it to spin, and Amanda's smile urged him to wickedness. He turned around on the bench, slapped his thigh, and smiled. Before he knew it, Miss Amanda Hodson was sitting on his lap. She squirmed slightly and, with a little giggle, told him what a fine specimen of a man he was.

He laughed at that. "A fine specimen, you say. I don't think I have ever been called a fine specimen before." He knew he was lying, but that did not seem to matter. He was feeling the rich warmth of the whiskey and the soft touch of Amanda. A great deal about this girl reminded him of Delilah Poitras.

Neither John nor Amanda paid any attention to the eyes of the good folk watching them. Two ladies taking tea got up and left the hall. Paullina Richardson watched from the kitchen. She was filled with consternation, but neither she nor Mr. Richardson were willing to risk offending Mr. Connolley. They wanted to ensure the continued patronage of Mr. Jacob Barlow.

"Mr. Connolley … John, I mean." Amanda's eyes sparkled, still damp. "I just want to say how sorry I am that you suffered such a brutal attack." There was sincerity in her voice, and John smiled. "The manner in which you were beaten was most cowardly, and I do hope Artemus Sprague can find the renegades soon, so justice can be done."

"Why, thank you, Miss Amanda," John said, waving to Mr. Richardson for another whiskey.

Encouraged by his smiles, Amanda pursued another line of thought. "I must say I am mystified … indeed, shocked … that Miss MacPhearson is goin' to marry Junior. Havin' nursed you back to health, one would have thought her inclination toward you would have grown stronger. I simply do not understand her. Her sudden decision to marry Junior after years of refusal has the whole town buzzin'."

John closed his eyes at the mention of Katherine, and his head drooped some.

"Mr. Connolley … John … I know you're suffering more from her betrayal than any of them blows from your attackers. If I might, suh, quite frankly … Miss MacPhearson is a fool. Everyone knows how mean-spirited Junior is. Folks just put up with him 'cause he's a Crawford. Seems like money can excuse a man for anythin'." Amanda looked at John and saw this as the right moment to make her move. "You just remember, John, when your heart's at ease, there is a new woman in town. One who is more interested in the quality of a man than the size of his bank account."

John looked up at that. "You are a fine lady, Miss Amanda. You have matured much since last we met." Studying her a moment, John noticed just how much two months had added to her bosom. She was well-endowed for fourteen. He blushed at his consideration of her beauty and chastised himself for having thought so impurely.

As if reading his mind, Amanda leaned forward to kiss John. He devoured her lips. Suddenly stopping, Amanda gasped. With a wicked grin and an insufficient flush, she whispered, "I feel you, Mr. Connolley. You want me for a wife."

That was a sobering moment for John. He had let himself be drawn in by this little girl, and he flushed with shame. Anger boiled, and he flipped her from sitting up on one knee to lying facedown over the other. He gave her a few good smacks, then put her to standing. Amanda gulped back tears and hung her head. John gripped her chin in his hand and forced her to look at him. "Thems were the words of a hussy, Miss Hodson. I got no respect for that kind a' talk from a lady." Amanda gasped and tried to speak, but John put a finger to her lips. "There ain't nothin' you can say to make up for that. What's done is done." Poor Amanda flushed red and fought to keep her tears from becoming a wail. "Now you go home, little missy, and tell your daddy everythin'. Every word of it, you hear?" Amanda blanched, and John hardened himself against pity. "I expect to hear back from your daddy by day's end. If I do not have the pleasure of his company before then, I will seek him out. Do you understand me?"

Amanda was too choked by fear and mewling to speak. All she could do was nod. John spun her around, smacked her again, and sent her running. When the door chime announced her departure, John turned back toward the piano and lowered his head. The room took a few turns. "Richardson!" he shouted, a bit too loudly.

Mr. Richardson came running out to him. "Yes, Mr. Connolley?"

"How much do I owe you, suh?"

"Six whiskey and some catfish." Mr. Richardson took a moment to calculate it in his head. "That would be one dollar and seventy-five cents." John handed the man two silver dollars, refused the change, and got up. He staggered slightly, bumping into the piano. He grunted and set himself back down. "Are you all right, Mr. Connolley?" Mr. Richardson asked.

"No, suh," John replied. "My ribs are hurtin' some. I don't feel much like making my way back to the plantation right now. You figure you could get me one a' your rooms and send for Matthew?"

"Yes, suh. I'll send Luke to the stables. Your Negro can sleep there."

John, not liking the idea of Matthew being stuck in the town stables for the night, countered, "I would prefer it if you could put a cot in my room for him." Seeing Mr. Richardson's look of surprise, and not wanting to make it sound as if he were doing any slave a favor, he added, "It's more than likely I'll be needin' his assistance."

"Of course," Terrance Richardson replied. Motioning for John to remain seated, he added, "I'll get Judith to help you up to a room. Matthew will be round shortly to tend to your needs."

"I'd rather wait for Matthew, iffin that's all right wit' you."

"As you wish, Mr. Connolley."

After Mr. Richardson left, John took a moment to notice all eyes on him. He dropped his head into his hand and regretted having allowed himself to act in so lecherous a manner.

*   *   *   *

Matthew half dragged, half carried his drunk master to his room. "John," he scolded once he had him laid out on the bed. "What do ya think you's doin'?" Matthew grabbed one of John's boots and pulled it off. Tossing it aside, he carried on with his harangue. "Judith is chatterin' an' screechin' like a magpie that won't shut up! She said you's actin' all improper in thar." John grunted as Matthew roughly yanked at the other boot and tossed it aside. "I cain't believe ya, John, kissin' a li'l girl in public like that!"

"Matthew," John slurred, "get outta here!"

"In one fell swoop, like a hawk divin' for a mouse, you gone done turned that li'l girl inta a whore!" Matthew chastised. "Ya proud a' yourself, Mista Connolley?"

John attempted self-defense. "She kissed me."

"Don't be tryin' ta justify yerself, John. Judith done tol' me what ya did. It weren't right, an' ya knows it. Gettin' that l'il girl ta sit up on your lap." Matthew grew stern. "It ain't fittin' for a man a' your stature ta be sittin' wit' women like that an' … kissin 'em, ta boot!" That John turned his head to avoid looking at Matthew only angered him further. "I's tellin' ya, it ain't fittin'! Iffin you're needin' relief, then ya ought ta make your way down ta that Margarette's. She gots herself a special entrance in de back for folks like you's."

John felt the sting of that insult.

Matthew kept up his attack. "Don't ya go ruinin' li'l girls." Scowling, he added, "She be spoilt now. Ya knows that, don't ya? Folks is talkin' like she's one a' Margarette's whores!" Matthew shook his head. "How's ya gonna fix this? I'd say marry de girl, but we both knows ya cain't do that. Not wit' that brand on your back! Ya may be white but iffin any a' your good folk see your *JB*, well, they ain't gonna want their daughter marryin' you's. Visions a' black babies'll dance in their heads. Shoot, wit' your little *JB,* no one's gonna believes you's white, even if ya is. That brand screams mulatto and ya knows it."

John swirled in guilt and self-recrimination.

"Damn you's, John." Matthew was relentless. "Ya ain't gots no right ta be actin' in so selfish a manner!"

"Leave me be," John muttered.

"I's leavin'," Matthew said as he crossed to the door. Before closing it behind him, though, he stopped to add, "I's real disappointed in ya, John." After a painful recriminating pause, Matthew added, "I thought ya better than this."

The room spun as John passed out.

CHAPTER 30

▼

APOLOGIES

When John awoke, his head felt as if someone had smashed it in with a sledge-hammer. His tongue felt too thick for his mouth and his teeth felt like a live oak covered in Spanish moss. His stomach was no better off. It was swirling around like a whirlpool. All John could manage to keep down for breakfast was a small bowl of grits, a cup of hot coffee, and a glass of water. *Surely, Lord, this is punishment enough for my transgression.* But John knew better. After breakfast he decided to make his way over to the Hodson residence. Mr. Hodson had not come to see him yesterday as requested. He could only surmise that Amanda had been too embarrassed or afraid to tell her father of their goings-on. In a way, he felt, this was only right. It was, after all, his responsibility, too. He needed to own up to his share of the guilt.

The Hodsons lived upstairs from their general store. One entered their home from the back of the building. A plain, wooden staircase led to the apartment. John paused a moment to collect himself. Once again John reviewed what he had determined must be said. Matthew was right. That little girl's dishonor was his fault. Had he not been so drunk, he would have never lured her to sit on his knee or kissed her so fervently. He flushed with shame, knowing right well his guilt. He knocked. Brian Hodson answered.

"Mr. Connolley," Mr. Hodson said in a cool manner. "Come in."

John stayed right where he was. "I just come to confess my actions, suh, and apologize to you." Mr. Hodson's silence and stern look suggested that he already knew what John was about to say. *No doubt*, John thought, *rumor has spread.* Once a rumor was ignited, it burned through town like a fire through dry cotton. John blushed and dropped his head in shame. "Yesterday I … yesterday afternoon at the inn … I … your daughter … Miss Amanda and I …" John's throat seized up.

"I know what you and Amanda did," Mr. Hodson said. His manner was severe. "Amanda told me everything, just like you instructed her to."

John looked up, surprised. "But you never—"

"It was not for me to come to you, Mr. Connolley," Mr. Hodson replied. "It seems to me the responsibility was on you to set this right."

John nodded.

"Now, suh," Mr. Hodson continued. "My Amanda was wrong in all she said and did. She willingly sat on your lap and initiated that kiss. From all accounts, more than I wish had been told, you drew on that kiss quite heartily. Are those accounts true, suh?"

"Yes, suh," John whispered to his boots.

"Still, the majority of the blame lies with my little girl. She was the one who did the seducing, and it is hard for a man to resist such temptations. Particularly when he is drunk."

John remained silent, too ashamed to speak.

"Amanda!" Mr. Hodson hollered. "Get in here!"

"No, suh, I …" John stopped himself from speaking further. Mr. Hodson was right. He owed Amanda an apology.

"Come inside, Mr. Connolley." This was not a request; Mr. Hodson's tone was demanding.

As John stepped over the threshold, Amanda stepped timidly into the room. She kept her head lowered, much like John, to hide the flush of shame.

The dimly lit room helped hide their embarrassment. All shutters and curtains were drawn to avoid outside eyes looking in. The only candle burning was the one held by Mr. Hodson. It seemed to flicker wildly against the barren walls. It was not much of a sitting room. Three pine chairs circled a small table upon which sat a miniature porcelain vase. A small hutch against the far wall held but a few ornaments—stock the Hodsons were unable to sell in their store. This was not a room designed by the wealthy and ostentatious. Clearly what money they had was spent on external affectations, such as clothing, in order to appear a part of the social circle within which they had somehow managed to gain acceptance. Brian Hodson and his good wife had recently been added to the MacPhearsons' guest list. Mr. Hodson kept his store stocked with Angus MacPhearson's favorite cigars in order to encourage this burgeoning friendship. For a man of moderate means, this friendship was a substantial accomplishment.

John felt a pang of guilt when he took in the state of Mr. Hodson's home. His actions yesterday may very well have destroyed what little chance Amanda Hodson had for a good marriage.

"Amanda," Mr. Hodson declared, "you are to apologize to Mr. Connolley."

"No, suh," John blustered. "It should be me apologizin' to the lady."

"Lady?" Mr. Hodson mimicked sarcastically. "That is very generous of you to call her that, suh ..." Following a cutting pause, he added, "... after yesterday. No"—Mr. Hodson shook his head—"you have apologized already."

John did not bother to point out that the man had refused to accept his sincerest regrets.

"Now," Mr. Hodson said, looking to his daughter, "it is Amanda's turn to apologize to you." When a short pause ensued, Mr. Hodson bellowed, "Apologize!"

Amanda jumped before she started talking to the floor. "Mr. Connolley, suh ..." The poor girl started to choke on her tears. Mr. Hodson, showing no pity, grabbed her chin to lift her eyes up. Amanda was forced to look Mr. Connolley in the eye. "I am very sorry for behavin' ... for behavin' ..." Her lips quivered. John's heart reached out to the poor thing.

"Say it!" her father demanded.

"... behavin' like ... like ..."

Mr. Hodson's hand gripped her chin tighter, causing Amanda's lips to pucker grotesquely. "Say it, girl!"

"... like one a' Margarette's wenches." Mr. Hodson released his daughter, and she dropped to the floor in a pool of tears.

John knelt beside her. "It's all right, Miss Amanda." Gently stroking her raven black hair, he added, "We both behaved badly." He sighed, stood, and faced Mr. Hodson. "I will never take advantage of your daughter again, suh. You have my word."

"I will take you at your word, suh," Mr. Hodson replied curtly. "Amanda, get back in that kitchen." Amanda leaped to her feet and ran through the kitchen door.

Dinah Hodson's voice, shriller than a magpie's, was heard all the way to the sitting room. "Your behavior is a shame to us all! You are the ruination of your family's good name. Do you know how hard your daddy and I worked to be accepted into good society ... and now this. We will never be invited back to the MacPhearsons' again! No decent folk will ever want to associate with us because of you." There was a scuttle of feet, and Dinah shouted, "Get back in here!" Clearly the girl had tried to escape her mother's wrath. "I am not done with you. Bend over that table and drop your stockings."

"It sounds like her mama plans to whop her again." Mr. Hodson sighed. "Between you, me, and that woman ... particularly that woman ... Amanda will not sit right for a week."

Amanda started screaming. The loud smack of wood against skin rang in John's ears. He turned to Mr. Hodson. "Miss Amanda's been punished enough, suh."

"Her mama does not seem to think so." The tone of Mr. Hodson's voice, however, suggested he agreed with John.

Amanda's howls intermingled with pleas for her mother to stop.

John had heard enough. He knew how hard he had spanked Amanda, and if her daddy and her mama had both spanked her since, this fourth spanking was uncalled for and cruel. He stormed across the room like a hurricane looking to rip the house apart, and swung open the kitchen door.

John was shocked by what he saw. Amanda was bent over the edge of the table, with stockings dangling around her ankles. Her skirt was thrown up over her head, exposing a red and swollen buttock. She had so many welts that they had begun to break open under the force of the wooden spoon. Blood streamed down her legs.

John grabbed Mrs. Hodson's arm. "Miss Amanda has been punished enough."

Dinah Hodson dropped the spoon instantly and stared up into John Connolley's fiery eyes. She was so stunned she could not utter a word. John let her go and knelt beside Amanda, lowering her skirt. Amanda's face was buried in her hands.

"It's all right, Miss Amanda," John said to comfort her. Amanda tried to bend down to pull up her stockings, but John stopped her. "You leave them off," he whispered soothingly. "They will just rub against your sores; that will hurt real bad. Come on, now, step out of them." Sensing her shame, he whispered in her ear, "No one is going to watch you, I promise, and my eyes are closed. You have my word."

Amanda slowly stepped out of her stockings.

"Are you done?" John asked.

Like a frightened little rabbit, Amanda quickly murmured a yes.

"That's my girl." John opened his eyes and gently stroked Amanda's hair. "Now run along to bed." Before she could escape, John grabbed her by the shoulders. "Don't you worry no more about none a' this," he whispered softly in her ear. "It's all forgiven." He kissed her on the back of the head and released her. Amanda shot out of the room like a rabbit chased by coyotes. She never once looked back at him. John stood up to face Mrs. Dinah Hodson. "If you strike that little girl again, Mrs. Hodson, I swear, I will come back here and do twice double to you what you have done to her."

"She shamed us, Mr. Connolley," Mrs. Hodson blustered. "She shamed us—"

John cut her off. "I mean it!"

"Mr. Hodson!" the terrified woman cried.

Brian Hodson entered the room. He had been standing just outside the door and had heard everything.

"You must not let him," Dinah Hodson urged.

"I am afraid, good wife," Mr. Hodson answered, "I will. Mr. Connolley is quite right. Amanda has been punished enough. She will not be penalized again." Mr. Hodson turned and offered Mr. Connolley his hand. "All is forgiven, Mr. Connolley. Let us remain friends." John shook Mr. Hodson's hand and left.

"Mr. Hodson," Mrs. Hodson wailed. "Whatever shall we do?"

"You worry too much, my dear," Mr. Hodson said, smiling.

"Whatever is there to smile about?" She asked, angry at her husband's light attitude. "Amanda is ruined. She will never marry now. No man will have her."

"Why, Dinah," Mr. Hodson laughed. "Did you not see how Mr. Connolley defended your daughter? Did you not see how tenderly he comforted her? Did you not hear him call her 'my girl'?" Brian Hodson chuckled confidently. "I do believe that man will marry her."

"He better," his wife said bitterly, "or your little girl may just as well end up a Margarette whore."

"Oh, he will marry her," Mr. Hodson said with all the confidence of a coon dog in pursuit of its quarry. Giving his wife a gentle shake, he added, "Trust me, wife. I will have this match sewed up by Christmas. Be easy as shooting a racoon from a tree." He mimed the shot and laughed as he watched his prey fall.

CHAPTER 31

▼

FALL HARVEST

Considering the late spring, harvest was abundant for the majority of folk. John was most fortunate in his yield. Even without rice or cotton, John was sure to bring in a profit. He was hoping that he would even have enough to buy Matthew. Mr. Barlow was willing to sell Matthew for twenty-seven bushels of tobacco, and with all John had harvested, he was sure to have ample. Getting it all to Savannah before it turned to rot, though, was another matter. He had built his cart big enough to hold a large yield, but still, he could only haul eighteen bushels in one trip. Many days would be spent driving to Savannah and back.

Brian Hodson had overheard John explaining his dilemma to Terrance Richardson one day over lunch. Seeing John's predicament as a fine opportunity, he addressed John. "Mr. Connolley, may I have a word with you?"

"Certainly, suh," John replied and motioned for the gentleman to sit down opposite him. John was seated at Mr. Barlow's usual table. Mr. Richardson always insisted that John eat there, as it kept up the remembrance of the great man's presence. "What can I do to help you?"

It had been some time since John had seen Brian Hodson. After that last uncomfortable encounter, John had avoided Mr. Hodson—a difficult task, considering the man owned the only general store in Laurel Creek.

"Well, suh, I could not help but overhear your conversation with Terrance Richardson. It seems you have yourself a bit of a dilemma."

"It is not much of a dilemma, suh," John said reassuringly.

"Indeed? I beg to differ," Mr. Hodson countered. "It seems you have no less than four trips left to make into Savannah. With all the traveling you have been doing lately, you must be exhausted."

"I am somewhat fatigued, but it must be done if I am to get all my tobacco to harbor on time."

"You are likely to lose more than a few bushels to rot," Mr. Hodson said with concern.

"Indeed, I am worried, but Matthew and I are working as fast as we can. Some loss is inevitable, considering my circumstances."

Mr. Hodson had a plan. "I could help you reduce that loss."

"Indeed?" John inquired. "How so, good suh?" Any chance of increasing profit could mean freeing Matthew. His interest was peaked.

"I was thinking ..." Mr. Hodson began. "Your predicament meets well with my current needs."

"How so?" John asked.

"Well." Mr. Hodson smiled, trying not to reveal the true intent behind this endeavor. "As you still have four loads left to deliver to Savannah, and I have stock to collect, we could team up. Using my three carts and yours as a fourth, I would no longer have to rent another or hire drivers like I normally do. With you and Matthew driving two of the carts, my nigga driving the third, and me and David on the fourth, why, I'm set. You, too, I figure." Pressing the point, Mr. Hodson added, "Heck, I save a few dollars, and you get all your tobacco into Savannah in one load. Less chance of rot, greater chance of profit." With a smile and open arms to portray an honest gesture, Mr. Hodson topped his offer off with, "We can complete both our transactions in just one trip. How does that sound to you, Mr. Connolley?"

"It seems a mighty fine offer," John acceded, "one I truly appreciate." Indeed, with Mr. Hodson's help, John could ensure his profit with enough left over for Matthew. Both men smiled and shook hands.

Mr. Hodson decided to push his luck a little further, "With extra time on our hands, why, this little scheme of ours would also free us up to do a little visiting. Forgive me for being so bold as to ask, but if you were willing to make the proper introductions, my son and I would sure like to see Mr. Barlow's estate. I hear tell Heartland is the finest plantation in all of Georgia."

John Connolley smiled; he could do as much for the man. This deal was really one-sided anyhow. John figured Mr. Hodson was making the offer more for a chance to meet Jacob Barlow than anything else. "I would be honored to make the necessary introductions, and, havin' lived at Heartland all my life, would be honored to give you a proper tour."

Mr. Hodson smiled. This was what he had been hoping for all along. He needed no assistance. Three carts, his son, David, and his Negro were all he needed. He was motivated by another need: the restoration of his daughter's reputation and to marry her off to the only man likely to wed her after August's unfortunate incident. A match with John Connolley would relieve his family of the stigma of Amanda's shame. More importantly, he thought, his daughter would have a man who would control her, not the other way around.

Tuesday was designated as the day they would travel. Mr. Hodson also offered up David and his Negro to help John load the carts. "The extra manpower will make the process more expedient. This will ensure all the carts are loaded and ready for early departure."

John accepted Mr. Hodson's kind offer, more than pleased with the way things had turned out.

*   *   *   *

When the four carts pulled into Laurel Creek, John was met with a surprise. Miss Amanda waited outside the general store, dressed in traveling clothes. Brian Hodson added her bag to the others. Mr. Hodson walked Amanda over to John's cart and asked if his daughter might have the pleasure of riding into Savannah with him. "I promised my daughter she could go shopping. She has been so well behaved these past few weeks." Smiling an apology to John, he added, "I simply could not disappoint her." Before John could politely refuse, Mr. Hodson continued, "There is no room for her with David and I, and, well, suh, even you must agree, it would be most inappropriate for her to ride with one of the niggas."

John considered asking why Mr. Hodson did not make David ride with William or Matthew, allowing Amanda room to sit next to him, but he knew such a query would be considered rude. Instead he graciously answered, "I would be delighted to have your daughter ride alongside me, suh."

Brian Hodson helped Amanda up onto the cart, winked at her, and left smiling. When everyone was ready, John clicked his tongue and snapped the reins to start the train of wagons moving.

John and Amanda rode silently for the first while. John was too embarrassed to talk, thinking only about their public display of indiscretion, while Amanda had to rustle up the nerve to carry out her father's instructions.

CHAPTER 32

▼

THE CLERK'S TALE

Miss Amanda was fearful of beginning, so she sat there silently, studying the text her father had sent along with her.

John, fond of reading, was curious. "What is it that you are reading, Miss Amanda?"

Relieved at not having to begin as instructed, Amanda looked up and smiled. "Why, it's *The Clerk's Tale*, Mr. Connolley."

"*The Clerk's Tale*," John said, quite astonished. "Why, that's pretty hard reading for a little lady."

"I do declare, Mr. Connolley, you are right. *The Clerk's Tale* is the most confoundin' piece of literature I have ever been forced to read."

"Why, who forces you to read it, Miss Amanda?" John asked politely.

"My daddy," she replied dryly. "He says a woman has a lot to learn from this particular story."

"Indeed." John concurred with Mr. Hodson on this one. *The Clerk's Tale* would instruct this little girl about the state of matrimony. "I reckon your daddy is wantin' you to understand the trials that may befall a wife."

"Indeed, thems were ... I mean, those were his very words," Amanda assured him.

"Your daddy is a sensible man, Miss Amanda; it would be prudent to listen to him."

"I do plan to read this story as he instructed me to, Mr. Connolley, but I cain't make heads or tails of it, with all these funny words. It sure ain't no … I mean, it sure isn't any English I ever heard."

John laughed. "Miss Amanda, you don't have to watch your tongue with me. Now, as for *The Clerk's Tale*, Geoffrey Chaucer wrote that. He was one of the first English writers. He wrote in what we now call Middle English."

Amanda smiled shyly and did as her daddy instructed her: "Would you be so kind as to assist me in understandin' this tale, Mr. Connolley?"

"Certainly," John replied. "I read Chaucer as a boy. It was hard at first, but once you get used to the language, you'll find it's quite easy to understand." Amanda did not appear convinced, so John encouraged her with a smile. "It will make for a pleasant ride to Savannah, havin' a pretty voice read to me."

Amanda read beautifully—too smoothly, in fact, for one who had no understanding of Chaucer's language. John began to suspect that she feigned ignorance in order to allow for conversation. Well, he could forgive her that. It would have been an exceedingly uncomfortable trip without the security of literature between them. Amanda's voice was so pleasing that when she paused for breath John was inspired to say, "Why, Miss Amanda. You have the voice of a nightingale."

Amanda blushed at the glowing compliment. Her daddy was right. John Connolley was not to be trapped by the ways of the flesh. She was going to have to appeal to his mind. *This here story*, as she figured, *is going to help me win Mr. Connolley's heart. More important*, she thought, *it will let me know how Mr. Connolley plans to treat his wife*. Smiling coyly she decided, *it is time to play my hand*. Sliding closer to John's side of the cart Amanda lifted the book for him to see. Feigning confusion she pointed to a passage, "What does that mean, Mr. Connolley?"

After he pulled the cart off the road John took the book out of Amanda's hands. Re-reading the passage he smiled as he explained, "The clerk is saying that young Walter's worst fault was that he wouldn't take a wife." John grimaced slightly, wondering whether this girl might be playing this story up against him. Still, if she wanted to battle wits with him, he was up to the challenge. That little girl had no idea what she was getting herself into.

"I see," Amanda said shyly.

Yes, suh, she is a sly one, John Connolley thought. *She understands this tale better than she's willing to let on.*

Amanda looked up and smiled, but before she could say anything, John decided to use her little plan against her. Pointing to another section and reading it to her for emphasis he countered, "Here Chaucer describes marriage as a burden of great labor for men."

"Oh, Mr. Connolley," Amanda contradicted, snatching the book out of his hands. "Chaucer means no such thing, I'm sure of it. First of all, he says here it's blissful. Does that not mean man is happy in his labors?"

This little girl was good, but John was not about to give up. "Actually, in this case, 'blissful' means blessed."

"Why, even better," Amanda piped up. "Marriage is the sanctity of our Lord … a blessed state every man and woman should enter into."

John laughed. Amanda was a tough opponent. It was like battling wits with Emily again.

"Besides that, Mr. Connolley, this here Chaucer fella goes on to state that marriage is not hard labor. Listen: he says 'noght of servyse.' Does that not mean not of hard service?"

"You have me there, little lady," John said wryly. "You are as quick as a gator snappin' up fish for his dinner. It doesn't seem like you need my help after all."

Amanda gasped, feeling too clever for her own good. "Oh, no, Mr. Connolley, you are a great help. I would never have figured out any of this without your kind assistance." Amanda's thick lashes fluttered, and John gave in. *Just like Mr. Barlow used to give in to Emily*, he thought. *Women. They sure know how to manipulate a man.*

"All right, you win this round." John chuckled. "Read on."

"Oh, Mr. Connolley, you make it sound like we are boxin' or somethin'."

"Ain't we?"

Amanda feigned shock. "Why, I simply do not understand your meanin', suh."

"You most certainly do," John insisted. "But please, continue."

Amanda didn't get much further into the tale before gasping in horror, "Oh, Mr. Connolley, is Chaucer sayin' Miss Griselda's a … a whore?"

"No." John shook his head.

"But he says, 'likerous lust'?" Amanda was truly confused.

John smiled, "He means quite the opposite. What Chaucer is sayin' is that Griselda never allowed her lust to run freely."

Amanda looked confused.

"You see, every man and woman feels lust, but only those who can control those feelings are worthy in the eyes a' God. Griselda was a pure and honest woman. She kept her passions restrained. Thus she was a woman truly deservin' of the state a' matrimony."

Amanda blushed, feeling chastised. The memory of her indiscretion stung. Tears formed, and lips quivered.

John realized he had touched on a topic too close to both of them. "What's wrong, little lady?"

"Oh, Mr. Connolley. I see now why Daddy made me read this. He wants me to know that no man will ever marry me. Not after …" Her words were choked by tears.

John was not sure what to say. He let her weep for a while until he could no longer bear her pain. He pulled the cart over to the side of the road. Being the lead cart, though, he had to explain himself three times: "Miss Amanda is not feelin' well." "She has gone faint." "She only needs a moment to collect herself."

Mr. Hodson wanted to check on his daughter, but Amanda pleaded with John not to let him. "She'll be all right, suh. Just took sick from the motion, is all. We'll just rest a bit and then catch up." Mr. Hodson nodded, trusting John's word.

As soon as the last cart was well out of sight, Amanda threw herself into John's arms and cried. "Now, Miss Amanda," John said soothingly, "I don't want you worryin' none. There are lots of young men out there who'll be wantin' to marry you. Why, as soon as your mama lets you come out, men'll come flockin' to you like geese flyin' to Georgia in November."

"But I don't want any other man, Mr. Connolley. I want you."

"Now, Miss Amanda." John's voice was stern but in no way rough. "Be reasonable. I am thirty years old. Sixteen years your senior."

"Penelope's husband was thirty-eight when they married, and she was fourteen. Why, next to Mr. Hilton, you're a spring chicken."

"I would be one to say your sister married too young."

"You would be the only one!"

"Now, hush. I know you are fourteen, and that may be marryin' age for some, but I don't see it that way. As far as I am concerned, you are still a little girl. Now, your mama told me you were to wait until you turned sixteen, and I reckon you ought to listen to her." Amanda's head dropped, and she resumed crying.

John cupped her chin in his hand. "Give yourself a few years, Miss Amanda. Enjoy your youth." He sighed at her stubborn countenance. "Do not be in such a hurry to grow up. Fruit picked green tastes bitter. I know a woman who married young, an' she's not happy now that she's older." John looked at her sympathetically. "You deserve to be happy, Miss Amanda."

"You could never make me unhappy," Amanda muttered through tears.

"Enough now. Here," John said, as he retrieved a handkerchief from his pocket, "blow your nose."

Amanda complied.

"There's a good girl. You feel better? Can we keep ridin'?"

Amanda nodded.

"You keep readin,' my dear. I swear you got the voice of a songbird."

Amanda threw herself into the tale, feverish with the thrill of having been called "my dear" by John Connolley. She read studiously until she was nearly three quarters of the way through the story. Barely able to contain herself she uttered, "Oh, John." Although she had done her homework, reading the tale twice before she was to read it to John, she only now discerned its deeper meaning. Poor Amanda was pale, her hand upon her breast. "What does this mean? It frightens me."

"I am not surprised," John responded. "The marquis has just tested his wife by taking her infant daughter away to be murdered."

Amanda gasped. "Oh, Mr. Connolley," Amanda cried. "Why would Griselda allow this?"

"She must. It is her husband's will. Do you not remember the promise she made to the marquis on their wedding day?"

"She agreed to obey his will ..." The poor girl's voice trailed off.

John finished for her. "... in all matters."

Amanda began to cry.

"What I think your daddy is tryin' to say here," John continued, "is that a man may demand ungracious things from his wife. His will may not be somethin' you want to obey."

"Oh, Mr. Connolley," Amanda lamented. "This is horrible, just horrible. It makes me never want to marry."

John smiled, feeling the hook easing itself from his gill.

Teary-eyed, Amanda looked up beseechingly. "You would never expect such a horrible thing from your wife. Would you, John?"

"Of course not!" John answered without thinking. "A child is a blessing from God. To kill your own child would be a most heinous crime."

"It comforts me to hear you say that, Mr. Connolley."

Amanda smiled, and John realized he had just bitten down and swallowed the bait. The hook sunk deep in his throat, and Miss Amanda was happily reeling him in. John grimaced and snapped at the reins. He was a big old catfish, stubborn and set in his ways. He was not planning on being so easy a catch.

Nearing the end of the tale, before Walter, the dreadful marquis, had amended his ways, Amanda slammed the book shut.

"It was terribly cruel of Daddy to make me read this tale," she declared. "I swear, Mr. Connolley, I can bear no more. The man has convinced the poor creature that both her daughter and son have been murdered. Now, after havin' divorced her and sent her home to live in penury, he writes to her an' asks her to come prepare his home for his new bride. I do declare the man is truly monstrous." She turned to John, once again with watery eyes. "I cannot help but cry at every page."

"You are a tender heart," John sighed. "It speaks of goodness in you."

"You know, Mr. Connolley, I have been thinking."

"What about?"

"That promise Walter insisted Griselda make before he married her."

"Uh-huh."

"Well, it really was a rash promise, don't you think?"

"She should have taken more time to think before makin' it, I agree."

"Griselda never should have kept it."

"You mean to say she should have broken her word?" John asked.

"I do! To let her husband kill her children like that, and then express no sorrow … why, that is a sin. Surely she will go to hell for it."

"But Walter never killed her children. You know that. He sent them to live with his sister."

"Well, I know that," Amanda said adamantly, "but Griselda didn't. As far as she knew, that nasty ol' sergeant was takin' her babies away to slaughter 'em and feed 'em to the wolves. Why, there would be no dishonor, suh, under such dire circumstances, for a woman to disobey her husband's rule."

"I daresay you may be correct, Miss Amanda," John agreed. "But what say you to Abraham's rash promise?"

"Abraham?"

"Abraham's promise to the Lord could be considered as rash a promise as the one Griselda made to her husband."

"I don't understand."

"Why, little girl, didn't your daddy make you do Bible studies?"

"Yes, suh," Amanda answered, but her blush suggested she never paid it any mind.

"Abraham's story is in the first book of the Bible, Miss Amanda." John was as stern as a schoolmaster chastising a wayward student. "Genesis twenty-two. Listen as I recite it for you. 'And it came to pass after these things, that God did tempt Abraham, …'"

"Tempt him?" Amanda asked, cutting him off.

John grimaced. "Tested him, just like Walter tested Griselda." He continued, "'And he said, Behold …'"

Once again Amanda interjected. "Not like Walter tested Griselda, I'm sure," Amanda said determinedly.

No point reciting the whole thing, John figured. *Not if she plans to keep cutting me off at every turn.* Leaping into a summary, he continued, "Well, Abraham was an ol' man. He an' his good wife, Sarah, only had one child. Their boy, Isaac, was born after Sarah was convinced she could never have children. But God loved Abraham so much, he granted them a baby."

"Oh, no, John. Don't tell me the Lord asked—"

"He did," John said, confirming Amanda's fears. Amanda gasped as John recited verse two: "'And he said, Take now thy son, thine only son Isaac, whom thou lovest, and get thee into the land of Moriah; and offer him there for a burnt offering ...'"

Amanda shuddered. "I don't believe it! I cannot!"

"It is the written word, Miss Amanda," John assured her most sternly. "God asked Abraham to sacrifice his only son, Isaac. Abraham was to take the lad, who was about ten years of age, up the mountain. When they got to the appointed spot, God told Abraham to build an altar, place Isaac on top, then take his life and burn him as an offerin'."

"I simply cannot, will not, believe our Lord would ask such a thing ... not of a faithful servant," Amanda uttered in complete dismay.

"Well, he did," John assured her, "but he didn't let Abraham go through with the act. As Abraham was raisin' his knife to kill Isaac, the good Lord stopped him."

Jubilant, Amanda declared, "I knew our Lord would never expect such a thing."

"The point is, Miss Amanda," John said, imposing on her revelry, "Abraham was ready to kill his own son. He had the knife in his hand. He raised it. And if God hadn't stopped him, he would have killed his Isaac." John paused to let the gravity of Abraham's circumstances set in. "So," John asked, "was Abraham foolish to obey God?"

"Why, no ... I ..." Amanda was dumbfounded; speech failed her.

"What if the Lord did not stop Abraham? What if he had let him kill his only son?"

"But ..." Amanda was confused. "What are you sayin', John?"

"You see, the Lord only asked that Abraham be willin' ta sacrifice his child. He gave Isaac back when Abraham showed God he would be obedient and faithful under all circumstances. You see, the story of Abraham is a lot like *The Clerk's Tale*." Poor little Amanda was so confused, John had to make the connection for her: "Griselda's story is a parable about remaining faithful an' obedient under all circumstances. It reminds us that we all need to do what the Lord our God commands of us without question, for the Lord will not lead you astray."

"But God gave Abraham back his child's life," Amanda reminded him. "Walter stole both Griselda's babies, leavin' her to think they were dead."

John could not help but laugh. "Read on, my dear. You will soon see Walter is not all that evil in the end."

Amanda, ignoring John's request for more of the story, rambled on. "And what about all them other mean ways he tested her? Surely they weren't necessary. Why, the Lord our God would never have done somethin' like that!"

"No?" John queried.

Amanda gulped. *I really should've listened more in Bible studies*, she thought miserably.

"What about the Lord's testin' of Job?"

"Oh, dear me," Amanda cried. "I oughta listen more in church."

"At the very least, young lady, you ought to read your Bible. But enough of this. I think my point's been made. Read on for me. I would like to hear the end of this tale."

When Amanda finally closed the book, she started to cry again.

"What is it now, Miss Amanda?" John was getting a little distressed; this girl sure could cry a lot.

"Oh, Mr. Connolley ... when Walter holds Griselda in his arms, presses her against him, tells her them younguns are her children ... I cannot help but cry." She paused for a moment to weep. She reached into her bag for another handkerchief and cried even harder when she found she had none left.

John pulled the cart over to the side of the road. He undid his coat and pulled out his shirttail. "Here, Miss Amanda," he said softly. "You can wipe your nose on this." Amanda used John's shirt to wipe her eyes and blow her nose but could not stop herself from crying. John reached his arms around the girl and held her in a swaying embrace. Without John realizing it, Miss Amanda had successfully reeled in her catch.

CHAPTER 33

▼

THE BITTER TRUTH

It was half past three when John and Amanda finally pulled up to Mr. Barlow's manor. The others, having arrived at a quarter to twelve, were forced to make their own introductions—a rather embarrassing circumstance, but Mr. Hodson made the best of it. He believed John's lateness suggested success on his daughter's part. This could mean a marriage—one that would ensure connections he never dreamed possible for his family, from the sight of Mr. Barlow's estate.

Mr. Barlow, having received correspondence from John, expected Mr. Hodson. In his letter, John had asked Mr. Barlow to provide accommodations for the Hodsons. Brian Hodson, unaware of John's behest, insisted that he and his party continue on to the Riverfront Inn in Savannah. Mr. Barlow would not hear of it. Too much had been done on Mr. Hodson's part in aid of Mr. Connolley. Gratitude in the form of hospitality must be permitted. Mr. Hodson acquiesced, pleased that his children would be experiencing the finest of Savannah's society. Still, Mr. Hodson felt awkward accepting Jacob Barlow's offer. He ventured forth with an apology: "I do not believe Mr. Connolley informed you of my daughter's presence in the party."

"Your daughter?" Mr. Barlow searched the yard. "Where is she, good suh?"

Mr. Hodson flushed with shame, expecting reproof for allowing his daughter to ride alongside a man without chaperone. "She is with Mr. Connolley, and they seem to have fallen behind." Desperate to explain, he added, "She fell sick. I am afraid she is not used to travel, suh. I do hope everything is all right." Needing to excuse himself for leaving an ill child, he added, "Mr. Connolley assured me she just needed a little rest from the motion. They should be arriving shortly."

Mr. Barlow smiled. "And how old is your daughter, suh?"

"Fourteen, Mr. Barlow."

"Fourteen!" Mr. Barlow exclaimed. "Why, that is a fine age." Smiling, he added, "Strange that they take so long. We have already waited five minutes for them to arrive." Noting Mr. Hodson's concern, Mr. Barlow felt obliged to add, "Worry not, good suh. John Connolley is an honorable man."

Mr. Hodson winced, remembering how honorable Mr. Connolley had been after a few shots of whiskey.

"I can assure you," Mr. Barlow added, feeling the need to prove his point, "your daughter is safe with Mr. Connolley." Hoping to assuage the man's fears, Mr. Barlow invited Mr. Hodson and his son to dine with him. Mr. Hodson, unable to refuse such a gracious offer, followed Mr. Barlow into the dining hall.

There he was introduced to the eminent Raymond Poitras II, son and heir to the greatest trading baron along the Atlantic, and his beautiful wife, Emily—Mr. Barlow's daughter. Joining them was a slight lad of twelve, wiry and full of life. This was Raymond Poitras III, the future of Poitras Enterprises. Mr. Hodson could not believe his good fortune—to be surrounded by so much wealth and fine breeding! Neither he nor David spoke unless addressed, which was seldom. Emily Poitras's interest was directed toward the absence of the man she called brother, John Connolley.

"He has fallen behind," Mr. Barlow intoned. He loved being the storyteller and gave no opportunity for Mr. Hodson to explain matters. "It seems he rides with a beautiful young lady who faints somewhat at travel."

Emily beamed, her hopes for John revealed in a winning smile. "I daresay she would feel faint sitting next to a strapping man like our John Connolley. Perhaps her fainting spells are intentional."

"Oh, no," Mr. Hodson said, aghast. "My Amanda knows better than to behave improperly."

Emily, reaching across the cherry-oak dining table, took Mr. Hodson's hand in hers and gently caressed it. "Dear Mr. Hodson, I am certain of your daughter's propriety. I do not mean to suggest otherwise. I merely refer to those little guiles we ladies often use to attract a man's attentions. No one would hold such a natural strategy against your daughter. Indeed," Emily added, "I would think her quite a simpleton not to make use of such a perfect opportunity."

Raymond Poitras II, a mere two years Emily's senior, admired his wife's sagacity. "That, *monsieur*, is my sweet Emily. She used many such a guile to entrap me."

"Do you feel trapped, good suh?" Emily feigned insult.

"By no means," the gentleman exclaimed, his French accent thick and still working its guiles on Emily. "I feel none of the gentle chains you have wrapped around my heart. And when you tug at them, my dear, I willingly run into your arms."

Emily laughed gaily. "My husband, suh," she explained to Mr. Hodson, "is a true French romantic."

Thus began a series of entertainments designed to divert Mr. Hodson from the absence of his daughter. After a light lunch, Emily Poitras took Mr. Hodson and his son on a walking tour of her father's gardens. Heartland was renowned for its natural beauty. Mr. Barlow had retained much of the original forest in the two acres designated for walking and leisure. A fine gravel path cut through it, maintained by gardeners. Numerous flower plots cut into the tree line, along with a number designed for shrubbery. The path followed along a small creek that eventually led to the Savannah. It was a charming walk that kept one well protected from the sun, provided a mossy scent, and offered the advantage of running water to calm the senses.

Upon returning from their walk, Jacob Barlow and Raymond Poitras II joined the party for tea. It was near the end of this final distraction that John Connolley finally arrived with Mr. Hodson's daughter. Brian Hodson was the first out of his chair and onto the porch to greet them. "Mr. Connolley, you are quite late! Look at the hour! Why, it is now half past three!" Before John could hope to answer, Mr. Hodson continued with his flurry. "Wherever have you been?"

Although Hodson was scolding, his manner was light and his voice gay. He grew even more cheerful at the sight of his daughter's glowing countenance. He took her hand and helped her down from the cart. "My dear girl, I have been worrying myself sick over you. The last time I saw you, you were as pale as a ghost, and Mr. Connolley was trying desperately to revive you. I never should have left you."

"I am fine, Daddy," Amanda said cheerfully, and she gave her father a wink.

That one quick flick of an eye spoke volumes. Thrilled by its intelligence, Mr. Hodson threw his arms around his daughter and laughed. "I am so pleased you have regained your health." Still, Mr. Hodson knew better than to leave their late arrival unchecked, so he inquired, "Mr. Connolley, do explain yourself."

John stepped down from the cart, removed his hat, and twisted it in his fingers. "Mr. Hodson, suh ..." John was embarrassed at having let time slip past. "Your daughter kept takin' ill."

"It is true, Daddy," Amanda sang cheerfully. "Mr. Connolley here was so good as to pull the cart over three times during the course of our journey." She blushed. "I am afraid I was a terrible burden." John's smile suggested no such thing.

Mr. Hodson felt the success of his plan. He reached out a hand to John. "Thank you for taking such good care of my daughter." Mindful of polite society, he added, "I do apologize for burdening you with such a sickly child. I should have left her at home."

John, having been schooled in high society, responded appropriately. "To deny Savannah of such a tender beauty would have been a sin, Mr. Hodson." Amanda blushed, Brian Hodson beamed, and Emily hoped desperately for a match. John furthered his compliment by adding, "Miss Amanda was no burden, for when she was not feelin' faint, she was readin' to me. Your daughter, Mr. Hodson, has the voice of a songbird."

Amanda's blush resembled the breast of a scarlet ibis.

Mr. Barlow, unable to contain himself longer, took this moment to step forward. "John," he said amiably, but with reserve, "welcome home, son."

John stepped forward, shook Mr. Barlow's hand, and replied, "It's good to be home." He smiled fondly and added, "Uncle Jacob."

The old man, overcome with joy, threw his arms around John Connolley and was received in kind. Emily, in tears, raced forward and joined the men in their hug. The crowd erupted in laughter. Releasing Mr. Barlow, John took Emily in his arms, lifted her up and swung her as he often had when they were younger. She laughed aloud like a child. Emily's husband was somewhat taken aback by this display of emotion. Mr. Barlow took a moment to assure him that Emily and John were like brother and sister—all love between them filial.

When John finally returned Emily to her feet, she grabbed his hand and began pulling him inside. It was as if she were twelve again. "Do come in for tea," she sang merrily.

Raymond, not entirely convinced of the innocence of his wife's interest in John Connolley, intercepted her. "Allow your brother to take a moment to rest, my dear. Good sir," he said, extending a hand to John, "I am Raymond Poitras II. You know my parents, I believe."

"Indeed," John said, taking the man's hand. "I have had the honor of playin' for Mr. Poitras and your lovely mother on many occasions."

"He is a marvelous piano player," Emily piped up. "Very unusual for a man."

Raymond defended John. "As unusual as Haydn, Mozart, and Beethoven? They too are men, my dear."

John had to intercede. "I could never hope to emulate the greats, suh."

"No?" Raymond raised a brow. "According to my mother, your fingers flutter like butterflies against the fire."

John blushed. He had heard Delilah Poitras use that expression before ... and not in connection with his music.

Raymond, misunderstanding John's flush for modesty, persisted with his argument.

"My father often laments that if Mr. Barlow would have only given you to him—"

Emily gasped.

Raymond, clearing his throat, attempted to hide his error. "—allowed him to take you to France ... Papa was sure he could have made you a virtuoso, renowned across all of Europe." Raymond bowed slightly. "I would be honored if you would play for me tonight."

As soon as John nodded his assent, Mr. Barlow led the party inside. There was still a two-hour wait until dinner. Emily warned John that she had plans for their entertainment. Without any insight into what that might be, John and Amanda were whisked away, each shown to their respective rooms to freshen up.

✳   ✳   ✳   ✳

After a short respite, Emily knocked on John's door. She had Amanda in tow. "John, do join us for a short walk. Your young friend, Miss Hodson, has not yet seen Daddy's garden."

John agreed, and Emily's husband joined them. "It seems, *monsieur,* that we are two very lucky men. I with my exquisite wife to accompany me, and you with a beautiful china doll. Such ruby lips, such raven hair ... and her eyes! They are so like my mother's."

"Why, Raymond, if I did not know better, I would think you were flirting with Miss Hodson here," Emily chastised. There was a hint of jealousy in her voice. The Poitras blood was fiery with passion. She loved her husband but kept a tight rein on him for fear he would turn out like his father. Even having surpassed eighty, Raymond Poitras I continued to sire many of his slaves.

"My love"—smoldering looks from Emily always melted Raymond like ice under a July sun—"I am a great admirer of beauty, but desire no one but you.

You will always be my favorite." After kissing his wife's hand, Raymond turned to John. "Come, *monsieur,* take your lady by the arm. We will walk with our works of art."

Amanda, taking full advantage of Raymond Poitras's suggestion, reached up and slipped her arm into John Connolley's.

Emily and Raymond led the way through the garden forest. With every turn, another plot of flowers was exhibited. In many a tree hung small bird feeders, and soft chittering was a common sound. It was the perfect romantic setting, and John determined not to allow himself to be distracted by this girl. *Little girl,* he kept reminding himself. *I will not give in to the inclination of love! It is impossible. Emily should know better. Why is she pushing this child on me?* John's internal lament continued. *I simply cannot enter a state of matrimony. Emily knows that!* It angered him that Emily was playing so cruelly with a young girl's heart. And his own! Losing Katherine, even when he knew he could never have her, had been— was still!—one of the most painful experiences of his life. It pained him continuously. *It cannot be forgiven,* John thought bitterly, *if Emily insists on pushing a bond between Miss Hodson and me.*

Amanda, oblivious of Mr. Connolley's concerns, ooohed and aaahhhed over every flower, bird, view of the creek, and small bridge that extended the path to the other side. For Amanda, this walk was an affirmation of John's love.

Finally alone, John retreated to the security of his old room. He had never forgotten Ol' Henry's words: "Ya gots yourself a room here, boy ... your own room, where ya can escapes this world." This room had been his respite through harsh times—a place of solitude and quiet. John needed it now to help ease the feelings that had erupted during his walk with Amanda. Emily and Raymond took every opportunity to abandon him to Amanda's wide eyes.

John looked around his room for the first time since arriving. Very little had changed since he had left ten months ago. The bed still sat in the center, and the room was still sparsely furnished. Beneath his feet, the brown-skinned lady with the strange red dot on her forehead still adorned the rug. He smiled down at her and tipped his hat. "Ma'am." She had been a great listener in his youth.

Separation from home, the only home he had ever known, brought with his return a flood of memories—memories of his mama. She would have counseled him. Reminded him who he was and of his responsibility. She would never have let him entertain thoughts of marrying that little girl. John smiled fondly at the thought of his mother. Evelyn Connolley had been a loving mother. She had died too young, abandoning him to a harsh world. He did not blame her, though; nobody chose yellow fever. Images of Evelyn filled his mind. Her soft brown hair, crystal blue eyes, and soft skin permeated his senses. He remembered sitting on her lap with his ear pressed against her breast, listening intently to her heartbeat.

"Mama?"

"Yes, baby?"

"What happens if it stops?"

"Why, I'd die, of course."

John remembered fear swooping down on him with the talons of a hawk, gripping tightly against his heart. "Don't die on me, Mama!"

Evelyn laughed. "Of course I'm not goin' to die on you, baby … not 'til I'm old and gray."

Well, she was never old and gray. Evelyn died when she was but thirty-two years of age. John sighed. He fought hard not to cry. A few tears managed to squeeze out against his will. He always felt crying was something he could never allow himself. It had nothing to do with feeling weak; it was more like admitting defeat.

A hand reached around John's waist. He turned to face Emily. "I knocked, but no one answered, so I let myself in. I hope you do not mind."

John shook his head.

"I saw you standing here. You were just staring into space. What were you thinking about, John?"

She got no answer. John was too busy admiring the circumference of her face and the delicate length of her neck. His fingers gently caressed her cheek. Her golden locks were free, no longer pulled up into the stately bun she preferred to wear now that she was older. It was hard for John to believe she was mother to six wonderfully wild children, as she liked to describe them. Only the eldest, Raymond Poitras III, had been allowed to travel with them. "You're still so beautiful," John whispered.

Emily blushed. "Hug me, brother."

John embraced his sister. "You didn't always call me brother," he teased.

Emily slapped him playfully. "Oh, you are terribly wicked for reminding me of that!"

"We were young."

"You must never tell my Raymond," Emily warned. "He is frightfully jealous of you."

John laughed.

"I am serious, John. He finds it hard to believe we see each other as siblings, because we are not blood."

"Your husband needn't worry. Our foolery ended the day Mama caught us."

"Oh, Mama Evelyn was mad," Emily winced at the memory. "Did you know she spanked me? That was the only spanking I ever got in my entire life. I threatened to tell Daddy, and she urged me to. She said I could not explain away the spanking without revealing the truth of what we had done. I know it was just kissing and all, but she was right. I took my spanking, and Daddy never knew."

John laughed heartily at the story.

"What is so funny?"

"You gettin' spanked." John flicked his coattails back and sat himself down on the bed.

"I fail to see the humor in that!" Although she strove to be stern, Emily could not help laughing along with John. Seating herself beside him, she inquired, "Why should my injury please you so?"

"Shoot, girl. You got me whopped so many times, it's nice to know I got you licked at least once."

Emily turned pale at the memory. "Oh, John, I am so sorry. I was frightfully mean to you."

John shrugged it off. "We were little. Children can be mighty cruel sometimes."

Emily shook her head, refusing to be let off so easily. "No, my cruelty was uncalled for." Her eyes misted over. "Oh, John, how can you still love me?"

John put his arm around her shoulder and laughed. "Now, Emily, you are being too hard on yourself."

"Too hard? How can you say that, John, after what I said to you? After what I did?"

John tried to lessen her burden. "I have no recollection of—"

"You most certainly do!" Emily interjected, punching John hard in the arm for emphasis.

John grunted his displeasure.

"No one would forget something like that." Eyeing John sternly, as if he were guilty, she confessed, "Thomas Paine. Now do you remember?"

"Oh, yes," John said coyly. He had known all along what she was talking about. "That was rather unpleasant."

"I did that on purpose, you know."

"I know."

"I told you where the magazine was, then let Daddy know you were reading it. I knew he would be angry. I knew he would whop you good. I could forgive myself that. My little ones are always looking for ways to get each other in trouble, but …" Emily paused and started to cry. "… but what I said, what I called you that night. I can never forgive myself for that."

"Emily, it's OK," John said, holding her again. "It's all forgot."

"But I called you mulatto and a slave."

"You were right about me bein' a slave."

"But I said you were going to be my slave. Oh, John," Emily wept. "Can you ever forgive me?"

"Of course I can. I forgave your daddy, and if I can forgive him, I can forgive anybody."

"I simply do not understand how you can forgive him. Not after what he did. I will never forget your birthday."

John was silent, stroking Emily's hair.

"When he started whipping you, I ran into the house. I could not bear to watch. I saw Geoffrey struggling with your mama. I helped him hold her down. I cradled her in my arms the way she used to hold me. I whispered in her ear. I sang to her. I wept with her. Then Daddy told me you and I could no longer be friends. I screamed and hollered, made such a scene … but he would not relent. He claimed you had lowered yourself to the status of a servant. I knew he had done it, though, not you. I swore he could not stop me from seeing you, but he never had to. That damn brand kept us apart."

"Emily!" John was shocked at her cursing.

"I cannot help but curse, John. It was those markings, after Daddy whipped you … after he branded you … You refused to even look at me."

"It's OK, Emily." John tried to comfort her. "Everythin's OK now."

"No!" Amanda screamed. "No, it's not!" She slammed open the door. It wobbled as it hit the wall. Emily had left it ajar, and Amanda, having stood in the hallway, had listened in on their private conference. Her face was pale, her countenance ghostly. "Nothing is OK, if what you say is true. But it isn't true! What y'all said … it isn't true!"

"Miss Amanda," Emily turned and reached for the girl.

Amanda pushed her away. "Don't touch me. You're lyin'! Mr. Barlow loves John. He loves him like a son. Said he raised him."

Snarling, John ripped off his jacket. Tossing it aside, he pulled his shirt over his head and turned to show his back to the girl. "Look, damn you!"

Amanda fainted.

Emily gasped, ignoring the prostrate girl. Emily had only heard about the whippings; she had never seen them evidenced. The scarring was more than she had expected. "Oh, John," she cried. "Look at what Daddy did to you. How could he have been so cruel?"

Pulling his shirt back on, John scowled. "You think I am the only one Jacob Barlow has ever whipped? Hell, girl, he has over three hundred men and women out there who have suffered worse things than I can even imagine. And believe you me, your daddy made sure I could imagine a lot." Looking to the floor, he noted Amanda Hodson lying inert. "Look to the girl," he ordered, as he stepped over her.

John's pounding down the stairs roused the rest of the household. Jacob Barlow and Mr. Hodson were downstairs in the parlor, enjoying a whiskey and cigar before retiring. They met John at the front door. "Where are you going, son?" Mr. Barlow asked, dismayed.

"I am taking me a walk."

"It is a mite late for a walk," Mr. Hodson commented. "Look to the hour, John. It is nearly ten o'clock."

"Damn the hour!" John slammed the door behind him.

Taken aback by John's ill humor, Mr. Hodson was unsure how to react. Mr. Barlow tried to smooth things over. "I apologize for John's temper. He usually keeps it well contained. Something must have set him off. Let us go and see, shall we?" They climbed the stairs to find Emily coddling Amanda on John's bedroom floor.

Mr. Hodson, shocked at his daughter's ghostly appearance, cried out, "Amanda, darling, what is it?" His intrusion only made the girl wail more.

"Please, Mr. Hodson," Emily interceded, "your daughter is fine. She is just a little upset."

"Whatever has disturbed her?" asked the distraught father.

Raymond Poitras answered for his wife. He had been the first to show up at the scene. Having been in the next room, he had overheard most of what happened. "Do not worry, *monsieur*." His French accent dripped like honey from his tongue. "It was just a lover's quarrel."

Brian Hodson could not help but smile.

"John will walk off his temper and, as you can see, my sweet Emily, she will help ease your daughter's heart." Raymond smiled, waving his hands. "Lovers! They have these foolish quarrels all the time."

Mr. Barlow, grateful for Raymond Poitras's intervention, took Brian Hodson by the shoulder. "You see, suh? Nothing to worry over." Mr. Barlow quickly steered Mr. Hodson away from Amanda. Jacob Barlow knew better than to believe the tale of a lover's spat.

Raymond stood leaning against the doorjamb. "She knows the truth then, I see."

"Only a small part of it," Emily replied.

"The worst part, I imagine," Raymond sighed.

"Raymond, tell Papa to wait for me in the parlor. I must speak with Miss Hodson, try to explain to her."

Amanda moaned. She feared this story would be even more gruesome than that of *The Clerk's Tale*. At least Griselda's tale was fictional. But this ... what John had suffered ... only the good Lord knew what her John had suffered.

*   *   *   *

After calming Amanda down and sending her off to bed, Emily joined her father in the parlor. She had a few choice words to share with him. "Well, Daddy, are you happy with yourself?"

"Happy?" he asked, dismayed. "How can you even suggest such a thing? It grieves me no end to know how I have ruined that man." He sat down and rested his head in his hand. "Such hopes I had that we could marry him to that girl."

"Well, believe it or not, that girl is still willing to marry him."

Jacob was flabbergasted.

"It is true. I told her the story ... everything. I did not bother to spare you, either. No doubt you disgust her as much as you do me."

"Emily!" Mr. Barlow looked up, shocked. "How can you say such a thing?"

"I saw his back. I had no idea how brutal you had been. Daddy, how could you?"

"He was my slave, Emily. You always knew that."

That was a poor excuse, and Emily knew it. John's words echoed through her. He was not the only one. The only difference between him and the others was the color of his skin. Was her disgust at John's mistreatment enough ... or should she feel loathing on behalf of all those other whipped slaves, too? Emily shook her head. "I cannot think." Regaining composure, she turned on her father. "You will go shopping tomorrow. My Raymond has agreed to accompany you. You are to purchase a regard ring for John to present to that little girl." Not giving her father a chance to respond, Emily continued, "I will take Miss Hodson shopping. I plan to deck her in the finest gown Savannah has to offer." Pausing briefly, she added, "At your expense. I will present her to John tomorrow night at dinner." She looked sternly on the old man. Her father had never looked so withered or weak in her eyes. "You will do this for John, Father."

Jacob winced—such a formal address. Emily had only ever called him Daddy. "There will be a wedding." Scoffing at her father's feeble attempt to reach out to her, Emily added, "This is the least you can do to make up for your mess."

CHAPTER 34

▼

THE RAVEN BELLE

It had been a long day for everyone. Raymond Poitras II and Mr. Barlow took their duty seriously and visited every jeweler in Savannah to ensure the purchase of the finest stones. The ring, as Emily explained, required six stones. Such a ring always bore the birthstones of bride and groom, as well as both sets of parents. "Your birthstone," Emily explained, "will have to do for his daddy, since we know nothing about his real father." The word "daddy" was said with such scorn that Mr. Barlow winced. Every time he remembered the look of disgust in his daughter's face, he became even more resolved to find the perfect regard ring for John and Amanda. This union, he determined, would come to pass, and it would heal all wounds between him and John Connolley.

Emily, for her part, took Amanda on a whirlwind tour of the finest dress shops Savannah had to offer. A pre-made gown that fit Amanda was required, and Emily would not rest until such an item was found. Not only must it fit the girl perfectly and reflect the highest standards of society, it must also advance Amanda's appearance in age. John was too conscious of their age difference. A dress to veil that difference was essential. When undergarments, gown, gloves, bonnet, fan, and slippers were finally purchased, both Emily and Amanda were anxious to return to Mr. Barlow's estate to begin dressing Miss Amanda Hodson for dinner.

That afternoon, Amanda experienced pampering unlike anything she had ever hoped or imagined possible. After a long, lingering bath scented with lavender oil, Amanda was surrounded by Emily's maids and decorated with powder, perfume ... even face paint. They went so far as to heat an iron and curl her hair. All this occurred before Amanda was dressed in clothes she had never dreamed she would wear. Even the tying of the corset, though frightfully uncomfortable, was a moment of thrill for the little girl. She truly was a woman now. As she stared at herself in the mirror, she was astonished at how one simple undergarment could produce such a transformation. An already imperceptible waist had been cinched down two sizes, and the way the corset pushed up and promoted her bosom made her flush.

"Oh, Mrs. Poitras, is this truly decent to wear?"

"Of course it is." Emily could not help but laugh. "No one will see the corset, Miss Amanda. It is an undergarment."

"Oh, yes, I know ... but it tightens me up so much, and lifts my bosom so. I wonder if a woman should be so exposed." Amanda twisted and turned, so she could view her form from every angle. She did not want to admit the thrill she felt at looking so womanly.

Emily guessed at the girl's true intent, so she took little effort in comforting Amanda. "Your gown will cover your bosom modestly. Have no fear of that, Miss Amanda. The corset merely accents your form to help make you attractive to the more deserving sex."

"Will Mr. Connolley not think me too presumptuous? He is a very upright and modest man."

"Come," Emily said sweetly. "Put on your gown, and you shall see what I mean."

Once fully dressed, Amanda could not help but exclaim, "Oh, Mrs. Poitras! You have made me so beautiful."

"I have merely accented what was already there, Miss Amanda. And you may call me Emily, as we are now friends. Mrs. Poitras always makes me think of that wretched woman Delilah Poitras, Raymond's mother. No, it will not do. You must call me Emily."

Amanda clasped hands with her new friend and exclaimed, "Oh, Emily! I do wish Mr. Connolley would hurry and return!" She desperately wanted John to see her dressed like a fine Georgia lady.

The two women hugged. "With you in this dress," Emily whispered, "my dear brother cannot help but be enchanted. If he does not ask for your hand in marriage, I will declare John Connolley a simpleton."

"Oh no, Emily, you must never say that!" Amanda declared in all earnest. "For John Connolley is the finest, most gentlemanlike man I have ever met."

Emily laughed. "My word, little lady. You are enraptured by his charms. Though, I daresay, I cannot blame you. My brother is a prize indeed."

Amanda squeezed Emily tight in both thrill and expectation. "Oh, Emily, you have given me such hope."

✶   ✶   ✶   ✶

The gentlemen were late in returning. They had had a great deal of work to accomplish that day, unloading Mr. Connolley's freight and then reloading the carts with supplies for Mr. Hodson's store. It was nearly six o'clock when they finally staggered into the house. Exhausted and dirty, not one of them wanted any form of entertainment. A quick meal in the kitchen followed by baths and an early rest was the most any of them desired. For the first time in his life, Mr. Hodson actually envied his Negro, who was free to go and do as he pleased for the rest of the evening.

David, being young and easily irritated by exhaustion, allowed his displeasure at the prospect of a fancy dinner be known. "Daddy, no! We's too tired for this. Couldn't we just take supper in our room? I have no patience for high society and fine manners right now."

John repressed a smile. The boy was audacious, but he was only expressing everyone's thoughts at the moment. Brian Hodson was not about to forgive his son so easily, though, "You hush, child! I will be teaching you manners later if you do not apologize to Mr. Barlow this instant!"

The petulant youth lowered his eyes and muttered, "Sorry, Mr. Barlow."

"Now you run upstairs, David, and change your clothes. Mind you wash up first and wear them coat and breeches your mama packed for you."

This was too much for the boy. "Ahh, Daddy, do I have to?"

Mr. Hodson grabbed David by the arm and roughly swung him around. "You have to! Now get!" Darting out of his daddy's reach, David barely avoided the clout designed for his head. Brian Hodson turned and bowed to Mr. Barlow. "Please forgive the child, suh. He is not used to such exertion as was required of him today. Weariness has made him bold. Even still, he should know better than to speak so foolishly."

"Apology accepted, good man, apology accepted," Mr. Barlow said lightheartedly. "Go join your son, now. John, you had best get cleaned up, too. Tonight's dinner is in your honor, and I have instructed the cook to prepare a sweet potato and apple casserole." He paused to see John smile; sweet potato and apple casserole had always been his favorite. "Milly is nowhere near as fine a cook as your mama was, but she will not disappoint us. Now, please, hurry and get ready, as everyone is expected to wear his or her finest attire."

John winced, wishing he were twelve years of age so he could mutter his disapproval, too. There was no point arguing, though, as it would only drag matters out further. He wanted to inform Mr. Barlow that he had not bothered to bring his only good suit, but that would have been a lie. When Mr. Hodson had asked for introductions, John knew his suit would be necessary. Knowing Mr. Barlow as John did, he suspected another suit awaited him in his room. He was soon to find out he was right. A grey morning suit made of fine oxford cotton did indeed await him. He was also to discover a red linen shirt with matching cravat added to the package. Gold cuff links, shiny black shoes and a pair of gray stockings were waiting for him as well.

Mr. Barlow was a stubborn man and always got what he wanted. John grimaced as he bit back his displeasure. The sooner he was dressed … the sooner they would eat … the sooner he would get to rest. *Ahh*, he mused, *the logic that separates the mind of a twelve-year-old from that of a gentleman.* Laughing silently, he determined the twelve-year-old point of view to be the better one.

*   *   *   *

It was well past seven when the gentlemen were finally assembled in the front lobby to wait for the ladies. Emily was the first to enter. She was elegantly dressed but made sure her look was more stately than Amanda Hodson's. She refrained from wearing the latest fashion, donning instead a high waist. Although it accented her bosom, it was more effective at hiding the female form. If Miss Amanda Hodson was to be the belle of the ball, her appearance must shine brighter than a full moon against a clear sky. Next to Amanda, Emily hoped to look like a distant star. It was hard to downplay Mrs. Emily Poitras's beauty, though. Her blonde hair and blue eyes had always been attractive. She was a woman designed to attract a man's attention. Still, her job tonight was to pull all eyes to Amanda. As a result, the dress she wore was laced up, covering even her neckline. She opted for cream colors, as they would surely dull next to the pinks and blues of Amanda's fine taffeta. Even in this simple attire, Mrs. Emily Poitras was a true Southern belle—all elegance and grace.

"Gentlemen," Emily intoned as she reached the landing. "I wish to present to you Miss Amanda Aimsely Hodson." The gentlemen looked up as Amanda walked into view at the head of the stairs. Every eye, including those of her father and brother, was fixed intently on the beautiful creature above them. As Amanda began to descend, John stepped forward. He was mesmerized. Mr. Barlow stepped next to him and whispered, "Breathe, son." John had been holding his breath from the moment of Miss Amanda's entrance. Mr. Barlow took this moment to slip a small box into John's coat pocket. John Connolley, hypnotized by Amanda's beauty, did not even notice. Within moments, Amanda Hodson floated before him, taking a gracious turn that billowed and fluttered her skirt.

"This, gentlemen," Emily explained, "is the very latest in ladies' fashion. So new, in fact, that Miss Hodson is the first lady in Georgia to don what is called the natural waist."

John's eyes clung to Amanda's waistline. Her waist was cinched in so tightly, John was sure he could cup the whole thing in one hand. He wondered if she could breathe. Fortunately Amanda gave no sign of distress.

Emily was enjoying the role of fashion consultant. "A lot of the current fashion is still retained, though. Note the gown consists of two skirts."

Amanda blushed. She was not used to being the object of such study and admiration. Her hands fidgeted and grasped onto the sides of the outer skirt.

Amanda Hodson's gown was indeed the finest Savannah had to offer. Emily had accomplished her task. Amanda's neckline dropped modestly, exposing a hint of cleavage. With Amanda's shoulders partially exposed, her sleeves puffed out and tightened again at the elbow. Peach silk gloves matched the inner skirt that was moderately exposed in front. The gown, a rich navy blue, was elegantly decorated with embroidered flowers along the edging and bodice.

Amanda's hair was curled tight and dangling. Upon her head sat a small navy bonnet, with a peach-dyed ostrich feather that fluttered as she moved. Before her face she waved a delicate fan constructed of hand-painted silk. Little white flowers that matched the ones on her dress outlined the edge. A pastoral scene was painted in the center. When only a few feet from Mr. Connolley, she curtsied slightly.

"Mr. Connolley." Amanda's eyes fluttered. She knew there was power in her enchanting quality, especially inside this dress. "Would you be so kind as to escort me to the dinner table?" Their arms interlinked, John led the raven belle to her chair. Unable to take his eyes off her, John sat beside Amanda.

"We have a fine meal prepared in honor of our guests." Mr. Barlow stood at the head of the table and held a glass in his hands. "If all would stand, I would like to propose a toast." Both John and Amanda blushed. They were the only two seated, but they quickly rose to join the others. Everyone held a glass—the men, whiskey, and the ladies, wine. Even Raymond Poitras III and David, both only twelve, were allowed a small glass of liquor for the toast. "Tonight we celebrate John's first year as a landowner."

"Hear, hear!" the gentlemen answered.

"He has shown himself to be a formidable farmer, as his first yield brought in enough profit to earn back his initial expense, as well as purchase a field slave."

John grimaced. He had paid for Matthew, but his intention was to petition the Georgia government for Matthew's freedom, then present Matthew with his papers.

Unknowing of John's true intent, the gentlemen uttered a cheer of admiration.

"We are all very proud of you, son," Mr. Barlow said. Lifting his glass, he finished, "A toast to John Connolley."

The table responded, "To John Connolley."

John stumbled over his words. "T-thank you, Uncle Jacob ... everybody. This is too kind ... I-I ... please do not ask me to say a speech. Let us sit down, shall we, and eat."

All at the table laughed and complied.

Quail was served, along with sweet potato and apple casserole, rice and red beans, and chilled asparagus with sweet egg yolk and mustard dressing.

When dessert (a choice of chocolate mousse or Choctaw pumpkin cake) and coffee was served, Mr. Barlow gave Amanda a wink. The poor girl flushed, unsure of its meaning. "Miss Hodson," Mr. Barlow said, smiling, "I hear tell Mr. Connolley has a surprise for you."

John choked on his dessert. He had selected the Choctaw pumpkin cake, and a few bits sputtered out of his mouth. Amanda looked at him with expectant eyes. John stuttered. "I ... ah ..."

Amanda did not even wait for him to finish. "Oh, John ... Mr. Connolley, I mean." Her eyes fluttered. "Did you buy me a present?"

John carefully set his fork down, controlling the urge to simply drop it. He took a moment to wipe his mouth with his napkin—a small gesture, but it helped hide his panic and compose his nerves.

Mr. Barlow smiled. "A present! Every young lady loves a present."

"And surprises," Amanda giggled. "What surprise have you for me, Mr. Connolley?"

"The gentleman is shy," Mr. Barlow said. "You will have to put your hand in his pocket and retrieve the gift yourself."

Amanda, so excited by the most perfect day and thrilled to have it topped off with a gift from the man she admired, thrust her hand in John's coat pocket without any concern for propriety. John's hand raced against hers to reach for the gift. Amanda reached it first, and John's hand clasped around hers. Feeling the shape and size of the box, discerning immediately the likelihood of its contents, Amanda gasped, "Oh, John!"

Her smile diminished, though, as she took note of John's countenance. He was not smiling. His features were a mixture of anger and confusion. She surmised correctly that he knew nothing of this, and all was but a part of Mr. Barlow's amusement. "Let me go," she squeaked.

John turned to her. "Miss Amanda, I ..."

"Let me go, please." John released her hand, and like a dove flung about by a hurricane, Amanda dashed from the room.

Mr. Hodson rose instantly and moved toward his daughter.

"Mr. Hodson." John stood. "Please, allow me to retrieve her." Closing his eyes, taking a moment to breathe and settle himself, John added, "Your daughter and I, we need to talk, suh."

Mr. Hodson nodded, and John followed Amanda out into the yard. He found her sitting on the bench next to the garden path. Moonlight shone against her hair. Hands hid her face, and her body shook as it heaved with sobs.

John sat beside her and touched her shoulder.

The poor child nearly leaped out of her seat. "Mr. Connolley ... oh please, suh," she wailed, "leave me alone."

"Miss Amanda." John sighed. "I think it important we talk."

"You needn't say anythin'," Amanda wept. "I know it wasn't your design. I could see it in your eyes." She paused, trying to heave another sigh. "You never wanted to marry me. You have been tellin' me so all along. I just did not want to listen. And then when your sister ... she took me shoppin' for this dress ..." She lowered her head. "... for you to like me in it."

"Miss Amanda, I do. Truly I do. You look so beautiful. I have never seen you look so ... so grown up."

"Do you really think so, Mr. Connolley?" Amanda's eyes sparkled, pupils reflecting a full moon.

"I do." John's hand was still inside his pocket, gripping tight against the box. "But," John sighed, "Miss Amanda, even if we were more of an age, you know why I cannot marry." He had to look away from her red, quivering lips, from the rise and fall of her bosom.

"Oh, Mr. Connolley, I know why you think you can never marry. An' Miss MacPhearson, she must have proved that to you."

John ached. His stomach clenched.

"But it isn't true. I told you before there was a new woman in town … one who preferred the quality of a man." She sighed, hoping he would look at her. "It's still true. It does not matter to me what you used to be. I swear to you, with all my heart, I will keep your secret."

John glanced back at Amanda and felt his eyes trapped by hers.

Trying very hard not to smile, Amanda pursued her line of reasoning. "It's clear to me Mr. Barlow was wrong in his dealings with you. It is also clear to me that he has been doing everythin' in his power to make it up to you. Surely you have noticed."

"Yes, I have."

"And that is why you should forgive him, if you haven't already."

"You do have goodness," John said with a smile.

"Thank you, Mr. Connolley." Amanda stuttered a sigh. "You can set your mind at ease, Mr. Connolley. I wouldn't marry you right now even if you asked." She barged on, afraid John might interrupt and destroy her well-laid plans. "I am afraid Mr. Barlow is using me as a peace offerin'."

"What do you mean?"

"I told your sister last night I would still marry you if you asked me. I also said I didn't care about all that I had heard and seen. She must have told Mr. Barlow. I reckon he figures if he can give me to you, all debts between you will be settled." Amanda looked at John defiantly. "But I do not wish to be a gift. I am no peace offerin', Mr. Connolley. I just want to be the woman you want to marry. But if you do not want to marry me, then I do not want to marry you. I know that now. So you may keep your ring. I will not accept it. I don't even want this gown anymore. It was meant to help me attract you, and I couldn't do that. I just want to go home." Amanda buried her head in her hands again and began to cry.

John placed a hand on her shoulder, hoping he could comfort her. As soon as he did, though, Amanda leaped up from the bench and tried to race back into the house. John was too quick for her, though. He stood and held her by the waist. He was right: he only needed one hand to cup her waist. He sat on the bench and pulled her close to him. With Amanda standing and him sitting, they were almost eye to eye. "Miss Hodson, I truly never believed I could marry."

Amanda gasped. He was talking in the past tense. That suggested a change of heart had occurred.

"You are right," John continued. "Miss MacPhearson was firm proof of that … but you have given me hope." Reaching into his pocket, John retrieved the small box. He opened it.

Amanda's eyes opened wide. She had never seen so beautiful a ring, with six gems bedecking it.

John's fingers trembled. *How am I ever going to repay Barlow?* The band was fourteen karat gold, and the gems included a ruby, two emeralds, two diamonds, and an opal. "Miss Hodson, I didn't buy this regard ring … but I swear, if you accept me, I will pay Mr. Barlow every penny for it." … *Somehow.* John suspected the ring cost more than all the money he had saved up over the past fifteen years. "Miss Hodson, will you be my wife?"

Amanda wrapped her arms around John's neck and cried, "Oh, yes."

John placed the ring on her left hand, then gently kissed her cheek. "We need to ask your daddy for permission."

"Oh, he will say yes, John. I know he will." Amanda giggled happily.

"You are right, I'm sure," John agreed. Standing, he wrapped his arm around Amanda's and led her back to the big house. "Still, it wouldn't be proper to announce our intentions without acquirin' his blessin' first."

Inside the house, agitation reigned. Mr. Hodson stood by the fireplace, staring into flames that flickered anxiously across his face. His son paced up and down the floor next to him. Raymond and Emily stood holding hands, the gentleman whispering softly into his wife's ear in an attempt to calm her. Mr. Barlow remained seated at the table, staring in wonder at the blunder he had committed. Raymond Poitras III was the only one not to show any concern. He was dutifully eating the remains of everyone's dessert.

Distraught by what had transpired at dinner, Emily snapped at her son, "Raymond, stop that! You will turn into a portly youth if you keep eating like that."

Young Raymond looked up, startled at being sanctioned so harshly by his mother. He quickly darted out of the room to avoid further censure.

"Shh, *mon cherie*, you must not blame the child." Raymond whispered to his wife soothingly. "He is not at fault."

"No," Emily hissed. "We know where the fault truly lies." She glared at her father.

Mr. Barlow responded by placing his face in his hands.

All eyes jerked up instantly when John entered the room with Amanda. "Mr. Hodson." John's voice boomed against the silence. "May I have a word with you, suh?"

Emily pressed her face against Raymond's chest and crossed her fingers, hoping against hope this was what it appeared to be. Mr. Hodson composed himself, taking a moment to straighten his vest and coat, nodded his head, and followed John into the adjoining room.

Mr. Barlow stood and approached Amanda. "Is everything all right, my dear?"

"Let us wait for John and Daddy, shall we?" She smiled coyly.

Mr. Barlow winked, knowing all was well. Amanda Hodson had said "John" instead of the honorific "Mr. Connolley." That suggested a newly formed intimacy between the two.

"Of course," Mr. Barlow replied. "Please sit while we wait." He pulled out a chair for Amanda.

Within moments Mr. Hodson and John reentered. Brian Hodson was newly animated, no longer a countenance of sorrow. "Lady Poitras. Gentlemen." He waited a moment for all eyes to look on expectantly. Mr. Hodson continued, "I am pleased to announce the engagement of my daughter, Miss Amanda Aimsely Hodson, to Mr. John Connolley." Amanda rose from her seat and joined John. Their hands clasped, and both smiled. Cheers rose from the small crowd.

David whooped. "Shoot, girl, you got 'im! I never thought you'd do it."

Amanda blushed.

Brian Hodson crossed over to his son and cuffed him on the head. "You hush up and act respectable. This is your sister's moment. I will not let you ruin it for her."

There was no worry of that, though; Mr. Barlow and Emily both rushed to Amanda and John's side. Handshakes, hugging, and kissing commenced, and all was gaiety and congratulations.

Raymond Poitras II, not wanting to be left out, raised his glass. "A toast to Miss Amanda Hodson, the future Mrs. John Connolley."

"Hear! Hear!" Mr. Hodson shouted, slapping his son's back. Amanda's good fortune had saved David from another whopping.

"As a wedding gift," Raymond continued, "I intend to give Miss Hodson a Negro girl to help out in the kitchen. It is sure you will need much help feeding a man as *grande* as Monsieur Connolley."

Amanda smiled sweetly. "That is a very kind offer, Mr. Poitras. However, I must decline your generous gift. If I know my future husband correctly, we will not be owning any slaves." Amanda was not worried. *Why, with so much wealth surely Mister Barlow can afford to hire me a servant. My own servant!* The very thought made Amanda giddy. Amanda turned and smiled up at John. "Am I correct, Mr. Connolley?"

John smiled. Amanda's words filled him with love and admiration. "You are absolutely right, my love. You know me well." Turning to Raymond, John extended a hand. "Your offer is appreciated, Mr. Poitras, but a slave will not suit our lifestyle."

"Of course." Raymond nodded. "I will just have to think of something equally extravagant to give to your future wife."

"I know what I shall give to Miss Amanda as an engagement gift," Mr. Barlow announced. "The opportunity to ride home in style. John, you will escort your fiancée back to Laurel Creek in my carriage." Mr. Barlow took Amanda by the hand. "This way you will not have to face the elements. And"—Mr. Barlow winked, as this was the best part—"the seats have silk cushions."

"Oh, John, may we, please?"

John shook his head. He felt sorry for Amanda. She looked so eager. "I would love to escort you home in Mr. Barlow's carriage, but I must drive one of the carts."

"Nonsense," Mr. Hodson shouted. "My David here can drive your cart. Right, son?"

David was thrilled. "I sure can, Daddy." He had been waiting for his father to give him responsibility for some time now.

"There," Mr. Barlow rumbled happily. "All is settled. John and Amanda will return to Laurel Creek in style."

Brian Hodson leaned in close to Amanda, whispering, "This will not only exonerate you in your mother's eyes … I daresay it will elevate you to the status of favorite."

Amanda squealed in delight. "Oh, John, this is so exciting! I have never ridden in a chariot before."

The room erupted in laughter.

John kissed her hand to keep Amanda from feeling too foolish. "Although it is only a carriage, my love … tomorrow, for you, it shall be a chariot."

CHAPTER 35

▼

THE HARVEST BALL

The Harvest Festival was always a long-anticipated celebration in Laurel Creek. Money was made off the fat of the land, and the good folk of this fine community enjoyed celebrating a good yield. That year's crops had been bountiful, regardless of the depression that had hit the south of late, and Laurel Creek had much to be thankful for.

The day's festivities started with the Harvest Derby. People lined the streets to watch the horses set off. The race always began in front of Richardson's Inn, and the course took them west for a three-mile stretch along the creek, south around John Connolley's plantation, Majestic Beauty, and then back east toward town. The winner was the first to break the ribbon in front of Richardson's Inn. Junior raced Tenet and won. It was as everyone expected; Junior always won. His father put big money into horses for Junior to race with. As he did every year, Junior strutted around town like a peacock with his feathers spread, drinking and celebrating, bragging to everyone he saw.

That evening a dance was held in the town hall. Folks had moved John's piano from Richardson's Inn, as John Connolley had promised to play some for them. Other musicians had to come, though, as John insisted on dancing at least part of the night with his fiancée.

The whole town was abuzz with the news that John Connolley was to marry Miss Amanda Hodson. The majority of the town saw the marriage as the best possible thing for Amanda. She was turning out to be a wild one, just like her sister.

Penelope had not married well. Her husband was a reputed scoundrel, drunkard, and gambling man. Most folks had envisioned a similar fate for Amanda—if not the brothel—until John Connolley's proposal. Few understood why he would choose to take such a woman for a wife, but at least he was giving her respectability.

The dance hall was beautifully decorated. The local ladies had taken great care to arrange dried flowers, squash, and corn. Tables lined the walls, leaving the center of the room open for dancing. A small stage was set up at the front of the room for the musicians to play, with John's piano set in the center. The Richardsons had been called in to cater the feast. As with every year, they went all out for this occasion. They served the finest of meats, hors d'oeuvres, and dainties, as well as a selection of the best wines, whiskey, and rum in their storeroom.

The Richardsons' Negroes were decked in the finest attire. The women, draped in beige muslin with a white magnolia stitched across the breast, wandered the room, serving drinks and hors d'oeuvres to the revelers. There were also a number of Negro men dressed in black morning suits standing out front to park carriages and stable horses for the finer folk. Matthew was among them. John had asked him to volunteer. Ever since they had been bushwhacked, John had been nervous about leaving Matthew alone. True, Matthew was now a free man of color, but that did not change people's attitudes. Laurel Creek still saw him as John's slave. No decent folk were willing to trust a black man with the letter *R* branded on his face. The only way John believed Matthew would truly be safe was if he worked alongside Richardsons' slaves at the ball.

When John entered with Amanda Hodson on his arm, a number of folk came up to greet them. Mrs. Atwell was among the first to express her well wishes. "Why, we are all so pleased to hear about your pending nuptials." Leaning her mighty bulk forward, she kissed Amanda on the cheek.

John smiled, ignoring the woman's hypocrisy. He remembered only too well how Gertrude Atwell had snubbed him at the MacPhearsons'. She was only putting on a show.

Mrs. Richardson rushed in to congratulate them. "Such a lucky girl, Miss Amanda, such a lucky girl!"

Amanda basked in her glory. John could not help but smile. He patted her hand and left her to share her happiness with the town ladies. Amanda was truly in the catbird seat. Newly engaged and dressed finer than any other woman, including Miss Katherine MacPhearson, Amanda knew she was the envy of Laurel Creek. She swirled for the ladies to show off the dress Emily Poitras had bought for her. She made sure everyone knew about her day of shopping with the illustrious woman.

"Miss Amanda," Gertrude Atwell exclaimed. "Your gown ... it is so interesting. The waistline is so low."

"And the neckline so revealing," finished Katherine.

Although Amanda's dress was modestly cut, its unique design allowed for Katherine's catty remark.

Amanda was not about to let her past rival infringe on her good fortune. "As Mrs. Raymond Poitras II explained to me, the natural waist is the latest style in London. Why, Emily Poitras herself picked this very gown out for me. She said it was just the dress needed to capture the heart of Mr. Connolley ... and she was right."

Suddenly the girl's unusual look became the utmost in fashion. Every lady cooed about its beauty. Katherine turned her back on the scene and walked away.

John joined Terrance Richardson over by the card table. Mr. Richardson handed John Connolley a whiskey. John accepted. He was much better at drinking now. He knew to sip slowly. He could make one drink last all night. In this way, he remained a part of the group without having to partake like a fool. "So, Mr. Connolley," Mr. Richardson asked. "It is true, then? You and Miss Hodson are to be married?"

"Yes, suh." John smiled. "I proposed to her in Savannah last Thursday and received her father's consent that very night."

"I am not surprised he approved," Mr. Richardson responded. "Why, if I had a daughter of marrying age, I would want her to marry you."

"Thank you, suh. That is very kind of you," John answered politely.

"Mr. MacPhearson," Mr. Richardson called out, waving the good man over. "Have you heard Mr. Connolley's good news?"

Mr. MacPhearson joined the two men. "Indeed, Mr. Richardson, the whole town can talk of nothing else." Mr. MacPhearson reached out his hand to grasp John's. "I wish you all the best, Mr. Connolley. I hope Miss Hodson makes you happy and provides you with many children."

"Thank you, suh," John replied. "I am certain she will."

"Is it true," Mr. MacPhearson inquired, "that you plan to wait two years?"

"Yes, suh," John answered. "Miss Hodson is still too young to marry."

"Tush!" Mr. Richardson replied. "Fourteen is a fine age and a sixteen-year age difference good for a man."

"Still," John persisted, "I believe it in her best interest to wait until she is at least sixteen."

"Good luck getting her to wait." Mr. Richardson added with a laugh.

"Indeed," John agreed. "She is a most determined young lady, and marrying me was her design. When a woman like that makes up her mind, there is very little a man can do to change that. Even still, she must wait two years."

Angus MacPhearson and Terrance Richardson laughed at that. Both men knew right well what it meant to be married to a hardheaded woman. Neither believed John Connolley would have his way in the end.

The music began, and couples started to assemble on the dance floor. "Excuse me, gentlemen." John bowed before making his way over to Amanda. He had promised her the first two dances.

The evening began with a waltz, and all the couples glided gracefully across the floor. It was followed by a much more lively line dance that required partners to switch. John found himself dancing a short swirl with Miss Katherine. She refused to look at him. He did his best to ignore her and keep his attention focused on Amanda. She was the lady who truly loved him; Amanda knew his secret and still wanted to marry him. Still, Katherine's scent lingered, and his skin tingled at the touch of her.

After their dances were over, Amanda excused herself. She had promised her brother, David, the next two dances. After that she was to dance with her brother-in-law. She would not be free to dance with John again for a good half hour. Before abandoning John, Amanda asked whom he planned to dance with next.

"No one but you." John smiled and kissed her hand. "While I wait," John added, "I will sit at the piano and help play the music that will tickle your toes." Amanda giggled and ran off to find her brother.

In another corner of the room, Miss Katherine was fighting off her intended. Junior had been drinking a lot of rum in celebration of his win. He seemed to forget they were in public and kept insisting Katherine give him a kiss.

"Frank, please," she urged. "The town's eyes are upon us."

"Let 'em look," Junior slurred. "Everyone knows you're my intended. We're engaged to be married … soon you will feel what it means to be my wife." He wrapped his arms around her waist and pulled her tighter. She could feel his passion, and the fear in her eyes only made Junior want her more.

"Junior, please. Let me go."

Katherine squirmed to free herself, but Junior's grip tightened. Anger flared in his eyes. He grabbed her face in his hand and shouted, "You are to address me as Frank." Sensing eyes turning their way, he lowered his voice and pushed

Katherine farther into the corner. "What I mean to say, Katie, darling, is that since you are to be my wife, you must call me by my Christian name."

Katherine was frightened. With eyes as wide as a doe's, she begged, "Frank, please, you are hurting me."

Her terror was so compelling that Junior pressed himself against her. His hip gyrated against her, and his free hand reached down inside her bodice. Panic-stricken, Katherine clawed herself free, leaving Junior a cursing, bloody mess. Without even looking, Katherine grabbed the arm of the nearest man. With eyes blurred by tears, all she saw was a black morning jacket. "Why, good suh, of course I will dance with you."

Pulling the confused Negro onto the floor, flustered and stunned, Katherine swung Matthew between her and Junior. When she looked up and saw who it was she had chosen, she joined the chorus of gasps that had erupted from the folk surrounding them. Katherine, so stunned by what she had done, was gripping Matthew with hands like shackles.

Matthew tried to get Katherine MacPhearson to let go of him without hurting her. It was a sticky situation. He knew he could never dance with a white woman, but pushing Katherine off might harm her. That would lead to another set of problems. Before he had time to figure his way out of the situation, though, a pistol was aimed at his head.

"Get your stinking hands off of my fiancée, nigga," Junior growled.

Mrs. Atwell screamed at the sight of the gun and fainted. Her husband was heard calling for smelling salts.

Artemus Sprague, always weary, crossed over. "What is the problem, Junior?"

"As you can see," Junior snarled, "that nigga has got his filthy arms around my girl."

Suddenly the crowd parted. John was demanding folk get out of his way. He rushed forward to see Matthew and Katherine entangled. Both had been too stunned by Junior's threat to move.

"Matthew, what is going on here?" John asked.

Junior answered before Matthew had a chance to speak. "It is evident, Mr. Connolley, that your nigga is molesting my lady."

John ignored Junior. "Matthew?"

Matthew and Katherine came back to their senses. Katherine, turning on Junior, demanded, "Frank, put that gun away."

"I will do no such thing," Junior growled. Katherine yelped as Junior grabbed her by the arm and yanked her roughly beside him. "Artemus"—Junior used his gun to point—"this here nigga molested Miss MacPhearson. I want him hung."

"Mr. Connolley ..." Sheriff Sprague began.

"He did no such thing!" Katherine cried out. "We were dancing, is all." She tried to free herself from Junior's grip, but his hand clamped down on her like an alligator against a leg.

Junior glared at her. Katherine would pay for suggesting that she would willingly dance with a black man. Not only would they not wait for their wedding night, but he intended to teach her proper manners.

"It makes no difference, Miss MacPhearson," Sheriff Sprague responded. His voice held the same disgust all good folk felt at Katherine's admission. "It is against the law for any colored man to touch a white woman the way that nigga was touching you."

"But it was not by his design," Katherine pleaded.

Junior was so angered that he violently shook the woman. "Why are you protecting this nigga?" He lifted his pistol and would have hit her across the face with it, had John not stopped him by wrestling the gun from his hand.

"Back off, Mr. Connolley." The sheriff clearly sided with Junior.

Angus MacPhearson stepped in. "Katherine, you come to me." When Junior refused to release her, Mr. MacPhearson's voice became threatening. "She is not married to you yet, Junior. You best be releasing her to me."

As soon as Junior let her go, Katherine ran straight to her father. "Daddy, please! You have to stop this. Please do not let them hang Mr. Connolley's Negro."

"You will not hang my man," John demanded.

John was not pointing the gun, but the fact that he was holding it made Artemus Sprague leery. "You best hand me Junior's pistol, Mr. Connolley."

After handing over the weapon, John repeated his demand. "You will not hang my man."

With the sidearm safe in his possession, Mr. Sprague grew brave. "There is nothing you can do about it, Mr. Connolley." Spitting on the ground, he added, "Except buy yourself another nigga. The law has been broke, and your boy is going to hang."

Matthew's eyes bulged with fear. "Don't let 'em hang me, Mista Connolley," Matthew begged. "Please don't let 'em hang me." Frank Crawford Sr. and one of his hands held Matthew back. They already had Matthew's hands bound and a rope tossed over his head.

Katherine, terrified, blurted out desperately, "John made Matthew dance with me." John was mystified by this declaration, but said nothing when she mouthed the word "please."

Angus MacPhearson, noticing the silent communication, turned on his daughter, demanding, "Explain yourself, girl!"

"Mr. Connolley, ah …" she sputtered. "He … ah … he saw Junior and me, and I think he was jealous. So he sent Matthew over to ask me to dance. He … he …" Stumbling some, she ranted on, "… he was unable to ask me himself, as he was playing the piano."

By this point, the whole room was witnessing the scene. Amanda Hodson could not bear to listen to Katherine's tale. "That's a lie!" Amanda screamed. "My John would never have done a thing like that. He no longer cares about you!"

Again Katherine looked to John and whispered her silent plea.

"Jealous?" Angus MacPhearson roared. "Why, the man is engaged! What has he to be jealous of?"

Answering, Junior sputtered. "Oh, he is jealous, all right. He is always looking at my girl. I can believe that foolish story." Standing on his toes in an attempt to look John in the eye, he spat derisively, "Everyone knows you are only marrying that Hodson slut because I won the best girl."

John stepped forward, and Artemus Sprague advanced between them. "There will be no bullyrag here, Connolley."

"Oh, he is jealous, all right," Junior taunted, "and he is trying to ruin my lady by making his nigga touch her."

"That just means," Sheriff Sprague reasoned, "that Mr. Connolley here ordered his nigga to put the noose around his own neck."

Junior's laugh cackled and wheezed.

John stepped forward. His back was straight, and he looked like a bear standing on back paws. Looking down on Artemus Sprague, he insisted, "You will not hang Matthew."

Junior, sensing that John might just win this battle, crossed over to Matthew and removed the noose. Swinging it overhead, Junior lassoed John with it. "Then we will just have to hang you for ordering your nigga to dance with my Kate!" He wrapped the rope around his arm and yanked it hard enough to pull the great man to his knees.

John grabbed for the rope tightening around his neck. Struggling for breath, he desperately tried to loosen it. Amanda and Katherine raced to his side. Both women struggled to help free John.

Angus MacPhearson, angered by the sight, stepped forward and demanded John's release. When his words had no effect, Angus MacPhearson turned on Sheriff Sprague. "Artemus, you will not hang Mr. Connolley. He has committed no act of murder, nor has he stolen any horse. You cannot … you *will* not … do this!"

Artemus Sprague nodded. He may not have liked John Connolley, but he always held to the letter of the law. As far as he was concerned, John Connolley was only guilty of being a fool.

"Release him!" the sheriff demanded. When Junior failed to listen, Sheriff Sprague spun on the younger man and shouted, "Now!" Junior dropped the rope, and John was finally able to get the noose off.

Throwing the rope to the ground, John stood up and faced the sheriff, his breath raspy. "I will not allow you to hang Matthew."

"I understand," Artemus Sprague said, "but the law has been broke. How do you propose I bring forth justice? Flog you?" He turned to the good folk watching and encouraged them to laugh along with his fine joke.

John let out a long sigh. "If that is what it takes to save Matthew's life, then so be it."

Matthew's eyes nearly popped out of his head. He wanted to shout, "You cain't!" but the words choked in his throat. The threat of the noose was too overwhelming.

Sheriff Sprague ceased laughing at this point. Turning back to face John Connolley, he ran his hand along his chin, pondering the situation at hand. "This is an interesting twist." He took a moment longer to study the great man before asking, "So, Mr. Connolley, do you take full responsibility for all that has happened here today?" Artemus Sprague insisted on clarification before whipping a white man.

"I do."

The sheriff turned to face his brother-in-law. "What do you say, Junior? Would you be willing to accept a flogging of Mr. Connolley in lieu of hanging his nigga?"

Voices from the crowd started shouting, "Lynch the nigga!"

Junior raised a hand to silence them. "No." Junior walked up to John Connolley and smiled. "I like the idea of whipping Mr. Connolley. It will teach him to stay away from my lady."

Both Amanda and Katherine screamed at once, "No!"

Rushing to John's side, Amanda begged, "No, John, no. You must not do this."

"I am sorry, little darlin'," John said, looking down on his future wife, "but I have no choice." Then, turning to Sheriff Sprague, he asked, "Do I?"

"I am afraid, Miss Hodson," the sheriff explained, "that Mr. Connolley here is right. He either takes the lash, or we hang his nigga."

"Then we hang the nigga, John," Amanda insisted.

John stared down at the child he once thought a woman. Too shocked to even reply, he just listened as she rambled on.

"He's just a slave."

"He is a man, Amanda," John exclaimed. "A good man. And whether he was a slave or not, it would not matter one bit. He is a human being. Besides, I freed him. You know that!"

Amanda refused to listen. "We can always get another one. But us ..." Tears burgeoned. "What about us?" Amanda, noting Katherine's look of contempt, whirled on her. "How dare you judge me!"

John hardened. He turned Amanda to face him. "I will not let Matthew hang."

Amanda reached up on her tiptoes. John bent down some so she could whisper in his ear. "Oh, John, please. I can live with your secret, but I cannot bear to share it."

John stood straight. He looked down at Amanda, "I understand." He placed Miss Amanda Hodson into her father's arms. "Everything comes out in the wash eventually, Miss Hodson. It is best we found this out now."

Amanda's cry was heart wrenching. Plucking the regard ring from her finger, she gave it back to John Connolley. Turning to face her father, she begged him to take her home.

Brian Hodson stared at Mr. Connolley. He was dumbfounded by everything that surrounded him. Just moments ago, his daughter had been the happiest woman alive, engaged to be married to the man she loved ... and now his daughter had given back her regard ring. Even more confounding was the fact that his once future son-in-law was going to allow himself to be whipped just to save some Negro. None of it made any sense.

"Mr. Connolley," Mr. Hodson protested, "surely you do not intend to go through with this?"

"I do."

"But surely one nigga is not worth losing a wife over. Repent, suh. Let them hang the rogue, and take back your fiancée."

"I will not."

Mr. Hodson muttered an oath.

"I can no longer marry your daughter, suh. Not at the cost of a man's life."

"A nigga's life!" he said, spitting at John's feet. "You would give up my little girl to save a nigga? You are a fool!" Turning to face his son, Mr. Hodson hollered, "David! Take your sister home. Dinah, you go with them."

"But, Daddy," David whined, "if there is to be a floggin', I want to watch."

"Get going!" Mr. Hodson ordered. Then he called back his wife and pulled her aside, whispering fiercely, "You help Amanda pack her things. We'll be sending her to Savannah with Penelope. Maybe that useless husband of hers can help us find Amanda a match."

Mrs. Hodson nodded in agreement, scrambled for her children, and without so much as a curtsy, rushed them out of the hall.

Katherine turned to her father. "Daddy, you must stop this."

Although Angus MacPhearson had no wish to see John flogged, he had no positive answer to give. "And what would you have me do, little darling? The law has been broken, and the only other option is for Artemus to hang Matthew. Clearly Mr. Connolley will not allow that. I may be the only one, but I respect Mr. Connolley for what he is willing to do. It is never right to kill a man heedlessly, especially when it was caused by a young woman's foolish behavior."

Katherine blushed. Her father had seen right through her.

Angus MacPhearson looked sternly at his daughter. "Mr. Connolley was engaged. His acting out of jealousy does not make any sense."

Katherine threw herself into her father's arms. "Oh, Daddy, I made Matthew dance with me." She sobbed into his shoulder. "I just wanted to escape Junior. Everything I said about John making Matthew dance with me was all a lie."

Mr. MacPhearson pushed his daughter forward. "What are you talking about, girl?"

"Junior was behaving badly … kissing me and touching me like … like I was already his wife"—Katherine lowered her eyes in shame—"like we were in private." Katherine began to sob. "I just had to get away from him, and Matthew was the first man I grabbed. I did not even look to see who he was. All I saw was the coat. I dragged him onto the dance floor with me before I knew what I had done." Katherine wept. "I could not tell the truth, Daddy. I was so ashamed." Amid heaving sobs, Katherine begged, "Please stop this, Daddy. Do not let them whip John … not for my mistake."

Although Mr. MacPhearson sympathized with his daughter, he had to be realistic. "There is nothing I can do, little darling. Junior said Matthew molested you. The crowd, seeing his arms wrapped around you, wants vengeance. And since Mr. Connolley is not willing to let them lynch his Negro, the only recourse left is for them to flog your man." Katherine went limp in his arms. Her father held her tight. He knew the guilt was tearing her apart. Even though Katherine shook in his arms, and his heart went out to her, Angus MacPhearson chose not to console her. *This here is her doing. As much as it pains me, my Katie deserves to suffer anguish for what she has done.*

John placed Amanda's ring in his pocket before removing his jacket and vest. He paused for a moment before lifting off his shirt. As soon as Katherine heard the cloth ripple, she released herself from her father's grip. She desperately tried to hide John's back with her body. Her arms reached around his chest, and he held her hands in his. John closed his eyes as he felt her tears against him. Try as she might, Katherine was just too slight to hide much of anything. *JB* screamed from John Connolley's shoulder. Ladies dropped like flies hit by the swatter. Dr. Odland, having just revived Mrs. Atwell, had to turn around and administer smelling salts again. He was cursing; the woman weighed heavily in his arms.

Angus MacPhearson walked over to John, inspecting his back in the process. "I must say, Mr. Connolley, this is certainly an interesting piece to the puzzle. Gives the whole picture meaning, it does."

John remained silent.

Artemus Sprague and Junior walked around to see what all the fuss was about. "Guns!" the sheriff ordered as soon as he saw John's brand and back. Before the words were even out of his mouth, he had Junior's pistol pointed at the man's head. Within moments three other pistols and two shotguns were pointed at John Connolley. "It is a hanging offense to pass yourself off as a white man, boy," Artemus Sprague explained before adding, "You goddamn mulattos sicken me."

Junior turned to Katherine and laughed. "You are in love with a nigga." He spat his words as daggers. "Why, you should marry him!"

Katherine removed her regard ring and threw it at Junior. "I would," she cried, "but he would never ask me now. I do not deserve his goodness."

John closed his eyes.

Artemus Sprague smiled. "Someone bind his wrists. We got ourselves two niggas to hang tonight."

Matthew groaned. *I always knowed it'd come ta this,* he thought.

Katherine turned. "Mr. Connolley is not colored, Sheriff. Just look at him. He is white."

"I am looking at him," Sheriff Sprague said as he inspected the scars on John's back. "It only takes a drop of colored blood to make a man a nigga, Miss Katherine. Yes, suh, it only takes a drop. I have heard about how white some of you mulatto can get, but I never thought I would see one."

"Mr. Connolley has no colored blood," Katherine cried. "Mr. Barlow proved it."

"Then why is he refusing to defend himself?" Junior quipped.

"Would anyone believe me?" John asked sardonically. He knew only too well there was nothing he could say in his own defense. People were too easily influenced by the markings on his back. That damn *JB* said it all as far as the good folk of Laurel Creek were concerned.

Desperate, Katherine searched the room for help. Her eyes lighted on the doctor. "Dr. Odland!" She shouted as she pointed. "He knows. Dr. Odland knows Mr. Connolley's blood is as clean as yours or mine."

John looked down on the woman, releasing his anger. "Clean blood, Miss MacPhearson? My blood is as red as any other man's. So is Matthew's." John looked back to Artemus Sprague. "Hang me if you like, suh, but I suspect Mr. Barlow will have something to say about it if you do."

The threat of Mr. Barlow's vengeance caused the sheriff to pause. "Odland," he hollered. "Get over here!"

Dr. Odland pushed his way through the dumbfounded crowd. "I heard what Miss MacPhearson said, Sheriff. She speaks the truth. John is white. Mr. Barlow showed me papers to prove it. You best not hang him."

Artemus Sprague rubbed his chin thoughtfully, "Well, I never saw any papers. What I do see is a brand that clearly indicates this man to be property. Only slaves are property, and only niggas are slaves, except for the odd savage. Junior"—the sheriff smiled—"it looks like you get to lynch John Connolley after all."

Junior cackled and wheezed in anticipation.

Angus MacPhearson, sensing a mob forming, crossed to the door and retrieved his rifle. Aiming it just above the sheriff's head, he shot a hole in the roof. "No one is hanging anybody!" The stunned crowd gave him the time he needed to reload.

"Put that gun away, MacPhearson," Sheriff Sprague growled. "You are not the law around here."

Mr. MacPhearson shook his head. "You are not doing a good job of being the law, so I have to have my say. Now, you have two witnesses that confirm Mr. Connolley here as white. That tells me you have no recourse for hanging him."

"Their word is not good enough," the sheriff insisted. "I need to see those papers, too."

"Mr. Connolley," Mr. MacPhearson asked, "do you have those papers at your place?"

"Yes, suh," John replied. "They are in my desk drawer."

"Then I will send someone to collect them for you." Addressing Artemus Sprague, Mr. MacPhearson added, "In the meantime, Sprague, if you hang Mr. Connolley here without waiting for the evidence, Mr. Barlow will be most upset."

"Not even Jacob Barlow is above the law!" Artemus Sprague spat.

"Indeed, you are correct. However, if you hang Mr. Connolley here, and he is in fact white, I can assure you there will be a reckoning from Mr. Jacob Barlow … a revenge unmitigated." Looking directly at his old friend, Frank Crawford Sr., he added, "A revenge I will not stand in the way of."

Frank Crawford walked over to his son-in-law and whispered in his ear, Junior straining to hear. The sheriff rubbed his chin thoughtfully, then decided, "We will wait for your man to bring the papers, Mr. MacPhearson."

Mr. MacPhearson immediately issued the order, and one of his hands raced from the room.

Turning to John, the sheriff sneered, "You will not be hung for a nigga just yet. But whilst we wait for your papers," he added resolutely, "we are going to whip you for the crimes of your boy here."

Junior jumped in at this most opportune moment. "Let me be the one to whip him, Artemus." He sounded like a child begging for candy.

"I do not care who whips him," the sheriff replied, "just as long as it gets done." Still eyeing John Connolley, he added, "Get on out to that whipping post, boy."

Before John could acquiesce, Mr. MacPhearson hollered, "No one is getting hung, and no one is getting whipped, either!"

Frank Crawford stepped forward, dragging Matthew alongside him. He shook the bound man at Mr. MacPhearson as he shouted, "Are you suggesting we let Connolley and his nigga walk free for accosting your daughter?"

Angus MacPhearson was not going to back down. "Katherine told me what happened, and Matthew was not the one who accosted her."

"He is lying, Daddy. I saw that nigga grab my Katherine and drag her on the dance floor."

"Shut up, Junior!" Mr. Crawford had no patience for his son's stupidity.

"Katherine," Mr. MacPhearson turned toward his daughter. She had her face buried in Patrick's chest. "Come over here, girl."

Katherine moaned, her body quivering. Patrick released her, but she did not move.

Crossing over to his daughter, Mr. MacPhearson whispered harshly in her ear. "This here is your doing, little girl. Now, Junior was wrong for manhandling you, but it was your decision to grab Matthew, then lie about it, that has put Mr. Connolley in this mess. Now get over there and stand up for your man. For if you do not, you truly do not deserve him."

Quelling her tears, Katherine released her grip on Patrick and walked over to Artemus Sprague with the stately bearing of a queen—which crumbled the second she began talking. "Junior … he …" Turning blurry eyes to her father, she pleaded, "Oh, Daddy, please do not make me say it."

Angus MacPhearson was relentless. "Where is your courage, woman?"

Katherine closed her eyes and let it all blurt out. "Junior … he … he was treating me like a husband would treat a wife, in private. I ran into Matthew's arms, seeing only the morning suit. Matthew did not accost me. Junior did."

"Lies!" Junior shouted. "Daddy, she is lying!"

"Explain those scratches on your face!" Angus demanded.

John reddened as soon as he heard Katherine's story. As his muscles clenched, the room took a step back.

Junior yelped, but before he could leap behind his father for protection, Frank Crawford turned on his son and cuffed him. Stumbling backward, Junior turned and hid in the crowd.

Mr. Crawford, still brandishing a firearm, pointed it at John. "Back off, mister!" When John showed signs of relaxing, Frank Crawford turned to face his old friend. "So, Angus, is this how it is going to be between us?"

Angus MacPhearson's reply was simple. "It looks that way to me."

"Josephine!" Frank Crawford yelled.

The poor woman squeaked and ran straight to her husband's side.

"Find that sniveling coward of a son of yours and meet me outside." With that he turned and walked out the door.

Without a word, Josephine acquiesced. She knew the mood her husband was in. If he was not tired after he was finished with Junior, she knew she would be next.

The sheriff sneered, spat at John's feet, and followed in the wake of his family.

After the Crawfords departed, Mr. MacPhearson turned to John. "Put your shirt on, son. This bloody mess is at an end."

As soon as his shirt hid his face, John uttered a sigh of relief. He was not sure how much more his body could take. Too many beatings had already left him feeling like a crippled old man more oft than a man of thirty. He took a moment to thank God for this reprieve.

"Mr. Connolley." Katherine's voice quivered. "I am so sorry for what I did."

"It is all right, Miss Katherine," John replied softly. "You do not need to apologize."

"No, Mr. Connolley, I do. You see, everything that happened tonight is all my doing."

John's voice was gentle. "You are being too hard on yourself."

"No. Do not excuse me. The choice I made in June led us down separate paths, bringing us back here today. Because of me, your man was nearly hung. Because of me, you nearly hung with him, and Artemus would have surely whipped you if Daddy had not interfered. Dear John, can you ever forgive me?"

"Forgive you?" John whispered. "I do more than forgive you, Miss Katherine. I love you."

The room was stunned. John Connolley, a man with the markings of a slave, had the audacity to tell Miss Katherine MacPhearson that he loved her.

"Oh, John," Katherine wept. "I love you, too."

The room gasped. Miss Katherine MacPhearson had replied in kind!

CHAPTER 36

▼

DEMON RUM

The Harvest Ball had been a disgrace. The humiliation Junior had heaped upon him was too much for Frank Crawford to bear. Mr. Crawford, after slamming his way through the front doors of his plantation home at Pine Grove, turned on his son, "You fool! You bloody, bloody fool!" Mr. Crawford's voice echoed and boomed.

Junior shuddered beneath his father's daunting glare. "But, Daddy," the desperate youth pleaded, "Katherine was lying."

After smashing the rum bottle he had emptied and cradled on the way home, Mr. Crawford picked up a richly carved high-backed chair and threw it at his son. Junior barely managed to leap out of the way. The chair shattered like glass against the front door. "It does not matter one iota that she lied," Mr. Crawford bellowed. "Did Katherine MacPhearson come across looking like a fool?" Selecting another high-backed chair, Crawford Sr. smashed it against the black slate flooring. Ripping free one of the legs, he aimed it at Junior. "Did Connolley? No! It was me who was made into a fool before the entire town. Me! For believing in you! Trust me, son. I will never make that mistake again."

"Daddy, please," Junior simpered.

Josephine, who had been hiding behind the brocade curtains, lunged toward her husband's arm in a desperate attempt to wrestle free the intended weapon. Frank Crawford flung her like a rag doll against the center table. A large porcelain vase filled with cattails and palm leaves smashed against the floor. Josephine slid through the water and debris. The poor woman found herself caught between the wildcat and its prey. Only a mother's instinct emboldened her to stand. Mrs. Crawford never got further than her knees. A series of blows rained down on the woman; each word was a hit against her stomach and ribs. "Never. Again. Shall. You. Come. Between. Me. And. My. Disciplining. This. Child!"

Junior leapt to his mother's defense. He could suffer his father's wrath but he never could stand to watch his mother get beaten. Pulling his father off Jospehine, Junior managed to get in a few blows before his father cracked the chair leg against his jawbone. Landing on his hands and knees, Junior spat out a mouth full of blood and two teeth.

Crawford Sr. hovered over him. "So the whelp is finally trying to be a man, is he? Well, it is high time I made you into one!" Indeed, Frank Crawford Sr. had had all he could stomach of Junior. He even questioned whether the boy was really his blood. He was no longer willing to look at his "baby girl" of a son. Junior's face, he determined, had to change. Even if the interior of his son remained effeminate, before this night was over, Junior would bear the image of a man. He threw the chair leg aside. For this he would use his hands. Fists rounded against the young man's face, smashing against cheekbones, jaw, and nose, pummeling down on eyes. By the time the hour struck twelve, Junior was a bag of broken bones on a blood-stained floor.

Dr. Odland's arrival came as a shock to Mr. Crawford. He demanded to know the name of the rogue who had sent for the doctor. The "fool nigga" who had gone to fetch him begged Dr. Odland to hide his identity, knowing full well Mr. Crawford would further his revenge on him.

"Who sent for me," Dr. Odland reiterated, "is of no consequence. I am here now. Show me to your wife and son."

"Fine," Crawford Sr. hollered. "Don't tell me the bastard's name! But I swear to God above and the devil below, if I ever find out who brought you, I will plant his head on a spike as a warning to the rest of my Negroes!"

Dr. Odland blanched at such a cruel recitation, believing the man capable of such a grisly threat. Move aside, Mr. Crawford," the doctor replied curtly. "Or am I to assume your plan was to murder your son?"

As Mr. Crawford stepped aside, a wicked sneer rippled across his lips. "Your patients await you, suh."

*   *   *   *

Upon first sight of Junior, Dr. Odland found the struggle to retain the contents of his stomach impossible. He had to empty himself a few times before he could begin the process of reconstruction.

The young man was left blind in his right eye. His nose was flattened with very little bone left for rebuilding, and his jaw now slanted to the left, diminishing his once-famous smile. Frank Crawford had been successful; his son now bore the appearance of a dangerous man.

His brain, addled by the beating, had also changed. Junior had always been a mean cuss, but now he was violent to all he knew. This new, twisted mentality, coupled with intense anger and hatred, turned Junior into a deadly demon. There was only one place for a man like him, and when the call to arms came in 1812, Junior leapt at the opportunity to escape his father and embrace the right to kill. Death came to greet him on January 8, 1815, in the Battle of New Orleans. Junior was one of seventy-one Americans to die in the battle that brought honor and victory to America. Frank Crawford felt no pride in his son's contribution to this memorable event. Nor did he grieve the news of his son's demise. He merely beat his wife for having failed to produce a worthy heir.

CHAPTER 37

▼

MATTHEW'S REQUEST

On the morning after the Harvest Ball, Matthew sat at the kitchen table, waiting for John to wake up. He had sat there all night, pondering the previous evening's events, determining what he had to do as a result.

"Mornin', Matthew," John muttered, as he wiped the sleep from bleary eyes.

"Mornin', John." Gesturing to the chair across from him, Matthew continued, "Please sit down. I needs ta talk ta you's."

"What is it, Matthew?" John was concerned. His friend seemed quite grave.

"I's been thinkin' 'bout what ya did for me last night."

"It was nothin', Matthew. Forget it."

"Nothin'?" This blatant dismissal of the threat against their lives angered Matthew. "It weren't nothin', John! Ya saved my life. I take that sorta thing seriously."

"Of course. I'm sorry, Matthew. I guess I meant to say let's not worry 'bout it."

"But I gots to. They almost hung you's. Y'all was willin' ta let 'em whip you's. Ya gave up yer lady … all jes' ta save me." Matthew lowered his head. "I's sorry, John."

"Don't be, Matthew. This was bound to come out someday. If she cain't live with my past, how can I live with her?"

"Still," Matthew persisted. "Ya coulda had a wife and children. I done stole that from you's."

"Now listen here." John was stern. "You did nothin' wrong. It was all—" John paused to sigh—"Miss Katherine … and me, too, I guess. She lied, and I let her. I couldn't let them hang you, Matthew. Not for somethin' you didn't do."

"I thanks ya, John." Matthew was nearly in tears. "I owes ya."

"You don't owe me nothin', Matthew."

John was firm, but so was Matthew. "No, suh, John, ya gotta listen ta me. Ya done saved my life …"

John cut him off. "You saved my life, too, remember? The night Junior beat me. You could have run, but you went and got Mr. MacPhearson instead."

Matthew persisted. "Ya saved me twice. First ya brung me here when Massa Barlow was sure ta hang me … then ag'in last night. An' ya freed me." Waving a hand to silence his friend, Matthew continued, "No, suh, John Connolley, I knows ya paid Barlow for me. That man don't free nobody. How much I cost you's?"

John refused to answer.

"I wants ta know, John. I needs ta know, an' I plans ta work for ya 'til I's paid every penny."

John objected, "Matthew, that'll take years."

"I don't care. I's gonna pay back every cent, ya hear? I's workin' for ya 'til then. No, suh … ya ain't gettin' rid a' me that easy."

John smiled. "I'd sure be glad to have your help, Matthew. You're a fine man and a good friend."

"So it be settled, then," Matthew said. "How much I cost?"

"Twenty-seven bushels of tobacco."

"Ooowee, that much." There was almost a note of pride in his voice, then recognition set it. "Ya sho is right … it's gonna take me a long time ta pay all that." Determination set in. "But I's gonna do it. Ya jes' watch. Someday I's gonna be free."

"You already are free, Matthew. Them papers been signed. I'm your sponsor. You can live and work free in Georgia for the rest of your life. Now, if you want to pay me back, you can. I'll hire you on. But you ain't no man's slave no more."

Matthew echoed John's words. "I ain't no man's slave no mo'."

CHAPTER 38

▼

MAKING LOVE

It was awkward for John to sit there with his arms folded on the kitchen table, watching his wife avoid him. Katherine bustled about their little kitchen, desperately trying to keep busy, but there was nothing for her to do until Patrick and Matthew arrived. Still she rushed around, wiping an already clean counter and rearranging the plates she had set on the table. Twice she picked up the frying pan to put it on the stove before setting it back down on the counter.

Katherine had failed to perform last night—their first night of conjugal bliss. John did not hold it against her. She was so frightened when he had tried to enter her she cried out, begging him to stop. Lying with her back to him, she had cried. No soothing words could make her stop. Katherine eventually fell asleep, but John had remained awake most of the night. He ached for relief and eventually took himself outside.

When John returned, he discovered Katherine awake. "Where did you go?" she asked timorously.

"I just went for a short walk," John replied. "I needed some air."

"I am suffocating my husband," she wailed. Throwing her face into her pillow, Katherine once again began to weep.

Kneeling beside the bed, John whispered, "Please, wife, do not cry. It is never easy the first time. We can go slow. We can try again."

"No! Please, no," Katherine begged. Her eyes were puffy and red, her face filled with terror. She thought he meant right then.

John swept her up into his arms. He hated seeing her so. She was shaking like a leaf. "I just want to hold you. I will not make you do anythin', I promise." As desperately as John wanted to make love to his wife, he had no desire to hurt her. Having her repulsed by him was worse than death. He would give anything for her to want his body next to hers. *Married life ain't so easy*, he thought wryly.

John gently rocked Katherine until she fell asleep in his arms. He must have fallen asleep himself at some point, for when he opened his eyes, Katherine had already risen. He could hear her rustling about in the kitchen. She had turned crimson when he entered the room, keeping her eyes downcast.

Holding out his hand, John called, "Katherine … wife. Come here."

Katherine obeyed but refused to look at him.

Putting his arm around her waist, John pulled her down onto his lap.

Caressing her chin, he lifted her face. She immediately closed her eyes. "Wife," he said softly, "look at me."

Katherine burst into tears, hiding her face in her hands.

"Tell me, what is wrong?" John asked softly.

"I am not a good wife," Katherine lamented.

"How can you say that?"

"I could not … I would not let you … a wife has no right to refuse her husband." Through a gush of tears, she added, "Oh, John, how can you love me?"

"Because you are beautiful, kind, an' lovin'. I would not trade you for any woman."

Her eyes opened briefly.

"There is my favorite smile."

Katherine shut her eyes as soon as John made eye contact.

"Please, wife, look at me."

"I am so ashamed, John. You deserve better than me."

"I could say the same, and with more reason than you."

Bleary eyes opened wide in wonderment.

"You gave up everythin' for me," John explained. "Wealth, society … an' you accepted my shame when you married me."

The defiant glint John so admired flared up in Katherine's eyes. "You have nothing to be ashamed of, John Connolley." She actually balled her hand into a fist and punched him in the chest. He grunted in response. "Never let anyone ever tell you that! I do not care what other people say. You are a good man, and I love you."

"And I love you. I am OK that things did not work last night. We will get there. We have a lifetime ahead of us to make things work."

Katherine withered like a bluebell struck by frost. "But I … it hurt, John … and I was so scared. I am afraid to try again."

"There is nothin' to be afraid of. I am not goin' to hurt you. I will be gentle … I promise."

"But you were gentle last night, so kind to me … and it still hurt. Oh, John, I know I have to do it, but … I-I am so frightened."

"Do you trust me?"

Katherine nodded. Her eyes squeezed tight; lips trembled.

"Then come with me into the bedroom," John whispered seductively.

Katherine froze at the suggestion. The negative connotation surrounding last night's failure hindered her. John sensed her unease. "It's all right Katherine. We can stay here. We're in the kitchen, though. Do you mind if I try something?

Katherine nodded her approval.

"I am just goin' to do somethin', OK?" John reached down and lifted up Katherine's skirt.

Katherine's heart started to race. Her muscles tightened as she squeezed her legs together.

"Can you relax for me?" John gently inquired. "I just want to put my hand here. Just my hand. I am not goin' to do anythin' to hurt you. I promise. I just want to start small, with my finger."

As he tried to enter her, Katherine squirmed. "John, please." She was like a frightened chick fallen from the nest, desperately searching for her mama's wings to hide her.

"I will stop. How about I just rest my hand here?"

Katherine nodded.

John kissed her gently. Slowly, almost imperceptibly, John's fingers began to caress her. Katherine started to moisten, her body relaxing into his arms. "Is that OK?" he whispered into her ear, hoping his breath would help excite her. "Do you want me to stop?"

Katherine shook her head. Her breathing deepened, causing her breasts to swell. Her legs relaxed. Her neck arched. John leaned in to kiss it. John's finger slipped inside, and Katherine gasped.

"There, that was easy. Did it hurt much?"

Once again she shook her head.

Slowly rotating his finger, he asked, "Do you want me to stop?"

Opening her eyes, she whispered though quivering lips, "No."

"Kiss me."

Hungry lips united. Katherine's teeth pulled on John's mouth as his fingers began dancing against her. Imagining he was playing Mozart's Piano Sonata in A Major, John rhythmically tapped out the rustic harmonies of the finale, *alla turca*. Katherine moaned. It was intoxicating to feel her squirm against him. He hardened and wished he could enter her. He could be patient, though. The last thing he wanted was to make his wife bitter.

Holding Katherine's breast, John used it like a percussion instrument. Katherine's lips let go of his as her body arched. Her eyes opened wide. Deep, heavy breaths were accented with stifled moans. John watched as a flush raced up from her cleavage over her neckline and face. She grabbed his hand, causing his finger to slide back inside. It went in so easily, John leaned in to her ear and asked, "May I try again?"

Katherine sat there, pressing his hand against her, nodding her assent.

"Stand for me."

Releasing her grip, Katherine stood so John could undo his pants. Gasping at the sight of him, she quickly closed her eyes.

"It's OK," he whispered. "You are my wife. You can see me."

Katherine tried to open her eyes, but could not bring herself to do it. He was enormous, and it was impossible to imagine him fitting inside her. Determined not to give in to her fear, she asked timidly, "What do I do?"

John smiled. He enjoyed explaining things to her. "Face me."

Katherine complied, eyes still closed.

John lifted her skirt up to her thighs.

Katherine quivered.

"It is OK," he whispered. "We can wait."

"No, John." Katherine opened her eyes. "I want to."

"Step your leg over. There you go. Now bend your knees for me."

Katherine did as she was told, and when she was low enough, John rubbed himself against her. Shaking from renewed pleasure, Katherine started to moan, trying to stifle the sound by biting her lip. John held her hips and began pushing himself inside. Katherine swallowed and tried not to cry.

"Does it still hurt?"

Katherine nodded.

"Do you want me to stop?"

Shaking her head fervently, she allowed John to guide her body downward. Once fully immersed, he started to pulse. Katherine smiled. The vibrations were reviving her recent pleasure.

"There, was that so bad?" John asked in soothing tones.

Katherine responded by kissing him. As John was slowly lifting and lowering her body, Katherine opened her eyes and watched with astonishment the look of joy radiating on her husband's face. He had given her such feelings of pleasure, and she wanted him to feel the same. He pulled her body closer, so she was rubbing against him. The swelling passion ignited, causing her body to arch. They moaned in unison.

John opened his eyes. Through heavy breaths, he asked, "Are you OK?"

Katherine was crying.

Lord, he asked himself, *why do I always make women cry?* "Katherine, I am sorry. I pushed it too far. I did not mean to hurt you."

"You did not hurt me. These are tears of joy." She kissed him. "You made me feel so beautiful. I cannot believe I shied away from you last night." After a deep kiss, Katherine promised, "Oh, John, I will never shy away from you again."

John laughed, pleased with his wife's transformation. Clasping his hands around her buttocks, he pulled her in for another kiss. "Come, we must separate," John said wisely. "Patrick or Matthew could walk in on us any moment."

"May we …" Gasping, Katherine blushed at her boldness.

Smiling, delighted that his wife now desired him, John whispered, "Tonight."

One more kiss ensued before Katherine reluctantly released her husband. As soon as she stood, though, she gasped again. Quickly gathering up her skirt between her legs, she ran back into the bedroom. John could not help but laugh.

Katherine's voice scolded, "How dare you laugh at me, Mr. Connolley?" Popping her head out from around the corner, she unsuccessfully scowled at John. "Make yourself useful and go fetch me some water for coffee."

"Yes, ma'am." John rose, doing up his trousers as he crossed the front room. Blessing his timing, he greeted Matthew at the front door. "Mornin', Matthew."

"Mornin', John. Did ya sleep well?" John nodded. "An' de missus?" Matthew's grin was mischievous. John would have shoved him if he had not been holding a pail of milk in one hand and a pail of eggs in the other.

"Just fine, Matthew. How'd you enjoy sleepin' in the hayloft?"

"Wit' that bed ya put up thar, it be like havin' a place a' my own. I likes it real fine."

"We'll build you a place soon. Over the winter, I reckon."

Matthew smiled. *My own home!* He still found it hard to believe he would have a house of his very own. Grinning, he asked, "Where'd ya like me ta put this here milk an' eggs?"

"Eggs on the table an' milk in the pantry, next to the separator."

"Sho thing. Where ya off ta?"

"Fetchin' some water for my wife ta make coffee with."

"Ya wants me ta fetch it for ya?"

"No, thank you, Matthew."

As John left, Matthew crossed to the table to deposit the pail of eggs. As he entered the pantry, he discovered Patrick MacPhearson crouched against the wall. The youth was as pale as the milk Matthew carried.

Before Matthew could speak, Patrick silently implored him to be quiet.

"Mista Patrick," Matthew whispered, "what ya doin' in here? You's all whey-faced. Ya sick, suh?"

"No ... I ... I just came in ... are they still in the other room?"

Matthew glanced over his shoulder to look into the kitchen and parlor. "No, suh. John's gone ta fetch some water, an' Mrs. Connolley, your sister, suh ... she ... well, I don't rightly know where she is."

"I do," Patrick replied in a hoarse whisper.

"What you mean, Mista Patrick?"

"I came too early. I came in the back way, like I always do ... and ... I almost walked in on them."

"Walked in on 'em? Doin' what? Ohhh ... in de kitchen?"

"In de kitchen," Patrick parroted.

"Looks like ya was in de wrong place at de wrong time, Mista Patrick. Well, they don't needs ta knows ya saw."

Patrick winced.

"Come on, lemme help you up. Sit down here at de table."

"Not that chair!"

"Try an' liven up some, Mista Patrick. Ya don't want 'em suspectin' ya knows."

"I cannot stay in here," Patrick groaned. "How can I look at my sister now?"

"Mista Patrick. They's husband an' wife. What ya seen were all natural."

"In a kitchen? On a chair?"

"Hush now, the missus might hear. Set down. Ya jes' rememba' they's married. This here's thar home. Ya gots ta be comin' in de front door, an' knockin', from now on."

"You are right, Matthew. I will be more careful in the future."

"Now come on, we's gots ta meet Joh—Mista Connolley down in that swamp. He wants ta be plantin' rice thar next year, so we gots us some clearin' ta do."

CHAPTER 39

▼

GERTRUDE ATWELL

Katherine sat, smiling politely. Her cheeks were smarting from the effort, but her mama had taught her the importance of decorum, regardless of how crass your guest might prove to be. Gertrude Atwell was proving just how asinine a well-bred lady could be. She never said anything directly, but the insinuations were enough to make Katherine blush. From the moment Mrs. Atwell walked through the door, she had been all consolation.

"Oh, Miss MacPhearson ... Mrs. Connolley, I mean. Do forgive me. It will take some getting used to, your being married and all. But how are you feeling? I heard ... word is all around town ... it is all anyone can speak of ... every tongue is flapping. Why did you keep this a secret, you naughty little creature? You, getting married ... and to Mr. Connolley, of all people. Oh my! We all know ... I mean, everyone has seen or heard ..."

About his back, Katherine thought grimly. *Yes, I am sure the whole town is all a-titter over that one.*

"Well, enough of that," Gertrude said through an embarrassed giggle. "I am sure he is a good man. He keeps a large sum of money in my Joseph's bank, after all. A man with over a thousand dollars to his name cannot be all that bad, now can he? He never touches it, either, my Joseph was saying. Frugal!" she added pointedly. "That is a fine trait in a man. You know you will never want for nothing with a thousand dollars in the bank. Is he planning on adding more to that account, I wonder?"

He most certainly will not! Katherine thought grimly. She knew where that money had come from. Mr. Barlow had confessed that fact to her in June. Keeping her thoughts well concealed, Katherine smiled sweetly. "Mr. Connolley has made no mention of any future deposits."

Mrs. Atwell, failing to conceal her chagrin, barged on. "Well, no worries. Still, his background is hardly becoming of a MacPhearson. I must say I am surprised your daddy approved of the match."

"My daddy respects Mr. Connolley—"

"Oh, I am sure he does," Mrs. Atwell interjected. "Your marriage is proof enough … unless you slipped off and eloped without his knowing?" Gertrude eyed Katherine searchingly, half looking for the affirmation. When Katherine pointedly ignored her suggestion, Mrs. Atwell pushed on. "No? Of course not. You are a good girl. One raised such as you would never cause such distress and dishonor to her family. But Mr. Connolley? I mean … well, we all thought you were going to marry Junior. You were engaged to him, after all. Now there is a man … such a man, my lady. A man of wax, as William Shakespeare would say."

"Indeed, most people seem to think so," Katherine replied dryly. *How appropriate,* she thought, *that it is the nurse you are quoting. Neither woman can restrain her mouth.* It made Katherine think of one of Juliet's lines: *And stint thou too!* Not that Mrs. Atwell was likely to slow her onslaught of words any more than the nurse ever did.

Suddenly the bulky woman shuddered, gasping a sigh. "At least he used to be. Poor thing." Shaking her head in dismay, she continued through suppressed sobs, "Such a pity about his accident. They say his horse reared up and kicked him in the face."

Katherine grimaced. *They may say that,* she thought bitterly, *but we all know the truth.* She took a moment to thank God for having helped her escape a life chained to that family.

After a brief pause of reverent respect, Mrs. Atwell continued. "Junior was such a lovely youth … so handsome and charming. Oh, well … even without his former good looks, he is still a wealthy man." Her emphasis on the latter suggested Junior's monetary value outweighed even his physical appearance. "A fine match for any young lady. But you have married a fine man, too. John Connolley does, after all, have a sizable sum of money in my Joseph's bank. And he owns his own land, small though it may be. But I am sure he will develop it into a mighty plantation in no time, just like your daddy did." Without even drawing a breath, Gertrude rambled on, "I hear tell he owns a slave now. He will need more than one nigga if he wants this place to grow. Has he purchased a little nigga girl to work the kitchen for you?"

Katherine barely had time to shake her head.

"No! Oh, my. Well, being just newly wed, the marriage so sudden and all, I suppose Mr. Connolley has not had time to find you a little girl yet."

Katherine was angered by the woman's feigned ignorance but managed to keep her choler inside. "Mr. Connolley, as you know, will not be purchasing a Negro child ... or any Negroes for that matter."

"Oh, of course not. But your daddy, no doubt, has plans to give you a nigga or two."

It took great willpower not to roll her eyes, but Katherine managed somehow. "No, ma'am. Mr. Connolley has flatly refused any gifts of persons."

"Well, that hardly seems fair, now does it? Why, with him owning a hand for the field, it seems only right he give you a little girl for the kitchens." With a quick perusal of the adjoining room, Gertrude added a mental note to reduce the plural to the singular. John Connolley's small house confirmed her belief: poor Katherine MacPhearson had fallen on hard times.

"Mr. Connolley," Katherine responded curtly, "owns no slave. Matthew is a free man of color. He has purchased his freedom from my husband."

Not even bothering to hide her shock, Gertrude Atwell blurted, "Where did a nigga like that get that kind of money?"

"My husband saw fit to lend it to him. Matthew is now working for Mr. Connolley in order to pay off his debt." Struggling to maintain decorum, Katherine smiled and motioned for Mrs. Atwell to take a seat in one of the wing chairs.

Mrs. Atwell filled the chair; portions of her hips and thighs spilled out underneath the arms. "An indentured servant, is it? Well, almost the same as a slave. If he reneges on any of his payment, you can easily convince the court to make him property."

"My husband would never ..."

Like a hawk diving for a mouse, Gertrude Atwell honed in on the words "my husband." "It's so hard to believe ... you are a new bride. One day married."

"Yes," Katherine replied, as she moved toward the kitchen to retrieve a plate of biscuits. Before Katherine could even offer any, Mrs. Atwell snapped up a cookie, stuffed it in her mouth, and continued talking while eating. "And not even a honeymoon. I know Junior would have taken you all over the world if you would have married him." Another cookie, followed by yet another, popped inside Gertrude Atwell's mouth.

Katherine was stunned at how much, and how quickly, this woman could consume. No wonder she was no longer the slight little colt Joseph Atwell had presented to the community ten years ago. "But I did not marry Junior, as you know. I married Mr. Connolley."

"Yes," Mrs. Atwell replied, with crumbs of biscuit flying from her lips. "And he was to marry little Amanda Hodson. Lord only knows what will happen to her now. She always was a wild little thing ... a libertine just like her sister. Well, we all know where she is going to end up ... Margarette's!" More crumbs sputtered with her final exclamation.

Katherine winced. "Her father, I heard, has sent her to live with her sister in Savannah."

"Well," Mrs. Atwell grunted over another biscuit, "we all know what happened to that one. Penelope's life is certainly not one any young lady would envy. Such is the future for Miss Hodson, if you are asking me."

I most certainly am not, Katherine thought cynically.

"But you will never suffer such a fate, will you, Mrs. Connolley? Not married to such a formidable man as Mr. Connolley. Why, I have never seen such a big ..." Gertrude Atwell coughed, having suddenly choked on another biscuit. Katherine leaned forward to offer aid, but Mrs. Atwell waved Katherine's hand away. "I am fine, child." Mrs. Atwell's smile faded and turned conciliatory, "And such a slight child you are. Pure innocence. I remember the innocent days. And I remember the loss of that innocence." Mrs. Atwell leaned her mighty bulk as far forward as the confines of the chair would allow. Taking Katherine's hand in hers, she continued, "Last night was your first night as a married woman," she whispered sympathetically. She patted Katherine's hand.

Poor Katherine blushed, desperately trying to find a way to avoid the upcoming conversation.

"It must have been ... difficult. I understand the trials a woman must endure. Believe me, child, I do. It is a cross every woman has to bear. And still, Mr. Connolley ..." Suddenly the woman shuddered, massive rolls of fat jiggling. "The sheer size of him. Why, your cross must be larger than most women's."

Katherine gasped. Livid, she pulled her hand free of Gertrude Atwell's condescending caress and stood. "I will ask you to please respect my husband's privacy. His size and the cross I have to bear is none of your concern." She was just about to ask Mrs. Atwell to leave when she heard John clearing his throat.

John Connolley was standing in the kitchen with one arm around Matthew and the other around Patrick. All three men stood there, red in the face, having heard the last of the ladies' conversation.

Another gasp crossed Katherine's lips as soon as she saw John's leg. A long gash ripped open his trousers and cut deep into the flesh of his left calf. His pant leg was stained to the boot with blood and mud.

"John! What happened?"

"We were clearin' the lower swamp of trees. Patrick here slipped in the mud while takin' a swing with his ax."

Patrick lowered his eyes in shame.

"It could have happened to anyone of us," John said, hoping to ease Patrick's guilt. It really had not been the young man's fault. "His ax ended up in my leg instead of the ol' oak."

Patrick, abashed, lowered his head.

Katherine moved swiftly, standing in front of John before he finished his explanation. Her fingers hit straight for the buttons on his trousers.

John's hands were as fast as hers, and he clamped them down on hers. He shot a glance at Mrs. Atwell.

Katherine understood instantly and turned gracefully toward her guest. "Mrs. Atwell, your company has been a delight, but as you can see, an accident has occurred, and I must now tend to my husband."

"Allow me to assist," Mrs. Atwell grunted as she squeezed herself out of the chair. She waddled over.

Mortified, John shouted "No!" and stopped the poor woman in her tracks. So stunned by this outburst was Mrs. Atwell that she even took a few steps back.

Katherine immediately set to work smoothing things out. "Mrs. Atwell, as much as I appreciate your kind offer of assistance, please try and understand, my husband is a very private man." Walking over to the older lady, Katherine wrapped her arm through Gertrude Atwell's elbow and led her toward the door. "There is no need to worry. As you can see, I have Patrick and Matthew here to assist me if required. You would, however, prove most useful if, when you get back to town, you would send word to the doctor to come out right away."

Gertrude Atwell was far from placated, but she accepted Katherine's excuse with some grace. "Of course, Mrs. Connolley. I will do as you ask." Without even bothering to face John, she added a quick, "Good day, gentlemen."

As soon as Mrs. Atwell was gone, Katherine issued orders. "John, get those trousers off. Matthew, you help him."

"I do not need help undoin' pants," John exclaimed. Katherine ignored him, but thankfully Matthew listened, and John was free to unbutton his own trousers.

"Patrick," Katherine ordered, "I want you to fetch me a basin of water and some clean rags." As soon as John's trousers were a tangled mess around his feet, Katherine began again. "Matthew, get your master—"

John cut her off with a stern look.

"—I mean, Mr. Connolley, a chair."

Matthew had the chair placed instantly.

"Good. Now John, sit for me."

Patrick returned with a basin of water and a sheet he had torn into strips.

"Thank you, Patrick. Put the basin on the table and set those rags next to it. Matthew, grab me that bottle of whiskey." Then, as an afterthought, she added, "And a glass. Pour him a drink." Katherine paused in thought. "Patrick."

Riddled with guilt, Patrick leaped in the air at the curt sound of his sister's voice. Katherine felt no sympathy. "Go into the spare room," she ordered. "Next to my sewing kit is the bag Dr. Odland gave me. I need a needle and some cat-gut." She looked her husband in the eyes. "I am going to have to do some stitching, John, and it will hurt. Matthew, pour him another drink."

John took the glass and swallowed the shot. Beginning to feel the warmth of the liquor, he smiled mischievously. "If I didn't know better, wife, I'd think you were trying ta get me drunk."

"You hush. I am trying to get you numb. Pour some whiskey in the glass for me, Matthew."

Both men looked at her.

"Not to drink! I am going to pour it on John's wound to clean it. Dr. Odland believes cleaning the wound helps it heal." Matthew handed her a glass half full of the golden liquor. Before pouring, she warned, "John, this is going to hurt. Do you want something to bite down on?"

"No, I'll be OK," he reassured her, but he stiffened, stifling a yelp, when she started pouring the whiskey over his wound.

Katherine turned accusing eyes toward her brother. He had just returned with her bag in hand. "Patrick, were there any wood chips on the blade of that ax?"

Patrick stammered for a bit and then answered, "No, ma'am. I think it was clean."

Irritated, Katherine shot back, "Thinking is not good enough, Patrick. Do you know?"

"Now, Katherine," John said soothingly, "take it easy on Patrick. He feels bad enough as it is."

Katherine inspected the wound more thoroughly, using tweezers in case she had to remove any splinters.

John winced but refused to cry out.

Katherine stood, turning on her brother, and cursed. "What you boys are doing out there is just plain foolish. Damn you, Patrick!"

John took his wife's hand, turning her to face him. With a slight tug from John, she knelt down beside him. He took Katherine's face in his hand—not too roughly, but with a grip strong enough to let her know he was angry. "First off, Katherine, I never want to hear you curse again. Is that understood?"

Katherine nodded. Her eyes moistened, but it did not deter John from his purpose.

"Second, what happened was not Patrick's fault. It was an accident. It could have happened to anyone. Third, what we do out there is not foolishness; it is our livelihood. Fourth, we are not boys. We are men!" John was almost too adamant with the last, and the tears Katherine was fighting back sprang forth. "And lastly," John said softly as he wiped the tears from her eyes, "thank you for takin' charge, gettin' rid of that woman, and fixin' me up like you are." John caressed her cheek with his fingers.

Katherine flushed and whispered, "I am sorry, John."

John leaned forward and kissed her. Whispering in her ear, he asked, "You plannin' on fixin' my leg?"

Putting her shame aside, Katherine leaped back into action. "Paddy, where is my kit? Matthew, pour John another drink."

Soon John's leg was stitched, with a bandage neatly wrapped around it. "Well, you two," Katherine chastised. "What are you standing around here for? Surely you have work to do, and a fair sight more with John injured. Get to it."

"Yes, ma'am!" Patrick and Matthew chanted in unison as they both rushed out the pantry door.

By this point, all the whiskey Katherine had been pouring down John's throat had started to take affect, and he was beginning to feel randy. He grabbed Katherine by the waist and sat her down on his good leg.

Katherine could tell exactly what her husband was up to. As he was only in short breeches, it was easy to feel his intent. She squirmed slightly to free herself from his arms. "Now John, you let me go. You are in no condition for this sort of foolishness."

"Kiss me, wife."

Katherine tried to protest. "You want more than a kiss, I can tell." Still, she acquiesced and pressed her lips against his. Somewhat at a loss for breath, she tried reasoning with her husband. "You are in no condition—"

John cut her off with another kiss. "I have me an idea," he said when he finally released her lips.

Katherine swayed slightly on his lap. After her experience earlier in the morning, John's touch had a way of igniting a fire inside that was impossible for her to put out. "What might that be?" she asked tentatively.

John leaned in and whispered in her ear, causing her to tremble. "Do you trust me, wife?"

Breathing deeply, she replied, "I trust you, husband."

"Then help me into our room."

CHAPTER 40

▼

PINE GROVE

John and Mr. Barlow sat on the teak chairs on the small veranda, facing a rippling field of tobacco. John still planted tobacco, as well as rice and cotton, now. They were watching a bunch of flies swarm over the corpse of a small bird that had fallen from its nest. A family of tree swallows had settled on the edge of John's roof.

"I had best clean that up. Little Evelyn will cry if she sees one of her baby birds is dead."

Mr. Barlow nodded solemnly. "I reckon young James will be mighty disappointed, too, being he is the one who discovered the nest."

"He will be upset," John agreed. Standing and crossing over to the corpse, he picked it up and flung it into the nearby bushes. "Both younguns like to watch them play with feathers."

"How is that?" Mr. Barlow asked.

"These tree swallows like to drop a feather off the roof and catch it before it hits the ground. It keeps the little 'uns mesmerized for hours." John let out a slight laugh. "I have to admit, I enjoy watching them, too." John sighed as he looked in the direction of the dead chick. "But it is Evelyn we really have to worry about. That little girl will cry over anything. Once she starts wailing, it is nigh on impossible to calm her down."

"She is a tenderhearted little thing," Jacob said, "much like her grandmother was."

John smiled at the mention of his mother. "Most little girls are, I reckon," he mused.

"Well, now that the bird is out of sight, there is nothing to worry about."

"I am not so sure," John said, returning to his seat. "James has named every one of them birds. He will figure it out soon enough. I just hope he is not so cruel as to tease his sister."

"Where is my little man?" Mr. Barlow asked with pride. Jacob Barlow loved John's firstborn. He was a big child—fourteen pounds at birth—who clearly resembled his father. Every time Mr. Barlow saw the lad, he was reminded of John's youth, when he had shared a true father-son relationship with John Connolley.

As a result, James had become Mr. Barlow's favorite grandchild, surpassing even Raymond Poitras III. There were no feelings of jealousy from Emily's family. Living in New Orleans, her children seldom had an opportunity to visit. The youngest Raymond was also of an age where a grandfather's interest was not essential for his happiness. He was nearing twenty, and when he was not helping his father run the business, he was seeking out hunting partners and ladies to dance with.

"James is inside helping his mama bake you a cake."

Mr. Barlow grunted. "You should not let him work in the kitchen like that. That is not the proper way to raise a man."

"My mama taught me to cook when I was little. She always said a man ain't always gonna have a woman around to do his biddin'."

"Do not talk foolish, John. You have a fine little man in there, and you are allowing your wife to raise him like a woman."

"Are you suggesting I am less of a man because I can flip an egg or cook up grits? Shoot, Uncle Jacob. Learning how to cook is not going to kill the boy."

"If I had known what your mama was up to, I never would have let that woman keep you in the kitchen."

"What is done is done, and I am no worse for wear. Besides, when Katherine gets sick, we still eat a decent meal. She says so herself. That is high praise coming from her."

"Yes, suh, you are one lucky man. Your wife can sure cook up a fine meal. Still, you ought to hire her some help. She comes from a fine family. It is not proper for a gentle lady to do common labor."

Incensed, John replied, "Katherine does not view being my wife as common labor."

"Now, John, that is not what I meant. She ought to be running a household, not working it. I know you are opposed to owning slaves, but surely you can afford to hire your wife some help."

"We can afford it," John replied, "but she does not want any help. I have already asked her."

"She has two little 'uns to look after and another on the way," Mr. Barlow countered. "She cannot keep doing everything by herself."

"When she wants help, I will hire someone."

"You ought to hire someone anyway. Remember, she has already lost two."

John sighed. Those were painful times. Katherine still grieved the loss of those babies.

Mr. Barlow persisted with his argument. "You especially need help for those times when your wife does take sick. It is not proper for a man to work in the kitchen."

Mr. Barlow was in lecture mode, and John knew the best thing to do was smile and nod.

"And now you are letting her teach your son how to cook. It is not right for a man to be schooled in housework. That is a woman's domain. Men have no business in there."

"Well, you need not worry yourself, Uncle Jacob. I know from personal experience that the novelty of helping your mama wears out real fast. It will not be long before he will want to work in the fields with me. As for my playing housewife ... I am too tired by the end of the day to lend a hand." John sighed, worry lines forming across his brow. "It is going to be even harder work now that Matthew is done paying me. He is likely to move on."

"You were a fool to free him."

"I reckon you are wrong about that."

"You need the extra hand."

"I will hire someone else. He might stay on, though. He is thinking of settling down in these parts."

"What is he going to do?"

"He wants to free his wife."

"He married that MacPhearson Negro ... what is her name?"

"Sarah."

"Well, that ought to keep him working for you for a while. She is sure to cost a thousand dollars or more. She is still good breeding age."

"He already has the money."

"What? How the hell does a Negro pay off a debt and still save over a thousand dollars? It is impossible."

"I gave it to him."

"You what?"

"You heard me."

"Where did you get that kind of money to give away?"

"I gave him that money that has been sitting in the bank all these years."

"That is your money! Your children's money!"

"Whore's money!" John hissed. His voice was a harsh whisper, as he did not want Katherine and the children to hear. "And I will never touch it!" John paused to regain his composure. "I figured there is no reason to leave it sit there for that greedy pig Atwell. Matthew more than deserves that money. He works hard, and he has been a good friend. Shoot, Uncle Jacob, he saved my life. Them Crawfords left me for dead. They meant for me to die tied to that old oak. Matthew could have run. He might have made it, too. But he went to get Mr. MacPhearson instead. No, suh … do not say anything, Uncle Jacob. I owe that man my life."

"You are plumb crazy to give that kind of money to a Negro. They lack proper sense to manage it."

"Matthew plans to use it wisely enough. He is going to buy his woman, then petition for her freedom."

"You see, there is his first mistake. His wife is well tended to. She has herself a good home with the MacPhearsons. He does not have to pay for her keep. He sees her often enough for a Negro. Why is he wasting all that money just to buy her? These Negroes lack all good sense. He should be investing that money."

"There is no point arguing about this, Uncle Jacob. You and I will never agree."

"You think you have this all figured out?"

"Yes, suh, I do."

"You are a fool!"

"I whored for that money, Mr. Barlow!" John whispered fiercely. "I reckon I am free to do with it as I choose. And I chose to give it to Matthew."

"And Matthew is willing to take your money just like that, no questions asked. Dirty, greedy little nigga!"

"Do not put Matthew down!"

"I will not apologize for calling a Negro a nigga. A spade is a spade, and that Negro is going to take you for all you are worth."

"For your information, suh, I had to fight with Matthew to get him to accept that money. Argued with him for years! *Years!* He wants to earn it. Work for it, he says. But I will not let him. Not for that money! I told him it was payment for all those years you worked him as a slave. It is barely enough, if you ask me. He thinks it is your money. I told him you gave it to me when I first moved out this way. I lied. It sickens me to lie, but I will never tell him where it really comes from. I do not want anyone knowing about that. I would die if Katherine knew."

Mr. Barlow blushed. He had revealed John's secret to the girl years ago.

"I told Matthew I was too proud to use that money. At least that was the truth. And now I do not need it. I told him I proved I could make it on my own, and I did. Then he goes and says he wants to do the same thing. Said I should be taking that money as payment for my slave years. So I told him you paid me for my work ever since I were fourteen. 'How much did Old Man Barlow ever pay you?' I asked. 'Not one red cent! Nothing! The only thing Barlow ever gave you was a whip and a brand ... first on your back, then on your face. No, suh,' I said. 'That money is yours. You earned it, and you are going to take it.' Finally he nodded and accepted." John smiled. "It was Sarah who changed his mind. He went and married her. A man has a right to live with his wife."

"Do you really think Angus MacPhearson is going to agree to this sale? Negro women of breeding age are mighty valuable."

"Katherine has already spoken to her daddy on Matthew and Sarah's behalf. Matthew is over there right now securing the deal."

"You already gave him the money, then?"

"Yes, suh. It is a done deal. There is no turning back the hands of time now."

"I told you he would waste that money. A Negro buying a Negro ... who ever heard of such a fool thing?"

"It happens all the time, Uncle Jacob ... men buying their wives and children. Matthew is not buying Sarah to own her. He is purchasing her so he can free her."

"Makes him an even bigger fool."

"I do not expect you to understand."

A crash and a scream ensued, bringing a sudden end to their conversation. Suddenly little Evelyn ran out the front door. Frantic, she stumbled down the steps of the veranda, tripping at the bottom. She scraped her hands and knees against the rough gravel, releasing a high-pitched squeal.

John hurried down the steps to pick her up. Comforting her, he asked, "What is it, little girl? Look what you gone and done." His voice drowned beneath Evelyn's wails. "Let me wash these cuts for you." John carried his child over to the water pump and encouraged her to hold her hands underneath the water.

There was quite a bustle going on inside the house; scurrying and screams commingled with the banging of furniture. "John," Katherine screamed. "John, get in here."

Ignoring his wife's plea, John continued to tend to his daughter's needs. "What is all the fuss about, Evelyn?"

The little girl was too overcome by her own high-pitched wails to answer.

Katherine appeared at the front door. Her hair was in disarray, her eyes wild and frantic. "Mr. Connolley, you get in here this instant."

"You are in big trouble now, son," Mr. Barlow laughed, still relaxed in his teak chair, not reacting in the least to the turmoil around him. "When a wife addresses her husband so formally, there is always hell to pay."

Katherine scolded the old man. "I would ask that you not curse in front of my children, Mr. Barlow."

Mr. Barlow smirked slightly as he shrugged his shoulders. He was wise enough to keep the rest of his laughter to himself.

John stood, holding Evelyn as far away from his ear as possible. "What is all the fuss about? You would think a swarm of bees just broke into the house."

"Worse, Mr. Connolley. Another mouse!"

John laughed.

"You find the discomforts of your family amusing, do you, suh?"

"It is just a little mouse, Katherine."

"That little mouse has caused great uproar, frightening both little Evelyn and me."

"That poor little critter is more frightened than the two of you put together."

"That poor little critter is a disease-ridden rodent. I do not want that vermin inside my house. Do you want your children dying of yellow fever?"

John winced. That was how his mama had died.

Katherine did not stop for any sympathy. "You get in here right now and kill that thing!"

"All right, I will catch the little fellow for you. Here, take Evelyn. Maybe you can calm her down."

Katherine held out her arms and gathered in the wailing child. "Hush, now, Evelyn, your daddy is going to kill it for us."

"I am not killing anything," John hollered as he entered the house. "I will catch it and set it free."

"Kill it, Daddy," little Evelyn wailed.

"You listen to your daughter," Katherine said harshly. "I do not want that thing coming back again."

"It will not come back."

"Oh, it will be back. I swear that is the same vermin you freed last week."

There was another crash from inside the house. "James," John hollered. "Get on outside, son. Let me catch the critter. Go on outside and visit with your granddaddy."

James responded with a squeal of triumph, "I got 'im, Daddy! I got 'im!"

"You have not killed it, I hope?"

"No, suh, Daddy. I got it inside this here sheet."

"Good work, son. You take him out back now and let him go in the rice field."

"Yes, suh, Daddy!"

Katherine burned with anger. "I swear, John," she hollered at the door, as if it were the man himself, "if that mouse returns, I will kill you!" Storming over to Mr. Barlow, Katherine placed Eveyln in his lap. "That man infuriates me so!"

Calmly walking through the door, John stopped and took a moment to admire his wife. Even angry, Katherine was the most beautiful woman he had ever laid eyes on. He still could not believe she had married him, that she loved him regardless of his past. Her eyes flashed with defiance. Her hair was a tangled mess that resembled a crackling fire. Her bosom was swollen, and her stomach protruded; she stood proud and strong, regardless of her condition. Most women were ashamed to be seen pregnant … but not his Katherine. She bore his children with pride. John smiled.

"Do not try your smiles on me, Mr. Connolley. I will not forgive you so easily."

John stepped down off the veranda and kissed her gently. "How about I head over to the silo and catch you a corn snake?"

"John!" Indignant, Katherine balled a fist and went to swing it.

Laughing, John caught her hand, pulling her in for a hug.

Katherine struggled against him. "I do not find your jokes amusing, Mr. Connolley." She scowled at Mr. Barlow. "Even if your good uncle does."

Mr. Barlow's laugh converted into a series of coughs. It took him a moment to collect his breath. "Mrs. Connolley, your husband is indeed a scoundrel. But I shall make amends for him. I will get you a cat."

Little Evelyn perked up at the idea of a kitten in the house, "May I play with it, Granddaddy?"

"Of course you can, little darling." Then, with enforced gravity, knowing the next topic might spark controversy, Mr. Barlow added, "I can do you even better, if you allow me."

Katherine and John turned to face him.

"I can set you up in a grand plantation house with a dozen cats."

"A grand plantation house?" Katherine's face brightened. "Oh, Uncle Jacob, whatever do you mean?" Crossing over to the teak chairs, Katherine sat down next to the old man. She looked warily at her husband. "Wipe that sourly look off your face, John Connolley. Sit down and listen to what your uncle has to say."

John refused to sit. "What, may I ask, is wrong with my house?"

"Rodents, for one thing!" Katherine replied instantly.

"Size for another," Uncle Jacob added. "You only have two rooms and another youngun on the way."

"I am planning to build on."

"How long have you been saying that, John?" Katherine asked delicately. "The fact is, you do not have time. Even with Matthew's help, there are simply not enough hours in the day for everything you have to do."

"If y'all were not so damn adamant against my working Sundays, I could get to it."

"John!" Katherine admonished. "Do not curse in front of our children."

Before John could even offer his apologies, Mr. Barlow leaped in with his remark. "No, suh," he insisted. "Sunday is the Lord's day!"

"Your uncle is right, John. Besides, Sunday is the only day you get to spend any time with your children. Would you really want to give that up?" She leaned over and kissed her daughter's cheek, who was still sitting in Mr. Barlow's lap, to add emphasis.

John softened some. "How can we keep such a big house?"

"Hire some help," Mr. Barlow answered.

"We could hire Sarah to help me run the house," Katherine offered.

Mr. Barlow and Katherine were bombarding John. He was starting to feel overwhelmed. "A plantation home means a bigger plantation. I can barely keep up with the land I got. How can y'all expect me to work even more land?" Before anyone could answer, John barged on, "I will not take on any Negro slaves! We are going to make it on our own, Katherine. We will not own slaves."

"I am afraid my husband is right, Uncle Jacob. We could never run a large plantation without the use of slaves, and owning men is not an option."

"Well," Mr. Barlow reasoned, "you do not have to work the whole township. You can rent out most of the land to sharecroppers."

John looked up, startled. "A whole township?"

"A whole township." Mr. Barlow smiled.

"What is the name of this plantation?" John asked.

"Pine Grove," Mr. Barlow announced triumphantly.

"The Crawfords' plantation," Katherine whispered.

"Not anymore." Mr. Barlow basked in his victory. "I bought Frank Crawford's land ... all his stock, Negroes included ... the big house ... and furnishings. I got quite the deal due to the man's current state of desperation."

A hint of a smile appeared on John's face. "You sure took your time destroying the man."

"Revenge must be savored, son. Though I do wish Junior could have suffered more."

"Surely the beating his father gave him was retribution enough. But if that did not suffice for you, then indisputably his death must have. It was providence, Uncle Jacob. Even you have to admit that."

"Indeed. In a battle where only seventy-one men were killed ..."

"Seventy-one Americans," John corrected. "Over two thousand British soldiers died that day." John shook his head at the grisly memory, "It was a charnel house."

"Seventy-one Americans," Mr. Barlow agreed. "That Junior was one of them seems to indicate that the good Lord used the Battle of New Orleans to exact your revenge. Yet, I hardly feel avenged."

"Would you have preferred I had beat the small man to a pulp rather than his daddy, or that I had been the one to desecrate his body on the battlefield? No, Uncle Jacob. I follow in the Lord's path. Christ did not come down off the cross to smite those who nailed him up there. I do not need to be the one to execute revenge. Besides, I remember having to identify Junior's body." John shuddered at the memory. "There was very little left of him; I could only make out half of his face. If you could have seen the frothy gray mass oozing out of his skull, you would have felt thoroughly avenged."

Little Evelyn squealed in horror, burying her face inside her grandfather's chest. Mr. Barlow cooed softly to calm her. "Hush, little baby."

"John! Please! Little Evelyn does not need to hear such gruesome details. Nor do I! Besides, it is unwise to talk so unseemly of the dead."

"My apologies, wife." John truly was abashed. He had no desire to discomfort Katherine or his daughter.

"Are we to live at Pine Grove then, John?" Katherine asked, intent on changing the topic.

"I shall give it to you, son. All but the Negroes," Mr. Barlow added judiciously. "I know you will refuse them. And if you did accept them, you would just waste a fortune in investments by giving them all their freedom like you did with Matthew."

"Mr. Barlow, I cannot accept such an exorbitant gift."

"Mr. Barlow?" Jacob Barlow sighed. "Let us not return to Mr. Barlow."

"Uncle Jacob, I have worked hard these past nine years to establish myself in a community where I am looked upon with disdain. Only your name and Angus MacPhearson's influence have allowed me to remain here with begrudging acceptance. I have built a good life on this little plantation, earning enough money to care for my family. I do not require your gifts."

Katherine slumped slightly, but immediately straightened her back, "My husband is right, Uncle Jacob. John is a good provider. My children and I want for nothing. We are clothed and well fed."

John smiled. Katherine's support meant a great deal to him. He was reminded once again why he fell in love with this formidable woman. He took a moment to thank God for bringing her into his life. This simple prayer had become a daily exercise.

"Indeed, it is evident John has done well for y'all, and I do not mean to suggest otherwise. It is just that I am an old man. I can no longer manage the two townships I already own and cannot conceive of managing a third. It would benefit me greatly if John would consent, at the very least, to manage Pine Grove for me. I will not give it to you, son. I do not wish to offend your pride. I bequeath this land to you, though, upon my death."

"But how am I to manage a township when I can barely run what little land I own?"

"Sharecroppers, son. Become my landlord. Katherine here will help you. I am sure she has a head for that sort of thing, her father having one or two tenants himself."

"Indeed," Katherine piped up. "I could assist you in that capacity … if such a plan is agreeable to you, John."

"You could still grow your own crops," Mr. Barlow added. "Choose a prime section of land, and rent out the rest to worthy tenants."

"Matthew …" John mused. "Perhaps he could rent a section."

"Now you are talking, son." Mr. Barlow smiled, hoping his offer would prove acceptable to the proud man.

"Oh, John," Katherine smiled sweetly. "Does that mean yes? Are we to move to Pine Grove?"

"I shall consider it."

"I shall take that as an affirmative," Jacob Barlow announced.

"Do not push me, suh. When I have decided, I shall inform you both."

"Oh, Evelyn," Katherine squealed. "We are going to live in the big house! It is a grand manor, and you shall have your own room."

"I have not agreed to the proposition," John struggled to interject.

"And I shall have a big kitchen to cook in."

Mr. Barlow laughed. "You had best acquiesce, son. Your wife has taken your leaning for an assent." Observing a scowl forming on John's brow, Mr. Barlow added, "Look at how happy it makes her, son. Does your wife not deserve to live in a fine house? Consider all the money you shall make renting out that land, John. Why, there will be enough to send your boy to the finest schools. Think of your wife and children, son … not your pride."

John looked over to his wife, her eyes pleading. How could he deny her after all she had sacrificed? "I agree. We shall move to Pine Grove. I will manage your land with my good wife's aid. I have one condition, though."

Katherine and Mr. Barlow looked on expectantly.

"We must change the name from Pine Grove to Majestic Beauty."

Katherine flung herself into John's arms, "Oh, yes, husband. Majestic Beauty it is. Oh, John, you have made me so very happy."

John could not help but laugh along with her. "Let us celebrate, then. Katherine, run inside and fetch Arlo."

Evelyn's eyes widened at the mention of her favorite doll. "Are we gonna dance, Daddy?"

"Indeed we are, little darling. Arlo's feet are itching to take a turn. Will you take a turn with him?"

"Yes!" Evelyn cried with glee, leaping off her granddaddy's lap.

"Who might this Arlo fellow be?" Mr. Barlow inquired.

Katherine answered his question by returning to the veranda with a crudely carved marionette. It stood two inches taller than Evelyn. John took control of the strings and had the doll bow to his daughter.

"Where in tarnation did you get that thing?" Mr. Barlow asked.

"I made it," John replied. "I saw one once. You took Emily and me to one of them traveling theaters when we were little. I begged you to buy me one, but you refused. 'Damn fool waste of money,' you said."

"John, this here is a happy time," Katherine scolded. "I will not have you spoil it with cursing."

"Sorry, wife." It still brought a thrill to John's belly, calling Katherine wife.

"I remember," Mr. Barlow laughed. "I had to whop you, too, to get you to stop begging."

"When Katherine was pregnant with James, I started building one. It was not easy to construct, let me tell you. I went through a lot of wood before I got to Arlo here. And little Evelyn was already born by then. She took to him like a bloodsucker takes to your leg."

Exasperated, Evelyn cried, "Make Arlo dance with me, Daddy."

"All right, little darling. Put your left hand on his right shoulder. Hold his left hand with your right. Now Arlo is going to put his hand on your waist. Katherine, darling, will you sing us something?"

Katherine's voice rang sweet and true, a slow Floridian waltz for her daughter to dance to.

"Now step back, Evelyn. Use your left leg. Good girl. Step out with the right foot. Step forward on the left. Back in with the right. Good girl!"

Mr. Barlow smiled. "Why, that is a mighty fine way to teach a lady to dance."

"Now open up, hand in hand, and walk forward. There is my little lady."

John had Arlo walk his daughter over to her grandfather.

Mr. Barlow leaned forward and picked the child up. "My, what a good little dancer you are!"

Sitting prouder than a princess, little Evelyn responded, "Thank you, Grand-daddy."

"You have made a fine life for yourself, John, despite all of me."

"Indeed, stepping beyond our past has been hard ... particularly with my choice to keep you in my life."

"Why, son? Why have you forgiven me?"

"Your sins are black, and you still reap the fruits of your iniquity. You are like Claudius, who prays to God but refuses to let go of Gertrude or the crown. He, too, knows his sins can never be forgiven. No, you have not been forgiven; not by yourself, perhaps not even by God. But I can forgive you. I choose to forgive you. I choose to let go of the past. I choose to remember the early years of my life, when you were like a father to me. You are the only father I have ever known, and as your son, I must forgive you. We are, as you have always said, family. If Christ can forgive those who nailed him to the cross, even those who did not regret their actions or change their ways, then I can learn from his experience and try to forgive you. You are my Gethsemane; you are my Roman soldier, my Pontius Pilate, my Passion. In your own way, you led me to Christ. Even now, as I stand here and wonder how he did it, I can hear him say 'Father, forgive them; for they know not what they do.'"

John sat down on the steps and shook his head. "I hated you, Uncle Jacob. So many times I wanted to kill you. I could envision my hands strangling the life out of you, but I chose not to. I could no longer allow that hatred to consume me. When I turn to Jesus, I see how hating you is like a cancer in my soul. It will destroy me. I can never love you as I did when I was young; I know you too well for who you are. But I can forgive you, if not for your redemption, at least for my own. I have chosen to walk in the path of the Lord. As I ask for forgiveness, I know in return that I, too, must forgive: 'Forgive us our sins; for we also forgive every one that is indebted to us.' The Lord also says, 'But if ye do not forgive, neither will your father which is in heaven forgive your trespasses.' You have asked me for forgiveness. I choose to grant it to you. Unconditionally. I know you have not changed toward others, only toward me. I know I cannot change you. Only you can choose to change yourself. Only you can look inside to see the darkness of your soul. Only you can grant yourself the light. Someday you, your descendants, the people like you will see the wrongs you have committed. Someday the world will change. We cannot live like this forever. All this hatred is swelling up inside us. All this fear will strangle our good country. Indeed, this country is headed for an explosion. I know fear and hatred can never be eliminated, but it does need to be controlled. I cannot control our nation, but I can control my own life. With you, at least, I can let go. I do not want the fear or the hatred to control me anymore."

"Granddaddy?" Evelyn asked, distressed. "Why are you crying?"

Katherine reached over to take her daughter out of Mr. Barlow's hands.

The old man slumped over, weighted down by his sorrow.

John watched Mr. Barlow weep in his misery. There was nothing he could do to comfort the old man.

It is for him to wrestle with his own demons.

978-1-60528-004-2

1-60528-004-6

LaVergne, TN USA
29 October 2009
162471LV00004B/1/P